In the Big Scheme of Things
by
Kevin Macan-Lind
ISBN: 978-1-8384686-9-9

Copyright and Disclaimer 2021
All rights reserved. No part of this publication may be reproduced, stored in a retrieval system or transmitted in any form or by any means, electronic, mechanical, photocopy, recording org otherwise, without prior written consent of the copyright owner. Nor can it be circulated in any form of binding or cover other than that in which it is published and without similar condition including this condition being imposed on a subsequent purchaser.

This novel is a work of fiction. The characters are the product of the author's imagination and any resemblance to actual persons, living or dead, is unintended and entirely coincidental.

The right of Kevin Macan-Lind to be identified as the author of this work has been asserted in accordance with the Copyright Designs and Patents Act 1988.

A copy of this book is deposited with the British Library.

Published By: -

i2i
PUBLISHING

i2i Publishing. Manchester.
www.i2i.publishing.co.uk

To my wife, Linda

Acknowledgements

Diana Watts, Stuart Kinsey, and Piers Chipperfield. With gratitude to my editor, Mark Cripps, and my publisher at i2i Publishing, Lionel Ross. And for their advice and encouragement, authors Peter James, Linwood Barclay, and Gyles Brandreth. Last but not least, because she's so well-read, my wife Linda; potentially my biggest critic but paradoxically, also my biggest support.

The fear of death follows from the fear of life. A man who lives fully is prepared to die at any time.

Mark Twain

Chapter One

I had read the email message with a mixture of excitement and trepidation. Having sent my latest, finished manuscript to a dozen prospective publishers, this had been the first person from a publishing house to offer some potentially positive news in the five years that I had been penning novels and submitting them for review. The request from Jeremy Browne at Gambon & Clarke Ltd of Holborn to call him had led me to walk down High Holborn to find their offices to attend the appointment.

Their address in Red Lion Street consisted of a black front door at street level, nestled between an Italian restaurant on the left and a greengrocer on the right. I pressed the entrance buzzer to the side of the door and responded to the receptionist's inquiry accordingly, 'Hi, my name is David Jones and I have an appointment to see Jeremy Browne at eleven o'clock.'

'One moment, please,' came the reply.

Whilst I complied with the request, a young woman arrived on the pavement next to me, opened the door with her key, entered and promptly shut it again, leaving me still outside. The receptionist then buzzed the door open and announced, 'Please come up.'

I entered and saw stairs immediately in front of me. Climbing to the first floor, I entered a room approximately ten feet square which housed a wooden desk behind which sat a very pretty girl in her early twenties who smiled at me as I approached.

'Hello,' she said, 'you must be Mr Jones.'

'David, please,' I said.

8

'Please take a seat and I'll let Mr Browne know that you've arrived.' She waved an arm towards a sofa with a coffee table in front of it. I sat down and surveyed my surroundings. They were small offices spread over the floor I was on with a staircase up to a second floor, presumably. The reception area had a number of framed book covers on the walls, none of which were familiar to me. To my right, a window afforded sunshine to flood the girl's desk and computer. The three magazines on the table in front of me: *Horse & Hounds, Vogue* and *Golf World,* held no interest for me. I opened the briefcase on my lap and started to check its contents.

'Mr Jones, please come in.' In the doorway to the right of the receptionist's desk stood a man of similar age to my own, about forty. I closed my briefcase and stood up. Approaching him, I said, 'Mr Browne, I presume,' and I chuckled.

Jeremy Browne, his brow furrowed, replied, 'I'm sorry, is something amusing you, Mr Jones?'

'Yes, I suddenly thought of the famous greeting between Dr Livingstone and Henry Stanley in Africa,' I responded.

'I see,' he remarked, turning around.

We entered his small office and we sat opposite one another across his desk which was covered in files, paperwork, a laptop, a takeaway coffee cup and a telephone.

'Would you like a tea or a coffee, Mr Jones?'

'Please call me, David,' I said. 'No thank you. I had one at Antonio's,' I replied, even though I hadn't.

Jeremy Browne ran a hand through his hair and took one of the files, placing it in front of him.

9

'Okay then, David, let's make a start, shall we?'

I smiled and then the phone on his desk rang.

Jeremy looked out of his window as he answered, 'What? I told you last week that we needed them by Friday.'

I awkwardly pointed to my chest and then the door and raised my eyebrows, querying whether I should leave him alone with his telephone conversation. He shook his head and continued with his call, 'Greg, this is your last chance and I am not your mate.' He looked at me and shook his head, rolling his eyes.

He continued with his telephone conversation. 'I see. Well, I suggest you present yourself to my office within the next two hours. I will allot ten minutes to you out of my busy day in order that you may try to save your print contract. I doubt that you will, but let's see.' With that, Jeremy Browne slammed the phone down and lit a cigarette.

'Sorry about that.' He put on some glasses and pulled out a document from the file. He pushed it towards me and said, 'Sorry again, David, it's not for us I'm afraid. As you know, this is your third try with us.'

'Have Mr Gambon or Mr Clarke had a read of it?' I replied.

Jeremy smiled. 'You haven't done your homework, have you?'

'What do you mean?' I asked.

'Gambon & Clarke, publishers, was started by those two gentlemen in 1863, David.'

I took back the manuscript and put it in my briefcase.

'I'm puzzled then, Mr Browne. Why did you invite me in today?'

10

Jeremy picked up his phone and said, 'Julie, could you arrange a couple of coffees, please? Thanks.'

Turning to me, he said, 'I have a proposal to make and consequently, made a presumption for you to join me in having coffee.'

'Okay, so you didn't like *The London Boys* but you have other ideas for me?'

''*The London Boys* had merit, David, but didn't quite cut the mustard, as they say. I'm sure you'll appreciate that we get sent hundreds of manuscripts every year and we end up choosing only a couple of dozen to publish.'

At that point, a knock on the door interrupted proceedings.

'Come in,' Jeremy called and Julie entered with a tray containing the coffees. As she put them down on the desk, he said, 'Thanks, Julie.'

'Milk and sugar, David?'

I shook my head and smiled. We each took a cup and saucer of coffee and Jeremy Browne continued, 'I will now get down to business. I want to give you some background on the proposal that I wish to make to you. Last week, I went to the National Publishing Association's conference in Birmingham. It's always good to try and keep up to date with the latest trends, see fellow book publishers, meet up with printers, etc. Not unexpectedly, still very popular, in terms of book sales, are children's books, as has been the case for about five or six years now. But one of the delegates there who I've known a while came up with an idea which is what I want to discuss with you, David.' He paused and sipped his coffee.

I did the same and waited for him to continue.

11

'Very well. This genre, I believe, has merit beyond being a published book, or two. Before I launch into that, let me share some information with you. I have some contacts in the film industry in the States and I called a couple of them last week. They are both film producers and they are keen to see what we can come up with. They have screenplay writers on hand to put the finishing touches on whatever I send over to them. It's not a done deal exactly but we've all known each other for about ten years so it's very exciting. It's an area that they're both experienced and have produced a number of films in the genre which are leased around the world, mainly for television broadcast. And I think that this is something for you to get your teeth into, David.'

I drained my cup of coffee and put it back on the saucer.

'Well, I can't wait. Please tell me more,' I said enthusiastically.

'What do you mean?' he asked.

'You mentioned a particular genre,' I queried.

'Yes', Jeremy paused and poured himself another cup of coffee, 'like some more, David?'

I declined, 'Er, no thanks, very kind.'

The phone on Browne's desk rang and he listened to Julie who had taken a call on reception. Browne put his hand over the mouthpiece and whispered to me, 'Sorry, David, I'll just deal with this before we carry on.' Into the phone, he said, 'I told you never to phone me at the office. Whatever it is, it will have to wait, all right? I'll call you this evening.' He replaced the receiver and sat shaking his head as he returned his attention back to me.

12

'Apologies, David. Right then, I'll proceed.' Jeremy Browne picked up a blue folder from his desk and handed it to me. I leafed through the six pages contained in it and quickly absorbed the contents.

'A Christmas-themed book? Perhaps *The London Boys* book was too didactic for you, but you think that something at the other end of the spectrum, like a Christmas story, would suit my style?'

'I note your scepticism, David, but I think that this project helps both of us, actually.'

Jeremy reached across the desk to retrieve his folder and continued as he pulled out one particular sheet of typed paper which he held up in my direction.

'This is a contract between Gambon & Clarke Ltd and yourself, David Jones, for you to write the manuscript of a novel and for us to publish, get it printed and distributed. I suspect that you haven't been commissioned to write something before, with a decent sum of money at the end of the day. Am I correct?'

I nodded my head and smiled. 'You're right, Jeremy, and this helps us both, how?'

'Well, I know how keen guys like you are to get something published, see their name in print and I can see an opportunity for Gambon & Clarke to put a toe in the water of a market that is growing exponentially, year on year. First of all, there's the Christmas period book market and as I've mentioned, the lucrative film industry too.'

At this point, the telephone on his desk rang and Jeremy picked up the receiver, 'Yes, Clare, Mr Jones is with me at the moment.' After a minute's pause, he said, 'No, we're not quite at that stage yet', he nodded and continued,

13

'I'll call you back in about half an hour, Clare.' He gently replaced the receiver.

'Sorry about that, David.'

I shrugged my shoulders and replied, 'You must have a raft of current authors who you publish that you could have talked to about this project. I gestured with my forefingers when I said the word project.'

'They're all busy right now.'

'Oh, I see. So, you tried them all first and you were left with me?'

'It wasn't exactly like that, David. Would you like another coffee, or something else?'

I shook my head and smiled as he continued.

'I would offer to show you around the offices at this stage but as you can see, we're a very small publishing house on just two floors of this building. The reception area and my office are here on the first floor and on the floor above us is the MD's office and an open-plan area with four staff, so not much to see!'

'Clare?' I asked.

'Clare is one of our manuscript readers and editors. Been with us for five years. Very astute and a hard worker.'

I glanced at my watch and Jeremy noticed this.

'Well, David, are you interested? Do we have a deal?'

'I don't want to appear negative but it's not really my area of expertise, Jeremy.' He opened the file in front of him and took out the contract. 'This has been signed by me as office manager and by Mr Paterson,' here, he pointed his pen skywards, 'as managing director. All it needs now is for you to sign it at the bottom. David, your area of expertise is creative writing, something that you're very good at.'

14

'But *The London Boys* didn't quite cut the mustard, is what you said earlier.'

'It was timing, that's all. A lot of manuscripts came in at the same time as yours and our business plan didn't allow us to publish more books than we are scheduled to do.'

'I see.'

As Jeremy Browne pushed the contract document towards me, he said, 'Look, I tell you what. If you sign the contract and agree to write the Christmas-themed book, I will make a commitment to you today to agree to publish *The London Boys* as a follow-up. How does that sound?'

I picked up the contract and read it again.

'You've been very fair, Jeremy. Just one question. If I was to work on a story for you, when would you be looking to publish it and consequently, working back timewise, what would be our deadline?'

'We would need to get the book into the shops and to be available online by September, in readiness for the Christmas market.' Jeremy glanced at the diary on his desk and continued, 'Today is April 5th, so shall we say deadline next year to be April 1st, which will give us the opportunity of reviewing your submission, working on any revisions, sending it to the printers and then getting it distributed to book shops, distribution outlets like Amazon for example and getting it over to the States for them to see if it's suitable for a treatment to be made into a film.'

'Ha, ha, ha', I replied as I slowly clapped my hands together sarcastically. 'April 1st. All Fools Day. How appropriate!'

Jeremy frowned and said, 'What's the problem, David?'

'So, I've got to scurry back home, get some ideas together for this alien subject, get a plan down on paper, and then write the story, all in twelve months?'

'Well, how long do you need? Frederick Forsyth only took a couple of months to write his best-selling novel, *Day of the Jackal*. A year not enough, David?'

I reached out and grabbed the contract on his desk and then took my fountain pen from the inside pocket of my jacket, unscrewed the lid and signed my autograph at the bottom with a flourish. Handing it over, I replied, 'I will work very hard, Jeremy. It'll be worth it to see *The London Boys* in print too. Thank you, again.'

I stood and we shook hands.

'Just picking up on what you were saying, surely there's about a year between the hardback version being published and the softback?'

Jeremy put the signed contract back into his file and placed it in one of his desk drawers.

'David, this isn't going to be published in hardback first, it's going to go straight to our subsidiary, Amadeus, who publish all of our paperbacks.'

'But ...'

Jeremy cut me off before I could continue with a raised hand as he said, 'It's a management decision combined with the need to get this show on the road. Mr Paterson ...' here, Jeremy once again, prodded his pen skywards, 'has years of experience in this field, especially with new authors and the economies of scale.'

I nodded and said, 'Well, that's been fascinating, Jeremy. I'm over the moon, seriously. I can't wait to get cracking on the book.'

16

'One thing I need to mention before you go, 'Jeremy added, 'You'll need to weave a good looking, young couple into your story, for our film producer friends to find it attractive enough to invest time, effort and money into developing the project. Are you familiar with the format? Have you seen the typical Yuletide offerings that appear on television in the lead up to the Christmas period?'

'Er, no.' I frowned and continued, 'You're worrying me, Jeremy. I want to do a really good job, but I don't share your enthusiasm for either my abilities or the proposed story-line.'

At this point, the phone on his desk rang and Jeremy picked up the receiver again, 'Hi, yes thanks, Julie. Ask him if he'd like a coffee. I won't be much longer here.'

Replacing the receiver, he looked up at me and said, 'Look, David, I understand your concerns, I really do. What I can do is get half a dozen DVDs of films of this ilk and get them over to you. See it as homework if you like but I think they will really help you to understand what we need to see from you.'

'Your next appointment is here so I'll get out of your hair,' I said.

'No need to rush off, David. Watch the films and let me know what you think.'

'Thanks, Jeremy.'

'Obviously, we'll have regular catch-up calls and emails. And once again, I'm sorry we can't proceed immediately to publish your *London Boys* book.'

'Well, in the big scheme of things, I don't suppose it really matters too much.' I assured him. My saturnine expression seemed to trigger something in the book publisher opposite me.

17

'David, I wouldn't worry too much about anything. I never do. In fact, that's always been my philosophy.'

I grabbed my briefcase and glanced out of the office window and saw that it had just started to rain outside. I retrieved my coat from the chair next to me and then opened the door to exit the office. 'It's been a pleasure, Jeremy. I can't wait to receive the Christmas DVDs. I'll let you know what I think.'

'Would you tell Julie to let me have ten minutes before I see Mr Foster, please? I just have to compose an email message.'

I entered the outer office and passed on the message to the receptionist. I looked at the person seated in the reception area who was sipping a cup of tea and reading the copy of *Vogue* which had been placed on the table. The young man, presumably Mr Foster, glanced up at me and scowled for some reason. Nevertheless, I smiled in return and said to him, 'Good luck'.

As I made my way to the door to descend the stairs to ground level, I turned and said, 'Thanks, Julie. See you again one day, I hope.' I raised an eyebrow to her as I gave a final look towards the unhappy *Vogue* reader and made my exit.

Chapter Two

I had been home from London for two days. The train journey back to Bedfordshire had been without incident. I had actually found a seat. The train had been on time and it had stopped raining. The half-hour journey had allowed me to ponder my recent meeting in Holborn. At least, it had been a positive one, or had it? One year to write a story, the subject matter of which I had absolutely no enthusiasm about whatsoever.

The day after my return home, a courier had delivered my homework. The promised half a dozen DVDs had turned in to ten and I had started to watch a couple of them. I knew that I could only bear to watch a maximum of two per day. I had other things to do, after all. I had furiously scribbled notes as I watched them in an attempt to understand the format and the appeal of these films to their audience.

Ironically, I had just completed the last chapter of my latest offering and would get copies of the manuscript out to publishers in my usual manner within the next few days.

I made myself a cup of coffee, placed one of the DVDs into the player, *Mary Christmas Comes to Town*. I pressed play. A knock on my front door made me stop the DVD player and place my cup down on the coffee table. As usual, like most people, the first thought that comes to mind in these situations is who can that be?

Opening the front door, I was confronted by two men, one, a police officer in uniform, the other one, in plain clothes who showed me an identification card.

20

The tall, plain-clothed one, said, 'Good morning. Can you tell me, are you Mr David Jones?'

'No, I'm Samuel Franklin Cody,' I replied.

'I beg your pardon?' he said and at this point, a warrant card was produced. He continued, 'I'm Detective Sergeant Paul Craven. Would you know where I can find Mr Jones by any chance, sir?'

'I'm sorry, I'm David Jones,' I confirmed.

The two police officers exchanged a look between themselves and the uniformed one continued, 'I hope you're not trying to waste police time, Mr Jones? Why did you give a false name when you answered the door?'

I gave an embarrassed laugh and replied, 'Sorry, it's my sense of humour, or lack of it! I'm a writer and I've recently been doing some research on someone called Samuel Franklin Cody, for a proposed biography. Interesting bloke. Have you heard of him?'

DS Craven took a step forward, 'Would it be possible to come in for a moment so that I can explain why we're here?'

I opened the door fully and they both entered.

'Please sit down, Mr Jones,' DS Craven instructed me.

As I did so, without invitation, they sat down together on the settee opposite me.

'So, what's this all about then, officers?'

'On Tuesday of this week, you visited Gambon & Clarke Ltd in Holborn?' I nodded and DS Craven continued, 'You met someone there called Jeremy Browne. How well did you know him?'

'How well did I know him? What do you mean? Isn't he there anymore? Oh, my God, you don't mean …'

DS Craven nodded to his colleague who was taking notes.

'PC Kranic will be helping me with my report following our interview today, Mr Jones.'

'Interview? That sounds rather serious. Am I helping you with your inquiries, DS Craven?'

'I'm sure that you would rather assist the police than hinder them, wouldn't you?'

I took a sip of coffee nervously and asked, 'Would you gentlemen like a coffee too?'

'No thank you,' DS Craven responded, ' So, how well did you know Mr Browne?'

'You're still using the past tense, so I'll have to assume he's either dead or gone missing. Tuesday was the first time that I had met him.'

'Have you got some ID that we could see?' DS Craven asked me.

I stood up and went over to my chest of drawers to retrieve my passport. 'This okay?'

DS Craven took it from me and flicked through the pages. 'I'll keep this for a couple of days if that's all right, Mr Jones?' he said.

I replied, 'It sounds like I'm a suspect of some crime or something. Can you tell me what exactly has happened to Mr Browne?'

'The investigation has only just begun and I'm not able to share any details at this stage,'' DS Craven responded. 'I think we'll be here a while, so perhaps we will take up your offer of two coffees, please, white, no sugar.'

'Of course.' I left them to it in the lounge and when I returned with their drinks, DS Craven had his hands

22

behind his back as he stood scanning the books on my shelves.

I placed the mugs and a plate of biscuits on the table.

On hearing my return, DS Craven returned to his seat and said, 'Have you always had an interest in crime fiction, Mr Jones?'

'Crime fiction? No, not really. What do you mean?'

'While I was waiting for you to return, I was scanning the titles of your books, that's all.'

'I have an eclectic taste,' I explained.

'You have a lot of Agatha Christie,' he said as he pulled out a notepad and continued, 'Val McDermid, Ian Rankin, Raymond Chandler, Lee Child, Michael Connolly, James Patterson and err, Peter James.'

I sighed, 'I'm more of a collector. I've only read a few of them and intend to read the rest when I have the time. I'm a budding writer. That's why I had gone to see Jeremy Browne in London, the other day.'

'Yes, I'm glad you brought that up', PC Kranic said, speaking for the first time. 'How did that meeting go, Mr Jones?'

'Okay.'

'Really? We understand that your latest manuscript was rejected, just like the previous ones. 'Didn't that make you feel angry, upset?' he asked me.

'No, not at all. I'm getting used to it, I guess. Anyway, he did give me a contract to write a Christmas-themed book. I've got a copy of the contract, if you would like to see it.'

'We've got a copy of it', DS Craven stated.

'And he promised to publish my offering, *The London Boys*, as a thank you to me for agreeing to write the Christmas one.'

'There is no mention of that arrangement in the contract, Mr Jones.'

'Well, no, but he said it to me verbally and I had no reason to disbelieve him. And he offered to help with the Christmas book by sending me copies of films that have been produced of a similar nature because I had no idea of their style.'

'And why did he want you to write this book for him?'

'He had no one else to do it.'

The police officers exchanged looks again.

DS Craven then said, 'As a struggling author, I was wondering about how you finance your lifestyle, Mr Jones. You live in a nice house, albeit of modest size. How do you cover the payments of your monthly bills, for instance? I hope you don't mind my asking.'

I looked down at my shoes as I replied, 'Sadly, I lost my wife two years ago. There was an insurance policy in place. I also do some editorial work on my father-in-law's magazines. I looked up to see PC Kranic whispering something to his colleague.

'I see. I'm very sorry to hear about your wife, Mr Jones. Do you mind telling us what happened?'

'Cancer. Not much more I can say really.'

PC Kranic picked up a couple of the DVDs from the coffee table and said, 'What are these and why are they in unmarked plain covers?'

'It's what I told you about just now. They're the Christmas movies that Jeremy Browne promised to send to me so that I could understand the genre better.'

'I think we'll take a couple of these back to the station to check them out just to be sure,' he said and placed them into his folder.

At this point, DS Craven said, 'There are a few formalities we have to go through now, Mr Jones. A note of your father-in-law's name and contact details, please. In a short while, we will all need to go back to the station. The usual procedure, nothing to worry about.'

'I'm not worried,' I said. 'I haven't done anything wrong. I notice that you haven't touched your coffees, by the way.'

'No.'

'And what usual procedures exactly will we be going through?'

'We'll be putting together a statement for you to check and sign once you're happy.'

'Happy?'

'Happy with the wording', PC Kranic explained, 'and we'll be wanting to take a set of your fingerprints, obviously.'

'Obviously.'

'Normal course of events, sir. Right now, I need to take this opportunity to issue you with a caution: You do not have to say anything. But it may harm your defence if you do not mention when questioned something which you later rely on in court. Anything you do say may be given in evidence. Do you understand, Mr Jones?'

'No, I don't. Are you charging me with something? Am I under arrest?'

DS Craven smiled and replied, 'No, not at the moment.'

'Is this a murder investigation then? Surely you can tell me that.'

'Bedfordshire Police have been contacted by the MIT to carry out localised inquiries and to report back to them.'

'MIT? What's that then?'

'Major Investigation Teams are the specialised homicide squads of the Metropolitan Police in London. They are looking into the disappearance and possible murder of your friend, Jeremy Browne.'

'That has nothing to do with me.'

'That remains to be seen. Let's hope not.'

'Which police station are you taking me back to then?'

'Bedford.'

PC Kranic interjected, 'Well, Kempston, actually,' as he apologetically corrected his superior. 'That's where Bedfordshire HQ is. It's where we're based too.'

'Well, I've finished my coffee even if you haven't, so if you'll excuse me, I'll have to pop upstairs to the loo before we set off.'

DS Craven nodded and glanced at his watch as I exited the room.

***

When they were left alone in the room, PC Kranic turned to his colleague and said, 'Well, what do you think?'

'I really don't know. I'm usually a good judge of people, Stan. Our David Jones seems like a nice bloke to me, but something is playing on my mind and I can't quite put my finger on it, you know?'

'I don't trust him but that's me all over, isn't it? That's why I wanted to become a copper in the first place. I look forward to getting him back to the station. Perhaps, he'll crack then.'

PC Kranic then picked up his mug and took the first sip of this coffee, 'Ugh, that's cold and not very nice anyway!'

'Well, it's been sitting there for twenty minutes at least. What do you expect? Right, we'll be on our way in a few minutes when Mr Jones comes down.'

'Did you believe him about those DVDs?'

'I don't think that he would just leave them lying around if they were anything salacious. Don't forget, he wasn't expecting a visit from us, was he?'

DS Craven got up to look out of the window. The sun was shining and the weather for the past few days had been unusually fine for this time of the year. He looked at his watch again and said, 'Stan, you'd best go and chivvy him up. Knock on the door and tell him we've got to be going.'

'Yeah,' PC Kranic left his colleague looking at the field opposite the house as he went up the stairs. Seconds later, he was shouting back down the stairs, 'Sir, sir, he's not here! He's gone!'

DS Craven left the room and took the stairs two at a time. The door to the bathroom was wide open and the room was vacant.

'Shit!', DS Craven shouted. 'Right, check all of these other rooms, under the beds, inside the wardrobes, anywhere that could conceal a man. I'll call for a back-up to meet with us here. I'll go downstairs and check the gardens and the road outside.'

Finding nothing, Craven went back to the police Range Rover and sat down behind the wheel. He brought his clenched fist down hard on to the dashboard and issued forth, 'You little shit, Jones!' Craven shook his head as he watched his colleague, Kranic, searching in and out of the neighbours' front gardens trying to find their prey.

He smiled wryly to himself and started to contemplate what the hell he was doing in a role like this. Yes, he was a police officer, but he never wanted to be one. His father – a former policeman himself – had been in a position to influence his getting the job with Kent Constabulary, in Maidstone. Craven had had what can be called a chequered past. He'd spent some time abroad and mixed with certain elements of the underworld. As a young man, he'd succumbed to the dubious pleasures that can be found amongst the casinos of Monaco; wine, women, and song! He guffawed out loud. His reverie was curtailed as PC Kranic approached the driver's door and Craven wound down the window, 'Go over the road and search the ditches and the field opposite,' and he waved his hand dismissively.

Craven's unseemly past had appeared initially to be an asset to the Kent force, working as they did with the UK border control in trying to weed out people-traffickers and drug smugglers. But once again, Craven had sailed a bit too close to the wind on one particular operation in the view of Kent's chief constable. The resultant showdown had culminated with his transfer out of Kent: 'Get the hell out of my county, Craven and I don't care where you end up. Just piss off,' the chief had exploded.

The matter was not considered one for dismissal, or some sort of remedial training. Craven was dogmatic and so highly principled that he commonly refused to back down on something if he felt that he was correct. At Kempston – Bedfordshire Police's headquarters – he had convinced the hierarchy that he would be an asset and whilst appearing to be on normal duties, he would also be working secretly on undercover matters too.

One thing, however, was always in the back of his mind. He owed money to some very unpleasant characters, across the channel.

Chapter Three

After about four hours, I felt that sufficient time had elapsed for me to emerge from the neighbours' shed that I had secreted myself in. Having previously escaped through the rear bedroom window of my house and climbed down the trellis attached to my property, I had decided to lie low and contemplate my situation. Everything had happened so quickly and seemed to be racing out of control. I had done nothing wrong and now I had received a visit from the police about a possible murder for which I appeared to be the prime suspect. Ridiculous! And in my confused state, whilst it had seemed a good idea at the time, I had fled the scene and escaped arrest. I pulled out the mobile phone from my jeans and made the call I'd been pondering over.

'Amanda, hi, it's David.'

'How are you?' she asked.

'Where do I start? You won't believe the day I've had. Too much to tell you over the phone.'

'Okay. We can get together this evening, no problem. If that's all right with you.'

'No, it's not actually, Amanda.'

'Well, I'm at work at the moment but if it's an emergency, I suppose I could try and get away and meet you somewhere.'

'That's no good either. I can't get into my house at the moment and consequently, I can't get to my car keys. I could meet you about five-hundred yards away from my home, if that's any good?'

Amanda paused and said, 'You're worrying me, David. You sound really strange.'

'You'll find out why when we get together.'
'Right, I'll make my excuses here and I'll be with you in about an hour's time. Let's say 4pm?'
'Great. Thanks, Amanda. If you park up by the bus stop down the road from me, I'll come and find you.'
'Are you in any trouble?' she asked.
'Well, I don't think so. It's just all the other buggers, isn't it!'
'I can't wait to see you, David. You take care. I'll have a word with my manager and get on the road. See you in an hour!'

I looked at my phone again and noticed six missed calls from an unfamiliar number. There was also a voicemail message. I clicked on it and the message was from DS Craven, 'If you get this message, Mr Jones, please call me. There was no need to run away. We just needed to get some more details from you. Nothing to worry about, you know. Please call me.'

I deleted it and then called the number back. It was to a mobile number and not the main police station. It was answered after just one ring, 'Craven.'

Hello, it's me, David Jones. You left a message to call you.'

'Yes, Mr Jones', he responded excitedly. 'Thank you for getting in touch. Where are you?'

I smiled and said, 'Nice try, DS Craven. You've turned this into the script of *The Fugitive*. Totally unnecessary.'

'What? *The Fugitive*? I don't follow you.'

'Oh, come on, you must know the story. First of all, it started as a TV series in the sixties and then starred Harrison Ford in a movie. This is how it goes. After being wrongfully convicted for the murder of his wife and unjustly sentenced to death, the central character escapes from custody and sets out to find his wife's killer, catch him and clear his own name, while being pursued by a team of U.S. Marshals. Does that sound familiar?'

'No, I don't know what you're talking about.'

'I meant my story. My being wrongly accused of murder and escaping custody whilst being pursued by the authorities.'

'Deary me. You've really got to calm down. I think you've been watching too much television, Mr Jones.'

'Probably. That's why I'm ending this call now in case you're trying to put a trace on it.'

I ended the call and ten seconds later, it rang again. It was DS Craven's number on my screen and therefore, I ignored it. I went back into the shed to sit down. I knew that the Jenkins' were away at the moment and that they would never know their part in my circumvention. I left it half an hour and wended my way towards the street. Amanda's red mini duly turned up and I emerged between some hedges, opened the passenger door of her car and sat down next to her.

She turned towards me and said, 'Oh David, tell me what's happened.'

'We've got to get away from here, Amanda. Please drive to anywhere that's got a café. I'm gasping. Oh, and I haven't got any money by the way. I thought I'd better warn you. My wallet's at home or with the police.'

Amanda engaged first gear and pulled away from the kerb as she said, 'Police? What on earth have you been up to?'

As we drove along the road, I told her about my tribulations. 'I just don't know what to do, Amanda.'

32

We pulled up outside a café and we went inside finding a table near the window. We ordered coffees to start with and Amanda reached out across the table to hold my hand.

'Have you eaten at all today, David?'

I shook my head and she continued, 'Right, we'll get a meal and afterwards, we'll get in touch with the police.'

'Yes, I guess I can't just leave it. I'll give them a call when we've finished here.'

'No. We'll go back to your house and see if anyone's there. If not, hopefully, they've left it secure. As you won't be able to get access, I'll drive you over to Kempston and we can have it out with them.'

'What?'

'Well, you said to me that you were totally innocent of any implication in this Browne's disappearance, or murder! We've got to get this sorted, David. Firstly, you've got to get your door keys and passport back; and secondly, you've got to clear your name. You must be worried sick.'

The meals arrived and we didn't speak again until we'd finished. Amanda settled up with the waitress and we left the café to return to her car.

'Amanda, before we set off, let's talk. I'm not really worried, you know. I suppose it's because I've done nothing wrong. I'll give them a call.'

'No. This is serious, David, I'll drive you over there right now. Answer their questions, let them get a copy of your fingerprints if that's what they want and get your passport and keys back. Give them a ring to let them know what you're intending to do. We can pop back to your house when we know a bit more.'

'Thanks. It's good to have a plan.'

33

'Okay, whilst I drive us along to the police station, you make the call.'

I nodded and Amanda proceeded to start us on the journey to Kempston. I got my mobile out and switched it back on. I noticed another four missed calls and one new voicemail message from DS Craven. Before I made the call, I listened to his message, 'Hello, Mr Jones, as you're a fan of film and TV, as they say, you can run, but you can't hide. Just bear that in mind, sir and turn yourself in. Going on the run is not doing yourself any favours. You've got to realise that. Call me back as soon as you get this message, please.' I returned the call and it went straight to voicemail. I left a message, 'DS Craven, sorry to have missed your call. I was otherwise engaged with someone else. We are on our way to see you now in Kempston. See you soon.'

I put the phone in a convenient place inside the car in case it rang again.

'David, earlier when you were going over this morning's visit by the police, you told them about your wife dying and the little job you've got with your ex-father-in-law. But did you mention me at all? That we'd been an item for six months or so?'

'Err, no. At that point, I didn't have any reason to. Yes, I told them about Donna because they queried my affluent lifestyle, ha ha.' I squeezed Amanda's thigh and continued, 'but we weren't getting on very well leading up to her illness, as you know.'

'And you gave the police your ex-father-in-law's name and number?'

'Yes, I told them that Alan works from home now but has a small advertising sales team working from an office in Biggleswade. And hey, hang on a minute, little job?'

34

'Well, you said it didn't take you long and wasn't that often either.'

'Okay.' I grabbed my mobile as I turned to Amanda and said, 'Listen, I've changed my mind about going to see the police. I'm sorry. Can you turn around?'

'No, I can't, you big baby. First of all, we're on the dual carriageway; secondly, they've got your house keys, car keys and passport; and lastly and most importantly, they need your fingerprints and for you to go over a statement they've concocted. If you don't appear now, all hell will break loose. If you're as innocent as you claim to be, you've got nothing to fear.'

'If?'

'Look, you're my boyfriend. I'm bound to be biased but I wasn't with you on the day in question.'

'Oh great.'

At that moment, my mobile rang with its irritatingly shrill ringtone that I had been meaning to change for the last month and I answered the call, 'David Jones … yes, hello … in about ten, fifteen minutes, I suppose. Okay, see you then.'

Amanda smiled and said, 'DS Craven?'

'Yes, he'd gone home but is now back at his office at Bedfordshire Police HQ.'

'Not long now, David.'

'As the hangman said to Dr Crippen.'

'Pardon?'

'I feel like the condemned man.'

'He wasn't called David, was he?'

'I don't think so. I'm not an expert on murder, court cases and sentencing, you know, whatever you think.'

Amanda pulled into the car park and killed the engine.

'When you go in there to talk to them, I don't think that you should mention me.'

'What do you mean, Amanda?'

'Well, you said that you haven't mentioned already that you have a girlfriend. Therefore, if they ask, tell them that you got a lift here from a friend.'

I frowned and put the phone in my jacket pocket. As I put my hand on the door handle to exit the car, Amanda put her hand on my arm and said, 'Hey, don't look so worried. You'll be fine. And don't forget these two things; firstly, I love you; and secondly, I work for a firm of solicitors.'

'Oh my God, do you think that I'll need one of those, Amanda?'

'That's what happens in these scenarios, isn't it? It's just that there may come a point in there where, however well you're coping with the questioning, you may want some additional help from someone next to you who knows the law, that's all.'

'Thanks.' I opened the door and just before I closed it, said, 'I love you too.'

I left Amanda in the car park and walked to the entrance. I approached the reception area and standing behind this rather modern facade was an ageing police officer who must have been in his early sixties but looked older. Seeing that he had a new customer, he quickly tried to tuck his shirt into his trousers to smarten himself up but failed.

He smiled at me and said, 'Afternoon, sir, how can I help?'

36

'I'm here to see DS Craven, it's David Jones.'
'I'll just see if he's here. If you take a seat over there,' he waved an arm in the direction of some comfy, modular sofa seating in police blue, 'I'll let him know where you are.'
I sat down and glanced at my watch. Surprisingly, there were no magazines or police newsletters to read, so I perused the posters and notices on the wall. A Sergeant Terry Hall had won this month's 100 Club lottery and a notice showing the image of local criminal, Dwane Kwezezi, indicated that he was wanted in connection with a series of house burglaries, car thefts and violent disorder. As if officers reading this poster needed to be told it went on to remind them that, 'Violent Disorder and Affray are serious behavioural offences of the Public Order Act (POA)'. The final line stated that 'Mr Kwezizi should be approached with caution'. Some wag, police staff or otherwise, had added in biro 'if at all!' Looking at his photograph, that probably wasn't going to happen any time soon.
After ten minutes, I approached the desk again and, reading his name badge, said, 'Hi, Peter. Any news?'
He looked up with an astonished look on his face and replied, 'Do I know you?'
I smiled sardonically at him, 'Yes, I married your daughter last year.' Seeing a mixture of confusion, anger, and hate descend over his pudgy face, I continued, 'Your badge. Your name, Peter Fynch, it's on your name badge.' As he glanced down to check to see if I was telling the truth, the phone next to him rang and he answered it.
'Yes, sir, he's here waiting for you in reception. Okay, I'll tell him.'

PC Angry then looked up to address me, 'That was DS Craven on the phone. He says he'll be about another ten minutes.'

I shook my head and said to my new friend, 'You know, Peter, no wonder there's so much unsolved crime in this country. What do *you* think?'

Having had his afternoon ruined, he did well to get himself under control sufficiently to reply, 'Don't call me that. Please sit down again.'

'Why not? Isn't that your name then? Have you picked up someone else's badge?'

Even I could tell that Peter didn't want to converse in friendly banter with me as he was starting to make his way out from behind the counter.

I continued, 'I tell you what, Peter, or whatever your name is, I'm going to go outside to let my friend know that it looks like I'll be a while yet.'

As I exited the main doors, I failed to hear his latest remarks. I had made my mind up to leave the whole site as I had once again, gone off the idea of going through some sort of interrogation. Once out on the main road, I thought that I had better call Amanda, 'Hi, just to let you know; I'm not in the police station now.'

'Blimey, that was quick. Good news?'

'Err, not exactly. I haven't seen anyone yet. There was going to be a delay and I guess I saw it as some kind of omen.'

'You must have told someone that you were leaving.'

Well actually, I just said to the guy on reception that I was going to let the friend that had driven me to the station know that there was going to be a delay. I didn't name you as I didn't think you'd want to get involved.'

38

'So, are you on your way back to my car then?'

'No. I'm about half a mile away now, on the main road.'

'What? Have you finally lost your mind, David? First of all, you didn't wait to see DS Craven to discuss this and get your keys and passport back, like a normal, rational, sane person would do; and secondly, you go on the run again, for Christ's sake!'

'I'm sorry.'

'You're sorry? Sorry?! I can't take this anymore. Agh!'

'What's the matter?'

***

In response to the three taps on her window, Amanda wound it down. Two police officers stood beside her car and a WPC leaned down to speak, 'Good evening. Can you tell me, are you waiting here to pick up a David Jones, by any chance?'

'Well, I was. I'm not so sure now.'

'What do you mean, madam?'

'Two reasons really: First of all, we're in a relationship but I'm questioning whether I want to remain in it bearing in mind his recent activities; and secondly, he's not here is he. He's on the run again. I just can't cope with this.' At this point, Amanda burst into tears and thrust the mobile phone into the hand of the WPC and said, 'Here, talk to him. He's on the phone.'

***

'Mr Jones? A young lady has just handed me this phone to speak to you. Please don't hang up; just listen to me. DS Craven is now available back at the office to talk with you. PC Fynch on the front desk raised the alarm and said that you couldn't wait. I would urge you to reconsider your decision and to return to HQ, please.'

I paused as I waited for some cars to pass by as I crossed the road. WPC White then spoke again, 'Mr Jones, are you there? Can you hear me?'

'Yes. Look, I feel so stupid. This is not me, okay? Twenty-four hours ago, I was a normal, some would say, fairly boring sort of bloke, I suppose and now, I'm on Bedfordshire Constabulary's "Most Wanted" list ...'

'Calm down, Mr Jones. You're nothing of the sort. I'm sure that this can all be sorted out if you come in to talk to us.'

I didn't reply and I ended the call. It was starting to get dark and I began to realise that I had no clear idea as to what my best plan of action was going to be. I had no house keys, no car keys and was now about fifteen miles from my home, even if I could get into it. If I could get back to my neighbourhood, my only prospect of shelter tonight was going to be the Jenkins' shed. Great. I suppose that I could trek back to the police car park to try and find Amanda, but I shouldn't think that she'd still be waiting for me or even wanting to speak to me. I decided to try and call her anyway. I dialled her mobile but after about fifteen seconds, it went to voicemail. I suspected that she had seen who was calling her phone and had decided not to pick up. I really had burnt all my bridges. The prospect of the next few hours came to my mind now. Where would I find food, shelter? At that moment, the shrill ringtone started again. It

40

seemed even more urgent now to my fragile state of mind. Could this be Amanda?

'Hello?'

'Mr Jones, this is DS Craven speaking. I've been told that you've gone walkabout again. I don't know what you think you're up to, but we can't mess about like this.'

Things now got even worse. It had started raining and I looked heavenwards. The clouds coming in from the west were really dark and it was obvious to me what I needed to do.

'Okay, I'll come in. Can you come and pick me up then?'

'Are you joking? No more games, please.'

DS Craven sounded pissed off, so I acquiesced to his request, 'I promise that I won't mess around anymore. I want to come in and ensure that I can convince you I've got nothing to answer for.'

'Well, that will make a change. You know, it makes our lives so much easier when our customers agree to be more compliant.'

'Sorry. I'm having a bad week and the rain is getting worse …'

I heard a sigh at the other end as DS Craven continued, 'Oh, go on then. I don't know why the public think we run a free taxi service. Where are you exactly?'

'I don't know really. I took a right turn out of the main entrance way and just kept walking. Just before I got to the first roundabout, I crossed the road and that's where I am now.'

'Right, I'll send PC Kranic out in a car to try and find you. Remember, no more games, Mr Jones.'

41

He ended the call. Whilst I waited for the police car, I started to imagine them putting together the words and using my passport photograph on a potential 'Wanted' poster to place on the noticeboard next to Dwane Kwezezi's one!

Chapter Four

I had been allowed a visit to the toilet and was now seated in what had been labelled, Interview Room 2, on the door. The relatively modern building was similarly designed internally as well. I glanced around the room which was approximately twenty feet by ten feet in size but was already showing signs that it had seen quite a bit of use over the last few years. I was seated in one of the four chairs that complemented the very basic table in front of me. DS Craven and one other officer re-entered the room and sat down.

'Mr Jones …'

I interrupted and said, 'David, please.'

'No, for the purposes of this evening's interview, I think that we should keep this fairly formal,' he replied.

With the nod of his head, he indicated the officer next to him and continued, 'This is my colleague, Detective Constable Eldrid. Now, before I proceed, Mr Jones, can I arrange a cup of tea or coffee for you? We may be here a while.'

'Thank you, yes. Tea, please. No sugar.'

DS Craven picked up the telephone on the desk.

'Hi, three teas to Interview Room 2, please Mary.'

He then started to get a couple of files out from his briefcase. 'I've updated DC Eldrid on activities over the last few days,' he continued. DC Eldrid nodded in concurrence as he studied me intensely. I didn't like the look of him but then why should I? At about forty-five years of age, he was older than his colleague and I got the impression that he possibly resented the fact that he was unlikely to progress

44

further up the rungs of his police career. My musings were interrupted as the door opened and a woman, I presumed to be Mary, entered the room carrying a tray with the teacups. As soon as the tray was placed on the table and she had left the room, DS Craven said, 'Okay, everyone, help yourselves. Without further ado we've got to get down to business. We've had enough delays.'

DC Eldrid was still staring at me and hadn't touched his teacup. I tried to ignore him as I took mine and had a first sip. DS Craven took his cup and for now, put it to one side. 'Right. Now, Mr Jones, I'm recording this evening's proceedings in accordance with policy.'

He handed an A4 sized sheet of paper which contained the interview policy of Bedfordshire Police, called a 265a Notice. Then, he pressed a button on the top of the tape recorder next to him and continued, 'Today's date is Thursday 9th April, the time is 7.48pm, in Interview Room 2 at Bedfordshire Police HQ. Those present, are DS Paul Craven, DC Grahame Eldrid and Mr David Jones. Mr Jones, first of all, would you kindly confirm your full name, date of birth and current postal address for me, please?'

'David Kingdom Jones. 6th June 1986. 47 Beaumont Road, Langford, Bedfordshire.'

DS Craven gave me a wry smile and said, 'Kingdom?'

'Yes.' I sighed as I trotted out the mantra that I had given numerous times throughout my life. 'At the time, my parents lived in Portsmouth and I was born at the Queen Alexandra Hospital there. Obviously, my second name is from Isambard Kingdom Brunel. Hopefully, you've heard of him?' I raised an eyebrow.

45

'Yes, of course.' This was the first time that DC Eldrid had spoken since he had entered the room and I placed his accent as being either Essex or East London.

I carried on, 'You see, Brunel was born in Portsmouth too and with my father being an engineer, one thing led to another.'

DS Craven got back to business. 'Before we formally commence the interview, I would like to remind you that you were given a police caution earlier today.'

I nodded as I looked at the empty chair next to me. 'Do I need a solicitor here with me?' I asked.

'I don't know. What do you think?' DS Craven replied.

'Well, as you say, I watch films, TV dramas and read some books so I'm vaguely familiar with how things play out.' I took another drink of my tea before I carried on. 'I'm sure you're supposed to tell me if I have a right to have one present, or something?'

'I was coming to that. It's been a long day, for all sorts of reasons.' The two police officers exchanged confidential glances to one another. DC Eldrid took the piece of paper handed to him and said, 'Mr Jones, you have a legal right to speak to a solicitor, whether over the phone or in person. I suppose that depending on how you feel about the crime you may or may not have committed, the advice and guidance a solicitor gives you at this stage can make a significant difference to the outcome of your case.'

He paused and I looked at the two officers in turn. Getting no further reaction, I commented, 'Look, I just don't know what to do. Obviously, I've never been in this situation before. What do you suggest?'

46

'And obviously, we cannot advise you one way or the other, Mr Jones,' DS Craven confirmed.

Presumably, because the interview was being taped, DS Craven piped up, 'We urge you to exercise this right. It's free, so you might as well. If you decide to go for it, we cannot question you until you have received advice. However, you can decline legal advice and if you do, you may change your mind later.'

I shook my head and looked out of the window. It was very dark outside now and the rain was pounding against the window. How had my life spiralled out of control so quickly?

'What's the matter, Mr Jones?' DS Craven looked almost as worried as me.

'I don't know what to do for the best. If I request a solicitor to come in to help me, it seems like an admission of guilt. If I go for it, how does it all work then?'

DC Eldrid answered, it appeared to me, almost begrudgingly, 'Your lawyer can speak to you privately, either on the phone or in person, at any time while you remain in police custody. You can also request to have a solicitor in the room with you while you are being questioned.'

'You need to make a decision one way or another,' DS Craven said as he pushed another sheet of paper towards me. 'Perhaps this will help you to decide.'

It was the statement that they had prepared for me to go through and if I was happy with it, to sign. I read through it. It was a basic statement of the facts and didn't seem too contentious to me. However, I pushed the paper and the proffered pen back to the police officers' side of the table.

DS Craven gave one of his exaggerated sighs and said, 'What's the matter now, Mr Jones?'

'I'm still thinking about your last question. You know, do I need a solicitor now, before I sign this statement, or not?'

I put one of my hands up to my forehead and rubbed it gently. After about ten seconds, I sat back in my chair and looked up towards the ceiling.

DS Craven glanced at the clock on the wall and said, 'It's getting late. When was the last time that you had something to eat, Mr Jones?'

I looked at my watch: Eight-fifty in the evening. I screwed up my brow to try and remember and my stomach came to my assistance.

'Well, it was when I went out with Amanda to have something and that was about 2.30pm in the afternoon, I suppose. I must admit I'm starving now. I was all right until you mentioned it!'

'Right, I'll get DC Eldrid to take you down to the cafeteria to get something to eat.'

'Cafeteria? It's all right here, isn't it!'

DS Craven said, 'I am stopping the tape recording. At 8.50pm Mr David Jones and DC Grahame Eldrid are leaving the interview room.' Accordingly, it was turned off and we both stood up to leave the room. I then said, 'Of course, I haven't got any money with me as it's at home and I can't get access. You've got my keys, don't forget.'

'Don't worry, this one's on us. You're here at our invitation.'

The cafeteria was on the ground floor. A good selection of hot and cold food was on offer and the cafeteria was staffed by just one person, a middle-aged woman who smiled when we approached the counter. As I glanced up at the display showing the available selection, PC Eldrid said, in his usual dour manner, 'Just choose something small. We'll want to get back to business as soon as possible, okay?'

I raised my eyebrows and said to them both, 'Just a cheese and tomato sandwich, please.'

'Ham and cheese for me, Maria. Thanks. Oh, and two coffees too.'

We took the tray to a table nearby and started on our evening meal. He wasn't a great conversationalist for which I was grateful. Once we had finished the sandwiches, he grabbed his takeaway coffee and said, 'Right, let's go.'

As we walked to the stairway, I commented, 'Good little facility you've got here.'

'It's open 24/7. Has to be. Hundreds of people work here, different shift patterns, so it's a must have.'

We got back to Interview Room 2 and DS Craven was holding two small pieces of paper.

'We've received two telephone calls. One from an Alan Wade.'

'My ex-father-in-law.'

'And one from Amanda.'

'My girlfriend.'

'No, your ex-girlfriend.'

'What?'

'We had quite a long conversation. Sorry to be the bearer of bad news, David.'

'Steady on, you just called me David.'

I looked from DS Craven to DC Eldrid and back again. They were obviously gauging my reaction to this news as they awaited a comment from me.

'What did she say, exactly?'

'She's pretty cut up, actually. Basically, she doesn't want to continue in a relationship with you. Since you left her in her car crying, she's had a bit of time to think about things, weighing up the good times with you over the past six months versus the bombshell you delivered today and the potential life with you in the future.'

'How ironic.'

'What do you mean, Mr Jones?'

'Oh, I see. It's back to Mr Jones, is it? Ha, ha, ha. I was about to ask you whether I could make a phone call. I was going to call Amanda as she works for a firm of solicitors.'

'So, you've made a decision then?'

I looked up at the clock on the wall. It was ten o'clock in the evening.

'Yes, I have. I notice that you haven't started the tape recorder again.'

'If you're happy to proceed, I was just about to mention it, so let's go ahead.'

I shook my head. 'No, I've decided not to go ahead.'

DC Eldrid then said, 'We said, no more games, Mr Jones, if you remember.'

I banged my fist down on to the desk and everything on it jumped up.

'No more games? I can't speak to Amanda apparently, so I'm giving up. I've had enough. You'd better turn your machine on again.'

'What do you mean?'

'I want you to record what I'm saying. It's rather important, don't you think?'

'I'll decide when to start recording, Mr Jones. I'm in charge of this investigation.' DS Craven turned to his colleague and nodded. DC Eldrid pressed the record button.

'Go ahead. Recording re-commenced at 10.05pm: DS Craven, DC Eldrid and David Jones in attendance.'

'Right, I've made my mind up. I'm in no fit state to carry on with all of this. I'm not feeling very well. It doesn't look like I'll get access to the solicitors of my choice, even if I decide to go down that route. I'll sign the statement that you prepared for me, even though it's not perfect, if it gets me out of here.'

'We haven't asked you our questions yet, so I don't think we're about to end the interview any time soon, Mr Jones,' DS Craven raised his voice slightly for the first time today.

I banged my fist down on the desk again but with even more vigour this time. 'You're not listening to me,' I shouted. 'I'm not feeling well. Let me go home. Give me my keys and passport back.'

DC Eldrid retorted, 'Keep your voice down. We'll go through the statement again and you can make whatever amendments to it that you want and then you can sign it.'

'No. I'll say it again. You're not listening to me, are you?' I stood up, 'I'm out of here,' I said and started to move towards the doorway. The two policemen moved as one, to block my potential exit.

'Sit down, Mr Jones.'

'No. Now what are you going to do about it?' I folded my arms and stood my ground.

'As I said before, you're not under arrest at the moment but that could change very soon.'

'You can't intimidate me. I'm here helping you with your enquiries, voluntarily at the moment. I'm so glad that this conversation is being recorded, DS Craven. You've already taken up a massive part of my day and there must be a law or some guidelines somewhere which dictate how long the police can interview suspects. I'm sure a lawyer would have a field day going through a transcript of this tape!'

'So, now you want a solicitor?'

I sat down again and rested my forehead on the table. The officers sat down opposite me and all was peace and quiet for two minutes. I raised my head and sat back in my chair looking from one to the other.

'I'm so tired. Unless you're going to charge me with murder, DS Craven, I have to insist that you release me.' I smiled, hoping that that would illicit some sort of response.

'Who said anything about murder?' DS Craven responded.

'Now who's playing games ...?' I retorted. 'You said that the MIT had instructed, or invited you, to look into matters in your local area?'

DC Eldrid glanced at his colleague before replying, 'The Major Investigation Team doesn't just look into deaths that have been reported to them. We can't divulge too much information at this stage.'

'No, so we're all just wasting our time, aren't we! I'm sure that we've all got better things to do.' With that, I stood up again and made my way around the side of the table. Before I could get to the door, DC Eldrid grabbed my arm and shouted, 'Sit down!'

I pulled my arm free of his grip again and said, 'You've just assaulted me! You're not very bright are you, DC Eldrid? You shouldn't have done that as I'm sure your superior officer here will confirm.' I raised an eyebrow at DS Craven.

'Shall we all calm down now?' he replied. 'DS Eldrid please go and get us all a cup of tea or something.'

When DS Craven and I were alone, he said for the sake of the taping, 'Tape recording stopped at 10.25pm, DC Eldrid has left the room.' Turning to me, he continued, 'David, we need to make some progress here. I know that you're tired but so are we.'

'David? David? And you accuse me of playing games! You said that there had been a second telephone message, a call from my ex-father-in-law, Alan Wade?'

'Yes. He returned my call and we had a chat about you, his daughter, the marriage, his work and your ongoing relationship with him and the magazines.'

'Was he okay? How did he react to the news that I was being questioned for something?'

'He sounded fine but obviously concerned about you. Tell me more about Donna, what she was like?'

I looked at DS Craven wistfully and then towards the window. I couldn't see outside as it was too dark, but the rain had stopped. 'Donna was the love of my life. We had been friends at school and then started going out together. When we left at the age of seventeen, it carried on. It was Alan's idea that his first daughter be named Donna after *10cc's* hit of the same name. He was a big fan.'

'*10cc*, a pop group in the seventies, right?'

At that moment, the door burst open and DC Eldrid entered the room with two uniformed policemen. 'Okay, that's him. Take him away.'

DS Craven shouted, 'What the hell do you think you're doing?'

I pushed the two officers away as they tried to grab me by the arms and I said, calmly, 'Try anything like that with me again and I'll set my friend, Dwayne, on to you.'

'I'm in charge here. DC Eldrid. I am instigating a PD 284, a Suspension of Police Officers Procedure, against you. You have acted beyond your realm of responsibility and I am removing you from this investigation. Get out of this room now! The two officers can stay here for a minute whilst I talk to them separately. Go home and I will see you in my office at 10am tomorrow.'

Without further comment, DC Eldrid left the room and the door, open. 'Right, you two, a quick word in your shell likes in the corridor outside, please.' Turning to me, he said, 'I'll be back in a minute for a little chat. Don't run away!'

After the door had slammed behind them, I was left in the room alone. I started to go over the last few hours in my mind. It had been like a police drama on TV and not a very good one at that. What was the last thing Craven had said? 'Don't run away.' Hey, don't put ideas into my head!

Chapter Five

Amanda put the phone down. She had been talking for the last hour and a half with her best friend, Steph. It was late but because of the last thing that Amanda had said, Steph had insisted on going around to see her. Twenty minutes later, she was on the doorstep and being invited in.

They hugged and Steph said, 'Go into the living room, I'll make us some coffee and I'll bring it in.'

'Coffee? Forget that! I've got some Pinot Grigio in the fridge, glasses are in the cabinet above.'

A few minutes later, sitting next to each other on the settee with a glass of wine in their hands, they resumed their earlier conversation.

'You okay now? You were pretty upset on the phone tonight. And in view of what you told me latterly, don't have too many of these either,' Steph said, waving her glass about.

With that, the tears started flowing again and Amanda produced a new, dry handkerchief from her trousers to dab at her cheeks. 'I'm sorry.'

Steph put her arm around her friend's shoulders and said, 'There's no need to apologise. We've been through so much together over the years. I'm always going to be here to help and anyway, you haven't done anything wrong!'

When the sobs had stopped, Amanda continued, 'It's bad enough realising I've wasted the last six months of my life on a relationship that's not what I thought it was and has got to end, but then to come to terms with a potential pregnancy and what my options are around that scenario.'

56

'Two things, Amanda. Firstly, are you sure that you want to end it with David? He's in a bit of a spot right now, but for all we know, he's innocent. Your decision about that situation impinges on the next one. You said on the phone that you're late. How late are you? I seem to remember that you've been in this state before. I mean medically, not with previous relationships.'

Amanda drained her glass and refilled them both. 'I don't know about David. I thought he was different. We were getting on well, making plans for a possible future together. We even talked about the possibility of selling our respective houses and buying one jointly that we could move in to. We didn't talk about marriage or anything like that. It was too soon for that, I felt. Ha! Perhaps he wouldn't have been interested anyway! As to your second question, my period is about four weeks late. And yes, that has happened to me before whether I've been in a relationship or not.'

'Okay then. First things first. Tomorrow I suggest that you have a pregnancy test done and that will either put your mind at rest or …'

'Not! You're right though. I'll do that as soon as I can. I've just decided something, Steph. I'm going to give David a call to find out what's going on.'

'It's midnight, Amanda and goodness knows where he is now!'

'Well, I can leave a message, if necessary.'

'And of course, when you find out a bit more tomorrow if the test is positive, you'll have to let David know.'

'I'll cross that bridge if I need to. Excuse me a second, I'll call him now.'

Amanda dialled his number and the call went straight to voicemail, 'Hi, David, it's Amanda. I hope you're all right. Sorry about earlier today. I just can't cope with situations or people at the moment, for all sorts of reasons. Anyway, speak soon.'

Steph had rounded up the glasses and the wine bottle and taken them into the kitchen.

When she returned to the living room, she smiled at Amanda and said, 'Feeling better now?'

She nodded and stood up.

'I'm so grateful, Steph. I don't know what I'd do without you.'

'It's been a long day for you, I think you should try and get some sleep now. What will you do about getting a test done tomorrow?'

'Oh, I'll go down to Boots. They've got test kits that you can buy in there for five or ten pounds. I overheard one of my colleagues at work when she was talking to a friend on the phone recently.'

As Amanda was showing Steph out of her house, her landline phone started to ring. 'Right, I'd better get that. It's probably David. I'll call you tomorrow, Steph. Thanks again, bye.'

She rushed in and answered the phone which was on a side table next to her settee. She looked at the clock opposite her: One-twenty in the morning.

'Er, hello?' DS Craven apologised for the lateness of the call and asked whether she had had any contact with David Jones in the past few hours.

'No, sorry. Why? Don't you know where David is then?'

He didn't want to say too much but said he would call again later in the day. Amanda just looked at the telephone receiver in her hand when the call ended abruptly.

***

DS Craven returned to the interview room to find it empty. He left the room, slamming the door behind him. Thinking, or hoping, that David Jones had needed to visit the toilets, he made that his first port of call. Finding them empty too, he pulled out his mobile and called Jones' girlfriend's number which he had previously saved alongside others relating to the current investigation.

That call had not borne fruit either. What on earth was Jones playing at? He then went back to his office and placed the case's files and tapes in one of his desk drawers. At one-thirty in the morning, staff were thin on the ground, but he could see through the windows of his office that in the open plan area, a number of his detective colleagues were working on cases, some on the telephone, others on their paperwork. He decided to go and see them.

As he walked over to them, they all looked up and stopped what they were doing. He waited for the last telephone conversation to end and then said, 'Okay, chaps, listen up, please. I am currently carrying out an investigation at the behest of a London MIT. I was being assisted, by DC Grahame Eldrid whom I have removed from this case. Far from impressing me with his performance, he went over and above his authority and I have, unfortunately, had to **instigate a PD 284 against him**.'

'A **Suspension of Police Officers Procedure?**'

'Yes, Susan.' Craven wandered over to DC Susan Parkes' desk which had various bits of paper scattered around. 'Working on anything exciting at the moment?'

She ran a hand through her blonde tresses and looked up, 'A potential rape case. I'm following up on an allegation by a woman involving her ex-boyfriend.'

'How's it going?' he asked her.

'Quite well, actually. I've taken statements from both parties and some of their mutual friends. I have some sympathy for him actually but I'm keeping an open mind, obviously. It shouldn't take too long. Her evidence seems a bit flaky to me. So, what's happened to Grahame?'

'He's gone; he's history. This case, working with me, was his last chance, basically. I've monitored his performance over the past year or so and I haven't liked what I've seen. He wasn't my first choice to tie up with me on this case, but I knew that it would give me the opportunity of getting up close and personal. I will be seeing him later this morning, at 10am.'

'So, the case you're working on, MIT. Wow!'

'Yeah, it's a weird one. And it should be relatively simple to check out but our main possible suspect keeps disappearing. Firstly, from his own home, secondly from this police station.'

'The Scarlet Pimpernel!' Susan smiled.

'It's not funny. It's embarrassing. I'm going home now as I've got to get some sleep. Back here at 8am.'

She grabbed Craven's arm and said, 'Paul, I've only just logged on and there's not much more that I can do on my rape case, so I've got a bit of time if you need someone to help.' DC Parkes smiled enigmatically.

60

'Well, I'll need a new partner on this one, that's why I came out to talk to the team so, yes, welcome aboard. I've just got to make a call. Come into my office in ten minutes, okay?'

DC Parkes tidied up her paperwork and put the file in her desk drawer. She then announced to the three colleagues nearest to her, 'I've pretty much done all I can on the Bridger rape case for now and DS Craven needs some help now that Grahame's off his team, so I've agreed to join him. He's off home in a minute to get some rest, so I'll just go and get an update on what he's been working on.'

Craven had just ended his telephone conversation when DC Parkes knocked on his door and he gestured for her to enter. He handed her the case file and spent ten minutes bringing her up to date. She said that she would make a number of inquiries and discuss the progress, or otherwise, on his return. Craven left his office and then the department. As he started on his journey to find his car in the car park, his mind wandered from David Jones and his possible whereabouts, towards Susan Parkes. She was an attractive woman, recently divorced and he was single too. He hoped that he hadn't mistaken a certain chemistry between them. Food for thought …

***

Having been left alone in the interview room for ten minutes, it had not been my original intention to abscond again, but I was tired and disconsolate and the door was ajar for goodness sake! I had edged out into the corridor and there had been no one about. I decided to go back down to the cafeteria area. It was like the Marie Celeste. I called out, 'Hello, anyone about?'

Hopeless, no one there, so I entered the kitchen area and walked back through to the rear of that room, on the ground floor. I entered a store cupboard and sat down on the floor behind some large catering boxes containing coffee, biscuits, baked beans and crumpets. I got the impression that I could attempt to run away again but I didn't want to. What would be the point? Where would I go? I put my head back and closed my eyes. I must have drifted off to sleep. I didn't know for how long, ten minutes or two hours, I couldn't be certain. I was brought back to the real world by someone gently prodding me with a kitchen utensil.

'Oi, wake up,' a young female cook said, 'no funny business. Officers are on their way to get you.' Her eastern European accent went well with her long, dyed blonde hair. She smiled at me and seemed to have some sympathy too as two PCs arrived to pick me up.

'David Jones, please come with us back to the interview room. A detective is waiting there to continue the interview.' This Scottish chap with a red beard said to his colleague, 'Okay, better call DC Parkes and let her know we've found him and that we'll be with her in Interview Room 1 in about ten minutes or so.'

We all traipsed back up the stairs and I entered the interview room. This one was different in that it had no window looking out on to the world outside. It was the same size of room though and had a similar table and four chairs to the other interview room. One difference though was the striking blonde sitting down awaiting my arrival. She looked up from her paperwork as I entered and opened up the dialogue, 'Mr Jones. Hello, please sit down, my name is DC Parkes. Just to let you know, DS Craven has left the station to go home and get some much-needed rest.'

'Lucky him,' I replied. 'No, I won't sit down, thanks. I'll probably fall asleep.'

DC Parkes smiled at me, 'I'm sorry to hear that. What seems to be the trouble?'

'I'll tell you what the bloody trouble is,' I had raised my voice and instantly regretted in reacting so truculently, 'but I've been here for hours helping the police with their inquiries and I've been here voluntarily, don't forget.'

'And we're very grateful, Mr Jones, I'm sure. I've read through your file and I've spoken with DS Craven and it seems that some of the interviews have been truncated to say the least, haven't they? Firstly, the one at your home and twice from the police station itself. You're getting yourself a bit of a reputation!'

'I'm hoping that you are going to take notice of what I'm about to say. DS Craven and DC Eldrid didn't, oh, by the way, what happened to him?'

'I'm not in a position to discuss other officers, I'm afraid.'

'And I'm afraid I can't discuss anything with you or anyone else! I'm shattered. I haven't been arrested for anything, or even accused of anything as far as I'm aware. So, I request the return of my house keys and passport, please. To my credit, I could have run off earlier, but didn't, I just went downstairs to the cafeteria area for a rest.'

'It's not possible to return your keys, I'm afraid.'

I was still standing and I turned to put my hand on the door handle.

'Don't!' DC Parkes shouted. More calmly, she said, 'If you sit down here, I'll make a telephone call.'

I did so and she went to the doorway to beckon a PC over to ensure that I wasn't a flight risk again. It was the friend of PC Red Beard that I'd met recently. We viewed each other warily. I asked him a fairly innocuous question, but he ignored me whilst not taking his eyes off me. I changed the subject and said to him, 'Shame about the Hatters this season, eh?' Getting no response, I commented, 'Watford fan then?'

Eliciting no response, I gave up. Five minutes later, DC Parkes returned. Wearily I said to her, 'What did he say then?'

'Who?'

'DS Craven.'

'I didn't want to disturb him, it's 2.30am. I spoke to Chief Inspector Bryce who had wanted an update from me.'

'Right, as I'm not prepared to talk anymore, I want to know what you're going to do about getting me home. And I'll need my keys to get in, obviously.'

'I understand that your lift is not an option anymore.'

'No, not from the person that brought me here. And as you say, it's 2.30am. So, I'm certainly not going to call anyone else!'

'We certainly haven't finished talking with you, Mr Jones.'

'I need some rest, just like your colleague does and anyway, the treatment that I've received from you lot is bordering on cruel or downright illegal or something.'

She shook her head slowly, her blonde mane following her movements.

'Let me tell you something about how it all works. Once an interview has taken place, although the questioning has finished, the suspect is not released immediately. The interviewing officers will relay what has happened in the interview to the custody sergeant and he will decide about what is to happen next, whether to release on bail, under investigation, to caution, or refer to the Crown Prosecution Service for charging advice.

This whole process can take a long time. However, the police can only hold someone for questioning as long as the custody officer believes that the detention without charge is necessary.'

'Well, thank you for your textbook response.'

'In your case, you will appreciate that we are missing some pieces of the jigsaw. We haven't finished interviewing you yet. Therefore, we won't be discussing this with the custody sergeant.'

'Stalemate.'

'Not exactly. DCI Bryce had received a call from Holborn nick following up on whether any progress had been made and sadly, there hasn't been much for him to report, has there?'

'Holborn Police Station, where's that then?'

Looking down through her paperwork, she replied, '10 Lambs Conduit Street. Do you know the area then?'

'No.'

'Why did you ask then? No, don't tell me. I realise that we can't expect you to stay here awaiting the return of DS Craven. You look dreadful, Mr Jones.'

'Thanks very much!'

'On the understanding that we can continue our discussion soon, I am prepared to release you, but you are still under caution, don't forget. I am not prepared to commandeer a police car to get you home, but I will arrange a taxi for you, at our expense. Go home, get some rest and we will all reconvene later today. Here are your keys.'

As I put my house keys in my pocket, DC Parkes continued, 'We will be retaining your passport for now, for obvious reasons.'

'I have got things to do you know, so I can't wait to get back home.'

'I will escort you down to the front entranceway. The taxi will be there in a few minutes.'

Chapter Six

I had arrived home and decided to go straight upstairs to get some sleep. I had been awake for about forty-eight hours and was shattered. It still took about an hour to drift off to sleep as I mulled over what had happened to me over that period; the initial police visit; my resultant disappearance; my meal with Amanda and then our journey to police HQ; my fleeing the scene and then being brought back; the truncated interview; my sojourn in the cafeteria and return; and my return home. My breakup with Amanda, according to DS Craven at least, played on my mind the greatest.

I slept until nine o'clock when I was awakened by a knocking on my front door. Two things irritated me; I had a doorbell and the arrangement that I had made with DC Parkes was that we would be reconvening our discussion at three o'clock this afternoon. I grabbed my dressing gown and by the time I'd got that on and had walked down to the ground floor, the tap-tap-tapping had started again. I got to the front door, grabbed the handle and pulled it open.

It wasn't the police; it was one of the neighbours. I sighed and said, 'What is it? How can I help?'

'Well, actually I came around to see if everything was all right with you.'

'Yes. But I was asleep if you'd like to know.' I looked up and down the street.

'I'm sorry, I wasn't aware.' Mr Norman from number forty-five looked suitably chastised as he backed away.

'I assume that the police car outside piqued your interest. But there's nothing to worry about here. Please pass that on.'

I smiled at him as I closed the door, confident that nosy Norman wouldn't be bothering me again any time soon. I was still very tired and clearly tetchy, so I ascended the stairs again as I had decided to get some more rest before my three o'clock deadline. After about half an hour, my mobile phone started ringing, that awful, discordant, ringtone. I hadn't even realised that I'd left the phone on. I got out of bed and retrieved the phone from my jacket which I'd hung on the back of the chair. Just as I picked it up, the ringing stopped. Typical. I looked at the screen to see who had called. Amanda. Amanda? She never calls me in office hours during the week, so I returned the call immediately.

After one ring she picked up. 'Hi, thanks for calling.'

'I was both surprised and amazed to get a call from you. Sorry, I just couldn't get to it in time. I was in bed.'

'It's all right for some. I didn't interrupt anything, I hope!'

'Very funny. No, I've had a very trying time with the police and they haven't finished with me yet.'

'I see. I assume that you've got your keys back and you're home again. Er, would it be possible for me and Steph to come over at some point to see you?'

'Both of you? Is something the matter, Amanda?'

'Well …'

I interrupted, 'It's just that they're coming around again at three o'clock, that's all.'

'It won't take long.'

'I'm not going to get any rest this morning, so can you come around now?'

'There's no need to be like that. I was going to say I don't think I'll bother, but it's important, unfortunately.'

'Amanda, calm down. I'm fine. I'll put the coffee on if that's okay with you?'

'We'll be there by 10am.' With that, Amanda ended the call and I was left staring at my mobile wondering what was happening. I went to the bathroom to do my ablutions and then dressed quickly. I just had time to make the telephone call that I had been pondering about for hours. I looked up the number for Gambon & Clarke Ltd and made the call.

'Good morning, would it be possible to speak with Mr Paterson, please?'

'Who's calling?'

'My name is David Jones.'

A pause ensued before the female continued, 'Um, Mr Paterson is a very busy man as I'm sure you'll appreciate so I don't think that I can put you through. I'm sorry.'

'Before you go', I leaped in as it was clear to me that she couldn't wait to get rid of me and end the call, 'Yes, I'm sure he's a busy man but I think he'll want to speak with me. Please tell him I was with Jeremy Browne the other day.'

'You were with Jeremy?'

'Yes, I came to your offices earlier this week.'

I was put on hold for what seemed like ten minutes but in reality, was probably more like two. Eventually, the receptionist said, 'Mr Jones, I'm sorry …'

'Wait! I've got a contract with Gambon & Clarke to write a book and I demand to speak with the managing director.'

At this, the call was ended and the line went dead. 'Bugger me!' I shouted out to my empty household. As far as I was concerned, the matter did not end here. I went to the kitchen to prepare the coffee. As soon as it was ready, the doorbell rang.

I went to the door and let Amanda and Steph enter.

'If you ladies sit down there,' I indicated the settee, 'I'll get the coffees.'

When we were all seated and with mugs of coffee in front of us, Steph opened up the dialogue, 'David. You're probably wondering what I'm doing here. Moral support.'

I looked from one to the other and frowning said, 'Moral support? Do you really need that, Amanda? Am I such an ogre?'

'It's because I'm a bit nervous. Something has happened and I feel that I need to tell you about it.'

I waited for Amanda to continue and I presumed that she was choosing the right words or something as the silence in the room was palpable, so I broke the impasse, 'You've given your message a pregnant pause, Amanda. I assume that you're building up to something groundbreaking ... oh my God, it's not a pregnant pause, is it? I mean, tell me I'm barking up the wrong tree, for heaven's sake. What is it you've come to discuss with me? Is it your job? Your Mum, Dad?'

'Yes, I've been worried for a while about my situation. My period's late, David, so there is a possibility that I'm pregnant.'

71

'Well, have you had one of those pregnancy tests, you know, the ones people buy in the shops?'

'Yes, I have and it shows I'm pregnant.' Amanda extracted a tissue from her jeans and dabbed the corners of her eyes.

'Well, how accurate are they? Shouldn't you get a second opinion from your doctor?'

'Don't worry, I've looked into all of that. I've thought of nothing else for the past forty-eight hours, thank you. Home tests are around ninety-seven per cent accurate and sometimes, one can get a false positive result.'

'Ha! Well, there you go then! There's probably nothing to worry about. See your doctor and get another test to put your mind at rest.'

'Put my mind at rest? What if that comes back positive too?'

'You'll have to cross that bridge if you come to it.'

Steph could hold back no longer, 'I think it's more a question of you both crossing that bridge, don't you think? Not just Amanda.'

'Hang on a minute, who's to say I'm the father?'

'What?' Amanda screamed out, 'How dare you!'

'Well, I don't know what you get up to all day, do I? Yes, we're in a relationship, or we were until the other day. DS Craven could hardly contain himself when he told me that you didn't want anything more to do with me.'

'I thought you trusted me,' Amanda said as she stood up. 'Come on, Steph, let's go. I don't want to be here anymore.'

As they walked to the front door, I called out, 'I'm sorry about this morning. I'm still very tired, I guess. Let me know how you get on at the doctors.'

72

Amanda turned as she was leaving and said, 'No. That's my business, David and mine alone, you've made that quite clear.'

I watched them walk slowly back to their car and I closed my front door. Returning to the living room, I picked up my mug of coffee and drank some. I wasn't going to waste it; it was my favourite brand and still hot. I had a few hours to kill, so I mused that I might even drink theirs too!

We hadn't parted on the best of terms, but I was convinced that Amanda and I could salvage something from the apparent wreckage. I would leave things alone for a few days and then give her a call. I knew that I wouldn't be able to concentrate on my Christmas story whilst I was waiting for the police to arrive this afternoon and in any case, they still had a few of my DVDs to return to me. I hadn't finished my research yet. I still wasn't certain that this subject would fire up my creative juices but was willing to give it a try. I had a contract, after all. I had one other project to complete, which was far more exciting. I would get my laptop and my notes out this afternoon once the police had gone. In the meantime, I would make a couple of telephone calls.

'Hi, Alan. It's David. How are you?'
'Hello, David, I'm fine. Where are you exactly?'
'At home.'
'So, they've released you then?'
'Yes. They explained to me that they'd called you yesterday but not the content of the conversation exactly.'
'You know what they're like. They wanted to know what I felt about you, as your former father-in-law and about your relationship with Donna; the exact circumstances of her death; that sort of thing.'

'Hopefully, that helped them a lot. Thank you. By the way, I'll be getting a visit from them in a few hours.'
'What's all that about then?'
'It's all pre-arranged. For all sorts of reasons. We didn't conclude our business yesterday. I won't go into that.'
'If I can be of any assistance in any way,' he assured me.
'Well, you know where I am if you want me to help you with *Modellers' World* or *Antiques & Collectables*, Alan.'
'No, I think we'll be all right for now. A new guy started working for me a couple of weeks ago and he's showing a lot of promise. Shall we leave it that I can call on you if need be?'
'I'm sorry? I've worked for you on several publications over the past five years and now it's don't call me, I'll call you? This wouldn't have anything to do with the little chat that plod had with you, would it?'
'No, not at all.'
'Is this how you think Donna would have wanted you to deal with me?'
'There's no need to be like that, David and no need to bring my daughter into it either. I have tremendous respect for you, but I don't really want to discuss this matter with you over the phone. You're a freelancer, David and I wanted someone here with me in the office on the payroll. You always said to me that you didn't want to be tied down only working for one organisation. You wanted your freedom, now you've got it. So, shall we arrange an appointment for us to meet to discuss this further?'
'I don't think there's any point, do you, Alan?'

I ended the call. I was still mulling over whether I wanted to engage the services of a solicitor, or not, in my relationship with the police. It was quite clear to me that my link to Amanda was tenuous at best now and consequently, the firm of lawyers that she worked for. Perhaps that informed the decision for me, or perhaps the police would provide one to me. I couldn't remember what they'd said about that. I would ask them to reiterate that point when I saw them later, or I just wouldn't bother.

***

DS Paul Craven and DC Susan Parkes had discussed David Jones and this frustrating case on their way over to Langford to meet up with him again to continue the interview. Their car pulled up outside Jones' house at ten minutes to three and they continued to chat before they made their way to the front door.

'He'd better be in there,' DS Craven said, his hands grasping the steering wheel firmly. DC Parkes placed one of her own hands on his arm and said, 'Hey, Paul, chill. He'll be there, I promise. We had a big chat back at the station and he was as keen as we are to get this sorted.'

'Well, Inspector Thompson is on my case now.'

'Ian? He's okay. I worked with him at Thames Valley. True, he doesn't suffer fools gladly, but I like him.'

'All I know is that we had better get a result today. This investigation has already taken more than enough time, in his view.'

'Come on, let's go and see him, Paul,' DS Parkes held Craven's gaze and smiled.

75

***

I was jolted awake by the quick rat-a-tat-tatting on the front door. I had obviously dozed off again, sitting on the settee. I looked at the clock: Three o'clock in the afternoon. Ah, the police! Where had the last few hours gone? I went to the front door and let Craven and the attractive DC Parkes into my home.

I bid them welcome and offered to make them a drink.

'Thank you, Mr Jones, but I think we need to crack on.' With that, the two officers sat down and DS Craven took out a portable tape recorder from his Adidas sports bag and placed it on the coffee table between us.

'Right, please don't forget that you are still under caution, Mr Jones,' DC Parkes stated as she pressed the record button on the machine and continued, 'Today is Friday 10th April. The time is 3.03pm. Present are Mr David Jones, DS Paul Craven and DC Susan Parkes.'

I raised my hand in supplication and said, 'Please, before we can proceed, I have a question to ask.'

DS Craven looked at his colleague and raised his eyes towards the ceiling, 'Here we go. What did I tell you?'

DC Parkes said, 'For the tape recorder, recording ended at 3.04pm.' She pressed the off button and turned to me, 'Yes, David, what is it? How can we help?'

'I just wanted to say something about this business of having a solicitor present or not. I've been thinking about what I should do about it.'

'And? You've had long enough to think this one through. No more pissing around, Mr Jones. Time is running out. You've messed us around too many times. No more shenanigans, please!'

As he had raised his voice to me, DC Parkes had put her right hand on his arm and said, 'Hey, I'll take over, okay?'

I noticed two things: Craven seemed very stressed out to me, far more so than the current situation warranted, I felt; and the chemistry between the two officers in front of me. I turned my gaze from Craven to DC Parkes as I said, 'Sorry, I wasn't trying to be funny. I don't want to delay this process any longer than is necessary, believe me. I've also got things I want to do; you know.

I have a dichotomy. Concerning this legal advice business, my obvious choice, through Amanda, has now probably gone. Perhaps the police would provide one to me?'

'Well, you can definitely discount option one,' DS Craven jumped in.

'If only you knew,' I muttered, although I was still clinging on to my forlorn hope of retrieving the situation next week with her. 'Anyway, remind me of my options with police help in this respect.'

DS Craven sighed as he took out a handbook from his bag. 'Look, before I read this section out to you, Mr Jones, if you were wanting legal assistance in this interview today, you should have arranged it already.' He flipped through the pages until he found the appropriate one. 'Right, here it is.' He read me the policy concerning the provision of counsel by the police.

'So, if you really can't arrange, or pay, for your solicitor, I can probably get one here within the hour. What do you want to do?'

'It's not a question of not being able to pay. Hang on a minute, what exactly did you say to Alan Wade the other day?'

'Don't try and deflect my question. We need to get on and start making some progress or I'll arrest you for wasting police time.'

'I'm not deflecting your question, Mr Craven. It impinges directly on my ability to pay in the future as it now seems that I don't have a job anymore with A. Wade Publishing Ltd.'

'The contents of my conversation with Mr Wade are confidential and will remain so. I'm sorry to hear that you're no longer employed by him but that is nothing to do with me or our recent discussion. Oh, and it's DS Craven to you, not Mr Craven, okay?'

'I just hope that you haven't traduced my reputation, that's all.'

'Traduced?'

'Yes. Traduce, to speak badly of, or tell lies about someone, to damage their reputation.'

'You use a lot of big words, Mr Jones.'

'Seven letters, not really. No, I know what you mean. I'm well-read, I suppose and a writer at the end of the day. I need as many words in my vocabulary as possible in my trade. Sorry, I wasn't showing off or trying to embarrass you.'

'Look, I still think we've been side-tracked here,' DS Craven's voice went up a couple of decibels and once again, DC Parkes' hand rested on his arm. She picked up the police manual that had just been used and it was her turn now to flick through the pages before she found what she was looking for. Her big blue eyes first looked at me and then back down to the page in front of her.

'Let me read something to you.' She continued to lay out the implications of wasting police time. 'Now, I'm sure that you don't want that to happen, do you?' DC Parkes smiled truculently and went on, 'Time's up, Mr Jones. Your move. What do you want to do?'

'I've made a decision. I don't want to use one of your solicitors. The only other firm I've ever used is Wheeler, Mercer & Anderson. They handled the conveyancing when I moved into this place a few years ago.'

At this juncture, DS Craven stood up. He put his hand on his colleague's shoulder and said, 'I'm going out to the car as I want to make a couple of phone calls in private.' He left, shutting the door behind him heavily.

'Oh dear,' I said, 'not in a very good mood, is he!'

'It's not surprising, is it? He's under a certain amount of pressure from the guys upstairs. You've made things very difficult for us and indeed for yourself. I suggest you make some calls as well while we're waiting. Firstly, your Wheeler, Mercer people.'

'And Anderson. I'll have to go upstairs to dig out the old paperwork if that's all right. Won't be a minute.'

'Don't try anything stupid,' she placed her thumb and forefinger half an inch apart as she carried on, 'you're this far away from being nicked.'

With that, I ascended the stairs two at a time. A few minutes later, DS Craven entered the room I was in. He found me pulling out papers and files from my bureau. He stood in the doorway, hands on hips watching me. 'More time-wasting? Come on, downstairs, I've got some more questions for you.'

We went back to the living room and returned to our original seats.

'At least you didn't do a runner this time,' he glared at me and pressed the record button again, 'Taping restarted at 3.47 pm. In the room again, Craven, Parkes and Jones. Right, first of all, when you were at the station yesterday, you made a remark that you were going to get one of your mates to help you out, Dwane or something. What did you mean by that and who is he?'

'Dwane Kwezezi. He's not my mate. I got his name from one of the posters in your reception area. I saw it there when I was waiting. He looked an evil bastard and I thought it would be amusing to say that he was one of my friends when you lot were out looking for him!'

'You think that's amusing, Mr Jones?'

'Yeah. Well, it's my type of humour anyway, even if it's not yours.'

He looked at DC Parkes who was trying to stifle a smirk. 'Have you chosen a solicitor then?'

'That's what I was trying to find upstairs in my bureau.'

'It's another time-wasting exercise, Mr Jones. I'm sure their number's in *Yellow Pages* or on the internet.'

'I'll get my laptop and look them up.'

'Before you do that, I've got another question I'd like to ask. Earlier on today, I spoke with Stanley Paterson.'

'Who?'

'Stanley Paterson is the MD of Gambon & Clarke Ltd.'

'Well bully for you. I tried to get through to him and I was rebuffed.'

'Yes, he told me. So, what did you want to talk to him about?'

'I wanted to ask him about his colleague, Jeremy Browne. Oh and Julie, the receptionist.'

'I see. Well, they are both central characters to our investigation, so Mr Paterson knows not to discuss them with anyone except the police and definitely not with you!'

'The other thing, of course, is that I've got a contract with them to write a book, with the caveat that once I've done that, my other manuscript, named *The London Boys*, will also get published.'

DS Craven was sitting opposite me shaking his head. 'I've got a copy of this so-called contract. It's not worth the paper it's written on, frankly.'

'What makes you say that then?' I said rather irascibly.

'We are not getting into this subject right now as we have other things to deal with today. Basically, take a look at your copy of the so-called contract. Firstly, it's not on Gambon & Clarke's letter headed paper; and secondly, it's signed only by Jeremy Browne who doesn't have the authority to sign up new authors to publish their stories. Mr Paterson's autograph on it is a forgery.'

'I don't believe it!' I stood up and turned to ascend the stairs again.

'Sit down, Mr Jones!' DS Craven was standing now too and raising his voice again, 'We have got to crack on now. The MIT has been chasing Bedfordshire Police to make some progress and get results and consequently, my superiors are on my back.'

I could see how stressed Craven was and I returned to my seat. 'I was only going to get the number for Wheeler, Mercer & Anderson. Therefore, we can't carry on until I have some legal advice from them. I can see why you're getting upset, DS Craven. You haven't had much luck this week, have you? What with your colleague, the misanthrope DC Eldrid, kicking off like that.'

DC Parkes leaned forward to press the off button on the tape recorder.

'Tape recording ended at 4.08pm.'

DS Craven handed me his mobile phone as he said, 'There is the phone number that you need. I looked it up for you. So, get on with it, give them a call, on your phone, not mine!' He snatched his phone back as he shouted, 'You get one of them here by 5.00pm latest or I'll be issuing you with a fixed penalty notice for wasting police time. You have been warned! And you can tell them that too.'

I folded my arms and looked at him squarely. 'There's no need to be like that. As far as I am aware, I haven't been charged with anything. Anyway, don't you need a warrant or something to be in my house?'

DC Parkes, opposite me, uncrossed and crossed her legs again I reckon to distract me or something, which it did, before looking into my eyes to deliver the official police position on this matter, 'Mr Jones, in general, the police do not have the right to enter a person's house or other private premises without their permission. However, they can enter without a warrant when in close pursuit of someone the police believe has committed, or attempted to commit, a serious crime. In this case, you invited us into your house, so there's no problem here, as you can see. So, as DS Craven has already said, make the call.'

I stood up and put my hand up to halt any potential pursuit. 'I'm just going into the kitchen to call them, in private, okay?'

***

When they were alone, once again, DC Parkes put her hand on her colleague's arm as she edged closer to him to whisper, 'You all right? He seems to be getting under your skin, Paul. He's nothing and he doesn't look like a criminal to me. Does he to you?'

'It's not just him. I think I'm losing it, Susan. My last two cases went pear-shaped and this one, looks like it's going the same way. I can't afford that. I had to give Eldrid a bollocking, because of his behaviour and unwarranted actions. He never seemed like an asset to my team and I have vowed to keep him away from me in the future. My blood pressure has gone through the roof in the last two days. Thank God you're here now.'

***

As I returned to the living room, DS Craven and DC Parkes leapt apart. I sat down. 'Well, that's that then.'

'Go on, what did they say?'

'Only one of the partners, Anderson, might be able to help but he's in court today, so I guess that makes the decision for me. I've run out of time in terms of getting a lawyer here by your deadline, so I'll just have to go it alone.'

'Good decision.' DS Craven said as he pressed the record button on the tape recorder. 'Time is 4.35pm. Present are David Jones, DS Paul Craven and DC Susan Parkes. I have a few questions for you to answer if you would, please.'

'Well, it depends on what they are, of course, but I want to move on as I do have things to do believe it or not.'

'We'll come back to that. Now, as you know, we have been tasked by the MIT to make inquiries into the disappearance of Mr Jeremy Browne and Miss Julie Pemberton who both work at the publishers, Gambon & Clarke Ltd based at 21b Red Lion Street, in London.' DS Craven paused and looked up from his notes to gauge reaction to this opening statement. There being none, he carried on, 'You visited these offices earlier this week, Mr Jones, what can you tell me about that?'

'First of all, I didn't know that you'd been asked to look into the disappearance of anyone at all. Having been left in the dark, I'd assumed that this was some sort of murder inquiry, actually.'

'I can see that,' DC Parkes chipped in. 'So, you have already stated that you went to London on Tuesday 7th April as you had an appointment to see Jeremy Browne about a possible book-publishing deal.'

I nodded and looked at them both before responding, 'I don't know if that was your first question or just making a statement. Anyway, of course, I can confirm I was there. Enough people saw me there so it would be nonsensical for me to deny it. Can I just say something? When I spoke to the solicitors a few moments ago, they told me that it is my legal right to not answer any of your questions or just reply with no comment. Is that correct?'

DS Craven gave another of his heavy sighs before replying, 'Yes, but it's not going to get us very far, is it? What could just be a half-hour interview may stretch out into several hours and potentially a repeat performance back at the nick. I'm sure we all don't want that.'

'Look, I'm a nice guy at the end of the day,' I said, 'I've done nothing wrong. I went to the appointment, came home and got on with my mundane life. Two days later, a couple of things happened: My post arrived which included about a dozen Christmas movie DVDs; you and a PC turned up here asking some questions and ended up taking away my passport.'

'Yes, that was PC Kranic. Unfortunately, you then gave us all a bit of a run around, didn't you? Wasted a lot of police time but at least you did turn up in Kempston,' DS Craven took out the two DVDs that they had borrowed from me and continued, 'We won't be needing these anymore and your passport will be returned soon, as long as we are happy that you won't be a flight risk. You've already got your keys back and you'll be able to get about again under your own steam. Just as well now that you won't be able to get lifts from your ex-girlfriend.'

'Not that it's any of your business but that is far from over. Amanda and I are still talking. It's funny, but I've had several girlfriends and I've never been dumped.'

'We seem to be getting off the track a bit here,' DC Parkes took out her notebook. 'You previously stated that you had left the publisher's offices on good terms with Mr Browne? And when were you supposed to have further contact?'

'There was nothing concrete in place about that except for occasional phone calls and emails. I was to watch the Christmas movies on the DVDs which were dreadful, the few I watched, anyway. Then, I was supposed to put some ideas together, get a plan down on paper, and then write the story. I was given a year to do that and once the book was published, it was then going to be reviewed by his American contacts for a film treatment to be written so that it be made into a movie.'

'Are you serious?' DC Parkes looked at Craven. 'I'm in the wrong job. See how easy it is. You have to have a vivid imagination to be a creative writer don't you, Mr Jones?'

I was getting irritated now that I was being accused of being mendacious and decided that I didn't need to put up with this anymore. I would take the solicitor's advice and now not respond to their questioning. I folded my arms and waited. After a thirty-second recess, 'What's going on, Mr Jones?' DS Craven looked stressed again, 'We have some more questions for you. How did Jeremy Browne seem to you on the day? Was he apprehensive, happy, sad?'

I looked at DC Parkes and smiled. I was determined that there would be a standoff at this point but Craven's phone trilled and he took the call and all I heard him say was, 'Right … I see … you're sure? …', he shut his eyes and then ended the call. Speaking to me, he said, 'I'm afraid that DC Parkes and I have got to return to HQ. It's your lucky day, Mr Jones. But I'll be back, be rest assured about that.'

They left my house without another word and I can't say that I liked the way he had said that last sentence to me.

Chapter Seven

It being Saturday, I had a shortlist of jobs to do; obtain my weekly newspaper (I never seemed to have the time to digest all the news on a daily basis); get a few provisions; and visit the library to carry out some more research of the local jobs market. It hadn't been my usual routine but in view of the recent news from my ex-father-in-law with his withdrawal of the occasional job that I had with his publishing company, I couldn't see any harm in it.

Unfortunately, one hour later, all that I had proved to myself was that searching online was going to be by far the most fruitful resource. The newspapers and magazines that I had devoured had nothing for me.

I still had a handful of book publishers to contact when I got home. I was about to put the finishing touches to the biography on Samuel Franklin Cody that I had been working on for the past year. There were a couple of other books about the Wild West showman and early pioneer of manned flight. He was most famous for his work on the large kites known as Cody War-Kites. These had been used by the British before the First World War as a smaller alternative to balloons for artillery spotting. However, I felt that I had unearthed a few nuggets worth airing in a new book on one of my heroes.

I was just about back to my car when I bumped into my friend, Helen Wilson. We hadn't spoken for a while and when she suggested we go for a coffee to catch up on news, I jumped at the idea. Helen and I had met at university in Brighton whilst I was studying for a degree in journalism. She had studied there for one year before transferring to

Leeds University to complete her degree course in criminal psychology. We'd stayed in touch over the years, exchanged birthday cards, Christmas cards, that sort of thing.

We ordered a couple of cappuccinos and two pastries.

'How have you been, David, you know since the passing of Donna?'

'I can't believe that next month, it'll be two years, Helen. My first relationship since then is going nowhere, or indeed has even perished, for all I know!'

Helen frowned. 'That's not like you. You're normally on top of everything, David. How long have you known her? What does she do? What does she look like? Tell me all!'

'In many ways, Amanda reminds me of you, actually. Not as pretty, obviously and even works in a solicitor's office. We've been an item for the past six months but the jury's out at the moment, using your parlance. I'm due to find out more tomorrow.'

'I think you gave me a compliment there. Thank you. Would I know her? Is she a solicitor then? Where does she work?'

'She's at Stollards but not as a solicitor, just a lowly typist, well a secretary, I suppose. Ha, ha. I may not be laughing next week but we'll see. Are you still local, Helen, or London-based now?'

'I float around a bit as I get called in wherever my expertise is needed, solicitors, the police, the courts. I've even done some TV work; documentaries and a couple of dramas, not starring roles, I mean legal expertise, background stuff, you know.'

'Not really, but it sounds great. Are you in a relationship at the present time?'

'Cor, you don't waste much time, Lothario! No, it always seems that when I'm available, you're in a relationship and when you're free, I'm all loved up! Never the twain shall meet, eh? No, I'm not seeing anyone at the moment and I'm not looking for anyone either, certainly not someone who may or may not be in a relationship and seems uncertain.'

'That's a shame, because of what I'm going through at the moment, I would appreciate some legal advice.'

Over the coffees and pastries, I had briefly explained my recent brush with the law and Helen had seemed quite sympathetic. With my first two options coming to nothing, I had decided not to waste this golden opportunity.

'I don't think so, David. If I didn't know you any better, I might have mistaken the approach as your seeing me as a cheap date with free legal advice thrown in!' Helen smiled as she continued, 'But of course, I haven't got that type of mentality. After all, it was my suggestion we go for a coffee, even though you're paying!' She leaned over and playfully slapped my arm.

'Helen, before we go on, there is something that I feel I ought to tell you. It's so great seeing you again.' I grabbed her hand, 'I always believe in being up front and honest with people. You're probably not even thinking along the lines that I am.'

'I don't know what you're talking about, David. Please tell me.'

'Well, I'm thinking of moving on. House-wise, I'm mortgage-free on my place in Langford and I've got some savings which means I can look at getting somewhere really nice out more in the countryside, or by the sea, even. I mean, I work from home so it doesn't really matter where I'm based.'

I continued, 'Have you got the same mobile phone number, Helen?' I patted my pockets and couldn't locate my mobile. 'Oh no, I can't find mine. I must have left it at home, please write mine down.' I gave her my number.

'Great, and mine's the same number as I've always had. Look, it's been lovely seeing you again, David. I hope everything turns out all right for you with Amanda and the police investigation. You will let me know, won't you?'

'Of course,' she said.

I looked toward a dark-haired character at the next table feigning great interest in the menu in his hand, while giving us both occasional looks, I suggested, 'Come on, Helen, I think that we should be going.'

I settled up and we left. It had just started to rain, so we parted quickly, vowing to stay in touch. We walked expeditiously in opposite directions to find our respective vehicles. I couldn't believe that it was now three o'clock. Time flies when you're having fun. Albert Einstein had said this idiom but I'm sure he hadn't been the first.

When I was home, the first thing I did was to search for my phone and I found it on my sofa. It had obviously slipped out of my pocket. I looked at the screen. There were five missed calls and three voicemail messages had been left.

I played the messages in order:

'Mr Jones, this is DC Grahame Eldrid speaking. There has been a development and we need to speak. DS Craven has been removed from the investigation and the MIT in London has informed Bedfordshire Police that a body has been discovered. Please call me on this number as soon as you can.'

'Hi, it's Jeremy Browne. Hope you're okay, David. Just touching base, as promised, to see how you're getting on with going through the DVDs and getting ideas together. Talk soon.'

'David, it's Alan here. Alan Wade. I may have some good news for you, so if you give me a call back, I'll spill the beans. Bye.'

I scratched my head. The other two telephone numbers, I didn't recognise and I consoled myself with the thought that whoever had called me would try again. However, the voicemail messages had worried me, intrigued me, excited me, in the order that they'd been received. I had put the shopping away in the kitchen and made myself another coffee. Obviously, I would need to return the calls before I could get on with the rest of my day.

DC Eldrid? I thought he'd been suspended or something. And DS Craven removed? A body discovered. Whose? I drained the contents of my coffee mug and made my first call. It was answered immediately with, 'Eldrid.'

'Hello, it's David Jones here. I'm returning your call, as requested.'

'Yes. Mr Jones, we need to talk, in person, here at HQ. Are you able to get here? If not, I can get a car over to you within the hour.'

'Hey, hang on. What's going on? What happened to DS Craven?'

'Never mind about him. He's sort of on gardening leave, not sacked exactly, but taken off this MIT case due to lack of results. Ironic isn't it, that he had me removed on a Suspension of Police Officers Procedure which was reviewed and overturned and now he's gone and I'm back! So, what's it to be, your car or one of ours?'

'You mentioned in your message something about a body having been found?'

'That's why we need to carry on with the interview, Mr Jones. No more messing around now. If you're thinking about having a solicitor present, I suggest you arrange one, as quickly as possible.'

'I can't organise something like that in an hour; I'll need two at least.' I looked at my watch, 'Shall we say six o'clock, at my place?'

There was a pause on the line and I could practically hear the cogs going around in Eldrid's brain. Eventually, he replied, 'Right, I'll arrange for a car to pick you up in Langford at 6pm. No more funny business. Chief Inspector Bryce is running the show himself now. See you later.'

With that, the call ended. I was desperate to return Jeremy Browne's call but in view of recent developments, I decided to call Helen first.

'Hi, Helen, it's David.'

'Hello, stranger, ha ha. It's like buses with you, isn't it? Nothing for years and then two come along at once! You've obviously found your phone. You're not stalking me, are you?'

'No, just got a question for you. Can you come with me to the police station, please? I've got more questions to answer and I need legal advice. I'm not after a freebie, Helen, I'm prepared to pay you, obviously.'

'Oh, David, I'm a criminal psychologist, not a lawyer.'

'What's the difference then?'

'In addition to helping law enforcement solve crimes or analyse the behaviour of criminal offenders, criminal psychologists are also often asked to provide expert testimony in court. One of the best-known duties of a criminal psychologist is known as offender profiling, or criminal profiling. Okay? As you can see, I can't really help you, but I do have some contacts in the biz, obviously. It sounds urgent. Would you like me to make a couple of phone calls to see if I can drum up some help for you?'

'You're an angel. That would be tremendous. If someone could be at my house by 6.00pm, we could go together. They're picking me up, you see.'

'Okay, I'll see what I can do, David. What's your current address?'

'It's still 47 Beaumont Road, Langford. I can fill them in on the way. Basically, I haven't been charged with anything, yet. I'm helping the police with their inquiries, as they say. But I haven't been very helpful to date!'

'Right, I'll get back to you as soon as I have something positive to report. You take care, speak soon.'

I was so glad to have connected with Helen. It had been convenient synchronicity, good timing, kismet, destiny, fate, whatever one wanted to call it. I didn't have a lot of time on my hands, but I would return the other calls now using my landline phone, keeping the mobile free for Helen's potential call. Jeremy Browne and my ex-father-in-law; which one to call first? Not knowing exactly what Alan had for me, in view of what the police had said to me, Jeremy's message tipped the balance in terms of intrigue and interest. I decided to try him first.

'Hi, Jeremy, it's David Jones, I'll let you know about my progress with the DVDs or not, but first of all tell me what's been going on with you, Gambon & Clarke and the police locally,' I began.

'I think I know what you're alluding to, David. There's been a flurry of activity round here over the last few days. I'm not sure how much I can tell you, but it sounds as if you know something?' he replied.

I continued, 'I'll tell you, shall I? I've spent the best part of two days being interviewed by the police in connection with a London MIT inquiry. They didn't tell me too much then, but I've had a message to say that a body's been found. I'm due to spend some more time with them later, actually.'

'Well,' he paused a while before carrying on, 'we're all very upset here at Gambon & Clarke Ltd. It's a cliché but we're like a happy family here and one of our members has been taken from us.'

'I'm so sorry, Jeremy. All I know is that a body's been found.'

I could hear a cigarette being lit at the other end and a pause, whilst, presumably, he exhaled before continuing, 'I'll tell you something now as I'm sure you'll hear more later on. It's Julie Pemberton, the girl on reception that you met the other day.'

'Oh God, she looked lovely. What happened to her? Have they caught anyone yet?'

'David, I don't want to say any more as the police investigation is ongoing. It sounds like you haven't had much time to work up ideas for the Christmas book yet, so perhaps you could call me again at some point next week?'

'Absolutely. I'm in shock. I can't believe it.' At that moment, my mobile phone screeched on the table by my side. 'Jeremy, that's my phone ringing. I'll get that and I promise to call you again next week. Bye.'

I answered the mobile. It was Helen. 'Hi, David, I've managed to speak to three different solicitors. One of them is available and he can meet with you later. You'll have to agree terms between yourselves. His name is Kenneth Benworth, of Benworths. A one-man band but knows his stuff and he's reasonably priced which I know you'll like, David. If you're happy, I'll call him back.'

'Oh Helen, that's great. Thank you so much. If you like, I'll let you know how I get on.'

'Please do. Good luck.'

I had a bit of time so decided to give Alan Wade a call as apparently, he had some good news for me. That would make a change. 'Hi, Alan, it's me, returning your call. I'm on tenterhooks. You've got some good news for me?'

'I was chatting the other day with a fellow publisher and he has a couple of journals that need an editor or at least, editorial support. I was telling him how erudite you are. Interested?'

'Well, it sounds promising. All depends on the area of interest, obviously. Tell me more, Alan, please.'

'The first one is an existing title, where the current editor is leaving the role at the end of the month. It's called *Mechanical Engineering Today*, not the market leader in its field, by any means. The second is in a pre-production stage and will be titled *Spanish Property Today*. You'll see a common theme developing here, David. I thought of you because I know that you speak Spanish and at one stage, you and Donna had had an ambition of owning a holiday home in the Costas somewhere. So, what do you think?'

'Thanks for bringing up Donna again and our unfulfilled dreams. "*Sin embargo, todavía podría estar interesada*".'

'Pardon? Don't try and be clever with me, David. What did you just say?'

'I said in Spanish, "However, I could still be interested". My only worries, Alan, are with the first one as it's probably not the main publication in the sector and now, in a diminishing market; with the second, it may be too late to introduce yet another magazine into an already flooded marketplace. I don't mean to be so downbeat about this. In fairness, I think I need to talk to them.'

'If you've got time. Are you out of the woods with this police business yet?'

'No, in fact I'm about to see them again today. If you can email their details to me, I'll make contact when I can. Thanks for thinking of me, Alan.'

I ended the call and went into the kitchen to make myself a sandwich. I had a suspicion that it may be a long evening. At ten minutes to six, there was a knock at the door. As I walked past the living room window, I glanced outside and saw a brown coloured Volvo estate parked just along the road. I opened the door and a man, in his early fifties, wearing a blue suit and holding a suitcase matching the colour of his car, stood before me.

'Mr Jones?' the man proffering his business card toward me, carried on, 'I'm Kenneth Benworth of Benworths, solicitors. Our mutual friend, Helen Wilson, filled me in as best she could about your situation.'

'Do come in.' I indicated a seat and he sat down. 'I'm pleased to meet you. Yes, Helen said you'd be in touch. The police will be here in a few minutes, Mr Benworth, the idea being that we travel over to their HQ together and we can talk in the car too. As I understand it, things have developed since I was last with them. I was led to believe that initially, the original MIT inquiry was a missing person one but now a body has been found. They didn't tell me whose, but I have subsequently been told the name.'

'And who told you?'

Another rapping on the front door, more stringent this time, interrupted our conversation so I just said, 'If that's the police, I'll tell you in the car on our journey.'

Once again, I opened the door and there before me, DC's Eldrid and Parkes. It was Eldrid who spoke first, 'Okay, Mr Jones your chariot awaits,' he indicated over his shoulder at the car outside.

I looked at my watch, '5.59pm. Wow, that's amazing. You try and get the police out and they turn up four hours late if you're lucky.'

'Don't start. Mr Jones. And who's this?' looking at the man standing next to me.

'That's my solicitor, Mr Benworth. He'll be joining us on the trip and advising me during the interview.'

'So, you finally got your act together!'

I raised an eyebrow at Benworth, 'See what I've had to put up with?'

The four of us got into the Range Rover and we sped off towards Kempston.

***

We were all back in Interview Room 2. I looked round and smiled at DC Parkes, 'Home from home! It feels like I've never been away.'

'That's the problem though, isn't it? You're always getting away.' DC Eldrid frowned at me.

'Right, let me give you an update before we start questioning you again. Detective Chief Inspector Bryce is taking a keen interest in this case now and reporting directly to the MIT in London. As you know, DS Craven is no longer involved.'

DC Parkes raised her eyes to the ceiling before addressing me, 'Mr Jones, as you can see, DC Eldrid and I are jointly investigating and carrying out any necessary interviews. She leaned over and pressed the button on the top of the tape recorder before continuing, 'Today's date is Saturday 11th April, the time is 6.55pm., we're in Interview Room 2 at Bedfordshire Police HQ. Those present are DC Susan Parkes, DC Grahame Eldrid and Mr David Jones and his solicitor, Mr Kenneth Benworth.' This, she read from the business card in front of her. 'You have already been informed that a body has been found?'

'Yes, Julie Pemberton's,' I confirmed.

'And who told you that?' She looked up from her notes, running one of her hands through her blonde locks and engaging me with a forceful stare.

'Er, Jeremy Browne.'

'You've spoken to Jeremy Browne? When was that then?'

Kenneth Benworth put a hand on my arm, looked at me and shook his head. 'I'm sorry, I need a few minutes to speak with Mr Benworth.'

DC Eldrid jumped in, 'No more procrastination, Mr Jones.'

'That's a big word, DC Eldrid!', I countered.

Benworth once again placed a hand on my arm before talking, 'Officers, as hopefully you will be aware, persons being interviewed in connection with offences have a right to consult privately with a solicitor.'

I turned sharply to look at Benworth and interpolated, 'Hang on a minute, who said I'd committed any offences? I haven't been charged with anything you know.'

'Not yet!' snarled Eldrid.

DC Parkes waited while I had a whispered chat with Benworth, then said calmly, 'We only have a few questions for you, Mr Jones. Then, you can be on your way if that's all right?'

'Yes, I've got things to do, so would appreciate that.'

'As you can see, this investigation has been escalated to a murder inquiry now with a bit of missing persons mixed in. Please tell me about the recent telephone conversation that you had with Jeremy Browne.'

'I'd left my mobile behind and when I retrieved it, I found a number of voicemail messages to return. DC Eldrid had left a message to say that MIT had found a body and then Jeremy Browne informed me that the person who had been found was Julie.'

'Why would he want to inform you about that?'

'Well, we were only going to discuss whether I had made any progress, or not, with the book idea, then I asked him about police activity locally. Give him his due, he didn't want to say too much but he did tell me about Julie, perhaps because he knew I'd met her earlier in the week. He and the rest of staff members were pretty cut up about it, naturally.'

DC Eldrid said, 'I wanted to tell you about the body find to garner some sort of reaction from you.'

'This isn't a game, DC Eldrid,' Kenneth Benworth said abruptly, taking me by surprise.

'I'm aware of that, thank you.'

I sat back with my arms folded and waited. DC Parkes picked through her notes again, 'Okay, next question, 'What can you tell me about Tom Foster?'

I frowned, 'Who?'

'According to the statement made by Mr Browne to the police in London, he met with a Mr Tom Foster the same day that he met with you. Apparently, you were in the reception area at the same time as him.'

'Oh, him. Well, only briefly. Miserable bastard from what I can remember of him.' I paused before continuing, 'He was there flicking through some magazines whilst he waited to go in to see Jeremy Browne. He didn't speak. I wished him well for some reason.'

'How would you describe him? Age, height, hair colour, that sort of thing.'

'I wouldn't know his height. He was sitting down. Younger than me, I would say, about twenty-eight? Brown, mousy hair. Why, don't you know what he looks like then?'

'We have a similar description of him from Mr Browne. And your opinion of Julie Pemberton?'

'She seemed very pleasant to me. I just can't understand why anyone would want to do such a thing to a lovely young woman like that.'

DC Eldrid chipped in, 'You found her attractive then?'

I turned to Benworth, 'Do I have to put up with shit like this from him? How long do I have to sit here? Bearing in mind that I'm not obliged to say anything to them, I'm being fairly helpful, don't you think? Well, when can I go?'

In a conciliatory fashion, he replied, 'The police can hold you for up to twenty-four hours before they have to charge you with a crime or release you.'

'When did the meter start to run? I've been with them, on and off, for the best part of three days. I've had enough.'

'During your time at Gambon & Clarke Ltd this week, was there anything else that you noticed that was out of the ordinary?' DC Parkes smiled in an attempt to calm the turbulent waters, I assumed.

'Whilst I was in his office, sitting across from him, he received a telephone call from one of his printers. They had a bit of an argument. Mr Browne clearly wasn't happy about something, a late delivery?'

'Do you know who that was?'

'Greg, I think, but I don't know the name of the printers. Of course, you could ask him about that.'

'Oh, we will, don't you worry. Thank you.'

'Have you got any more questions for my client?' Kenneth Benworth asked.

'Just a minute, please.' DC Parkes spoke for the recorder, 'DC Parkes and DC Eldrid left the room at 7.13pm.' She looked at her colleague and indicated to him that they leave the room.

Once we were alone, I said to Benworth, 'Well, how do you think things are going then? Will they let us go soon?'

He smiled and replied, 'I'm certain that they don't consider you to be a suspect and that you're here literally to help them with their inquiries.'

'That's good to know. Oh, they're back.'

The two DCs re-entered and sat down. DC Eldrid spoke first, 'It's your lucky day, Jones. You're free to go, for now.'

'It's Mr Jones to you. And if you decide that you want to waste my time and that of my solicitor at some stage in the near future, kindly furnish us with a list of questions in advance.'

'We don't work like that, Mr Jones, as Mr Benworth will corroborate on your way home. Thank you both for your time today, it's been most helpful.'

'So, we can just go?' I looked at the departing figure of DC Eldrid and I turned to DC Parkes, 'Of course, we just need a lift back!'

'By the time you get downstairs, there'll be a taxi waiting for you.'

Benworth and I walked down to the reception area. Peter Fynch was there again and I couldn't resist it. 'Hi, Peter, you okay?'

He looked up from his paperwork and on seeing who was speaking his demeanour rapidly went downhill. He didn't answer but looked at me nonplussed.

I carried on regardless, 'I see that you caught my mate, Dwane Kwezezi. Well, not you, obviously, but your armed colleagues, no doubt.'

'What's going on, David?' Benworth queried.

'Oh, I and this young man go way back, don't we, Peter?'

PC Fynch continued to ignore me and he pointedly returned to his boring papers which were, presumably, preferable to making conversation with me.

'Come on, David, a taxi has just pulled up outside. Let's go.'

Chapter Eight

Monday evening had arrived and found me surprisingly relaxed. The last week had been quite extraordinary. I felt that I had dealt with the police interrogation as well as I could have and that the ball was now firmly in their court again.

Kenneth Benworth had unravelled the legalities of the case for me during the journey back to Langford on Saturday. We had agreed on the terms of his engagement and I was pleasantly surprised by his impartiality. I was very grateful to Helen for having recommended him to me and I told her so when I had called her. We had agreed to meet up this evening and I'd opened up a bottle of Cabernet Sauvignon in readiness.

Yesterday, I had spent some time viewing three of the Christmas DVDs that had been provided to me and this had fired up my imagination. I had made some rough notes of a potential plan for a storyline which I intended to share with Jeremy Browne when I next had contact with him. Also, I had made a mental note to discuss the contract with him, because of comments made about its authenticity, or lack of it. He had not been in his office today, so I would try calling again tomorrow.

The one positive thing about this morning was the conversation I'd had with Big Cat Publishing about the magazine opportunities. A lengthy discussion had led to our making an appointment for me to visit their offices in North London, the following Friday.

A gentle tapping on my front door broke me out of my reverie. I quickly pressed the play button on my CD player and went to answer the door. Andrea Bocelli's dulcet tones accompanied me as I held the door open wide to welcome Helen.

'Hello, David. Wow, love the music.'

She looked and smelled great. Things were looking up. We hadn't discussed in advance that this may be a date as such, or not.

'Let me get you a glass of wine, Helen. Red okay? It's Cabernet Sauvignon, my favourite.'

'Great, thanks.'

We sat down in the living room and I decided to play everything by ear in terms of how the evening would go. I was potentially footloose and fancy-free again.

Looking around the room, Helen said to me, 'I can't believe that this is the first time I've been here, bearing in mind how long I've known you, David. I didn't know you were an art lover, for instance. Three van Gogh's on the wall opposite, I love it.'

'Ha! They're not the originals, of course. Donna and I moved here three years ago. Sadly, it wasn't long after that that she became unwell.'

Fall On Me by Bocelli was playing as the dreadful, strident ringtone of my mobile started. I made another mental note to change the discordant noise as soon as was possible. I excused myself with Helen and I answered it. I had not appreciated the interruption and my first response was fairly abrupt. At the other end of the line, Amanda said, 'Sorry. I didn't mean to disturb you, David.' She paused momentarily before carrying on, 'What's going on? I can hear music in the background. Have I interrupted something?'

I walked over to the CD player and turned the volume right down. 'I'm just playing some music, Amanda. I am allowed. How are you?'

'Well, I thought I'd call you. I had hoped that you'd call me today following on from our last conversation.'

'I thought you'd said that it was none of my business. However, I had allocated some time to call you tomorrow, actually.'

'That's good of you to fit me in,' Amanda snapped truculently.

I turned to Helen, pointed to the phone and rolled my eyes heavenwards. She smiled demurely.

As I hadn't replied, Amanda went on, 'Have you got someone there, David? No, I tell you what, don't bother answering that one. You will either tell me the truth or be forced to lie and I'll never know which is correct, will I? I was going to let you know something today, but I don't think I'll bother now. And please don't use up any of that precious time of yours by calling me tomorrow. I'm going away for a few days, David. Please don't ask me where, or why, because I won't tell you. Okay?'

'Amanda ...' I couldn't finish my sentence as the call was ended and the line went dead.

Helen replenished our wine glasses and I sat down next to her.

'Well, I think it was Alexander Graham Bell who once said, "When one door closes, another one opens." I don't know if I'll ever truly understand women, Helen.'

'What makes you feel like that then?'

I sighed and had a good slug of red wine. I held the glass up to the light and said, 'You can always rely on a good Cabernet Sauvignon. You get to know the grape, the region of the country it comes from, the colour, its aroma.'

Helen gazed at me as I mused, abstractedly. She was trying to read my mind, clearly getting nowhere. 'You're a complex fellow, David, aren't you? I've got a few questions for you if you don't mind.'

'Fire away.'

'I know what you were alluding to when you said about one door closing and another one opening but I didn't know that it had emanated from Alexander Graham Bell. How on earth would you know something like that? And you didn't answer my query about you not understanding women. Also, how come you're such a wine connoisseur?'

'Wow! Steady on, Helen.' I laughed and drained my glass again. 'Okay, well firstly, I literally read the fact about Bell only last week in April's edition of *Reader's Digest*. I retain useless information like that. I'm not a polymath!'

'There you go again, David. Polymath? I'm not thick, as you know, but what's one of those when he's at home?'

'A person of wide knowledge or learning. I have an enquiring mind, certain interests and ambitions. I'll be thirty-four this year and I need to make a number of decisions.'

Helen took her diary out of her handbag and said, 'When's your birthday then?'

'6th June.'

'Oh, D-Day! See, you're not the only learned one. You're right about one thing though, this wine is lovely.'

I poured another glass of red for Helen as I carried on, 'Your next question about my not understanding women. I don't know if I'm any different to most men. A few years ago, *Cosmopolitan* ran an article entitled *15 Things Men Don't Understand About Women.*' I caught Helen's look and I rapidly said, 'I saw it at the dentist's, honestly. I don't subscribe to any women's magazines!'

'I believe you, David, many wouldn't! "Men are from Mars women are from Venus".'

'The John Gray book. I read that and quite enjoyed it when I didn't expect to! So, I think I'll just regard the fairer sex as decorous enigmas. And as to your final query, I'm not a wine connoisseur, as such. But I do like wine. When I've holidayed in France, Italy or even Greece, I've visited local vineyards to get a better understanding and get to taste the local vino! I've got a couple of questions for you now, Helen.'

She crossed her legs, which were stunning. I was impressed that she'd made an effort this evening. We'd agreed to meet up tonight, but it wasn't meant to be a date as such, certainly not in my mind. My previous thought that my fortuitous meeting with Helen had been a perfect example of synchronicity seemed to be developing naturally and without effort. She returned my smile as I asked, 'I've got a few things to do tomorrow Helen, and I was wondering about your availability. I've got some calls to make and depending on the outcome of those calls possibly I'll have some work to do. But if you're free, I wondered if you'd be prepared to go with me to the graveyard where Donna is buried. It will be the first anniversary of her death tomorrow.'

'I'm sorry to hear that, David. I've got things to do in the morning, but I could be available in the afternoon, if that's any good.'

'That would be perfect. Thank you.'

'So, are you going to tell me about your phone call, from Amanda, was it?'

I smiled derisively and drained my glass before replying, 'First, she wants to speak to me, then she doesn't. Yesterday, she was my girlfriend. Today, I don't think she is! Apparently, Amanda wanted to tell me something important and then decided that she didn't. It's your "Men are from Mars women are from Venus" thing all over again, isn't it? I can't cope with that, I guess that's it then.'

'You look so lugubrious, David,' she said and then put a hand on my arm. 'Don't make any rash decisions, especially after consuming three glasses of red wine.'

'Oh, I think that any decisions have been made for me, don't you?' I put my hand on top of Helen's as I continued, 'This Kismet thing has a lot to answer for!'

Helen leaned over and kissed me on the cheek. 'No, no, don't get too excited. I've got to make a move. I've got an early start in the morning.'

My best hangdog expression could do nothing to alter the situation and it seemed rather appropriate that Andrea Bocelli's singing ended simultaneously as the last track of his album concluded. We both stood up and as we looked into each other's eyes, I sensed a moment between us.

It was Helen who spoke first, 'I'm happy to accompany you to the churchyard tomorrow afternoon, David, but I think you should try calling Amanda to see if you can salvage things.'

I sighed, knowing that I didn't have any enthusiasm for such a venture but agreed to try anyway. As we parted, we vowed to reconvene at two in the afternoon the following day at my house and that we would travel together to St. Andrews.

***

"The best-laid plans of mice and men often go awry". This quote came to mind as I smiled wryly to myself. It might have been the wine from last night, but I couldn't for the life of me remember from where the phrase had originated. I had finished off the bottle of Cabernet Sauvignon after Helen had gone home last night as I had counselled myself that it would have been a shame to waste it.

I had gone to bed after catching up on the latest news on TV, the usual fare, really: Boris Johnson was under attack from the Labour opposition for not sticking to his election promises on education funding; the Bank of England had reduced the base rate to its lowest level ever, with the reporter explaining how changes to the base rate could affect interest rates or payments on savings and mortgages; and Nissan had announced that a phased resumption of vehicle production would begin at the Sunderland Plant shortly. And this mattered to me, how exactly?

I had descended the stairs this morning in a relatively cheerful mood, not a state of mind that I was renowned for but that changed with the first telephone call that I had made after breakfast. From my scribbled agenda for today, I crossed off the first task, telephone Jeremy Browne.

We'd had a lot to discuss. With no answer from his mobile, I had called Gambon & Clarke Ltd and when I had asked to be put through to Jeremy, I had instead been put through to the MD.

'Hello, Mr Jones, this is Stanley Paterson. I understand that you wanted to speak to Jeremy Browne?'

'Yes. We had agreed to speak this morning. He had wanted an update on the book we'd planned and I'd got a few questions for him too.'

'I'm sorry, Mr Jones, but before I tell you the up-to-date position here, what is it you wanted to know from him? Perhaps, I can help?'

'I was just going to go over my ideas about the Christmas book and whether I would be going down the right road in developing one of them.'

'Sorry to interrupt you, but I've no idea what you're talking about. Christmas book?'

'Yes, when I met with Jeremy last week about my manuscript for *The London Boys,* he promised to publish it if I wrote a Christmas-themed book. We are to have regular updates as to my progress because of the deadlines and his discussions with the Hollywood producers, etc.'

'I don't know what you're talking about, Mr Jones.'

'But I've got a contract with Gambon & Clarke Ltd to write this book and I just …'

Stanley Paterson leaped in once more, 'Let me stop you there. First of all, you do not have a contract to write anything in the future or to have an already written work published by Gambon & Clarke. I oversee every contract here as each one has my signature on it. You don't have one of those do you?'

I paused as I went over the machinations of last week's meeting in London. 'No. This one's signed by Mr Browne and I have to assume that your one is a forgery.' I glanced at the worthless document in front of me.

'I'm sorry to have to tell you that you seem to have been misled by my former employee, as I'm sure you've already realised. Now, I'm going to have to end this call shortly. The police are due to be here in ten minutes to continue their inquiry.'

'I see. Mr Paterson, you just said former employee. Perhaps, you could give me that update you mentioned earlier.'

'I can't say too much as Jeremy is currently under investigation. And because of what I've gleaned in recent days, he no longer has a position at Gambon & Clarke Ltd. Your comments today confirm the validity of that decision.'

'I don't suppose that I could arrange to come in and see you, Mr Paterson, about *The London Boys* manuscript and this Christmas book idea?' I asked almost mockingly.

'I think you know the answer to that one!'

'Do you know anything about someone called Samuel Franklin Cody?'

'No. I really must go now. A member of the Metropolitan Police force has just arrived. Goodbye, Mr Jones.'

The call was ended peremptorily and my mood of happiness dissipated immediately. I screwed up today's list of things to do and tossed it into the waste bin by my desk. Two of the tasks listed related to the Christmas book and as that was clearly not going to happen now, it was redundant.

I needed to clear my head and I decided to go for a walk. The weather was good and within half an hour, I was walking past the rolling fields of the pleasant countryside. My bucolic surroundings gave me a much-needed boost. I had previously attempted to make three telephone calls and all had immediately gone to voicemail. If I was a paranoid person, I could read something into that! I stopped by a farm gate and watched a farm-sowing machine trawling up and down a field. It fascinated me for some reason, probably because although aware of such activity, I had never bothered to study it before. Such an important part of the food chain. Twenty or thirty minutes must have gone by, in what for me, was an unusual period of inactivity. I started to contemplate my sedentary lifestyle, writing using a laptop, checking emails, websites, sitting down in the same place for hours on end. It was with a heavy heart that I decided that it was time for me to head home for more of the same. I walked slowly but vowed to repeat the activity soon.

My life now, I felt, was a bit in the doldrums. And just when I was starting to wonder what I would do next, the decision was made for me: Four hard raps on my front door encouraged me to find out who the potential visitors were. And why didn't anyone use my doorbell for goodness sake!?

I opened the door and two familiar faces confronted me.

'Morning, Mr Jones, we need to talk to you,' DC Eldrid said, leading the way into my house with Susan Parkes bringing up the rear. 'Things have moved on.'

'Oh, do come in,' I smiled sarcastically as the two officers sailed past me and entered the living room. 'Do take a seat.'

'No thanks,' DC Parkes said laconically.

'So, what's happened?'

'All in good time.' DC Eldrid stood with his arms folded. 'First of all, Chief Inspector Townsend from MIT, based at the Met, has been in touch with us. He told us that you had tried to get in touch with Jeremy Browne. What did you want to speak to him about?'

'We had agreed to speak this morning about my book. But having spoken to his boss, I now realise that that's not going to happen.'

DC Susan Parkes stepped forward, 'Apart from his mobile phone number, do you have any other way of getting in touch with Mr Browne? You see, we urgently need to speak to him. He seems to have disappeared.'

'And Tom Foster? To lose one may be regarded as a misfortune; to lose two looks like carelessness!' I suggested.

'What? How dare you, Mr Jones!'

'It's from Oscar Wilde, my favourite. Sorry, I don't have any other way of contacting Jeremy. I don't know him very well.'

'I understand that Mr Paterson told you the facts of life when he spoke to you. I told you that you didn't have a contract with that company, didn't I?' DC Eldrid sneered at me as he spoke.

I snapped back at him, 'You can wipe that supercilious look off your face too. You've got nothing to be proud of, have you? Two men are missing, at least one person is dead. And I pissed off, very unlikely to want to offer you any additional assistance. Not going very well for you, is it, DC Eldrid? Don't forget what happened to your friend, DS Craven, will you?' I sat down in my recliner chair and waved my hand toward the sofa opposite me.

'Please sit down, unless you've concluded today's business and need to run back to HQ.'

Eldrid remained standing and edged closer to me, presumably to try to enforce his authority over me. DC Parkes, however, had decided to take the proffered seat.

'We tried calling you about an hour ago but got no answer, Mr Jones.'

'No, you wouldn't have, I was out. I wanted a bit of peace and quiet, so I didn't take my mobile phone with me.'

Eldrid had that look on his face again, 'Do you know what I'm thinking?'

'No,' I replied and pausing for dramatic effect, I continued, 'do you?'

It took a few moments for the penny to drop and then Eldrid suddenly leaned down and with both hands grabbed me by my shirt and hauled me to my feet. 'You little shit,' he shouted. As he pulled his right arm back seemingly in preparation for hitting me, DC Parkes leaped up and placed herself between us.

'Stop! DC Eldrid, go and sit in the car and wait for me there.' He hesitated and she continued, 'Don't even consider it.' With that, DC Parkes pushed Eldrid away from me and towards the front door.

Once we were alone, she said, 'Sorry about that, David, but you did provoke him, you know.'

'I'm sorry you stepped in when you did. Eldrid's a loose cannon. Not very bright. One just has to know how far to push and when to do it! I was envisaging the resultant police brutality case that I was going to bring to court!'

'You're both idiots,' Parkes said, crossing her legs again, sitting opposite me. I'm sure that the dress she was wearing was shorter than the one she'd worn before.

'Can I help you any further, DC Parkes? It's just that as today is the first anniversary of my wife's death and I'm going to the graveyard to take her some flowers.' I looked at my watch.

'We only came over here because we couldn't raise you on the phone. We didn't want to give you the opportunity of alerting Jeremy Browne, but it seems that your relationship with him is fairly ethereal anyway. I believe your story. I'll get out of your hair in a moment, don't worry. One piece of advice though. When I was at the College of Policing, one of the first idioms that was drummed into our heads was "Wisdom is knowing the right path to take". May I suggest that you consider adopting that too?'

'It didn't seem to do your friend any good.'

'My friend? Oh, you mean Eldrid. He's no friend of mine, David.' DC Parkes ran a hand through her golden locks, a gesture I'd noticed before. I also noticed that the top two buttons of her blouse were undone. Was she flirting with me?

'I don't seem to have been much use to you today, do I?'

She smiled, and said, 'You've been more help than you realise. I'll be in touch. If we need to see you again, David, don't worry, I'll make sure that DC Eldrid isn't with me.'

'I'm not worried about Eldrid.' I stood up and we shook hands. Our eyes met and the gaze was held for about two seconds.

'Thank you for your time, David.'

DC Parkes left my house and she re-joined her colleague. I sat down and picked up my mobile. As I was due to meet with Helen later, I decided to try calling Amanda to give her an update. As a pedant, I hated leaving loose ends, outstanding issues and unresolved matters in my mind. I called the number which I'd used hundreds of times over the past six months. The noise at the other end was a continuous electronic buzz. I frowned and looked at the phone. I went into the phone log to check the number and I accessed her name and number and tried again. Same result. So, I hadn't misdialled or had a memory lapse. Either the phone had been destroyed or the service discontinued. My only other option was to try her at her place of work, Stollards solicitors. I called them and was informed that Amanda was unavailable as she had taken two days off. Oh well, the ball was firmly in Amanda's court. I would just have to wait. And so would she.

Chapter Nine

'Cloak and dagger, I suppose that's how it's going to be now for the rest of our lives.' Tom Foster sipped at his coffee in the most unpropitious corner of the café that his boss had found.

'Well, that's your fault, largely,' Jeremy Browne adjusted the large hat that he was wearing and leaned in closer as he continued, 'what on earth went wrong?'

'Yeah, yeah, I'll explain all that in a minute. Things went tits-up for me last week in London. This is what I want to know: Is this how you see our lives panning out now for the both of us? Meeting up in God-awful places like this? Starbucks in South Mimms, for Christ's sake?'

'I appreciate that skulking around in strange clothes is incongruous to our surroundings, but necessary right now. I wanted us to meet up where there weren't too many CCTV cameras about.'

Foster shifted uneasily in his window seat as he quickly glanced outside. 'What are you, some sort of James Bond master spy?'

'What do you mean?'

'I've been calling your mobile, getting no answer, leaving messages and never receiving a response from you. Then, I receive a call this morning from an unfamiliar number and it's you! It's either a secret phone or a new number or something.'

Jeremy Browne extricated the phone from his jacket pocket.

'It's called a Burner. It allows you to create multiple numbers on your phone for whatever reason, where you may want to keep your personal number private. You can delete a number at any time, or you can create as many numbers as you please.'

'You're scaring me. How do you know about all this stuff? I don't.'

'You know Jack Shit about most things, it appears Tom. Let's just say that we move around in different circles, shall we? When I came up with my scheme originally and I identified you as someone qualified in helping to execute it, that was my first mistake. So, I take it back. This balls-up wasn't your fault, it was all mine.' Foster banged his fist down on to the tabletop.

'Oh, great, that's all we want, bringing unwanted attention to the two losers in the corner. In answer to your question though, yes, this will be your lifestyle for the time being as half of the Metropolitan Police force is out looking for us. So, I suggest that you get used to frequenting God-awful places like this until we come up with another plan or they get a couple of major incidents to pursue. So, tell me what happened; we'll be here a while today. You've got plenty of time.'

Foster began, 'You told me about Julie Pemberton's access to a small fortune and I followed her home after work. She opened her front door and I barged my way in. I then started to come across as a big tough guy in my attempt to get information out of her. That's where I went wrong, I suppose. It's not me and she must have guessed it. Julie laughed at me.' Foster looked around the people in the café and lowered his voice, 'Did you hear me? She laughed at me. Something inside of me must have snapped and I hit her.' Foster closed his eyes momentarily and when he opened them again, he found Jeremy Browne gazing at him

implacably. He said nothing, so Foster continued, 'She was crying, and we ended up in her bedroom, upstairs.'
'What?'
'No, nothing like that. Julie said that ...'
'Don't call her that. You need to impersonalise her and the situation. You need to purge her of such human characteristics as sympathy or any kind of warmth or you'll end up spending time in a funny farm, not prison.' Jeremy Browne had leaned across the table and grabbed Foster's left wrist as he had spoken to him and he now released it as he said, 'Okay, carry on, Tom.'
'Right, Julie. Sorry, she, had told me that the information and the documentation that I needed was in one of her cupboards upstairs, so that's where we went. She was still crying and holding a handkerchief to the side of her face. There was swelling just under her eye.'
'Stop it! Carry on with the story.'
'We'd been sitting down, her on a chair, me on her bed. I was just waiting for her to compose herself before she went to find the information that we needed. Suddenly, she leaped up and ran to the doorway. It took me by surprise but as quickly as I could, I chased after her. We were at the top of the stairs and she turned around to confront me as I arrived. She flailed out at me and screamed. I tried to defend myself and pushed away from the offending arm. Julie, sorry, she, lost her balance and try as I might, she careered down the stairs head over heels until she hit the floor below, coming to a final stop against the front door. I ran down after her and cradled her head in my arms, but it was obvious to me that she was gone. Her head just flopped around; her neck was broken, Jeremy.'

Tom Foster put his head in his hands as the conversation ended. Jeremy Browne went up to the counter and purchased two more coffees, then returned to their table.

'So, did you call the paramedics?'

'No, she was already dead and then I knew they'd call in the police. I would just be incriminating myself!'

'Listen, cretin, we're in big trouble here. Now is not the time for us to fall out.'

'What are you so worried about? I'm the one who did it, however unintentionally.'

'Let me show you something on my phone, Foster, I'm up to my neck in it too, "An accessory after the fact is often not considered an accomplice but is treated as a separate offender. Such an offender is one who harbours, protects, or assists a person who has already committed an offence or is charged with committing an offence".

It gets worse. Not only am I an accessory after the fact but I am also one before it, "A person who incites or assists someone to commit an arrestable offence".

So, we're in deep doo-doo's. What did you do next then, about the body?'

'I waited until nightfall and I got my car up to the front door. I kept checking that there was no one about and eventually, bundled her onto the back seat. I couldn't see very well as I was driving with tears streaming down my face. I came to an unfamiliar part of London and ended up on an industrial estate in Wandsworth. I was panicking. I just didn't know what to do for the best and I placed her carefully, as if that mattered now, behind some bins out of sight of everyone.'

'They didn't find the body until mid-morning the following day. When they discovered who she was, they contacted members of her family first, obviously and then we got a call at Gambon & Clarke. Everyone there was terribly upset. Julie Pemberton was a very popular person in the office.'

'Don't look at me like that. It was your idea.'

'I said, encourage her,' Browne gave the ubiquitous first two-finger movements of each hand indicating inverted-commas, 'to tell you about the money and how to get it, not kill her!'

'It was an accident.'

'There is no such thing as an accident.'

'Who said that?'

'I don't know.'

It had started to rain outside and they glumly looked out of the window, each with thoughts running through their heads. The car park was full, several popular fast-food outlets attracting business and with the South Mimms location being so close to both the A1 and M25 motorway, always a winning combination. At that moment, three police cars with their blues and twos flashing and sounding their horns, sped into the car park.

Foster stood up, nervously, 'Oh, no, here we go.'

'Follow me.' They walked to the rear of the property towards the toilet area. A corridor led to a door marked 'FIRE EXIT'. They burst through it and into the rear of the car park.

'Don't go anywhere near our cars.'

'Well, that was a great idea of yours about going somewhere with a small number of CCTVs about, wasn't it!

I bet they're everywhere around here. And you called me a cretin! You're nothing but a narcissist.'

Browne hit Foster as hard as he could on the chin, and he crashed down to the tarmac.

'Get up! And don't ever talk to me like that again. Understand?'

Tom Foster rubbed his face and gingerly got back on his feet. They didn't speak for about a minute until Browne said, 'Sorry. I guess the stress of the situation is bound to get to both of us.' Foster looked around the car park. 'What do we do now then?'

'I've been thinking about that. We need a bolthole to go to. Obviously, the police know our home addresses and the addresses of friends and family members. But I've got an idea.'

'Have you noticed something?' Foster nodded over Browne's left shoulder. He turned around and saw three police officers wrestling someone to the ground only fifty yards away next to a black BMW which was surrounded by the police cars they'd seen earlier.

'How ironic! So, they weren't after us at all!' Foster turned towards the doorway; the door was still ajar. 'Come on, let's go back in. I'll buy you another cuppa.'

'Okay, then I can make my phone call.'

'Their table was still available, the cups not yet cleared away. They sat down with replenished cups of cappuccino and Jeremy Browne took out his phone. 'Tom, I'm going to give David Jones a call. He's always all over me like a rash. He'll do anything I ask. We need to lie low; our cars are marked now. We can't risk using them.'

'What are you going to say to him? What's the plan?'

'You'll see, just listen.'

Browne dialled the number and it took a while for the phone to be answered.

'Er, hello?'

'Hi, David, it's Jeremy Browne, how are you?'

'Jeremy? I didn't recognise the number. Have you got a new phone then?'

'Yes. I did something stupid, don't ask what.'

'What's going on? The police keep questioning me about you; how well I know you; that sort of thing. They say that you've disappeared. I spoke to your boss, Mr Paterson and he said that you're no longer an employee at Gambon & Clarke.'

'It's a long story, David. We need to get together. That's why I'm calling you. I've got a problem with my car. Consequently, I'm calling to ask you for a favour: I want you to come and pick me up.'

'When?'

'Well, now! And I've got some good news for you.'

'No can do, Jeremy. Sorry. I've got a prior engagement.'

'Well, I'm sure it can be re-arranged. This is important, David.'

Browne heard a click. The call had been ended and Browne truculently shouted, 'What a pile of crap!' Foster put a hand on Browne's arm and said, 'You don't want to draw attention to us. Calm down and call him back.'

Two minutes elapsed and then he tried again.

***

The phone rang again and I immediately answered with, 'My prior engagement is far more important than whatever you've got to say. It's the first anniversary of my wife's death if you want to know and I'm leaving in five minutes to go to her grave. Okay?'

'I'm so sorry, David. I didn't know. I won't keep you. I'll catch up with you another time if that's all right.'

'Fine. I can't stop now. I'm meeting up with someone else. Bye for now.'

As arranged, Helen met up with me at the front porch-way of St Andrews. I had a small posy of flowers with me and we walked slowly together toward the grave situated close to trees planted along the back of the graveyard.

'Sorry I was a few minutes late, David. I'll explain all later. You look very smart today.'

I looked down at my clothes and smiled. 'Nothing special, Helen, it's just that since we re-connected recently, I haven't worn a shirt and tie until now! Here she is, over here.' I kneeled and replaced the dead flowers with my new ones.

Helen was wearing a smart two-piece skirt and jacket today and I commended her on it.

'Oh, I've just come here from my bank. I had an appointment there to discuss my investments, all very boring stuff. But, hey, let's not talk about that right now. We're here to see Donna.'

I nodded and brushed some leaves from off the top of the gravestone. 'You're right. I miss her, you know. I come and visit once a month and have a little chat. That may sound silly to you.'

'No, not at all. In fact, I'm impressed. I got the impression that you'd moved on with your life. You know, got busy, filling up your time as much as you could, writing, editing, etc. Finding other interests, Amanda, me, sorry, perhaps I'm being a little bit presumptuous?'

I laughed and took hold of her hand. 'I'll only be a few more minutes here, Helen, then we can be on our way. I've got a few things to tell you. This isn't exactly my usual milieu so perhaps we could pop into Luigi's for a cup of coffee?'

'You take as long as you want, David. I'll go back to my car and wait for you there. And I've got things to tell you too.'

We parted and I spent about ten minutes updating Donna on my latest news. As I turned to go a familiar voice said, 'Hello, David. Fancy seeing you here.'

'Alan, hi.' My ex-father-in-law and I shook hands.

'So, you've got another lady friend?'

'What? Oh, you mean Helen. We were friends at university and met again recently. She works in the legal field and was instrumental in my finding a solicitor recently when I was dealing with the police.'

'I see. How's that going?'

'Which? Helen, or the police inquiry?'

'Either, both.'

'Helen, she's great, but it's early days yet. Got to get rid of Amanda first!' I laughed and put the dead flowers in the bin. 'I guess the inquiry is ongoing but at least the heat's off me for now. How often do you come down to see Donna's grave?'

'Not as often as I should. I think about her a lot. I don't need to come here to be reminded of her. But it's one year today. Unbelievable, isn't it.'

I nodded, took a final glance at the grave and said, 'Okay, Alan, I've got to shoot off now. It was nice seeing you again.'

'Before you go, how did you get on with the guys at Big Cat Publishing? Did you call them?'

'Yes, we had an initial chat about the two projects. I reiterated the concerns that I had about the magazines, you know, the concerns that we spoke about. Anyway, we agreed to discuss it fully when we meet up at their offices in London, this Friday, actually.'

'Well, I hope that something comes from it, David.'

'Que sera, sera.' I turned and waved a hand as I made my way down the church pathway towards the road. Five minutes later, I was tapping on the passenger window of Helen's car to let me in.

'You okay?' Helen smiled in a beguiling way, as she often did, 'I'll drive us to Luigi's and drop you back to your car once we're finished, if that's all right?'

***

'It's five o'clock Jeremy, and even South Mimms is losing its allure.'

'Very funny.'

'Well, have you got a Plan B then, or what?' Tom Foster pushed his fourth empty coffee cup away from him, 'This is ridiculous. I feel like we're a very unhappily married couple and we haven't even had our honeymoon yet,' he said jokingly.

'You're right, we can't stay here. I'll give David Jones another call. He should be available by now.' Jeremy

127

Browne stepped outside to make the call as he didn't want to be overheard by any of the other customers.

'Hi, David, it's Jeremy Browne. How're things? Are you free now?'

***

'No, not exactly,' I rolled my eyes at Helen sitting across the table from me. 'How can I help?'

'Well, basically we need to ask a favour of you. As I said before, I've got a problem with my car and we need a lift, David. Actually, two favours to ask. We need somewhere to crash out too.'

'Hang on, hang on. What's all this 'we'? And where are you speaking from exactly?'

'It's all a bit complicated. The person with me is Tom Foster, you know, the chap you met briefly in the reception of Gambon & Clarke.'

'Friend of yours, is he?'

'Oh, known him for years. And we're currently in a café at the South Mimms service area, just off the A1. Do you know it?'

'I know it about as well as I know you, it seems. I've got about a dozen questions that I want to ask you, but I haven't got the time right now.'

'Listen, I'm up shit creek, frankly. If you can't come and get us, for whatever reason, I'll get a taxi. I've got some money. What I need from you is your agreement that we can stay for a few days at your house. I know where you live because I sent those DVDs to you.'

'Let me get this straight. You want me to offer you and this Foster character, accommodation for a few days?

There's clearly something wrong with your homes, or you daren't use them! It beggars the question of why, doesn't it! And why the new phone, Jeremy?'

'I told you. Something happened to my old one, so I had to quickly get a replacement, that's all. No mystery, you can trust me. I can understand your reticence, but there's nothing to be concerned about, honest.'

'I'll call you back shortly, Jeremy.'

I ended the call and apologised to Helen for the interruption. I then looked out of the window hoping to glean some inspiration from somewhere. There being none after a couple of minutes, I was grateful when Helen broke the impasse. 'You look worried, David and I don't like seeing you like this.'

I turned and grabbed one of her hands. 'I've made a decision. I feel that I'm up to my neck in something and I don't like it. I can't sort this out, but I know some people who can.'

'David, look, you've got a lot on your plate today and that's a shame because I had something I wanted to discuss with you.' Helen put her other hand on top of mine and looked into my eyes, 'Today's Tuesday and I have to go away on Thursday, on business. Perhaps you can sort your life out while I'm away.' She smiled and started to get up from the table.

'Wait! Please sit down again. I want to hear what it is you want to discuss with me. You're far more important than the six balls I'm juggling with right now.'

'Okay, but don't forget about your telephone call. You said you'd call back.'

'That'll have to wait. Go on, tell me your news.'

'Well, in the line of my work, I deal with my clients, usually solicitors, who are dealing with their clients, criminals! I'm not sure how much you know about my line of work, David.'

'Not much. I like watching crime dramas on TV as much as the next man, so that's the extent of my knowledge, basically.'

'Okay, well let me trot out a phrase I learned to let people like my mum and dad know what I was up to at university, it's the study of the views, thoughts, intentions, actions, and reactions of criminals and all that partakes in criminal behaviour. And that keeps me busy.'

'You're the loveliest parrot I know, Helen. So, where are you off to on Thursday, then?'

'I've finished a report for a firm of solicitors in Leeds and I'm going up there for a few days during which time I'll deliver my findings and opinions to the partners; I'll also pop in to see my sister who lives in Holbeck, just outside of the city. I was going to see if you fancied coming up there with me. She raised an eyebrow at me and smiled wryly.

'This Thursday? Oh, crap!'

'What's the matter?'

'It never rains but it pours,' I laughed sardonically.

'How do you mean?'

'You know. It's the epitome of the old proverb, isn't it? Misfortunes or difficult situations tend to follow each other in rapid succession or arrive all at the same time!'

'Sorry, you're talking in riddles. I don't know what you're talking about.'

'I've got an appointment in London on Friday to go over a couple of potential editorial jobs. I've also got this Jeremy Browne situation to deal with. And obviously, I'd rather be going to Leeds with you for a few days. And hearing phrases like I know where you live and you can trust me, scare me fartless.'

At that point, my mobile rang and I looked at the screen to see that the unfamiliar mobile number calling was becoming all too familiar to me now, unfortunately. I answered abruptly, 'What?'

'It's me again.'

'I know.' I paused, drained the last of my coffee, and carried on, 'Jeremy, I've given what you said to me earlier a great deal of thought. I've decided to help you and Foster out. I'm prepared to let you both stay at my house for a few days.'

'That's amazing. Thank you.'

'As I said to you, I'm a bit tied up at the moment so can't get down to South Mimms to pick you up. But if you can get a taxi to my place, I'll be there to let you in. Can't say fairer than that, can I?'

'You're wonderful, David. I'll look forward to getting down to business with you when we get a proper chance to talk.'

'Okay, looking at the time now, shall we say a couple of hours, 7.00pm? I'll look forward to seeing you then.' I pressed the button to end the call and I smiled enigmatically at Helen.

'You're up to something, David. Just when I think I've got you pigeonholed, you suddenly do something which takes me by surprise.'

'You ain't seen nothing yet! Please excuse me while I make a couple of phone calls, would you? I'm going to try and organise my life to allow me to go with you to Leeds, if you were serious about that?'

'I don't see how you'll be able to get around the obstacles to let you do that.'

'They're not obstacles; they're hurdles. Watch the master in action!' I pulled out a letter from my jacket and called the number for Big Cat Publications and asked to speak to the MD, Stephen Ketts.

'Hi, Stephen. Sorry to trouble you. It's David Jones and I was due to come down and see you on Friday. Unfortunately, something's cropped up which I need to deal with and I'm just calling to see if we can re-arrange the date in our diaries. I'm keen to have a discussion with you about your magazines as I've got some ideas which I've been working on.'

'I see. I trust it's nothing trivial, Mr Jones?'

'Trivial?'

'Sorry, I was trying to lighten the moment. Looking through my diary, how does the following Friday work for you? Same time?'

'That would be great. Thank you so much for your understanding, Mr Ketts, I appreciate it and will look forward to seeing you on the 24th, at 11am. I promise to make it worth your while.'

Helen looked very worried, 'I didn't mean to disrupt your life like this.'

'Ha! That's just part one sorted. Now for part two. Two more minutes and I'll be all yours.'

I looked through the names and numbers in my phone's call-log and picked out the one I wanted. It was answered after two rings.

'Hello? DC Parkes.'

'Hello, DC Parkes, it's David Jones. I assume that you're still looking for Jeremy Browne and Tom Foster ...'

'Yes. Why do you ask?'

'You'll be pleased to know that I have a plan. I'll explain it. I've been approached by Jeremy and he's got Foster with him. They are looking for a bolthole for a few days and he asked whether they could stay at my place. Well, I don't particularly want to babysit those two in my own home, frankly. In any case, I want to go away for a few days. So, this is what I've arranged: By seven o'clock this evening, they will be arriving at my house by taxi where they will expect me to let them in. Instead, you and some of your colleagues could be there to welcome them and then you can have whatever conversations you want to have! How does that sound?'

'Mr Jones, that sounds excellent. Well done. Right, we just need to come over and get your keys to lock up afterward.'

'I'm not there right now, but I can be there at 6pm.'

'Perfect. I'll brief the team and we'll make our way over to Langford. Thank you. It's very public-spirited of you.'

We ended the call and I looked at Helen who had her mouth wide open.

'Right then, I'll settle up here and then we can make our way back to my place.'

Chapter Ten

We all met up at my house in good time. Susan Parkes was accompanied by four male colleagues, including DC Eldrid and PC Kranic. I quickly packed a bag upstairs in readiness for my break with Helen. She had explained in the car journey that she intended to travel up to Leeds by train. The Kings Cross to Leeds train would be stopping at Stevenage and that was where we would be picking it up. As soon as we could, we left the property with the police officers inside. They planned to await the imminent knock on the door from Browne and Foster at which point, they would grab them and haul them inside the house for questioning.

Helen and I hightailed it out of town and headed for her home, just over the county border, in Hitchin.

'I've got a spare bedroom, David, so don't get any ideas! I've looked into hotels in Leeds and the Ibis is right in the town centre and close to Madeley's, the solicitors I'm seeing, so I'll call them and book a couple of rooms if you're still serious about going up there with me.'

'Of course, I am. I've never been to Leeds. What's it like?'

'Well, it's a city of course, so it's got a cathedral; half a dozen museums and of course, it's got Leeds United football club. I don't think you know Samantha Brand, a good friend of mine. She went to university up there and I went to stay with her a couple of times, so I'm familiar with it.'

'You're more and more engaging, Helen, as each day goes by.'

We pulled up outside of the house and we remained sitting there as she didn't seem motivated enough to go inside for some reason. After a couple of minutes, she turned to me and said, 'David, have you spoken to Amanda recently? I hope you don't mind my asking.'

'Funnily enough, I received something in the post from her only today.'

'Oh, what did she say?'

'I don't know. I haven't opened it.' I pulled the unopened letter from my inside jacket pocket. I looked at the familiar handwriting on the envelope and turned it over and over in my hand.

'Why don't you want to know what's inside?'

'I'm not a control freak but I fear that the contents may have unforeseen ramifications for my future.'

'Come on into the house, I'll make you a cuppa and you can decide what to do. You've got to open it one day!'

Once inside, Helen disappeared into the kitchen to boil the kettle and I heard her getting cups and plates out of her cupboard. Whilst she was busying herself, I was sitting alone in the living room and I retrieved the envelope again. I took out the letter:

Dear David,
As I write this to you, I realise that I haven't written a letter to you before, just a Christmas card, not even a birthday card. Oh, by the way, many happy returns to you for the 6th of June. Oh dear, I've given the game away. By writing the previous sentence to you I've alerted you to the fact that I won't be around for you at the time of your birthday.

We've had some highs and lows over the past six months, haven't we?

I hope that you feel that I may have helped you over these last few months as you have tried to come to terms with Donna's passing.

Anyway, the last few days or so have made me want to re-evaluate my life. I feel that when I needed you to be with me you weren't there for me, were you?

Even so, I wish you only well, David, with all that you want to do with your life in the future. I take this opportunity of wishing you all the best.

Please don't think ill of me,
   Amanda

I put the letter back into the envelope and returned it to my jacket. At that moment, Helen came in carrying a tray of teas and biscuits. 'Have you decided to read your letter yet?'

'Yeah, just did.' I smiled sardonically.

'What did Amanda say then, if you're happy to share its content with me?'

I stared off into the middle distance and said, 'Not sure, actually.'

'What do you mean, exactly?' Helen frowned, 'No need to be enigmatic with me, David.'

I smiled, shook my head and took the envelope from my jacket once more. 'Here, read it for yourself, see what you make of it.'

It only took a minute and Helen placed it on the coffee table between us. 'Oh, dear. You'd better try calling her.'

'*Mea culpa.*' I took out my mobile and tried her number. Thirty seconds later, I put the phone back in my pocket. 'Dead.'

'What!' cried Helen.

'The phone.' I picked up my cup of tea and took a sip. 'I tried calling her yesterday too and I couldn't connect then either.'

'Are you worried, David? I know that I would be if I'd received a letter like the one in your possession.'

'Thanks a lot. But that's not what I wanted to hear from you, Helen.'

'I've never known anyone retain their sang-froid as well as you've been able to.'

'Well, what can I do?

***

Police officers lay in wait inside the house either side of the front door. Once the doorbell rang, the door was opened quickly by one of the officers and first Jeremy Browne and then Tom Foster, were grabbed by their lapels and hauled into the house. During the ensuing melee, both suspects ended up on the floor each with two male police officers grappling with them. Each of the six assailants hurled verbal abuse at one another together with the occasional fist. Then, Jeremy Browne wriggled free and whilst lying down pulled something from one of his pockets.

'Oh, my God, he's got a gun! What the …' and it was Foster who was the quickest to shout out. Momentarily, all was quiet in the room and a brief hiatus in the activity was created.

Simultaneously, Browne shouted, 'Okay, back off.' DC Eldrid rushed forward and said, 'Calm down, take it easy.'

As he approached, Browne pulled the trigger and Eldrid was hit in the thigh. All hell then broke loose. The other officers all backed away with Eldrid clutching his right thigh and screaming various derogatory epithets.

'Shit, Jeremy, you've done it now, you idiot!' Foster screamed. DC Susan Parkes was speaking into her mobile requesting an ambulance to attend the property, 'Officer down! We need assistance NOW!'

'Okay, gorgeous. No funny business. That call's fine but no others. Got it?' Browne waved his semi-automatic handgun about. 'And you can shut up!' he turned to DC Eldrid, 'help is on its way, you big baby!'

'You nutter.' Foster then turned to the officers, 'I want you all to know that this has nothing to do with me. I hardly know him. He didn't tell me that he had a gun!'

'Ha, ha, so the little rat wants to leave the sinking ship!' DC Duncan Pratt laughed.

'Shut the fuck up!' Browne shouted as he let his gun go off, firing a bullet out of harm's way into the ceiling. Plaster and pieces of wood floated down to the floor. Pointing the handgun at Foster, he said, 'And you, you little shit, go and stand over there with the others.'

The blues and twos of the ambulance eventually pulled up outside and once again, things went quiet. DC Parkes raised her hand and Browne nodded to allow her to let the two paramedics in.

'I didn't know somebody had been shot,' the male one said, looking up at DC Parkes. 'We're just going to have to patch him up, stabilise him, and get back to the hospital as soon as possible.'

'We'll go and get the stretcher out of the ambulance,' PC Kranic offered.

'You'll do nothing of the sort. You're all going to stay where you are while they clear up here.' Browne looked uncomfortable and far from in control. Suddenly, his bellicose attitude had changed. He said to the female paramedic, 'Nearly done? Sorry, I can't let any of this lot out of my sight. You'll have to get the stretcher yourselves when you're ready.'

Browne looked at the five police officers together with Foster standing in a line across the wall opposite.

'Why did you do it?' the female paramedic asked as she put the finishing touches to the bandage that she was applying to Eldrid's upper thigh.

'Self-defence. They attacked me.'

'That's no excuse and you know it. You look like an intelligent man to me.'

'Appearances can be deceptive!' Foster shouted mockingly. At that point, Browne raised his gun and fired off one more shot, hitting Foster in his left leg. He collapsed screaming on to the floor.

'Another customer for you,' Browne smirked. He walked over to the others and said, 'Right, you lot, no more sarcastic comments. We don't want to be looking at creating another episode of *Midsomer Murders*, do we?'

DC Parkes frowned, 'I'd be dead against it, obviously. What's the plan now, then? Or did you always intend to cause mayhem, Mr Browne?'

'Everything was going fine until I trusted that tosser, David Jones. I'm not a very good judge of character, am I?' He then kicked Foster on his good leg. 'Not only is Jones a crap writer but he's caused all of this.' He waved his gun at the two prone bodies on the floor.

'He didn't do this,' DC Pratt commented, 'you did. You didn't have to over-react in that way.' The comment triggered Parkes to put a restraining hand on his arm to quieten her colleague. The male paramedic had started to placate Foster, administering anaesthetics, stemming the flow of blood and bandaging the leg.

Then, simultaneously, all five mobile phones of the police officers started ringing, bleeping and singing.

Browne reacted immediately, 'Leave the phones. Don't answer them!'

'Mr Browne, you've got to realise something,' DC Parkes said sedately, 'if they're not answered within minutes, HQ will send out the local firearms unit. Whilst you've been acting like Wild Bill Hickok, don't you think that your neighbours might have phoned the police and reported hearing gunshots?'

This comment triggered a break in the conversation. He then turned to DC Parkes, 'Okay, Goldilocks, get the bracelets off your friends and handcuff them all securely to one another. Whilst you're doing that, the paramedics can get PC Braveheart and this wimp, Foster, into the ambulance. And make it snappy now, we don't want this thing going off again.' Jeremy Browne was waving his Beretta 9mm around. DC Parkes frantically handcuffed the wrists of her colleagues together and sat them down in the corner of the room as the paramedics left the house to obtain the stretcher.

'By the way, my name is DC Parkes.'

'Shut it. Give me your handcuffs and turn around.' She complied with this request and Browne quickly disabled her and placed her sitting down with her colleagues. Once DC Eldrid had been placed inside the ambulance, the two paramedics returned to pick up Foster. Browne turned and left the room. His ambition was to look through the obvious places to try and find a place where

David Jones may have put his car keys, a hallway, a kitchen. It took only a couple of minutes to find the key and plastic fob relating to the Volkswagen Golf that was sitting twenty yards down the road outside. He returned to the living room just as the paramedics were leaving the property together with their cargo.

'Okay, chaps and … DC Parkes,' he said in an avuncular fashion, 'I'm sorry, but I'm going to have to leave you all now. Don't do anything I wouldn't! And don't tell anyone where I've gone. Ha, ha.'

Browne chuckled to himself as he slammed the front door behind him as he ran to the Golf. Police sirens could be heard getting louder and louder as their cars made their way toward the centre of Langford.

***

I was waiting with Helen on Platform 3 of Stevenage railway station, the King's Cross to Leeds train due to arrive shortly. We had been dropped off at the station by taxi and had decided to purchase two takeaway lattes to sustain us for the first half hour of the journey.

About twenty people boarded the carriages at Stevenage station and we found seats facing forward, easily. Our carriage was only a quarter full and we were able to speak to each other freely. 'I'm really looking forward to this trip, Helen,' I smiled as our eyes met, 'you know, a chance to get to know each other better. There's so much that you don't know about me and I bet there's things I don't know about you.'

'Ha, strangers on a train, you mean. Hey, you're a budding author. You ought to write a story about it.'

'Already been done, Patricia Highsmith wrote the book. You must have seen the film, Alfred Hitchcock directed it.'

'Oh no, not another one of your old black and white films?'

I looked out of the window, 'Yes, very good, great plot, all about the perfect murder, Helen.'

All was quiet for about five minutes and to break the impasse, Helen offered me a polo mint.

'Peace offering, David. I'm sorry, I know it's one of your specialist subjects. Tell me all about the genre.'

'No, you're just humouring me.'

'I'm not. Don't go all moody on me. It doesn't suit you.' Helen playfully slapped my arm. 'I really want to know more. Come on, it's a long journey. I want to learn. You be my teacher. I promise not to be a naughty girl!' She said this to me coquettishly and smiled at me flirtatiously too.

'All right then. Sit back. It's a film noir, which in French means dark film, a style of filmmaking characterised by such elements as cynical heroes, stark lighting effects, frequent use of flashbacks, intricate plots and an underlying existentialist philosophy. The genre was prevalent mostly in American crime dramas of the post-Second World War era. *Strangers on a Train* was typical of this genre, the film being released in about 1950, I think.'

'Wow, you ought to get a job with the BBC, reviewing films.'

'No, they would want me to review all the latest releases and that really wouldn't interest me at all.' I paused as a myriad number of reflections suddenly permeated my thought process.

'David, you look so sullen. What's up?' Helen placed a hand on my thigh again.

'Oh, I don't know. It's this time of the year, I suppose. This month always seems to bring me so much angst, Helen. Donna died last year, in April. My latest book manuscript has been rejected, in April. I'm embroiled in a police investigation, in April. I've donated my house to a couple of criminals to hide out, in April. My relationship with my girlfriend seems to have come to an end, in April. Can you see a common theme emerging here? April is the cruellest month …'

Helen smiled, 'T S Eliot!

> *April is the cruellest month, breeding*
> *lilacs out of the dead land, mixing*
> *memory and desire, stirring*
> *dull roots with spring rain.*

That's from *The Waste Land*, my favourite. I also covered poetry when I studied for my English Literature A level. Hey, come on, everything will be all right in the end and if it's not all right then it's not the end!'

She held my hand and held my gaze.

'You're just the tonic that a man needs.'

'You are a polymath, whatever you say. There's no denying it. You must like poetry, you're such a bright guy.'

'Flattery will get you everywhere. If I remember, it already has!'

Helen punched me lightly in my ribs, 'You rat. I take it all back. I bet that I've found the hidden chink in your armour, Mr Jones!'

'What do you mean? You think you've found my vulnerable spot?'

'Yes. Possibly.' Helen paused before continuing, 'It's okay, you know. You can't be good at everything. Not everyone writes poetry. Don't worry ...'

'Who says I can't write poetry?'

'Well, can you? There you go. I throw down the gauntlet!'

I laughed out loud attracting the attention of several passengers. 'Right, I accept the challenge, young lady. I will compose something for you.' I said in a playful way.

'It doesn't surprise me, David. When do you think it will be ready?'

'Not long. How about five minutes?' I pulled out an envelope and a biro and started scribbling.

Within the deadline, I had come up with something, 'Are you ready? It's an eight-line poem. Not my best work but all I could come up with in the circumstances:

> *That girl on the seat*
> *I'd really like to meet*
> *Such poise and grace*
> *Perfect body; beautiful face*
> *I won't need a shove*
> *Cos I've fallen in love!*
> *Will she ever feel the same?*
> *And want to take my name?*

'Oh, David, it's wonderful. I'm really confused now. Please don't say any more, now you've got me thinking too.'

I replaced the piece of paper and pen into my jacket and we both had a few moments of quiet contemplation. Helen clearly didn't want an atmosphere of awkwardness to fall between us and she was the first to speak.

'Today's Thursday and my appointment with the partners isn't until 11am tomorrow.' Helen patted the briefcase on the seat next to her. 'All ready. My presentation is in here and three copies, one for each of the partners.'

'I'm very proud of you, Helen. It's so good to find someone who's working in the same field as the degree they've earned.'

Helen put one of her hands on my thigh and looked into my eyes, 'Whilst we're giving out compliments, I've never known anyone with such shrewdness as you.' She smiled, leaned over, and kissed me on the cheek.

'I've got to talk to you about last night, Helen. I certainly wasn't expecting that to happen after what you'd said.'

'I'm full of surprises and I've got another one for you.'

'Surprises? Shocks more like!'

'Look, you've always been in a relationship when I was available and vice-versa. Now, at the moment, I'm not with anyone, not looking either, actually and you seem to be available, possibly, but I think that the jury's out in relation to the Amanda situation.'

We held hands and I was looking out of the window gazing at the countryside as we sped northwards. Suddenly, my attention was drawn away as three people made their way down the carriage to enter the next one. I turned to Helen and quietly said, 'Bugger me, talk about shocks!'

'What?'

'You've heard me talk about the investigation that I'm wrapped up in. Well, did you see the people that just passed by us?' Helen nodded and I carried on. 'I didn't recognise the first two but the third one was a police officer called Craven. I'm sure it was, well I think it was. He looked slightly different. Oh, I don't know.' I shook my head, turned and tried to look again at the retreating figures.

'Don't worry about it, David,' Helen squeezed my hand, 'it probably wasn't him and so what if it was? Did he even look at you?'

'No, we didn't make eye contact and consequently, it's made me doubt whether it was Craven or not. This whole situation is starting to make me feel cranky. I'm paranoid now.'

'You'll be fine. I'll look after you,' Helen smiled, 'Hey, let me tell you about the surprise I've got for you. I mentioned my friend, Samantha Brand. Well, I've been in touch and we're all going out for a meal this evening. She knows the area and says that TGI Fridays which apparently is very close to the hotel, offers a good menu choice and is reasonably priced too. It'll be great to see her again.'

'That's a lovely surprise. I'm not used to those!'

'I hope you'll like Samantha,' Helen squeezed my thigh again, 'but not too much, especially after last night.'

'Yes, about last night. I'm a bit perturbed if you want to know. Help me out if you can. Where does that leave us exactly, Helen?'

'It took me by surprise too. We were in the moment. We'd had a glass of wine or two and we certainly got re-acquainted properly after all those years!'

I looked out of the window again. It had started to rain. 'That hasn't helped me. First of all, the letter from Amanda, then the passion between us last night.'

I wanted to take a moment, so I excused myself and went for a walk down the corridor. Somebody had left a copy of the free newspaper, *Metro,* on the end seat by the door and I sat down and started to read it. It wouldn't be long before we would be at our first stop. The time passed quite quickly and as the train pulled into the station at Peterborough, I replaced the newspaper on the seat beside me and made my way back to my original position next to Helen. I got to about twenty feet away from her and she was just nodding and saying something to a couple of men as they were moving on down to the next carriage. My curiosity was piqued. 'Who was that then?' I asked, as I sat down again.

'Oh, nice to see you again. Have a nice time?'

'Not really. I just wanted to process a few things in my little head, that's all. I flicked through some pages of a discarded newspaper, not much in there of any interest though. So, who were they?'

'I don't know, exactly. They seemed very friendly, very polite.'

'Oh, good,' I reacted sarcastically. 'Were they the police? Did they show you any identification?'

'It wasn't like that. Just asked me where I was going, whether I was travelling alone, or not, that sort of thing.'

'I don't believe it. What a cheek. Did they ask about me?'

'No! Blimey, well you said it, paranoia, or what!' Helen smiled. 'Calm down, there's nothing to worry about. Now, we've got a bit of time before we get to Doncaster where we have to change trains. Tell me all about yourself, David Jones. I suspect that what I already know about you is just the tip of the iceberg.'

The rain continued to hammer down on the windows. The three people who had joined our carriage were suitably wet despite having the appropriate accoutrements with them. Fortunately, they had chosen to sit well away from us. The train continued on its way and I turned away from the window and looked at Helen, 'Reminds me of the song *April Showers*. I'll hum it and you join in when you want.' She screwed up her face. 'I don't know what the hell you're talking about.'

'You must have heard it before. It was written about a hundred years ago and been featured in a number of films. Covered famously by Al Jolson, Bing Crosby and ... Judy Garland!' I smiled but it wasn't reciprocated. I continued humming the tune, but I was stopped abruptly.

'David! Well, thank you for that. I'd had my suspicions but in the last thirty seconds, you've filled in all the blanks and more. There's something you ought to know about me. I'm not someone who enjoys old movies, especially black and white ones. I can appreciate that there are a few that are regarded by film buffs as classics, but I don't get it. I know that you like old films, old music, because you've talked about them in the past. But for me, it's *Spider-Man, Mission Impossible*, any *James Bond* movie, that sort of thing.'

'Okay, so you wish to know more about me. I'll speak for a few minutes but please feel free to stop me if you want to. I would regard myself as a collector, Helen. My passion is books. Interestingly, I collect a lot of paperbacks, mainly crime fiction but hardly ever read any of them. Perhaps I would take one away with me on holiday. My real interest is in reference books. I try to better myself, believe it or not! I like to read biographies, history books, especially war books, geography, science, art, literature and music. It seems to have been a family trait. My parents and grandparents loved their books and I've carried on the tradition.'

My mobile phone didn't ring very often. That should tell me a lot. So, when it did in the middle of our conversation, which had been carried out in muted tones, it took us both by surprise. I excused myself to Helen and asked her to remind me to change the current cacophony that I'd enjoyed for the six months I'd had the phone. I didn't recognise the caller's number.

'Hi?' I said.

'Mr Jones? It's DC Susan Parkes. Where are you? We've got a few things to talk about.'

'Sorry, I don't know where I am exactly.'

'Don't try and be smart with me. I'm calling with information about your house and your car.'

'I wasn't trying to be clever, DC Parkes, I'm on a train,' I glanced out of the window, 'somewhere in the Midlands. Tell me then, what's happened?'

'I was going to suggest that we get together for me to explain everything. When do you expect to be back?'

I looked at Helen, and smiled, 'I'm not sure. Could be a few days yet. You'll have to tell me over the phone.'

There seemed to be an ominous pause before the officer continued, 'Right, as you know, when you left us, we had a plan. In summary, I and four of my colleagues were to lay in wait to apprehend and question Jeremy Browne and Tom Foster. To cut a long story short, a fracas ensued soon after they arrived. Browne broke free, pulled out a gun, and mayhem was unleashed.'

'What! Guns? Was anyone hurt?' I was shouting and a number of our fellow passengers looked over in our direction.

'Yes. Your friend Jeremy Browne shot DC Eldrid in the thigh and later, he turned on his partner-in-crime, Tom Foster and shot him in one of his legs too. Unfortunately for you, your living room has suffered some damage as a result of this debacle. More of that later.'

'Hang on a minute. He's not one of my friends, nor is Eldrid but I wouldn't have wished that on him. So, what damage has occurred to my lounge, exactly?'

'I'm glad you're on a train, Mr Jones. Hopefully, you're sitting down. Er, there is damage to that room but that's not all, I'm afraid. I've started to put a list together of all the remedial works that will need doing.'

'A list!' I shouted again and Helen put a restraining hand on my arm.

'There's a lot more to tell you. Browne made sure that we were all manacled together so that he could make his escape. Which he did by making off in your Golf which was parked outside. The neighbours were obviously concerned with the number of gunshots they had heard and called the police.'

'Oh, my word. This is serious stuff.'

DC Susan Parkes tried to placate me, 'You're right there. The main responsibilities of firearms units are the response to emergency calls believed to involve firearms and the arrest of armed, dangerous or barricaded criminals in official raids and operations. Specialist Firearms Officers receive enhanced training in dynamic entry tactics, for hostage rescue. I've shared all of this with you as I now go on to tell you the whole story. Your front door was locked by Browne as he made his escape and the Special Firearms team had to smash the door down to gain entry, sorry. They established the house was risk-free then set about freeing us all.'

I paused a while and finally said, 'Wow. What about the damage? Who's going to pay for that? And what about my car? Has that been recovered yet?'

'Don't worry about the cost of repairs. That will all be covered. No, the Golf hasn't been found yet, but it will be.'

Chapter Eleven

Jeremy Browne put as much distance between himself and Langford as quickly as he could. He knew that he was a marked man now, wounding a policeman and that idiot Foster by gunshots. Of course, they would have put out an urgent alert throughout the police forces of Bedfordshire and the neighbouring counties to track down the VW Golf that he was driving. Automatic number plate recognition would be one of the tools in their arsenal. Consequently, he knew that the sooner he was able to ditch this hot car, the better. It didn't take a genius to work that one out. And he certainly didn't feel like a genius at that particular moment. He had recklessly gone for his gun in the heat of the moment. It was a typical fight-or-flight response, he supposed.

As he found his way on to the A1, heading northwards, the background to this situation came into his mind. He remembered that whilst at school, he had learned something about in a stressful situation, fight or flight represented the choices that our ancient ancestors had when faced with danger in their environment. They could either fight or flee. In either case, the physiological and psychological response to stress prepared the body to react to the danger. Browne certainly felt that he had been embroiled in a very stressful situation being jumped upon by burly police officers hell-bent on restraining and detaining him. It had been going on since time immemorial. He now had the dichotomy of travelling as fast as he could but also looking out for any police cars, as he obviously didn't want to be caught as the fleeing fugitive, Bedfordshire's current public enemy number one.

He mused on the fact that he didn't now have a plan. Mind you, when he had had one where had that got him? He spotted a police car in the distance and slowed the Golf down accordingly. He decided to keep about four-hundred yards between the two vehicles. A plan seemed to be emerging. When he could pull off the A1, he would ditch the Golf somewhere. He would have to acquire another vehicle and that might prove troublesome as he wasn't an inveterate car thief. The Golf had been his first foray into the world of thievery. Browne chuckled to himself, firearms offences, perhaps, but not anything minor, like stealing!

***

The train slowed down, then stopped at Peterborough. I grabbed the arm of Helen's jacket, 'Come on, let's hop off.'

'What are you on about, David? We're going to Leeds!'

'I know that.' I rolled my eyes at her, 'I just thought that we could take a breather; grab another coffee and then jump on the next train to complete our journey. They're every fifteen minutes, or so.'

She paused, considering her options, then finally, 'Yes, come on.'

We both hopped off and I shouted out, 'Serendipity!' as we alighted immediately adjacent to the welcoming and peaceful platform coffee shop. 'I love the juxtaposition of the hot, smelly, oily train and this tranquil, quiet mini-café.' We entered and ordered two coffees to go and a couple of croissants too. We viewed the digital platform and train timetable sign and saw that we had twelve minutes to wait for the next train. We sat down and continued our chat.

'Well, we were rudely interrupted on the train by that phone call from DC Parkes but I had told you a bit about myself. Now it's your turn, Helen.'

'I'm not sure how I can follow that. I was impressed that you had postponed your interview with the guy at Big Cat just so you can be with me and go to Leeds.'

'And to meet your friend, Samantha!'

'Hey, watch it!' Helen smiled and slapped my hand blithely. 'You're still an impressive guy though, even if you've got a roving eye! You're so erudite, David. I bet you're tired of hearing so many platitudes. As a young man, you've written books and edited magazines. I can't compete with that.'

'Compete? You've done so much in your lifetime, Helen. Got a good degree, using it in your work. I'm proud of you. And yes, I've written books, or tried to. Nothing published yet! Please tell me more about yourself, your dreams and your aspirations.'

'Oh, I don't know really. I went into law, I suppose because my father was a solicitor, well still is actually. I enjoy my work. A large part of what a criminal psychologist does is studying why people commit crimes. In recent times, I've also assessed criminals to evaluate the risk of recidivism or make educated guesses about the actions that a criminal may have taken after committing a crime.'

'Recidivism? I like to think I'm well-read, but remind me what that means again, please.'

'Sorry, it's shop-talk. It's how likely the person is to re-offend in the future.'

'Thanks. So, you're happy with your work. What about travelling, holiday plans?'

'I haven't been to many places. Travelled to Greece last year, well, Corfu anyway. And two years ago, I went with Samantha to the Costa Blanca. Loved it. May go back there one day. Oh, look, here's our train. Once we're in our seats, I'll carry on with part two.'

We ascended the steps and found seats in a similar orientation to our previous ones. We decided to eat our croissants and drink our coffees before continuing with our deliberations. A combination of looking out of the window and concentrating on the food and drink meant that I was not keeping abreast of our surroundings properly. I looked up suddenly when I became aware that three men were making their way down the carriage past us and then away from us. As the retreating figures arrived at the door to exit one carriage and enter the next, I turned to Helen and said urgently, 'Did you see that?'

'No, what do you mean?'

'I know what your response is going to be when I say that I'm pretty sure that those three characters, including the DS Craven, the one I mentioned before, were the ones we saw previously.'

'Well, so what?'

'How can that be possible? Don't you see? They were on the previous train that we were on.'

The penny dropped and Helen frowned at me, 'It probably wasn't the same men and anyway, the first time you saw them you said that you couldn't be one-hundred per cent certain that it was this Craven. Plus, on this occasion, you only saw them from behind and some ten or fifteen yards away at that!'

'I want to believe that scenario, I do.' I packed our discarded food and coffee detritus away in the spare carrier bag I had with me. I looked away from the carriage doorway and turned towards Helen again, 'I'll try and forget that for now. Let's carry on, shall we? You said that your story continues in part two?'

'Yes. One of my fellow university students went to South America after she'd graduated. Fired up my imagination. What do you know about Chile?'

'Very cold,' I said laconically.

'Cold?'

'Well, you know, chilly!'

'Are you being serious?'

'I've always been famous for my occasional bon mots! No, I'm sure the weather would be fine for you. Just ignore me.'

'We change trains at Doncaster, and we've got a bit of time until then.' Helen dipped into her bag and pulled out a magazine to read.

***

As Jeremy Browne made his way as swiftly as he could up the A1 within his self-imposed speed limit restrictions, he was constantly scanning the signage for a town, a shopping centre, an industrial estate, or leisure facility that might afford what he was looking for. He had been catching the updates on the shootings in Langford with one of the victims being a serving police officer, on the car radio. He was also wanted as an accessory in the murder of a young woman in London. Browne's description and that of the car he was driving had been circulated. Therefore, the sooner he could ditch it and acquire some new wheels the better. The latest bulletin stated that the Golf had been spotted travelling northwards on the A1. The next exit was signposted for one mile away and the latest news item expedited his decision. He exited the road accordingly. Ten minutes later, a perfect opportunity presented itself. He turned the car into a retail park and parked in the furthest space away from the shop's entrance as possible between a Transit van and an old Nissan Micra, which from its two flat tyres looked as if it hadn't been moved for some months. He now contemplated his options: to look for a car which still had its keys inside the ignition, a bit like winning the lottery, he mused; or awaiting an unsuspecting shopper on their return to their car so that Browne could then confront them and carry out his heist.

    His new life of crime CV did not include breaking into vehicles, playing with the electronics and hot-wiring, or whatever, to start a car's engine and make his getaway, as he had seen in so many TV shows and Hollywood movies. He wasn't Jason Statham and didn't want to be! He had walked about one-hundred yards away from the Golf across this massive car park and then waited for an unsuspecting victim to emerge. It only took a few moments for a young guy and his daughter to appear. He was laden down carrying two very full carrier bags of shopping and keeping a watchful eye on his five-year-old who was walking in front of him. As they arrived at his black Citroen DS3, he pressed the key fob in his hand and the doors and boot unlocked. Browne swiftly approached the man and pressed his Beretta 9mm into his side and said, 'Don't make a sound. Just listen to me. Hand me the key. Put your shopping and the kid into the car. Do as I say, and no one will get hurt, okay?'

Once the shopping was away in the boot and with the child safely secured in the child seat in the rear, Browne resumed with his instructions, 'Right. So far, so good. Now, you get in the driver's seat and I'll join you.'

Before he could get into the car, Browne witnessed three black unmarked police cars speeding into the car park and surrounding the VW Golf in the far corner.

'Talk about karma!' he laughed as he slid in and once again pushed the muzzle of the handgun against the man's rib cage, 'Okay, what's your name?'

'My name?'

'Yes, you do have a name, don't you?'

'It's Brian.'

'Okay, Brian. Listen very carefully. You are now going to drive slowly out of the car park, without drawing any attention to us, as you do so. You will enter the A1 and go north. I'll talk to you more as we go along but let me tell you this. If you do as I say, no harm will come to you, or your daughter. Need I say more?' Brian shook his head. He then looked in his rear view mirror and saw that his daughter, Amy, was playing with her teddy bear and was oblivious of anything being untoward.

When she realised her father was looking at her, she said, 'Daddy, daddy, who is this? And why is he so angry with you?' her face crumpled and she looked from one adult to the other. The start of her crying was stopped by her father leaning behind and grabbing his daughter's leg

'Amy, darling, don't worry, it's my friend, Andy, he's just playing. You know, cops and robbers. Silly, Andy.' He turned to his new 'friend' and said, "Now come on, let's not do this here, you're scaring my daughter. Put your toy gun away and then we can carry on.'

Browne complied, wanting to get the show on the road and he returned the Berretta to his jacket pocket. 'Okay, Brian, let's go.' As the car started moving, Browne turned around in his seat and he grabbed the child's teddy bear by its leg and wiggled it. 'Everything's alright now, we're going off to get some ice-cream.' Amy wrestled the teddy out of Browne's hand and held it tightly to her body. Brian looked in his rear-view mirror at his daughter who was still scowling at Browne. He called over his shoulder, 'Amy, we'll be home soon. Hey, Danger Mouse will be on TV. You love that, don't you!'

***

'Hey, we've got a few minutes to spare. I'll ask you a few questions that will help me to understand you a bit better, is that okay?' Helen smiled at me in that familiar way that was so enchanting.

'Fine, then I'll reciprocate. I really want to get to know you better!'

Helen raised her eyes at me in a resigned sort of fashion. 'All right, favourite books?'

'Hmm, that's not as easy to answer as one would expect. As a teenager, when I started getting into books my favourite at that time was *The Citadel* by A J Cronin, very emotional, well I was anyway! A book that I love and can go back to, time and time again is *My Family and Other Animals* by British naturalist, Gerald Durrell.'

'Yes, I've read that one. Loved it. Anything else?'

'I recently read *Laura* by Vera Caspary. Oh, wow. It's one of the finest and most unusual mystery novels ever written. Came out during the Second World War and was made into a great film starring Gene Tierney.'

Helen's eyes started to glaze over, so I said, 'Don't be like that. You did ask. Anything else?'

She laughed and then continued, 'Oh dear, I'm frightened to ask more, favourite films, then?'

'Again, almost impossible to answer. One of the classics obviously, *Gone With The Wind*, I suppose; Fritz Lang's *Metropolis*; and my final one is a poignant choice really. I was dragged along to see it by Donna because although it was a modern movie, she thought that I might like it because it was in black and white and silent! *The Artist* won Academy Awards for best picture, best director and best actor.'

'And did you like it? If so, what was so special then?'

'I loved it, the first silent film to win the award since *Wings* that won at the first Academy Awards. It took me by surprise,' I looked away before continuing, 'it was the last movie that we went to see together before ...'

'Oh, David, I'm sorry, I didn't mean to upset you.'

I composed myself quickly, 'All right, let's try just one more then.'

'If you're sure, favourite food?'

'I see what you're doing here, Helen, using your feminine wiles on me!'

'I don't know what you mean, I'm sure.'

'Well, you know what they say; the way to a man's heart is through his stomach!' I laughed. 'You're going to be surprised. For someone as hedonistic as me, I have such simple tastes.'

'My little bon viveur, spill the beans.' Helen touched my cheek.

'Right, top of the charts, jacket potatoes, bangers and mash, fish and chips, pizza and spag bol.'

'So, you really haven't changed much since university. I always had you down as someone who would've moved onwards and upwards.'

'Oh, don't get me wrong, I can enjoy Beef Stroganoff, or Chilli Con Carne like the next man. Don't worry, I have simple tastes, Helen.'

'Beast!' She lashed out at me again, affectionately.

I glanced up, looking down the carriage to the door at the end and squeezed Helen's hand and said loudly, 'Look! Did you see that?'

'What?' Helen craned her head round to try and follow my gaze. 'I hadn't seen anything.'

'Well, they're not there now, are they! Two of those men that I saw earlier were looking through the door glass down the carriage at us.'

'Are you sure? Were they the same people as before?'

'Oh, yes. I'm sure of that now, Helen. I had started to doubt myself, you know. But I'm not going mad, after all.'

'I'm worried now too. I keep going over in my mind the questions they were asking me. Innocent, meaningless ones at the time, but now I'm not so sure.'

The train slowed down as it pulled into the station at Doncaster. 'Come on, Helen, we've got to get off now. Let's see everyone who follows suit.'

We sat on a bench and took note of the passengers as the train disgorged its cargo. The electronic board above our heads displayed the various train destinations and times. We would have about fifteen minutes to wait for our connection to Leeds. Within five minutes of the train stopping, the carriages were all empty. I suddenly spotted our three dark-clothed strangers at the far end of the platform.

'Helen, quick, look down there,' I pointed at the characters as they disappeared through somewhere convenient some fifty yards away. 'Come on, let's see where they've gone.'

'Are you joking?'

'No! We've only got a few minutes before the next train.' I grabbed Helen's hand and we started to run down the platform. We were soon at the point where the men had disappeared. It was where stone steps led down to a pathway that ran beneath the railway lines and allowed people to access other rail lines and platforms. We peered down the steps which were empty apart from a middle-aged woman slowly making her way up the stairs towards us.

'Okay, you stay here,' I said to Helen as I started to make my way down. I met the woman halfway.

'Excuse me, I'm sorry to trouble you. I wonder if you can help, please?'

'Pardon?' she answered sounding a bit irritated.

'Did you see three men just now?'

'No. I saw about twenty. What do you want, young man?'

'Sorry, it would have literally been in the last five minutes.'

'Are you the police then? Are they criminals?'

'No, no, no. They're friends of mine, that's all. Nothing to worry about, madam.' I was getting nowhere, so I carried on down the steps until I got to the ground floor.

I looked right, then left, but my surveillance bore no fruit, so I turned around and made my way back upstairs. I was shaking my head as I made eye contact with Helen. 'The three stooges have indeed disappeared.'

We made our way to the appropriate platform and when the train to Leeds arrived, we found forward-facing window seats. It was about half full and a quick survey of our particular carriage did not show any evidence of the people that had been of concern to me.

'It's approximately half an hour now to Leeds.' Helen smiled wanly.

'I'd be interested to learn what a criminal psychologist makes of all this.'

'All what? Nothing's happened, has it? You've got suspicions about some characters on this train. You've tried to follow them, unsuccessfully. So, I don't make anything of it, David.'

The train pulled away and silence descended upon us once again. I noticed a woman sitting opposite me and we had eye contact. It was obvious that she had been listening to our conversation, as people do when they're on a train journey with nothing to read. I said to her, 'Does this concern you?'

'No, but it's starting to,' she replied, as she looked away and feigned interest in the countryside and the odd industrial building that was interspersed in this area of Yorkshire. My phone with that dreadful and incongruous sound, kicked off again (when would I remember to change it!). The woman opposite glanced at me briefly as I answered it. She did an atrocious attempt at pretending not to listen. The ceiling of the carriage was never going to be more interesting than someone's private phone call even if she could only hear my side of the conversation.

'Hello?' I queried, the number calling being unfamiliar to me.

'Mr Jones?'

'Yes, who's calling, please?'

'Good afternoon, sir. This is Inspector Ian Thompson of Bedfordshire Police. My team has contacted me with some information that concerns you. Your car has been located, parked in a retail car park just off the A1. It is currently undergoing forensic analysis.'

'What will that help you to do?'

'We have already visited his workplace in London and carried out a thorough investigative process there, and the examination of your car will just corroborate what we already know about Browne. Any saliva, blood, or fibres found in your Golf will help us to determine any genetic fingerprints.'

'I assume that you didn't find Jeremy Browne in or anywhere near the car, then?'

'No, he had already made his escape by the time that we had been alerted to its location. We will be in touch again once our investigations are over and when the vehicle may be returned to you.'

'Thank you'. But before I was able to pass on my message the call had been disconnected at the other end. I wanted to speak to Helen but before I did so, I spoke to the woman opposite first, 'That was a call from the police about my car; I thought you might be interested to get an update.'

She scowled at me, grabbed her handbag and left her seat, moving further down the carriage.

'That's better,' I smiled at Helen, 'now I've got a question for you. This police inspector on the phone just now mentioned that they would try and find genetic fingerprints. What are they then?'

'These exist in blood, bone, hair follicles, saliva, semen, skin and sweat. They are the same in every cell and retain their distinctiveness throughout a person's life. Interesting, isn't it. They know who they're looking for, but they just want to put as full a profile together as is possible on this Browne character. For someone so didactic, it's so pleasing to be able to teach them something!'

'It's good to know you've got such a high opinion of me!' I laughed and carried on, 'I'm lucky to know someone who moves in the right circles. So, what will happen now then?'

'Well, Browne is a wanted man. He's injured several people with gunshot wounds, including a police officer. He's armed and dangerous and you say wanted in connection with the death of a young woman in London. It doesn't get any more serious than that, David.'

It amused me that the woman who had been eavesdropping earlier was now missing all of this latest juicy information as she was so far away now. Helen carried on, 'He'll be on the PNC now.'

'PNC?'

'Sorry, the Police National Computer is used to facilitate investigations and sharing information of both national and local importance.'

'Wow. I keep thinking back to him sitting in that office in Holborn. He had a bit of an attitude but was still friendly if you know what I mean. I would never have guessed that things would turn out like this, so egregious latterly. This PNC system, presumably, is very comprehensive then?'

'Yes, it's used to record convictions, cautions, reprimands, and warnings for any offence punishable by imprisonment and any other offence that is specified within the regulations. The net will be closing. I have to say though, I'm amazed that he's evaded capture so far.'

Chapter Twelve

Paul Craven had never wanted to be a police officer. He had drifted into a career in law enforcement by default. His brief spell in the RAF had ended after only six months, by mutual agreement. He had been told that the exact circumstances would never be made public. It was, with a huge sigh of relief on both sides, when Wing Commander Brady had presented him with his discharge papers. The DD Form 214 had subsequently been locked away in his bureau at home as Craven had decided that it wasn't a document to be proudly framed and placed on the wall of his living room. His secret was his for now, but he had become aware that any of his next-of-kin could request a copy of the form online by going to the National Personnel Records Centre website. He smirked to himself as he recalled that the accompanying letter had stated that military personnel records were open to the public sixty-two years after they had left the military. Well, that wouldn't bother him, would it! He would be well dead by then bearing in mind the type of activity he was now engaged in.

Yes, he was a drifter. He liked that description. It conjured up an image of Clint Eastwood in his mind. Craven laughed out loud as he aligned himself to that character. Hey, he even looked a bit like the star! A former girlfriend had told him so. Therefore, it must be true. 'Ha!' he exclaimed again, attracting the attention of half a dozen fellow commuters waiting on the platform for the next train.

'What are you looking at?' he sneered at the nearest of them, a businessman of about sixty who quickly moved further away up the platform, wanting to avoid any kind of potential confrontation.

No, the RAF hadn't suited him for obvious reasons. How was he to know that the young lady that he'd been caught with in his car was the Squadron Leader's daughter? And it was fortunate for Craven that on their third date, he had learned some rather compromising information about her father which the Squadron Leader would not want to be made public. This was Craven's trump card when he was invited to interview by his CO. As a result of that meeting, the RAF and Craven had parted company and a suitable reference had been obtained.

After that, a short sojourn as a security officer in Monte Carlo had followed. His year in the Principality of Monaco had started him on the road to ruin. Interestingly, the citizens of Monaco are forbidden to enter the gaming rooms of casinos or engage in any gambling. However, Craven had chanced his luck at the tables in his spare time. After some initial success, his fortunes had quickly turned around and he seemed to be continually chasing his losses. He wasn't stupid though and he didn't want to follow people that he'd come across who had gambled compulsively and often had substance abuse problems, personality disorders, depression, or anxiety.

Monte Carlo had been a beautiful part of the world for him for those twelve months. As a good-looking guy in his early twenties, he had enjoyed the spoils of living in the area, albeit in his small hotel room in the Hôtel Hermitage Monte Carlo which had been provided to him as part of his employment as one of the six security officers on site. With a debt of 15,650 euros to try and pay off, he had decided to leave Monaco before things had got any worse and had bid a tearful farewell to his girlfriend, Monique Brodeur.

On returning to the UK, he had applied to join the police force, who were recruiting heavily at the time and he had been successful after his two interviews. His father being an inspector in the Suffolk constabulary hadn't done him any harm either.

Early successes and hard work had gained him promotions to his current rank of detective sergeant. The problem for Craven was that his heart wasn't really in it. And he had mixed too much with the criminal underworld, made some useful contacts, obviously, but overall, he knew that the world of gangs, drugs and violence was a short-term panacea to achieve his goals. Ultimately, he realised, this lifestyle would catch up with him, one way or another. His problem, of course, now that he was almost debt-free and hopefully, one day would have some money to his name, meant that it would be very difficult to extricate himself from this environment of syndicates, networks and the subculture and community of criminals referred to as the underworld. He had made some unsavoury connections and unwelcome choices during his time in Monaco. His friends in the Principality, the mafia, had promised to always stay in touch!

His mind was suddenly brought to attention as a train pulled up at the platform where he was sitting. He had sensed that Jones had become suspicious of him, albeit he'd had a change of clothes and the fact that they hadn't been nearby or had any eye contact. Craven and his colleagues had had a perfunctory chat with Jones' female companion during the train journey and this had been duly noted by him. Craven's two associates, Tommy and Dick, had departed at the station, leaving Craven alone. The jury was out in connection with these two cohorts and he had reasons as to why he was keeping an eye on them. He had purposefully let the train carrying Jones and his friend depart without him, to allay any fears that Jones may have had about his being followed. Craven would catch this next train and pursue his quarry accordingly. He wasn't worried; he always caught his man!

***

DC Pratt strode out of the supermarket doorway back to the awaiting officers standing by their vehicles near the VW Golf. 'Typical!' he shouted. 'Another ten minutes of my life and our investigation time wasted.'

'What's the matter, Duncan?'

DC Frank Cooper moved forward and put his hand on Pratt's arm which was pushed aside immediately.

'I've just spoken to some oik and then the manager of this Tesco's. Can you believe this?' DC Pratt turned and pointed to each of the four CCTV cameras attached to the roof line of the building in turn.

'I've just been in there to view the available CCTV footage of the car park to try and ascertain what happened to Browne and where he's gone.' His five colleagues listened avidly as he continued, 'Listen to this, "Oh, I'm so sorry, sir. The CCTV system packed up two days ago. Our monitors in the office went all fuzzy. Don't worry, we've contacted the company that installed it and they'll be here tomorrow afternoon to repair it".'

DC Susan Parkes ran a hand through her blonde locks and laughed, 'At least he called you 'sir'!'

'How often does this happen? A crime occurs and the sodding closed-circuit television system set up for surveillance either doesn't work or the tapes have been recorded over!' Pratt got into his car and slammed the door behind him. DS Barry Wainwright, heading up today's team and Paul Craven's replacement, said, 'Right, come on, back to base. No point staying around here any longer. We don't know what direction Browne's gone or what car he's travelling in.'

***

This being a murder investigation, Tom Foster had been brought to Investigation Room 3 as it had state of the art video recording equipment. Two days ago, he had been taken to Bedford Hospital to be patched up after the Langford shooting. His gunshot wound, although unpleasant, had been regarded by the staff there as insignificant. After registering his details, the initial assessment of his injuries by the A&E doctors made them pass Foster straight through into surgery. Although not life-threatening, they had decided to deal with him straight away especially as he had two police officers hovering nearby. Surgery to remove the bullet had followed a general anaesthetic so that he was unconscious and unaware of the procedure. DC Eldrid had been taken to an operating theatre nearby to have a similar procedure for his injuries. Within three hours, Foster had been given his release papers and he had been escorted back to Kempston.

The video recording equipment had been started on the nod from Inspector Ian Thompson.

'Today's date is Saturday 18th April, the time 10.00am. In Interview Room 3 are Inspector Ian Thompson, DS Jonathan Fox and Mr Tom Foster. Okay, now Mr Foster, for the record, we have taken your biometric data, including your fingerprints and DNA samples and read you your rights; you have agreed to be interviewed without the assistance of a solicitor. You have stated previously that you have not retained a solicitor of your own and that you have declined the services of one that could be provided by Bedfordshire police. Is that correct?'

'Yes.'

'To be sure, let me reiterate: If you are interviewed at a police station, you have a legal right to speak to a solicitor, whether over the phone or in-person at the police station. The advice and guidance your solicitor gives you at this stage can make a significant difference to the outcome of your case and so we urge you to exercise this right.'

'Not interested.'

'Mr Foster, I hope that you appreciate the seriousness of the situation you're in.'

'Go on.'

'This is not the moment to go taciturn on us.'

Foster turned to his left and looked out of the window. DS Fox slapped his hand down on the table and in that small room, the noise was deafening. 'Get real, Foster. You're in big trouble here. DI Thompson has several questions that he wants answers to. Sit up and pay attention!'

Foster folded his arms and glowered at DS Fox. DI Thompson looked at Fox and shook his head.

'Mr Foster, DS Fox is correct. This is a serious business. We are assisting a Major Investigation Team in

London as they are keen to get some information into the disappearance and subsequent death of a young woman, Julie Pemberton, and we believe that you can help us with our inquiries.'

Foster smiled, 'What makes you think that?'

'Your friend, Jeremy Browne, let something slip.'

'As I said the other day, that bastard is not my friend. I had no idea what a fucking nutter he is.'

'So, how did you two get together, then?'

'He had the idea of extracting money from his colleague but didn't want to get his hands dirty. Hence, he contacted me to do his dirty work for him. Believe it or not, I have, or had, a certain amount of sympathy for young Julie. She'd seemingly come into an inheritance from her uncle who had died at Christmas time. Browne had wanted to extricate all financial details of ISAs, bonds, bank accounts and PINs. He couldn't bring himself to question, threaten, or heaven forbid, torture her, to get what he wanted.'

'DS Fox leaned forward in his chair, 'And how did he contact you, to invite you to his office to have a little chat?'

'Ha, ha, ha.' Foster leaned back. 'You lot do make me laugh. I'm not saying, but you don't find people like me in the Yellow Pages!'

'We know that. Moving on, tell me about your conversation in the office and what the plan was.'

'No. As far as I'm aware, apart from taking me to the hospital to get my leg seen to, all you've done is brought me back here for questioning. I'm not wet behind the ears, you know. As you will have already found out, I don't have a record for *anything*.'

'Well, apart from speeding on the M1 and M25 motorways.' DI Thompson was leafing through some papers in the file before him.

'How can that be possible? I don't even have a driving licence!' Foster chuckled again as he looked from one officer to the other.

'Yes, very clever, Mr Foster. They are the only items against your name to date.'

'What I was trying to say is that I've been in similar situations before and I know that the police have to provide information about the offence or offences that suspects are suspected of committing. You haven't charged me with any offence yet, have you? Please correct me if I'm wrong.'

'Not yet', DS Fox replied abruptly.

'Another question for you, Mr Foster,' DI Thompson looked up from his paperwork and carried on, 'The body of Miss Julie Pemberton was found behind some bins in an industrial estate in Wandsworth, South London. What can you tell us about that?'

'I'm sorry to hear that.' Tom Foster then pulled a pack of cigarettes out of his jacket pocket and placed them on the table in front of him. 'Can I smoke in here, then?'

Thompson shook his head, 'No,' and pointed to the sign on the wall, 'It's against the law. We are required by law to display no-smoking signs in workplaces and work vehicles; take reasonable steps to make sure that staff and visitors are aware that they may not smoke on the premises or in our vehicles. So, the answer is NO! Now, may we carry on, please?'

Foster pocketed his cigarettes and said, 'I don't know anything about the young woman being dumped near some bins.'

'Mr Foster, firstly, I didn't say dumped and secondly, your vehicle was picked up on CCTV footage in the vicinity. What do you say to that?'

Foster ran his hands through his hair and said, 'Well, my car had been stolen the day before so that would explain where it ended up then.'

DS Fox looked first at his colleague and then said to Foster, 'And did you report this theft to the police?'

'I didn't have time and anyway, it wasn't worth that much. And it would have been a waste of my time, wouldn't it?'

'You have already admitted that you'd been employed by Jeremy Browne to do his dirty work, your words, so you'll see what this is looking like, don't you? You said that you had some sympathy for Miss Pemberton, so why don't you just come clean and admit what you've done?'

Foster paused before replying, 'I won't admit anything and I've changed my mind. I want a lawyer.'

'It's true. You can change your mind at any time if you initially choose not to have a legal representative, Mr Foster, so I will stop the recording, at 10.45am.' DS Fox went to cease the recording.

'If you haven't got a solicitor of your own, we are required to appoint one or pay your legal expenses. What do you want to do?'

'Yeah, go on then, you organise your tame one to come down here.'

'Please rest assured, Mr Foster, our duty solicitor, who is available twenty-four hours a day, is independent of the police.' DI Thompson got up from his seat and paused at the doorway, 'I've got a few calls to make so I'll leave you in DS Fox's safe hands for now.'

***

The train pulled into Leeds City railway station and the journey had been without further incident. 'Wow,' I cried out as I looked out of the window, 'very impressive. Look at that.' I pointed at the 'Welcome to Leeds' sign which must have been ten feet high. 'The station looks amazing.'

Helen smiled as she pulled out her *Guide to Leeds* handbook that she had retained from her days at the city's university. 'It's the third-busiest railway station in the UK outside London and in 2008, automated ticket gates were installed in place of the human-controlled ticket checking, to speed up the passage of passengers.'

We grabbed our bags and exited the train and as we walked down the platform, I gazed about me at the structure and modern roof. 'It's amazing, Helen. Obviously, I've seen a few stations in my time but I have to say I'm impressed.'

'Despite the improvements, it was recently proposed that the station could be remodelled for the proposed HS2 scheme!'

'Oh, don't get me on my hobby-horse, I'm dead against it. HS2. I mean, what a waste of money.' Helen didn't want to enter into a debate on the pros and cons of developing the rail network for the future and the idea of getting people transported quicker from A to B. They got through the ticket gates and made their way outside. A row of six taxis was waiting outside the entrance to pick up fares and they got into the first one. 'Ibis Hotel, please.' The journey only took a few minutes, but they had decided to treat themselves for this, their first trip away together.

Once settled in their room, I said, 'Helen, I need to freshen up after our journey, and to get ready for this evening. So, if you don't mind, I think I'll grab a shower.'

Helen smiled, 'Excellent idea, David. While you do that, I'm just going to pop back down to reception. They've got a good selection of gifts in a large glass cabinet. I only had a chance to glance at it earlier and I'd like to have a good look. I won't have much of a chance to look around Leeds town centre on this visit, and it's mother's big birthday next month.'

'Well, good luck with that.'

'It'll save time and I haven't forgotten that you told me you hate shopping!'

I put my jacket on the back of the bedside chair and started to unbutton my shirt. 'Hey, I feel another poem coming on! You be careful down there. I'll see you soon.'

Chapter Thirteen

'Why are you doing this?'

'Oh, Brian, don't spoil everything now. You've done really well, so far.' Browne pressed the muzzle of his gun into his chauffeur's ribs again. 'Just drive until I tell you to stop.'

They had travelled about a hundred miles north. Brian then said, 'I apologise in advance for what I'm about to say but my petrol gauge is only about a quarter full now. I wasn't party to your master plan when you put it together.'

'Don't try to be clever. You've no idea who you're dealing with. Drive to the next petrol station and keep your mouth shut.'

With that, silence ensued and thirty minutes later the DS3 pulled into an Esso station.

'Okay, this is how it's going to work. You're going to fill the tank up and go into the shop to pay. I'm going to stay here in the car with the kid …' Browne waved his Berretta M9 at the sleeping child behind him. Brian swallowed hard, and looked at Browne as he said, 'I'll tell you this. I don't give a shit who you are or what crazy mission you're on. If you harm one hair on the head of my daughter, I swear I will hunt you down …' With that, Brian left the car and shut the door. Browne looked at the sleeping child and then at her father filling up the car's petrol tank. Once completed, Brian went to the counter inside the shop which was fairly busy, paid for the petrol, and returned to the car.

'You seemed to be a long time in there.' Browne nodded his head towards the shop.

'There was a queue. Didn't you see it?'

'Oh, yes. I watched you. Don't you worry about that. Right, drive out of here.'

As the car continued its journey northwards the two adult occupants were left contemplating their individual situations and private thoughts. Brian Temple, graphic designer turned website creator, now also a single parent pondered his current predicament. He had enough problems in his life without all of this nonsense. He loved Amy so much and indeed showered her with more affection than a father would normally to try and compensate for the fact that her mother, Beverley, had left her daughter of six months to be with his best friend. He also considered the note that he had rapidly scribbled out and passed to the assistant at the petrol station. Brian hoped that it would be taken seriously and if so, that police cars would be surrounding them soon.

His passenger Jeremy Browne, however, was wrapped up in his own thoughts and problems. He had gone astray, made some bad decisions certainly, but wasn't the arch-criminal that he was making himself out to be. Always short of money, the temptation of potentially getting his hands on a cool quarter of a million pounds had been too much to ignore. It had been a shame about Julie, a nice girl, he mused. So many mistakes, the first one employing a cretin like Tom Foster to carry out his duties for him. His reflections were interrupted by the sound of the siren emanating from the car behind them.

'Better pull over, Brian. You're not exactly Lewis Hamilton, are you!'

'Ha, I'm not prepared to be your getaway driver anymore. I'm very happy to stop here. It looks like my plans are better than yours.'

Jeremy Browne looked at Brian and frowned as the penny dropped. 'Is this your doing then?'

Both cars pulled over to the hard shoulder and Browne shouted, 'Bastard!' as he shot him in the foot. Temple screamed as police officers surrounded the Citroen. Amy also screamed to accompany her father's outburst, more because of her father's shriek of pain than the firearm being discharged, as the noise from that had been minimised by the fitted silencer.

Pulling the door open, they dragged Browne out and retrieved the handgun. As Browne was wrestled to the floor and handcuffed, one of the officers made the call for an ambulance to attend the scene together with a paediatric nurse for the youngster in the child seat. One officer had grabbed the First Aid kit from his car and was applying some initial, basic care to the injured foot. An armed response unit pulled up in front of the two parked vehicles and was quickly brought up to date on events. They bundled Browne into the back of the blacked-out Range Rover and within two minutes, were on their way again.

***

DI Thompson returned to Interview Room 3 some two hours later. DS Jonathan Fox had remained in the room keeping Tom Foster company.

'Afternoon, gentlemen.' The senior officer commenced, 'Two things: Firstly, let me introduce Mr Darren Ramsden, one of our duty solicitors, who drew the short straw today!' Thompson made this remark without mirth in his voice or facially. 'Secondly, your erstwhile friend, Jeremy Browne, has been apprehended. His bad behaviour got worse. He couldn't stop trying to be like Billy the Kid. Anyway, he's fired his last shot now. He and his handgun are in safe custody.'

'The guys at MIT will be pleased.' DS Fox smiled.

'Yes, they've been informed of progress and await news of any statements being provided by Messrs Browne and Foster.' DI Thompson then turned to the duty solicitor and said, 'Okay. Harry, DS Fox and I will leave you alone with Foster to have a debrief to gain an understanding of his role in the disappearance and subsequent death of the young woman, Miss Julie Pemberton.'

As they left the room, Darren Ramsden shook Tom Foster's hand and said, 'Let me introduce myself. Here's my business card. As you can see, I'm based in Bedford. I'm part of a firm that also has offices in St Albans and Northampton. I've been a solicitor for fifteen years and been a police duty solicitor for the past two.'

'Well, thank you for that. Where do we go from here? I haven't admitted anything yet, but it started getting a bit hairy in here, so I said that I wanted some support. And why did he call you Harry?'

'It's Ian Thompson's attempt at humour. It's sort of an in-house joke between us.' Foster looked bemused. 'You know, Harry Ramsden's famous fish and chip shops?' Foster rolled his eyes and Ramsden carried on, taking some paperwork out of his briefcase and took his pen out of his jacket pocket. Throughout the next half-hour, Foster gave his version of events to his brief.

DI Thompson and DS Fox returned to the interview room, the timing being apposite, as Foster had just finished his summation of the facts as far as he was concerned.

'Okay, gentlemen, if you're ready,' DI Thompson nodded to DS Fox, 'recording started again at 1.30pm; DI Thompson, DS Fox, Mr Tom Foster and his legal adviser, Mr Darren Ramsden present.'

'I've had a chat with Mr Ramsden and I'm happy to carry on.'

'Mr Foster, we previously spoke about the discovery of the body of Miss Julie Pemberton in the Wandsworth region of London. You declined to admit your involvement in both the murder and disposal of Miss Pemberton.'

'Under advisement, my client is now willing to make a statement on the matter.' Darren Ramsden turned to Foster and said, 'Go ahead, Tom.'

'Yeah, all right. I want to make a clean breast of things. I'll admit my part in all of this but I'm certainly not going to be made to carry the can for the whole thing. This is mainly Browne's fault and hopefully, now that you've caught him too, you'll nail him for all the stuff he's responsible for.'

'What sort of stuff are you alluding to?'

'I'd had a few telephone conversations with Browne before eventually, we got together in his office only recently. He wanted to recruit someone as apparently his previous partner-in-crime had been apprehended on an unrelated matter to him. This opportunity to get his hands on this girl's money had presented itself and he didn't want to let it slip through his fingers. I haven't got the evidence, unfortunately, but I suspect that he's behind quite a bit. He's a Jekyll and Hyde character, I think. Monday to Friday, nine to five, he's a mild-mannered office manager but at other times, he's part of the underworld. And what's all the gunplay about?'

DS Fox smiled, 'So much for 'honour among thieves' then. What was the name of his former accomplice, Mr Foster?'

'I don't know, really I don't. I did ask him once, but he declined to tell me.'

DI Thompson put his notes to one side.

'Okay, let's move on. Tell us exactly the circumstances how Miss Pemberton died.'

'Well, I didn't murder her,' Foster glanced at his lawyer who nodded his encouragement to carry on, 'Browne told me about the small fortune that he wanted to get his hands on and I followed her home.'

'How did you get access, Mr Foster?'

'As she opened her front door, she was unaware that I was immediately behind her and I barged in simultaneously. As a hoodlum, I started shouting at her and pushing her.'

DS Fox raised an eyebrow and said, 'Hoodlum? What are you, five foot, six?'

'That was the whole problem. She'd seen me in reception back at the office and clearly hadn't been impressed by what she'd seen.'

DI Thompson interrupted, 'You're a bombastic sod, aren't you!'

Foster looked down at his clenched fists and then mumbled, 'Julie laughed at me, that was where it all started, I suppose.'

'You killed her for that? What a brave man you are.' DS Fox shouted sarcastically.

Foster was taken aback by Fox's impassioned outburst and as he rocked back in his chair, he responded, 'No, I admit that I hit her but that didn't kill her and I'm sorry that I even did that. We ended upstairs in her bedroom.' He paused to look at the two officers, 'Before you get any ideas, that was where she said the documentation was being kept, in a cupboard somewhere.'

'If, as you say, you didn't kill her, how did Miss Pemberton die exactly?' DI Thompson was making notes and didn't look up as he spoke.

'I obviously wasn't paying attention and at some point, she made a break for it and was suddenly in the doorway. I quickly got off the bed and joined her on the landing.'

'The bed?'

Foster snapped, 'Oh, don't get your knickers in a twist, I was just sitting on it while she went to get her documentation. Calm down.'

'This is a murder investigation, Mr Foster, everyone is understandably very stressed at present. Carry on.'

'Basically, we had a coming together at the top of the stairs and she started to hit out at me in an attempt to get away, I suppose. In the altercation that followed, she lost her footing and fell head over heels, literally, down the stairs. I followed her down as quickly as I could but when I got to her my perfunctory examination revealed that she had died. Her neck seemed to have been broken.'

'And what did you do then? Did you phone for an ambulance?'

'No. No point.' Foster put a hand up to his eyes, they had started to water.

Darren Ramsden pushed a box of tissues closer to Foster and he grabbed one.

'We'll be talking to Browne shortly, so we'll be able to see how much of your stories match up. You're both implicated in Miss Pemberton's death, you do know that, don't you?'

'Yes, he told me that.'

'What? You've already colluded on this?'

Foster sniffed again and dabbed at his eyes, 'Yes, we met up afterwards and discussed what had happened. Jeremy Browne wasn't very happy.'

'I think that this would be a good time to take a short break. DS Fox and I will go and talk with the MIT team and the CPS regarding the evidence we've got to date to decide where we go from here and what charges we may wish to make. Mr Ramsden, I suggest you discuss what's happened today with Mr Foster and the possible implications for your client. Recording ceased at 2.05pm.'

***

As arranged, Paul Craven met up with his cohorts at Venici's, a café situated some fifty yards away from the main entranceway of Leeds City railway station. Owned for the past twenty-five years by the Polizzi family, Venici's was currently run by the second-generation patriarch, Paulo Polizzi who, at thirty-five, still had ambitions of having a chain of Venici's throughout Leeds, Yorkshire and beyond.

However, the café on New Station Street kept him and his staff of six extremely busy, so there were reasons, not excuses, why there never seemed to be enough time to talk to bank managers about his ambitions of expansion or time to explore potential sites for new premises.

Paulo viewed the three characters sitting in the corner of his café next to the window with indifference. The tall one had ordered the coffees and when he had brought their drinks over to their table, they had barely acknowledged him. Very rude, he had mused, but it happened sometimes.

Paul Craven had been alerted by Tommy as to where Helen Wilson and David Jones had alighted the train and had followed them, at a safe distance, to their hotel. Dick had remained to book a room there and had re-grouped later on at Venici's to await Craven's arrival on the next train into Leeds City.

As he stirred his coffee, Tommy turned to his boss and said, 'So, what is it you've got against this Jones character exactly?'

'That's my business.'

'Well, it's ours too if things turn nasty and we have to make decisions, unpleasant decisions.'

'You're not paid to make any decisions, Tommy. You leave all the creative thinking to me, okay?' Craven smirked emphatically.

'Yeah, but what if you're not around at the time?' Dick chipped in, 'In the heat of the moment when things start to kick off.'

'Don't be ridiculous. You're not in Chicago! Carry out my instructions to the letter and you won't go wrong. Most of the time, I'll probably be with you anyway. If not, and there's a problem that you're unsure of, phone my mobile.'

'We're sorry, Mr Craven, we don't mean to upset you. We'll do everything you ask, you can be sure of that,' Tommy said falteringly.

'Oh, don't be so sub-servient. I can't stand that!' Craven banged his fist down onto the table and the cups and saucers trembled, almost as much as his aides. The dozen or so other customers in the café all turned their heads towards the commotion in the corner. Paulo Polizzi sidled over to them and spoke softly to Craven, 'Now, now, gentlemen, we won't be having any more trouble, or noise, will we?'

'What?' Craven responded abruptly, 'who the hell do you think you are?'

'I am the owner of this establishment, sir, and whilst you and your friends here are under my roof, I would ask you to behave respectfully and obediently.'

Craven slipped a hand inside his jacket and pulled out his leather warrant cardholder and flipped it open, 'As you can see, I'm a serving police officer and therefore, I'll do what I damn well please.'

'That cannot excuse such boorish behaviour. Indeed, you should know better.' With that, Polizzi turned on his heel and went back to his counter.

'Bloody hell,' Dick whispered, 'you told us you were off the force at the moment, taking a break or something.'

'I'm on gardening leave at the present, but he doesn't need to know that does he? Right, let's get down to business, shall we? Tell me what happened back at the hotel.'

'Well, as you know, I booked a room at the Ibis where Jones and his friend are staying and when we were able, unseen by the hotel staff, as she was waiting to get into the lift when the door opened, we muscled our way in with her and travelled up to the first floor, where all our rooms are. We bundled her into our room and after a bit of a struggle, we stopped any chance of her making a noise and then tied her up.' Dick smiled at his boss in a self-satisfied sort of way, which was probably the last thing that he should have done.

'Idiot! You're telling me she's tied up in that room?'

Dick was starting to realise that he may have made a wrong decision and didn't answer. Craven turned to Tommy and asked, 'And you were happy to go along with this bullshit?'

Tommy looked away self-consciously and remained silent which again, was probably the worst thing that he could have done too.

'I told you to follow her, note the room number that she was sharing with her friend, and that we've got a lot of things to tie up before we can move on.' Craven shook his head, 'in all my years in the force, I've rarely come across such incompetence. Don't you realise that there'll be CCTV footage of you two cretins in reception and hovering around the lift area with Jones' friend? I don't believe this. Get your arses out of here, make yourselves scarce, and await my further contact. Tweedledum and Tweedledee. I can't believe I'm even considering using you after this. I'll have to go to the Ibis to try and clear up your mess.'

Tommy and Dick slunk off out of the café in silence and Craven went up to the counter to settle up. Proffering a twenty-pound note he said, 'That should cover it. I apologise for earlier, you know, the noise and everything.'

'We try to run a nice, clean, comfortable, environment and try to serve great coffee. Our regulars seem to appreciate that and that's why I want to preserve it.' Paulo didn't smile throughout the exchange and it was obvious that the conversation was over, so Paul Craven turned and left Venici's.

**

After my shower, I left the bathroom to get dressed and entered the bedroom. I wanted to look smart, not too formal, but relaxed. I had decided to wear the new jacket that I had recently purchased in the Next sale. The assistant there had said the dark blue, tailored jacket that I'd chosen would exude sartorial elegance. I sat down in the seat and admired myself in the dressing table mirror. Yes, I nodded, open-neck white shirt, no tie, smart casual. I would do and was ready! I checked my watch. Where was Helen? Getting no reply from her mobile I called down to reception.

In answer to my inquiry, the duty manager seemed to hesitate. 'Yes, Mr. Jones, your partner was here earlier. I left her perusing our delightful gifts that we have on display here, and I was called away to the back office to take a telephone call. When I returned to the reception desk some three or four minutes later, Miss Wilson wasn't there. So, I can't say definitively whether she went outside or back upstairs to the room.'

'Well, I'm telling you she's not here which must be blindingly obvious even to someone like you! That's why I'm calling you.'

The duty manager hesitated as he went through some receipts, 'Er, Miss Wilson paid the bill using an American Express credit card. As she was putting away the card in her purse, I was called away to the back office to take a telephone call. When I returned to the reception desk some three or four minutes later, Miss Wilson wasn't there. So, I can't say definitively whether she went outside or back upstairs to the room.'

I did not like this worrying situation, so decided to descend to the ground floor and seek out the manager. Seconds later, the lift doors closed again and it made its way upwards. There was no sign of Helen in the reception area as I made my way over to the desk.

I looked at the guy's name badge: *Joseph Mendes, Assistant Manager* was his name and job title. I smiled broadly as I spoke, 'Afternoon, Mr Mendes, I don't know if it was you to whom I just spoke. It's David Jones, from Room 117?'

'No, that was my manager, Andrew Davies.'

'Well, may I speak with him, please?'

'No, I'm sorry, he's just had to pop out for a while.'

My smile disappeared, 'So, when will he be back then?'

'I'm not sure exactly, Mr Jones. Andrew had to step outside to make a phone call on his mobile, in private.' I nodded, 'I'll wait over there.' I indicated the seating in the hotel foyer. I would be able to keep an eye on the lift doors and also the front door to spot Andrew Davies when he returned.

***

'Okay, so what happens now?' Foster mumbled.

Darren Ramsden said, 'All right, technically, the referral to the CPS for a decision whether to charge a suspect is sometimes referred to as Pre-Charge Advice. This is the most frequent interaction between the police and the CPS. It is governed by the Director's Guidance on

Charging, elsewhere in the Legal Guidance, The Guidance is issued under the provisions of section 37A of the Police and Criminal Evidence Act 1984. It sets out arrangements prescribed by the Director of Public Prosecutions for the joint working of police officers and prosecutors during the investigation and prosecution of criminal cases.'

'Thanks for that, Mr Ramsden. So, we just wait now to see what they want to do next?'

'On occasion, a case referred to the CPS may require further evidence to be obtained before a charge decision can be made. In such circumstances, the prosecutor will advise the officer of the further material required to obtain a charging decision.' Darren Ramsden folded his arms and leaned back in his chair. 'Try and relax, Mr Foster. It's just a question of waiting now.'

Tom Foster got up and started pacing up and down the room. He paused at the window and surveyed its potential for escape. There was none, it was a uPVC double glazed secure unit without any means of opening or closing it. 'I've been hoisted on my own petard, whatever that means. Is that right?' Foster snapped sardonically.

'Why don't you sit down? I'm sure that they won't be too much longer, to provide us with an update, at least.'

Foster slumped down again on his seat, next to his solicitor. They didn't have long to wait, as suddenly, the door flew open and DI Thompson and DS Fox entered the interview room.

'Afternoon, I have some news for you,' DI Thompson sat down opposite Foster. 'The CPS are requesting further evidence from us given the seriousness of the crime, so we have been given the appropriate permission to hold you in custody for an additional seventy-two hours, Mr Foster.'

'This is going to be a living death.'

Darren Ramsden smiled as he looked at his client who he was sure hadn't realised the oxymoron he'd just created. 'Don't worry, I'll come back in a few days. I'm sure they'll call me back in when they're ready.'

DS Fox nodded. 'Right, follow me, Mr Foster.' They both left the room and DI Thompson said, 'Well, Harry, what do you make of him?'

'Foster? Run of the mill, dogsbody, let's face it. But I'm happy to assist where I can, as you know.'

'Something of interest has occurred concerning Jeremy Browne though,' Ian Thompson stroked his goatee beard in contemplation.

Ramsden frowned querying this nugget of information as Thompson continued, 'Immigration-delay disease. It's a genetic mutation that causes people to be born without fingerprints.' Thompson paused, 'As you know, almost every person is born with fingerprints and everyone's are unique. But people with a rare disease known as adermatoglyphia do not have fingerprints from birth.'

'Wow,' Ramsden smiled, 'is that going to cause a lot of problems for you in this case, Ian?'

'No. Chief Inspector Tom Townsend from the Major Investigation Team has taken Browne off our hands and they are dealing with him in a London police station, interviewing him and dragging a confession, sorry, statement, out of him.' Thompson chuckled to himself. 'Anyway, Harry, I'll let you get on now. We've both got lots to do. I'll give you a call about Foster in a few days, okay.'

The meeting ended allowing the two friends to get on with the rest of their day.

Chapter Fourteen

My mobile phone gave out its noise which was a bit like a strangulated chicken caught in a combine harvester. I vowed to change its ringtone this very afternoon. Enough is enough! I had been worrying about Helen. Hopefully, she was now returning my voicemails, 'Hello, Mr Jones?'

These were not Helen's dulcet tones but a male voice.

'Yes, this is David Jones.'

'Good afternoon, Mr Jones. This is Stanley Paterson from Gambon & Clarke.' He paused and when his opening remark didn't elicit a response from me, he carried on, 'You know, the book publishers in Holborn that you visited recently.'

'Yes, how can I help, Mr Paterson?'

'Well, I've got two things I want to discuss with you. Where are you? In London, by any chance?'

'Sorry, no. I'm in Leeds, actually.'

'Leeds?'

'It's a long story. Away for a few days with a friend. Can't you discuss things with me over the phone?' I was distracted by the front doors opening and a man and woman walked in, obviously customers and not the hotel manager. Just then, the doors of the lift opened and two rather large Asian women exited the lift. 'I'm sorry, Mr Paterson, I'm sitting in a hotel lobby and a lot is going on. It's hard to concentrate.'

'Well, I was going to go over some of your literary efforts today but if it's inconvenient, perhaps we can reconvene at some other time?'

Not wanting to miss an opportunity to discuss book projects with the company's MD, I promptly back-pedalled, 'No, no, it's okay. I'm all yours, Mr Paterson, please continue.'

'Thank you. Firstly, I want to discuss a piece of your work that you've already submitted and secondly, one that you haven't, yet.'

'Great. I got the impression from Jeremy Browne that the company wouldn't go for a book about someone like Samuel Franklin Cody.'

'I'm sorry, Mr Jones, I don't know what you're talking about. Samuel Franklin who?'

'Cody. Samuel Franklin Cody.'

'Excuse my ignorance, Mr Jones, I've never heard of him. I seem to remember, vaguely, that you may have mentioned this to me previously.'

I sighed and then launched into a short biography on my favourite subject.

'I'll reiterate for you. Yes, Samuel Franklin Cody was a Wild West showman and early pioneer of manned flight. He's most famous for his work on the large kites known as Cody War-Kites. These were used by the British before the First World War, as a smaller alternative to balloons for artillery spotting.'

'Yes, yes, I remember. It sounds like Jeremy Browne actually got one thing right during his tenure at the company then. He was correct, Gambon & Clarke Ltd is not the kind of book publisher to produce biographical tomes of that ilk. I'm terribly sorry. No, what I was going to tell you is that when I was clearing out Browne's effects, I came across *The London Boys,* one of your manuscripts, I believe. I read it last week and I liked it. Very insightful, Mr Jones.'

'Please, it's David. That's good to hear. Just the sort of news that budding writers like me want to receive.'

'I was impressed with the amount of background information and factual knowledge woven around a thrilling tale, David.'

'I've been accused of being a pedant in the past. How dare they! So, does this mean that you're interested in publishing my book, Mr Paterson?'

'I would like to discuss the terms with you. And if I'm to call you David from now on, I think you may call me Stanley in future, if we're going to start some sort of relationship.'

'Oh my God!' I shouted. While I had been engrossed in the conversation on my mobile, a man had entered the hotel, walked past me and was now disappearing up the stairs. I had taken my eye off the ball as I had got embroiled in the phone conversation with Paterson. It was a man wearing a coat similar to the one the character wore on the train to Leeds that I thought looked like Craven. I snapped my flip phone shut, ending the call and ran towards the stairs.

***

DS Barry Wainwright had commandeered an office and had requested that DC Susan Parkes join him. He had straightened his tie and checked his hair, then placed the mirror back inside his jacket. He was moderately pleased with the way he looked in a self-satisfied sort of way. DC Parkes entered the room and sat down opposite him; the first thing she noticed was the tray holding coffee mugs, coffee pot, sugar bowl and a plate of biscuits. She raised an eyebrow as she looked at Wainwright.

'Right, Susan. I thought that we ought to get to know each other a bit better,' he paused, poured the coffees and carried on, 'would you like any sugar with that?'

'No. And I don't want any coffee either, thank you very much.'

Wainwright frowned. 'Is there a problem, Susan? As the new boy in town, I just want to get up to speed as quickly as possible. You know, office politics and all that. Who are the good guys, who are the ones to avoid, that sort of thing?'

'I'm sorry, I don't get involved in any of that.' DC Parkes responded, folding her arms across her chest.

'I'm the sort of guy that likes to hit the ground running, Susan. I like to know who's on my team, that's all.'

'I'm a team player, always have been, DS Wainwright. Oh, and by the way, please don't call me Susan in front of the rest of them,' she said in a sepulchral tone, as she jerked her head towards the officers in the open-plan office that they could see through the glass partition.

'Fine.' DS Wainwright smiled at his colleague even though his expression did not necessarily corroborate with his feelings. 'At least we know where we stand, DC Parkes. Okay, let's try and make some progress, shall we? Tell me something about my predecessor, DS Paul Craven. What happened there, then?'

DC Parkes ran a hand through her hair and looked Wainwright squarely in the eye. She hadn't appreciated his hubris but had to acknowledge that he was her superior officer in the force at the moment. And she couldn't quite place the origin of his accent when he spoke in the vernacular. He was quite clearly a stranger in a strange land.

'Before we carry on, I agree, we ought to find out a bit about the people that we work with. For instance, I've always been from around here, born in Luton,' DC Parkes said and then smiled, 'Tell me. I can't quite place you, where are you from, Cornwall, Devon?'

'Dorset, actually. I transferred up here to be with my wife. She's a university lecturer, based at Milton Keynes, at the Open University, you know? We're separated now and getting divorced at the moment, ironic, huh?'

'I'm sorry to hear that, DS Wainwright.'

'Barry, please.' He smiled then topped up his cup of coffee. Holding up the coffee pot, he asked, 'You sure you don't want one? It's really not too bad as police station brews go.'

DC Parkes eschewed this latest attempt, 'I'm sure, DS Wainwright. Perhaps, we can get back to the investigation now. What's the latest?'

'Now that Browne and Foster have been separated and have been interviewed apart, guess what? They're not singing off the same hymn sheet anymore. No honour among thieves, eh?'

'Well, they're criminals and untrustworthy. What do you expect?'

'Anyway, MIT in London are interrogating Browne and giving him a hard time, apparently.'

'I'd like to have a go at Foster if I may. I've got some questions for him. Who's interviewing him at the moment?'

'DCI Bryce. He won't let you anywhere near him just now. He'll try and unwrap Foster's story by himself initially, if you know anything about Bulldog Bryce!' DS Wainwright stood up.

'Bulldog? What do you mean?'

'You haven't met him yet, have you?' He chuckled to himself as he paused in the doorway. 'I think our chat is over now, DC Parkes. But just be aware, I still want to know all about DS Craven. What happened. Your relationship with him. But this will all have to wait for now. Got to get on with our work. Do let me know if you haven't got anything to do, won't you?' He didn't wait for a response as he closed the door behind him. DC Parkes was left looking at the door and she took out her mobile phone to make the call that she had been putting off making for a few days. The timing was right now. She didn't want to delay it any longer.

***

Paul Craven had made his way up to the first floor of the Ibis Hotel. He worked his way down the corridor to Room 124, a few doors down from where David Jones and his female friend were staying. He had spotted Jones in reception and was fairly confident that he had glided through the busy vestibule area incognito. He tapped on the door not expecting a response or indeed, even to gain access. He looked up and down the corridor, then took a step back before kicking at the door lock with all his might. As it was a modern construction, the wood shattered immediately and the door opened. As he entered the room, he could see why the chain hadn't been applied for extra security. The young woman was lying on the bed, her hands and feet tied, masking tape wound around the lower part of her head preventing her from making any noise. Craven approached her and shook his head as he considered the two men's handiwork. He bent down so that their faces were about a foot apart.

'I'm so sorry,' Craven said, as he started to gently remove the tape from off her face. 'Please don't be scared. I'm a police officer. We'll soon get this sorted.'

As soon as she was able to speak, Helen shouted, 'Prove it!'

Craven stopped what he was doing and took out his warrant card, flipped it open and showed his photo ID. 'Detective Sergeant Paul Craven at your service,' He said. First of all, he untied her feet then moved to release her hands. Once free, Helen continued, 'What's going on? You'd better have a plausible story, DS Craven. Checking me out on the train on the way up here and your two friends kidnapping me. Allegedly, you're a law enforcer. When I studied law – I'm a criminal psychologist by the way – I seem to recall that abducting somebody and holding them captive broke all sorts of rules. What do you think?'

'Before I continue, I just want to ask you something. I'm sorry, what's your name?'

'My God, that makes it even worse. You and your band members have chosen to carry out this heinous act upon a defenceless young woman and it's a purely odious, wicked, attack carried out randomly, not targeted on any particular individual for any rhyme or reason!'

'It wasn't quite like that. Look, are you okay? Do you need any medical treatment at all?'

'Don't think that a change in your attitude now is going to save you, DS Craven. Too late to be penitent.'

Helen rubbed her wrists and ankles, then her lips, 'I'll survive, I suppose, no thanks to you though. In answer to your question, my name is Helen Wilson, not that it's any of your business though.'

Craven explained, 'Without giving too much away, I'm on secondment carrying out an investigation on these two characters, Tommy and Dick. I haven't discovered their real surnames yet; they've used several pseudonyms. And therefore, they're not my friends, all right? I'm working undercover and consequently, I'm sure that you'll appreciate why I can't say too much.'

'In the past, in times of trouble, I've always been praised for my resilience,' Helen responded while trying to judge her captor's sincerity or honesty. She decided that the jury was out on that one. She continued, 'Whilst I was tied up, I kept reciting Psalm 23 in my head, over and over again to help during my confinement.'

'Psalm 23? What's that then?' Craven asked.

'You know, "The Lord is my shepherd ", that one. It's all about God's protection, "I will fear no evil" etc. You're not a churchgoer then?'

'Er, no, sorry. I never had the time to go. I know that's no excuse, Miss Wilson. I certainly can't be accused of being a person with any piety.'

'You're correct there, DS Craven. I assume you're about to leave me in peace now and go and report the damage that you've done to my door. But before you go, you still haven't explained what you were doing by engaging me in conversation on the train journey.'

'Basic police work. Our procedures sometimes seem a little skewed to the public.'

'Don't patronise me. I'm not just a member of the public. My work life is spent wholly in the world of law, DS Craven.'

'We'll have to leave things like that then. If you're sure you're all right, I'll go down to reception and get them to organise some repairs to the door.'

Helen was left looking at the door swinging on its hinges as Craven made his exit.

***

Chief Inspector Tom Townsend from the Major Investigation Team smoothed the ends of his moustache and his bow tie in that order as he considered the detainee seated in front of him. Standing by the door, as was his wont, he smiled as he said, 'Mr Browne, I'm pleased to meet you at last. Now, I'm sure that this won't take too long and I'm sure that you'll be very pleased about that!' He took out his fob watch, noted the time and returned it to his waistcoat.

'Aren't you going to join us?' Jeremy Browne asked the tall, middle-aged officer in front of him. He glanced at the redheaded, female officer seated opposite and muttered, 'How's this all going to work then? Believe it or not, I've never been arrested before.'

DCI Townsend overheard the comment and he decided to join them at the table, sitting down next to his colleague. He then said, 'Please be aware, Mr Browne, you are in a serious amount of trouble here. You discharged your firearm and injured a police officer whilst he was in the course of carrying out his duty; you further injured your compatriot, not that that matters too much and as if that wasn't enough, you later decided to discharge your weapon one final time and chose to shoot your kidnapped taxi-driver. What's wrong with you? More importantly, you are enmeshed in the plot to defraud, kidnap and then kill a defenceless young woman. What have you got to say for yourself?' DCI Townsend folded his arms and leaned back in his chair.

'I'm sorry. This isn't me; you know? I intend to cooperate fully.' Browne looked down at his hands which were folded and resting on his lap. 'So, what happens now?'

Townsend turned to his colleague and inquired, 'Please confirm that all formalities have been carried out when the suspect was arrested.'

DS Moira Johnston flicked a stray bit of hair away from her eyes as she confirmed that all necessary duties had been carried out to the letter concerning Jeremy Browne's arrest earlier on in the day.

'Thank you, Moira.' The senior officer then turned his attention back to his captive audience. 'I'll explain the facts of life to you then, Mr Browne, as you claim not to have been in this position before. Ordinarily, the maximum that a suspect can be held without charge is twenty-four hours. However, this can be extended by a senior police officer by a further twelve hours. If we need further time for questioning, we must apply to the magistrates for that additional time, up to a total of ninety-six hours. I hope that's clear. If not, do let me know.'

'I just want to get through this. I'm not going to be difficult.' Browne looked from one officer to the other then continued, 'I suppose I've got some rights?'

DCI Townsend smoothed his moustache and responded, 'Yes,' he had been through this procedure a million times it seemed to him. 'You get free legal advice; you can tell someone where you are; have medical help if you're feeling ill; you can see the rules the police must follow; and have regular breaks for food and get to use the toilet. Happy?'

Browne nodded. 'You want to know where all my problems stemmed from?' Getting no response, he continued, blithely, 'I'm a victim of circumstances, that's what I am.'

'And what makes you say that Mr Browne?' DS Johnston smiled in an attempt to get to the truth as quickly as possible.

'I've always been short of money, you know. Everyone always had more than me; my rotten brother, my work colleagues, my so-called friends.'

'That's no excuse, Mr Browne,' Townsend interjected, 'and you know it. I intend to uncover your perfidy.'

'Whatever. Prodigal habits die hard. Heard that one before? My family were always accusing me of spending money freely and recklessly and being wastefully extravagant. I can hear my father's voice now, ringing in my ears.'

The female officer started leafing through papers in a file in front of her. 'Let's start at the beginning, shall we? Where did you get the Beretta 9mm handgun from? Or have you had it a while? Also, where did you meet your partner-in-crime, Tom Foster?'

'Look, I'm not one of your dyed in the wool hardened criminals. I had to do some research, as a consequence.'

'What do you mean?' DCI Townsend declaimed with force. 'Only someone with evil intent and a certain mentality would know where to look.'

'Well, you certainly can't find either of those items online, you know! I had to be careful, obviously. If I wasn't cautious in my inquiries, all sorts of alarm bells and police sirens would have been set off, that was my concern.' Jeremy Browne took a sip of water from the glass which had been provided at the beginning of the interview. 'As a publisher, well, as someone who works for a publisher, I have contacts who are authors of crime novels and I called one. Without giving too much away, I was able to explain that I was doing some research and he was willing to point me in the right direction. In this case, the East End of London. I acquired both the gun and the services of Foster at a pub called *The Ship* or *The Old Ship,* or something. And I had to go there twice! Not my favourite place. I've never been to areas like Mile End or Poplar before and hopefully, never will again. I met someone called Eric, probably not his real name, what do you think? He drove me around for half an hour or so presumably to get me confused, but I already was!' Browne gave out a short guffaw.

DS Johnston ran a hand through her red tresses, made a few notes in her file and looked at her colleague before continuing, 'And so you obtained the gun and Foster on a trip to this pub? Which you can't remember the exact name of, or its location, presumably?'

'As I've already said, I had to go there twice, on two separate occasions, okay?' Browne looked at the Scottish officer as if she was deranged. 'I got the gun first and on my subsequent visit there, I was introduced to Tom Foster. The agreed fee for both items was handed to Eric in used notes, twenties and tens in a brown envelope, as arranged. I haven't had any contact with him since and probably won't.

In fact, I had a query about the Beretta, so I called his mobile and it was dead.'

At this point, the door of the interview room opened and a uniformed senior officer aged in his mid-fifties, wearing silver-framed glasses swept into the room with formidable hauteur. His presence immediately halted procedures and DS Johnston pressed the record button, 'Superintendent Alistair Walsh has entered Interview Room 4 at Paddington Police Station, at … 3.15pm.'

'Good afternoon, everyone. I just need a quick word with DCI Townsend.' He bent down to whisper a few words into his colleague's ear and his response was to initially nod and eventually, he looked Walsh in the eye and said, 'Really?'

Townsend stood up and said, 'Okay, the meeting's over. There's been a development. Sorry, end the interview tape, DS Johnston. Mr Browne, we will have to detain you in the cells downstairs for now. We will arrange for you to have some food and drink if you like.

Chapter Fifteen

Venici's wasn't at all busy when Craven entered the café and he was able to sit at the same table as he had before, by the window. A very pretty blonde came over to take his order and he had been relieved that it wasn't Polizzi, the owner.

Just as his espresso was being delivered, his mobile phone buzzed in his pocket. Craven looked at the caller ID and it made him smile.

'DC Parkes! What a lovely surprise. Susan, how are you?'

'Okay, I suppose. Where are you, Paul?'

'Oh, Susan, you know me better than that.' He sipped at the coffee. 'Sorry, my lifestyle has made me very cautious. Why do you want to know? Is this an official inquiry, or a personal one?'

'I miss you professionally and I miss our closeness, Paul. I care about you, of course. I need to know that you're all right. Also, something here has started to concern me.'

Craven paused and raised his hand to attract the attention of the waitress. She came over and he pointed at his cup. 'Susan, I'm still on this so-called gardening leave for another two months. Will your situation wait for my return?'

'Not really. I need to see you but if that makes you a bit jittery, don't worry.'

Another espresso was placed in front of Craven and he looked up.

'So, what brings the police back to my humble abode?' Paulo Polizzi stood with his arms folded.

'Apologies, I'm on the phone at the moment.' Craven's withering look dismissed the proprietor and he returned to his counter. 'I'm sorry, Susan, I was distracted. Do carry on.'

'Don't worry. It'll have to wait. You're obviously busy, Paul and I've got to go now. Somebody's just turned up.'

Craven looked at his phone before replacing it into his jacket. He had a bit of time on his hands and he started to survey his surroundings. The owner had attempted to give the place a taste of Italy. Fair play, you had to give credit where credit was due. Four posters had been strategically placed to lend a certain ambience: One of gondolas on the canals of Venice; one of the Colosseum in Rome; an advertisement showing two attractive ladies from the 1960s with a Fiat Cinquecento; and one of Marlon Brando in *The Godfather*. Hmm, not so sure about that one, he mused.

The owner returned to Craven's table.

'I'm waiting for a colleague to meet me here if that's all right.'

Paulo Polizzi smiled and shrugged, 'I don't care as long as you purchase coffees and remain courteous during your time here.'

Craven nodded toward the Brando poster on the wall by his head, 'Not one of your relatives, is he?'

'You never know. You can't be too careful, can you? So, how may I serve you, sir?'

'I think I'll have a cappuccino this time.'

Polizzi turned and disappeared through the beaded curtain behind his counter.

***

Superintendent Alistair Walsh, from the MIT and DCI Townsend walked down the corridor towards a small office approximately twelve feet square which housed a table and four relatively comfortable chairs. One side of this box featured a large window affording good light when needed although today, the blinds had been drawn.

As they entered the room, Walsh turned to his colleague and indicating the seated visitor, said, 'Ian, as I mentioned, this gentleman has come forward to offer some background information about our friend, Jeremy Browne, following the recent piece on BBC's *Crimewatch* programme. Anyway, I've brought Mr Williams into this room for our little chat.'

'Yes, much more relaxed than a custody suite or interview room. Let me introduce myself, Chief Inspector Townsend of Paddington nick, pleased to meet you.'

'Hi, my name is Greg Williams.' After shaking hands, they all sat down eyeing each other warily.

Walsh spoke first, 'I'll let Mr Williams explain in his own words.'

'Yes, I saw the programme about that girl, Julie Pemberton, her kidnap and murder and that Jeremy Browne was involved. Well, I had a very acrimonious relationship with that character. Firstly, on the telephone and then the next day, he turns up at my company, Southend Printers Ltd.'

Thompson interrupted, 'Southend? But you're miles away from Southend.'

'It's a long story.'

'That's not important now. Please carry on, Mr Williams,' Walsh frowned at his colleague.

'He was ranting and raving about a missed deadline for some books we were supposed to be printing for him. Browne couldn't deal with the lateness of deliveries when they had been agreed in writing previously. To cut a long story short, heated words were exchanged and he ended up pushing me over onto the floor behind my desk. As you can imagine, I didn't appreciate that very much and I'm sorry to say that I used some colourful language.'

'This is the part that I wanted you to hear, DCI Townsend. Carry on, please.'

'Yeah, well, do you know what this nutter does next? He pulls a gun out of his jacket and starts waving it about. That's bang out of order in my book.'

'A handgun. What happened next?'

'Can you believe this? He points the gun at the telephone on my desk and blows it to pieces. Thousands of pieces. He says, 'Well, you won't be needing that anymore, will you? Number one, you never phone me; and number two, you won't be phoning the police today about my visit, will you? By the way, Greg, I know where you and your pretty little wife, Meg, live. I'm sure you wouldn't want anything to happen to either of you. Take this as your final warning, Greg. Get the books printed, packed, and delivered by Monday, as promised, okay?' Williams cradled his head in his hands and the police officers waited for him to compose himself before continuing. 'Obviously, I agreed immediately. I had never experienced such malevolence in my life before. We had had a genuine, unforeseen reason at the print works as to why we couldn't deliver the books by the original deadline. Was he interested in that? NO!'

'This has been a very stressful episode for you, Mr Williams, but you really need to try and calm yourself down a bit. Would you like to take a breather? Like a cup of coffee or something?'

'No, I'm fine, I think I'd like to carry on. When you said coffee or something, could I have a cold drink by any chance?'

'Yes, we've got orange or lemon or Coca-Cola if you prefer.'

Greg sighed and replied, 'No, I'll have a coffee, please. No milk or sugar, thanks.'

DCI Townsend picked up the phone on the desk and ordered three coffees, then said, 'All done, please continue.'

'Well, we'd never been late before, so I felt that his behaviour was a bit of an over-reaction, to say the least, totally over the top in fact. I vowed to fulfil this order but made a promise to myself that this would be the last. It's not worth it. We're a small company with two directors and four other employees. On the day that this maniac visited the works, I was all alone in the office. This was like something out of a gangster movie, not my sort of environment. I was out of my comfort zone. But when he threatened me and my wife with God knows what, that was the end of the relationship between Gambon & Clarke and Southend Printers for me. It was the only decision that I could make in the circumstances, don't you agree?'

'Indubitably,' Superintendent Walsh nodded as the coffees were delivered.

Greg Williams took his cup and carried on with his story, 'It's not worth it. I never want to hear their name or Jeremy Browne's ever again. That's how I felt, Mr Walsh, until I saw the *Crimewatch* programme on the telly.'

'It's Superintendent Walsh, by the way, but not to worry, do continue.'

'Sorry, I couldn't believe it. There I was, sitting down with Meg having a pizza and then that piece comes on the programme about that arsehole. As they said, Browne was in custody, I felt that it was safe enough, for now, to come forward with my two pennyworth. You know, what he'd done to my office and the threat he made to me and my wife.'

'Very understandable, Mr Williams. I commend you for presenting your narrative of these terrible events. As you say, we've got him safely under lock and key, for *now*. Your testimony as to his character and behaviour will add to the evidence we're collating and will aid our case against him. We need to clamp down on criminals like this and on people with egregious tendencies.'

'When you said he's locked up for now, what did you mean by that, exactly? You've got me worried again.'

'We'll be holding him here for a couple of days, at least. Don't worry.'

'Don't worry!' Greg Williams said truculently and stood up.

'Calm yourself, Mr Williams. Please sit down again. We'll be keeping a close eye on Browne, once he's released,' DCI Thompson said in an attempt to placate the visitor. 'Also, in view of the alleged threat you mentioned, we'll monitor any activity around your home too. We'll make sure he atones for what he's done in your office, amongst other things.'

Greg Williams wasn't convinced but his view was that he couldn't do anything about the situation. He would make sure that he or any other Southend Printers employee was ever alone at the print works. Also, he would make sure that Meg was properly protected.

***

The marked, yellow and blue liveried, VW police car pulled up outside the front doors of the Ibis Hotel. One plain-clothed officer and one uniform disembarked and strode through the large plate-glass doors to meet with the hotel's manager, Andrew Davies. Their arrival had not gone unnoticed by Paul Craven from his window seat located inside the nearby café.

The hotel manager was awaiting their arrival and he proffered his hand to the suited officer.

'Detective Constable Thomas Rice. We got here as quickly as we could, Mr Davies. You've reported a number of issues. How can we help?' His uniformed colleague had not been introduced and he busied himself by surveying the modern lobby and the people in it.

'Yes, perhaps if you follow me up to Room 124, I can fill you in on the way? It's not their room, but the one she was pushed into and attacked in.' The blonde-haired hotelier led the way to the lift and once inside, continued, 'You're about to meet two of our guests, a Miss Helen Wilson and her partner, Mr David Jones.'

DC Rice contemplated the hotel manager, now in close proximity inside the lift and couldn't take an instant liking to him for some reason. Admittedly, he was good-looking, aged about thirty and smartly dressed. Although the man had possibly applied too much aftershave that morning, Rice didn't think that Davies was gay or anything.

His training stopped him from putting people in pigeonholes and applying stereotypical biases.

'We received a report that a Miss Wilson had been attacked and tied up?'

'Well, sort of, anyway, we're almost there. I'll let Miss Wilson explain everything for herself.'

***

The group of men entered the bedroom, squeezing past the two workmen in the doorway repairing the damaged door, to find Helen and me sitting on the bed.

Helen had already had the opportunity of bringing me up to date about what had occurred and I sat in the chair by the window as she prepared to reiterate the story.

DC Rice introduced himself and frowning at the work being carried out, he queried the activity, pointing his thumb towards the workmen.

Helen began, 'I'll come to that in a minute. First of all, I was manhandled by these two hoodlums into this room, tied up and gagged, so that I couldn't cry out. The point is, they didn't ask me anything or explain why they had kidnapped me!'

'You're understandably still upset about this incident, Miss …' Rice consulted his notebook, 'Wilson.'

'How observant', I muttered.

'Pardon?' The uniformed officer turned and replied to my comment.

'You know. How astute. I'm sorry, we haven't been introduced. How rude. My name's David Jones and you are?'

'PC John Ozanne, Leeds Central Police Station.'

'French, eh?'

'Well, my father was, well still is, actually. We came over here when I was a boy.'

DC Rice interrupted the new friendship, 'I'm sorry, PC Ozanne, we need to concentrate on taking down Miss Wilson's testimony.'

Helen persevered with her story, 'The two bullies didn't seem to have a plan, or if they had one, weren't following it. They went off into a corner of the room and started muttering and whispering to one another. After about five minutes, they left the room, shutting the door behind them and ensured that it was locked.'

'So, they hadn't demanded anything? Bizarre.' PC Ozanne made some observations in his notebook.

'I was left alone in the room, tied up, for about an hour. Disgusting.'

'I agree.' DS Rice continued, writing up his own notes. 'And then you were rescued. Superman burst through the door to rescue you.'

'It sounds ridiculous, but yeah, that's exactly what it felt like at the time. This guy said he was a police officer and that we'd soon get everything sorted. But I'm not that naive, so I asked to see some ID. He stopped untying me and he took out his warrant card and flipped it open; it said Detective Sergeant Paul Craven, photo, everything. I work in the legal world and it looked genuine to me. The only thing is that it had Bedfordshire Constabulary on it!'

DS Rice looked at his colleague and nodded, 'Did he give any explanation for his behaviour, Miss Wilson, or his reason for being in Yorkshire?'

'He said something about being on secondment up here and was working undercover investigating the two hijackers that had attacked me.'

'Right, the first thing that we'll be doing when we leave here today is to contact Bedfordshire Police HQ to find out what they can tell us about the bona fides of this DS Craven. If you're sure that you're all right, I think we'll have to leave it there for now.'

When the two officers had left the room, I went over and sat next to Helen on the bed. I put a hand on one of hers and said, 'Phew! What an ordeal. Sure you're okay?'

'Oh, David, I just can't believe it. It was like something out of a Hollywood gangster movie. I hope those two bastards are caught soon, either by the police or by this Craven character, but I have a visceral feeling about him and the whole situation.'

The two workmen finished working on the door with its new lock and we bade them farewell.

'You didn't tell the police that you'd had contact with Craven in the train on our journey up here. I was very surprised about that,' I prompted.

'Nor did you, David. You were here. If you thought that that was so damned important, why didn't you jump in and say so?' Helen buried her face in a handkerchief. She was clearly very stressed by the activities of the last few hours and hadn't appreciated my unsympathetic attitude.

'I'm sorry. I'm sure they'll round them up soon, eh?' I put my arm around her. 'Hey, we're meeting up with your friend, Samantha, this evening. Still up for that? Think you'll be okay by this evening?'

'Oh yes, I'm not going to let Samantha down. She'll be a breath of fresh air for me. Let's go back to our room now.

I'll grab a shower and then get dressed up. It'll do me the world of good.

***

It was an unavoidable truth that the net would be closing in on him now and that it would just be a question of time before Craven would be trapped. He had witnessed the arrival of the two officers at the hotel and at the opportune moment, had surreptitiously exited the Ibis through a side door and into the adjacent car park. Ever conscious of the ubiquitous CCTV cameras, he slipped down between the parked cars to make his phone call. He took out his mobile, 'Tommy. It's Craven. Right, I've just sorted your mess out at the hotel, so now you are going to do something for me to make amends and to earn your keep for a change.'

'Okay, boss.' Tommy replied timorously. He knew not to get on the wrong side of him. He had witnessed what had happened to someone when Craven had carried out an amercement when Craven thought that he had been double-crossed.

'Right, listen to me. You are going to get a car and drive to the rear car park of the Ibis Hotel. I will look out for you but call me when you arrive so that no more mistakes can happen. Even Laurel and Hardy could manage that.' He ended the call and remained crouched down between cars. He'd estimated a wait of perhaps ten or fifteen minutes for his transport to arrive. Tommy's CV had listed carjacking; breaking and entering; high up on his list of achievements, so Craven was expecting a fast response to this latest demand. What he hadn't expected was, 'Hello. Who have we got here then? What are you up to?'

Craven turned and looked up toward the uniformed figure standing over him. He replied, 'Nothing. I've lost my car keys. I think that I may have dropped them around this area earlier.'

'I see. It's just that I was viewing the CCTV monitors inside the hotel and I watched you skulking around outside, nipping in and out of the cars out here. It didn't look like you were looking for keys to me, that's all.'

Craven rose from his semi-recumbent position and stood face-to-face with the hotel concierge. The proud hotel employee in his powder-blue tailored uniform that displayed his name on the badge on his left breast pocket said, 'Right, you best be on your way, sunshine.'

Slightly taller than him and better built, Craven said to him, 'Listen, Tony, I suggest that you scurry back to your little cubbyhole and stay out of my way. You don't know who I am or what I'm involved with and I haven't the time to tell you now or why I cannot afford to be arrested by the local police. And don't ever refer to me as sunshine!'

As Tony turned around to go back into the Ibis, Craven approached him from behind and grabbing his head with both hands, slammed it on to the car roof next to them. Tony slid to the ground, unconscious. Craven said apologetically, 'Sorry, Tony,' as he backed away and looked left and right across the car park. The incident had been swift and relatively silent and been over in a matter of seconds. The noise of the head hitting the car roof had seemed loud at close quarters but in actual fact, had not carried very far. Craven bent down and pushed his victim's body under one of the cars. He then stood to survey the damage to the car's roof next to him. The dent would be pulled out fairly easily, he mused. But bearing in mind the age of the Lada estate, the owner probably wouldn't even bother to get it repaired and that's if they even noticed the damage! He chuckled to himself as he walked away. His mobile buzzed and he answered it as a blue Ford Fiesta entered the car park at the rear entranceway.

'It's Dick, Mr Craven. We've got a car for you, as requested.'

'Good. I need to get out of here, fast. Are you in the Fiesta that's just arrived?'

'Yes.'

'Well, drive across the car park, near to the side entrance and I'll make myself known to you. We can talk more in the car later.'

***

Helen emerged from the shower and having dried herself, put on the towelling dressing gown provided by the hotel. I approached her and put an arm around her. 'You look stunning, Helen.'

She pushed me away and said, 'You can forget about any funny business, David. We haven't got the time and I'm not very happy at the moment for some reason. I'm surprised that someone as intuitive as you hadn't guessed that one.' My mobile phoned trilled melodiously. 'Oh, thank God, you've actually done something positive for once, you've changed that dreadful ringtone.'

I looked at the caller ID and said, 'I'm sorry, Helen, you'll have to excuse me,' and I left her in the hotel room.

Alone in the corridor, I continued with the call, 'Yes, who is this, please?'

'The person you've been looking out for, but you're so inept, you've failed miserably in tracking me down. I've found out that you like words. Here's one for you; you're so jejune.'

'Naive, yes. I'll give you that.'

'So, what do you want with me?' he said curtly.

'I don't exactly want you, as such, you're too egregious a person for me, DS Craven, don't get me wrong. I only wanted to find out why you're so fascinated by me. So, you've got my attention, go ahead.'

'I'm calling to arrange a meet, Mr Jones, not question you over the phone!'

'You've got to be joking. Why on earth would I want to get together with you?' I asked rhetorically.

'Oh, I think it would be in our joint best interest. I want something you've got and I think I've got something that you'd like.'

'I can't imagine that I would ever be remotely interested in anything that you may have, Craven. Look, I'm rather busy right now, so ...'

'Before you go, Mr Jones, I want you to listen to a tape recording that I've got which may help to pique your curiosity.'

I was about to end the call and my finger hovered over the mobile as Craven shouted down the receiver, 'Wait! You've got to listen to this. I have a recording to play for you. Are you there? Ready?'

I just wanted to get back into the hotel room and see Helen and this unwanted interruption had annoyed me. 'Yes. Go on.'

A crackle started, background static, and then, 'Hello … this is Amanda speaking … I've got to read out this message to you, David, "I am being held in a secure location until these gentlemen receive what they want. I am all right at the moment … please …" There the taped message ended, and Craven then said, 'So, David, do I have your undivided attention now?'

'Right, well I think that we've established what you've got that I may be interested in, even if Amanda is my former girlfriend. What is it that you want then?'

'I find myself in a position where I need to get my hands on a substantial amount of money and I know that you will be able to help me in that regard. And Amanda is now your former girlfriend? Wow, you don't waste much time, do you!'

'That's none of your damned business and I don't have any money anyway. So, you see, you're wasting your time and mine.'

'Ha, ha, ha. You have the proceeds of your wife's life insurance policy, some money in three separate ISAs, a deposit account at Lloyds Bank and some shares in Shell Oil. You forget, David, I'm a police officer.'

'Yeah, and a crap one, at that. It doesn't take a genius to work out that the money is tied up.'

'Oh, dear. You've upset me now and we were getting on so well up to that point, I thought.' There was a suspension in the dialogue as the cracking sound of the tape broke in, 'Agh'. The recording was ended and Craven then spoke again, 'I'm sorry that you made me play that to you, Mr Jones. I'll call you that as you don't seem to like my using your first name. Before you think of insulting me again, bear two things in mind: Firstly, even a lowlife like you wouldn't want an innocent party such as your former girlfriend to get harmed, would they? And secondly, you and I know that those funds can be accessed quite quickly in an emergency. But we wouldn't want this situation to accelerate to an emergency, would we?'

'You bastard, Craven. What have you done to her? Leave her alone. Pick on someone your own size. All right, what are we talking about here then, how much are you after?'

'Well, there is life in the old dog, after all. Just to reassure you, the sound you heard was just Amanda wriggling around whilst we were restraining her. Don't worry, she hasn't been hurt. I must say though, I'm hugely impressed. I can't wait until we can get together. In answer to your question, I need £100,000. You've got three days.'

'That's ridiculous.'

'No, I was going to ask for £200,000. I know you've got it, so just be thankful that I've been fairly constrained. So, just do it. Call me on Saturday, by 5pm, to tell me what I want to hear.'

The call ended and as I placed the mobile back in my jacket, Helen came out of the room and into the corridor. 'Hello, stranger. You all right, David, you look worried. Who was that on the phone?'

I hesitated and looked up and down the corridor. A couple carrying their bags passed by and I waited until they had entered their room before replying, 'I'm sorry, Helen, I'm going to have to grab my things from our room. I've got a few things to sort out.' I passed by her as I entered the room and Helen followed me in. I started packing my bag immediately.

'Aren't you going to tell me anything then?' Helen raised her voice and started to get emotional. 'Can't you tell me who that was? What the hell is going on, David? What are you going to do now? Where are you going? So, you don't intend to meet up with me and Samantha this evening?' Helen sat on the bed and folded her arms across her chest.

'I'm really sorry, Helen. It's to do with Amanda. I'll call you when I can, okay?' I left her in the hotel room and made my way down to reception. I needed to get a taxi.

Chapter Sixteen

Chief Inspector Bryce had called a meeting. All available detectives based at Bedfordshire Police HQ had turned up for what Bryce had identified as a 'crucial update and briefing'. Twenty-seven officers sat in the conference room to listen to their immediate senior officer. Bryce commanded respect. He was tall with blond hair, looking younger than his thirty-eight years. The audience was well aware of his record in the force and consequently, they were all in rapt concentration as Bryce started.

'Okay, listen up, ladies and gentlemen. Thank you all for attending this hastily arranged meeting but it is an important one and I wanted everyone here in Kempston to be on the same page, all at the same time.' No one spoke but some were looking from one colleague to another to try and gauge reaction. Bryce ran a hand through his hair then held up a file of papers in the air.

'Scotland Yard has been in touch with us,' Bryce continued as he surveyed the room, looking at the faces in front of him, individually. 'They have received a European Arrest Warrant and asked us for our assistance in executing it.'

DI Thompson was seated in the front row of seats facing Duncan Bryce and he was first to raise the obvious question, 'Who are they after, sir? He or she must be local if they've come to us for help.'

'Yes, Ian and it's one of us they're after. As you know, once an EAW has been issued, it requires another member state to arrest and transfer a criminal suspect or sentenced person to the issuing state so that the person can be put on trial or complete a detention period.' A low rumble of noise and chatter spread throughout the room.

'All right, calm down now,' DCI Bryce held up a hand and continued with hubris as was his usual manner. 'It's the French police we're talking about here, the military Gendarmerie with primary jurisdiction in smaller towns and rural and border areas. They've uncovered two bodies buried in shallow graves in southern France, just over the border from Monaco. Additionally, the suspect is also being pursued over financial irregularities.'

DC Susan Parkes raised her hand and said, 'It's DS Paul Craven, isn't it?'

Bryce nodded, 'Yes. Scotland Yard is keen for a speedy result on this one, so please get your heads together and pool resources. Ian, please head up this search. DC Parkes, perhaps you'd work with Inspector Thompson on this one as I understand you know Craven quite well.'

***

Paul Craven ended the call to David Jones and from the rear seat of the Ford Fiesta addressed the car's two occupants in front of him. 'Keep going, and put your foot down, Dick. Where did you get this old banger, anyway? Not that it matters.'

'From the car park next door. Tesco's.'

'Your parents knew what they were doing when they named you, didn't they, Dick!' Craven spoke with malevolence and looked out of the window at Leeds city centre as they sped onwards. Tommy turned around to speak.

'Where are we headed, boss?'

'*Carpe diem,*' Craven replied laconically.

'What?'

'It's Latin, or didn't you go to school? Loosely translated as "seize the day". Just get us out of this Godforsaken city. We've got to lay low for a day or so, well, I have anyway.'

'Okay, boss. Anywhere in particular then?'

'And stop calling me boss. Arsehole. Get us out into the countryside somewhere. I'll know when we get there. And until we do, shut the fuck up!'

The journey continued without further discussion. Dick and Tommy briefly exchanged surreptitious glances with one another.

***

DS Thomas Rice and his colleague from Leeds Police, PC Ozanne, had been called back to the Ibis Hotel by its manager. They had only just returned to the police station when a call had been received concerning an alleged assault on their concierge by the man who had been talking to one of their customers, Helen Wilson. This character, who had claimed to be working as a police officer on secondment to the West Yorkshire constabulary, was clearly out of control.

Andrew Davies looked up from behind the desk in his spacious office and smiled welcomingly as his two visitors entered. Rice and Ozanne sat down in the proffered chairs opposite Davies. Rice took in his surroundings and looked wistfully at the manager as he said, 'Okay, Mr Davies, you reported that one of your colleagues had been attacked by this DS Paul Craven. Is that correct?'

'Yes, our concierge, Tony Fuller, had gone out into the car park to investigate some suspicious activity around some of the cars which he'd seen on the hotel's CCTV monitors.'

'I see. Well, we'd better have a word with him then.'

'I'm sorry, DS Rice, I'm afraid that won't be possible. A member of the public found him moaning and groaning, sitting on the ground and holding his head. There was a certain amount of blood involved and they immediately called 999. An ambulance has taken him to Leeds General Infirmary.'

'That's a shame,' PC Ozanne muttered as he scribbled some more notes.

'I beg your pardon?'

Rice shifted in his seat, 'I think what PC Ozanne was alluding to, was the fact that we would have liked to have had the chance to question Mr Fuller regarding this alleged attack.'

'There's nothing alleged about it. We have the assault recorded on CCTV if you want to see it.'

'Excellent. Thank you, Mr Davies.' The triumvirate moved out into the outer office to view the footage which showed Craven slamming the concierge's head onto a car's roof. The tape was acquired by the officers as evidence and they exited the hotel shortly afterwards. Their next port of call was Leeds General to enquire on Fuller's health and to see if he had recovered sufficiently to answer any questions.

***

DC Parkes brushed some stray locks of hair away from her face as she answered the phone. She was sharing a medium-

sized office with DI Thompson as they continued their investigation into DS Craven's recent activities and possible whereabouts. She handed the phone's receiver over to her colleague, 'I think you'd better take this one, Ian. It's a Superintendent Walsh from the Met.'
'Morning. It's DI Ian Thompson.'
'I understand that you're involved with the Craven investigation. I have some information to add to your files. I have an update on Jeremy Browne and Tom Foster. We've had them both detained here at Paddington nick whilst we cross the 't's' and dot the 'i's' on our evidence gathering. According to the CPS, we've got enough now to proceed to prosecution, but this information will help you with your case, I think. And if, or when, you get hold of Craven, let me know, because I'll have a few questions of my own to ask him!'
'Thank you. We'll be in touch when we can.' Thompson ended the call, raised his eyebrows and said, 'What's the latest, Susan? Where are we exactly on this one?'
'I've been collating what information we've got already but it's a developing situation. Craven is a dynamic character. We've got our own evidence and more has come in from Leeds and now from London. We're liaising with Interpol and they've sent over all the files on their investigation. We're talking about a potential serial killer here and fraudulent activity on a grand scale.'
'We've got to stop Craven's pernicious activity,' he replied with suitable haughtiness. 'And to think that he was one of our own. Was he always like this, do you suppose, or did something happen to change his personality?'
'As you know, he and I have worked together here at Bedfordshire HQ and I would never have guessed he could

have been up to this sort of thing. Shows what a good copper I am.'

'Don't worry. When someone is as rotten to the core as Craven, you've got to appreciate that they're very clever, or they think they are. That's why we've got to try and stay one step ahead. We'll catch this snake in the grass.' Thompson left the room, closing the door gently behind him.

Susan Parkes looked up and said, 'We'll have to see. It won't be easy.'

***

Helen walked through the front door of TGI Friday's in Leeds to meet with her friend, Samantha. She looked around the restaurant and quickly saw her waving an arm in the air to attract attention. They hadn't seen each other for about two years and as soon as they were seated opposite one another they started talking and it was as if they'd parted only days ago.

'Oh, Helen, it's so good to see you.' Samantha grabbed Helen's hand and gave it a squeeze. 'But I know that something's bothering you. You were so happy and positive on the phone a few days ago. I can tell that all is not well. Within ten minutes of our catching up, you're not exactly your usual talkative self, Helen. What's wrong?'

'Nothing,' Helen smiled weakly.

'Don't be like that. I'm not stupid.'

The waiter arrived at their table with their food order. Once he had retreated and they were alone, Samantha took a good gulp from her glass of Zinfandel rosé and raised her eyebrows at her friend.

'Sorry. So much has happened to me in the last few days. I told you about David, the guy I knew at Brighton University. Well, after we bumped into each other in town recently, we had a couple of meetings subsequently. They went really well but I think I've altered my opinion of him, literally in the last twenty-four hours.'

'Interesting. Oh well, it's not like you've actually had sex with him yet, is it!'

A silence descended upon the couple. Now, it was Helen's turn to have some rosé.

'Oh my God! You have!' Samantha gave a muted scream.

'I'll tell you more after we've eaten. Promise.'

They mutually agreed to eat their meals before continuing their conversation. When Samantha had finished her Cajun Spiced Chicken Fajitas, she pushed her plate to one side and said, 'Right, go on then, Helen. Tell me all. I'm all ears.'

'Well, I had been looking forward to introducing David to you this evening. He was supposed to be here,' she glanced at the empty seat beside her, 'but a few things are going on which worries me and as you can see you aren't able to meet him this evening or perhaps ever, for all I know. It's all so complicated. Back home, he's become embroiled in a police investigation into someone he met recently connected with his book-publishing ambitions.'

'That's not so bad, Helen.'

'Oh, that's not all. The way up here was a nightmare,' Helen smiled cynically, 'he kept thinking that one of the passengers who was walking up and down the carriage was one of the police officers who had been questioning him recently or looked like him. At that point, I thought he was being paranoid but listen to this.' Helen paused as she had some more rosé, 'I've got something to tell you about the most frightening thing that has ever happened to me and once again, it involved this same character!'

Samantha frowned, said nothing, but placed a hand on top of one of Helen's to encourage her to continue with the story.

'Anyway, David and I had become separated. I had gone down to the hotel's reception area and on my way back to our room …'

'Our room?' Samantha added.

'Yes, I am thirty-two; currently free and single; and whilst not necessarily looking for a mate at the current time meeting up with David again seemed, possibly like fate, I suppose.' Helen took out a tissue and dabbed at the corner of her eyes.

'I didn't mean to judge you or anything. You're my oldest friend. I mean in terms of years of friendship, there I go again, upsetting you unintentionally. Me and my big mouth! I'm sorry, I didn't mean to interrupt you either. Please continue with what happened to you.'

Helen had composed herself sufficiently to carry on. 'Okay, I was on the first floor of the hotel but before I got back to our room,' she took pleasure in emphasising those last two words, 'these two brutes grabbed hold of me and manhandled me into another room, a few doors down. They tied me up, gagged and blindfolded me.'

'Helen, that's horrendous! One of the worst things I've ever heard, well, certainly to someone that I know. I mean, you see this sort of thing in dramas on TV, or in films but …' It was now Samantha's turn to pause and to drink some more rosé before continuing. 'Are you all right?' She squeezed Helen's hand more forcefully this time, 'You're here, so what on earth happened next?'

'That's where the story becomes even more bizarre. This nightmare must have gone on for about an hour. The two bastards had left me alone, by the way, then all of a sudden, the door explodes open, noise and wood splinters everywhere! You'll never guess who emerged into my room!' Helen paused for dramatic effect, 'Our errant police officer. My knight in shining armour was this mysterious DS Craven.'

'So, this person on the train that David had misgivings about was a bona fide law enforcement officer?'

'Well, that's just it. He claimed to be. Even had a current warrant card, but for Bedfordshire Constabulary.' Helen sighed, 'He seemed quite sympathetic, actually, but he was difficult to read. Claimed that he was just carrying out his basic police duties when he engaged me in conversation on the train. After he was sure that I was all right after my kidnap ordeal, he left me alone in the hotel room.'

Samantha squeezed her friend's hand again, 'Oh, poor you. You won't forget this trip to Leeds in a hurry! It's a shame, really, because I had got something in mind for us to do while you're up here and I don't suppose you'll be up for it now. And of course, there's the situation with David to worry about too.'

Helen drained the remainder of her wineglass before replying, 'Oh, don't worry about him. He's off sorting out something to do with his girlfriend, Amanda.' She gave an indifferent shrug and continued, 'Anyway, I'm far more interested in hearing about your suggestion, Samantha.'

'Well, you're aware of my passion for art. We're so blessed locally if one wants to see collections of paintings, sculptures and pottery. Also, currently, at the Leeds Art Museum, there's a big art exhibition featuring my favourite, Artehelenmisia Gentileschi!'

Helen went very quiet and took out her handkerchief again, dabbed the corner of her eyes and glanced over at the front door of the restaurant.

'Not the reaction I was expecting, I must admit!'

'Sorry, Sam, I'm miles away. So wrapped up in my thoughts and I must admit I haven't heard of this artist of yours.'

'She was an Italian Baroque painter and now considered one of the most accomplished seventeenth-century artists, initially working in the style of Caravaggio. And as I studied her for my degree, I can't wait to see it. It opened yesterday and I wanted to go there with you if you're interested?' Samantha smiled at her friend warmly. 'Look, I know that you've got your meeting with the solicitors tomorrow so how about we pop along to the museum the following day, grab a spot of lunch. How does that sound?'

'You're my best friend, Sam,' Helen sniffed, put away her handkerchief and continued, 'I'd love to do that. I'm up here for a couple of days and before I head home again, I want to visit my sister who lives in Holbeck.'

'That's not far away. Sounds great.'

'I haven't seen Trudy for about two years, or my niece, obviously. We'll have a lot to catch up on!'

'Have you thought about what you're going to do about the David situation?'

'Ha!' Helen roared, 'Nothing! What can I do? I've just got to wait and see. I dislike what I've become, Sam. I've prided myself in the past for being such a resolute person.'

'You are a strong person. You'll get through this. It's not like David is the love of your life or anything!' Samantha turned towards the waiting staff and raised her hand to attract their attention. 'I'll get this, Helen. My treat, I invited you. It's been so great seeing you again but I'm sorry to hear about your problems.'

Their waiter produced the bill and once Samantha had paid with her credit card, Helen said, 'That's very kind. I was going to suggest we both go back to the hotel for a drink or two, but I've probably had too much already; I've got a big meeting tomorrow!'

Samantha stood up, 'I agree. Come on, let's go. You go back to the Ibis and try and get a good night's sleep, okay?'

Helen snorted wryly, 'Huh, I'm screwed, in more ways than one. I'm not a good sleeper at the best of times and believe me, this is not one of the best of times.'

They left the restaurant, hugged and Samantha kissed her on the cheek, 'Helen, despite everything try and get a few hours' sleep. You've got a big day tomorrow. I'm sure it'll be fine.'

Helen nodded, turned and headed off in the direction of her hotel, without reply. After she had walked for about thirty yards, Samantha called out at the retreating body, 'Helen! I'll call you tomorrow evening to see how it all went and to organise the museum trip!'

Helen didn't turn around but raised her arm and waved, in agreement, as she continued on her journey.

***

The tension inside the Fiesta was palpable. For approximately half an hour, no one had said a word. Tommy and Dick weren't as stupid as they looked. Suddenly, Craven leaned forward and broke the impasse, 'Okay, you two, have you got your passports with you?'

His two cohorts looked at each other and simultaneously shook their heads and Tommy responded, 'No boss, you didn't say that we needed to bring them.'

'I ain't got one anyway,' mumbled Dick.

'Not in your own name, Dick!' chortled Tommy.

Craven sighed, then said, 'Get real. You're the last people I'd want to go away with! Right, see that petrol station up ahead, about two hundred yards on the left? Pull in there.'

As Tommy did so, Craven leaned forward further and with his handgun, pointed towards the empty car-parking places situated behind the main shop facility. Once the Fiesta had stopped, Craven spoke with acerbity, 'Listen up. This is very important. You must follow the following instructions to the letter. I don't need to remind you of what will happen to you if you don't.' He rubbed the Beretta against the back of Dick's neck and they both turned around and nodded in agreement.

'Good,' Craven smiled derisively. 'Turn around, face forward.' And Craven placed the barrel of his handgun at the base of Dick's head. 'I only need one of you. Why on earth I decided to employ both of you, I don't know!'

'No boss, please!' shouted Tommy. Craven laughed out loud again. 'It must have been a BOGOF deal!'

'What do you mean?' Dick had started to whimper now.

'You know, buy one, get one free!' Craven withdrew the gun and returned it to its place in his jacket. 'You don't appreciate who you're dealing with here!' Craven sneered at his two accomplices. 'However, you may well be of use to me, after all, one final time.'

Without turning around, Tommy said, 'Of course, boss, anything you need, you just say the words of what you want, we'll do …'

'Shut it!' Craven screamed and once his blood pressure had returned to an acceptable level, he continued in a more avuncular fashion, 'Right, I'm normal again now. I am now going to tell you what the plan is, at least your part in it. I am about to exit the car and you will leave me here while you drive off somewhere, anywhere. Go off and buy yourselves an ice-cream or something. Meet me back here in one hour, no sooner, no later, sixty minutes. I'm going to give you the benefit of the doubt. I presume that you can tell the time, both of you?' Craven looked at his watch, 'I've got 2.10pm, you got the same?'

Tommy and Dick checked their watches and nodded. 'Excellent! The first thing that you two have got right this year!'

With that, Craven left the vehicle, slammed the door behind him and waved his hand dismissively to send his cohorts on their way. As he watched the car speed away up the hill, Craven took the business card that he had picked up at the hotel out of his pocket and dialled the number displayed. His call was answered on the second ring, 'Hello, Rhino Taxis?'

'Yes, hello, I need a taxi to take me to Leeds-Bradford Airport, please.'

'No problem, sir. Whereabouts are you at the moment?'

'I'm currently at a Shell petrol station approximately ten miles north of Leeds City Centre on the way to the airport. Do you think you'll be able to find me?'

'Oh, yes. I know exactly where that is. You're on the A660. I can get someone there in about ten minutes or so. 2.30pm, all right? What name is that for, please?'

After a short pause, 'Er, Mr Lane. Ten minutes? That'll be fine. I'll look out for the car; I'll be on the forecourt, waiting.'

'See you soon, Mr Lane.'

***

DI Ian Thompson looked up from the paperwork on his desk as there had been a tap-tap-tap on his door. 'Come in,' his voice was raised but not austere and as soon as he saw who stood in the doorway, his mood instantly softened. 'DC Parkes, do come in.' Thompson indicated the seat opposite him as an invitation to sit down. 'We're not having much luck in tracking down your friend, Craven. Have your efforts turned up anything yet?'

Susan Parkes shook her head, 'I've got a couple of lines of inquiry still outstanding and one other person to check out, just haven't been able to track her down yet. And DC Duncan Pratt is trying to help out now too.'

Thompson scratched his goatee beard which was now flecked with grey, salt and pepper as he kept telling people. He frowned, closed the file in front of him and said,

'You know what's been eating away at me with this case, Susan?'

'No, sir. What's that then?'

'Well, I keep coming back to the basics of police detective work, you know, MMO.'

'Sorry, you've lost me,' Parkes then ran both of her hands through her blonde locks and sat up straight.

'It's where I've always started every criminal investigation. I look at what the suspect's motive, means and opportunity might be.'

'I would have thought that that was obvious, with all due respect,' she replied.

DI Thompson bristled at this response and spoke more harshly for the first time, 'There's a certain amount of pressure coming from upstairs on this one, DC Parkes and I won't hesitate in passing some of it on! I want to know what your movements are for tomorrow on this case.'

Susan Parkes smiled, gazed out of the window and replied, 'I'm off to the seaside, sir.'

'What?' Thompson stood up, 'I assume that the trip is work-related? It's all hands to the pump here on this one. I feel like I've got the sword of Damocles hanging over me on this. I need to share something with you. Scotland Yard is all over this, Susan.' Thompson once again tugged at the facial hair on his chin, in contemplation.

'Yes, don't worry. There's no slacking on this case, sir. We're following up on all known leads. You'll be interested to know that I took a call yesterday from a DS Thomas Rice from Leeds Police. Craven's been up to no good up there, it seems.'

DI Thompson frowned, 'Go on, Susan.'

'He attacked a hotel employee in Leeds city centre, hospitalising him! They're waiting for the guy to come round before they can interview the poor man properly.' Parkes shook her head slowly.

'They're certain it's Craven?'

'Oh, yes. It was all captured on the hotel's CCTV. They've seen it. No doubt at all.'

'And the seaside connection?'

'Tomorrow, I'm off to Sheringham on the north Norfolk coast. Do you know it?'

'Been there once, I think.'

'I've been there before, but that was in the dim and distant past. I've had a couple of phone conversations with Paul Craven's father,' Susan paused for effect. 'I'm off to see former **Chief Superintendent Keith Craven**, retired now, of course, ex-Suffolk Constabulary. He was instrumental in getting his son into the police force in the first place, as you know. He wants to tell me something and he's got something he wants to show me too.

Chapter Seventeen

My life had started to turn into something like a Raymond Chandler murder-mystery with deaths, kidnappings, blackmail and theft. Where and when would it all end? I had spent the last few days frantically getting some funds together for the deadline that Craven had imposed on me. I had decided to cash in my Shell Oil shares. They hadn't particularly performed that well for me over the last two years. So, I transferred the money from two of my ISAs into a separate account. Together with my now, closed, deposit account at Lloyds Bank, I had been able to cobble together £105,000 in readiness for the promised, or threatened telephone call, scheduled for five o'clock. I awaited instruction as to whether he wanted the money transferred to a dedicated account of if I was expected to withdraw it in cash. There would be questions raised by the bank, I was sure. If and when I got the demand from Craven, I would get the police involved.

    Back home now, I gazed around my living room and surveyed the damage to my modest home. I sipped at my glass of Beaujolais and started to go through the mail that I'd received over the past few days. I put some of it to one side including a Barclaycard statement, a British Gas invoice, a local pizza service flyer, an estate agent marketing leaflet and two letters, one typed with a police logo and one handwritten. I decided to open the police communication first as I deemed it probably, to be the most important. Bedfordshire Police had written to me about damage and the potential cost of the remedial works to restore the room and the front door to their former sartorial elegance. Apparently, I would be able to acquire alternative quotations should I wish but having looked at the building company on the letterhead and recognising them for having a good reputation, I decided that I would go ahead with the recommendation.

Wine made from the Gamay Noir grape never failed to please and I rolled the liquid around my mouth. I turned the second, smaller letter over in my hand. I didn't recognise the handwriting and I couldn't quite make out the postmark which could have given me a clue as to its author. I glanced at my watch: four forty-five. Not long to wait now, just time to pour myself another glass of wine and to read the contents of the mysterious communiqué. It was a short note written on the torn-out page of a notepad with a cheap black-ink biro:

David,

By the time you receive this note, it will be Saturday – write this day into your diary. This is your lucky day, David. I think that I know you pretty well by now. You will have carried out my instructions to the letter and amassed the amount of money that I needed urgently. Why your lucky day then, I can imagine you're querying?

Because by the time you read this, I will be far away. I cannot afford to stay in the UK a moment longer. I am being pursued by different parties, one of whom you are aware of (the police), and one that you are not. And believe me, you wouldn't want to know who they are.

Time has run out for me, David. Even if I had been able to get my hands on the money, it wouldn't have been enough.

You will probably show the police this note, that doesn't bother me as it won't provide any clues as to where I've gone, just why. You won't be hearing from me at 5 o'clock. Instead, you will receive a text concerning the whereabouts of your friend, Amanda.

So, I wish you well. Enjoy the money – it is yours, after all! Perhaps in different times, we may even have been friends!

Paul

P.S. You know what Oscar Wilde said: Every saint has a past, and every sinner has a future.

I leaned my head back on the sofa and closed my eyes. This was a lot to take in. I opened my eyes, had another good measure of the Beaujolais and looked at the clock on the wall opposite me. The hand moved inexorably towards the twelve. At the exact moment, my phone buzzed, and I felt the vibration in my pocket. The promised text had arrived. Of course, the Caller ID was unfamiliar, and I clicked on it to read the message.

AFTERNOON. YOUR FRIEND AMANDA IS UNHARMED AND CAN BE COLLECTED FROM THE NOVOTEL HOTEL ON THE A1 AT STEVENAGE. ROOM 11. TELL RECEPTION THAT MR SMITH HAS SENT YOU.

I decided that I would go immediately. I still hadn't got my car back, so I would need another taxi and of course, I had been drinking in any case. I wouldn't tell the police about the letter yet. I just wanted to check on Amanda and the veracity of her health. Whilst I waited for the local taxi, I made a call to the mobile phone number that had sent the text message and it hadn't surprised me when the response was a continuous electronic noise indicating that the phone had either been immediately destroyed or the SIM card removed.

***

At precisely ten minutes past three, Tommy and Dick returned to the petrol station forecourt and the Fiesta was immediately blocked in by two police patrol cars. The car stolen from the Tesco car park had been reported as such and been put on to the police national computer. It had subsequently been picked up on Automatic Number Plate Recognition driving along the A660. Authorised firearms officers leaped out of their unmarked black BMWs and ran over to the Fiesta yanking the doors open and shouted, 'Right, hands where we can see them. Don't move!'

The associates of Craven complied immediately and the expression on their faces mirrored their obvious surprise at being apprehended in this way. The violence and speed of this manoeuvre had worked in line with the training that these officers had been through.

Tommy and Dick were appropriately dragged out of the car and cuffed. They now stood and were frisked to establish any concealed weapons, phones, wallets and documents which might be used in evidence.

'You do not have to say anything. But it may harm your defence if you do not mention when questioned something which you later rely on in court. Anything you do say may be given in evidence.' As their rights were being stated to them, they both calmed down. Tommy raised his eyes heavenwards; Dick looked down to the ground and shook his head. They had heard all of this before.

***

The call received by Paul Craven had elicited a typical fight or flight response in him. But when you're dealing with the criminal underworld and in this case, the mafia, the second option was always going to be preferable! His contact Aretino Esposito had explained to him why the pressure that he and his cronies had been receiving from the authorities they now intended to apply to Craven. As he waited in the departure lounge of Leeds-Bradford Airport, most of the conversation still resonated with him. He lit a Gitanes, the brand that had become his cigarette of choice during his tenure in Monte Carlo and he gazed at the lighting above him. His thought process was obstructed by an airport worker who approached him, 'Excuse me, sir, smoking is not allowed here.' Craven gave the man a withering look as he drew on the cigarette again. The man, however, carried on, 'Airports in the UK do not permit smoking after passengers have entered the terminal building or have passed beyond the security checkpoints.'

Craven exhaled a plume of smoke into the air then said, 'Anything else?'

'As with most other UK airports, Leeds-Bradford does now offer travellers the use of a designated outdoor smoking area, sir.'

Craven sighed heavily and disdainfully produced the police warrant card in his name which he flipped open, then proffered towards the airport worker's face. 'Piss off, little man. Go and bug someone else.' Other travellers nearby were now becoming interested in this exchange and Craven glared at them before he said to the worker in more hushed tones, 'I'm in the middle of a police investigation at the moment and carrying out surveillance on a very dangerous criminal.' Craven looked to the left and then the right, then continued, 'And you are in danger of jeopardising eighteen months of hard work by three police forces by your insistence on following the rules. Makes you feel good, huh?'

'I'm sorry, I'm just doing my job, sir'.

Craven carried on smoking then looked up at the airport employee who remained standing in front of him. 'You still here?' Craven stood up and grabbed the man's shirt. 'Listen, cretin, you've got five seconds to disappear. Understand?' The employee, now showing some spunk, said, 'Don't do that to my shirt. See that badge?' and pointed to the logo which had the word SECURITY embroidered underneath. Spotting a firearm tucked into Craven's waistband, he hissed officiously, 'Don't worry, I'm 'outta here. I've got something very important to do!'

Craven returned to his seat; his fellow passengers sat muttering to one another about the events of the past five minutes. Craven smiled and lit another Gitanes. He could now return to his contemplation of the telephone call that he had received yesterday.

Aretino Esposito had started with, 'Craven, time's up, my friend.'

'Don't worry. It's all arranged. The money should be with me tomorrow. I'm waiting for a phone call now.'

'Shut up and listen. I and my colleagues are being squeezed hard now. The money you owe us should have been with you by now and it's not enough, anyway. When we catch up with you, we are going to get hold of your balls and squeeze very hard my friend and I will tell you why. This week, police from four different countries carried out raids on our little empire of money-laundering and drug-trafficking. It's appeared all over the press in Italy, France and the United States. Of course, they described Operation Salami, two years in the making, as a 'decisive strike against one of the most powerful criminal networks in the world.'

'Quite a feather in their cap, then.'

Esposito shouted down the phone, 'Does this amuse you, Craven? You may think of yourself as a big fish in the little puddle where you come from but let me tell you this, you are just plankton and will be dealt with as such.'

'I see how this development has affected you, Aretino.'

'You have no idea,' he said and after a lengthy hesitation, 'and yet, in the big scheme of things, I see it as just another hurdle to overcome in our ambition to be the major player and entrench our dominance of the cocaine trade and continue to forge links with organised crime groups in Latin America, Turkey and Albania.'

Craven stared at the mobile in his hand and started to ponder about the megalomaniac at the other end of the line. Espirito was still wittering on, so he returned the phone to his ear, '… we have ambitions to be able to control as much as eighty per cent of all the cocaine entering Europe.'

'Thank you for sharing all of this with me, Aretino, but I'm at a loss as to why you're doing so.'

'Idiota!' Esposito exploded again, 'And do not call me by the first name ever again. Those days are over. Before you ask, I will tell you why you have caused me so much angst and why I was so keen to speak with you today on the phone, before our meeting up, to give you time to think.' He chuckled to himself and in the background, Craven could hear a measure of some kind of fluid, probably alcoholic, being poured into a glass. Espirito carried on, 'You see, you've made some fatal errors. Not least of which was your poor handiwork in disposing of those two bodies in southern France. Possibly unintentionally, you led the Gendarmerie and the Guardia di Finanza to our front door. So, thanks very much for that.'

'The Guardia di …?'

'They're the militarised police force responsible for dealing with financial crime, smuggling and the illegal drug trade.' Espirito drank some whiskey, 'My organisation has been compromised, Craven, but our origins in an Italian backwater still hold true, thank God! We still maintain bank accounts in Monte Carlo, Paris and Rome. We are transplanting operatives to Colombia, Spain, Germany, the Balkans, Canada and Australia.'

'So, you're carrying on your activities as normal?'

'No. We're carrying on in a modified state. Three days ago, the heads of our syndicate, from each of the important countries met to discuss the best way forward.'

Craven looked up during the call and spotted some activity at the far end of the terminal. Three or four men in dark clothing were looking around, clearly searching for someone or something. Were they police officers or others? Oh shit.

'And the best way forward?'

'Doesn't involve you, Craven. The reason that I've chosen to engage you in such lengthy conversation is to buy some time to keep you occupied whilst my associates make their way to try and find you. You see and you'll know all about this if you're any good at your job, I have the use of cell tracking technology that gives worldwide geolocation on any phone. Useful in my line of work.' Espirito said in a pejorative manner, 'I have no further use for you. You were always a minor player in the master plan. You do understand that, don't you?'

Craven decided to make his move and started to stand up but two hands from behind him forced him to sit down again. Within seconds, three others had approached and one sat down on either side of him. The tallest of the three and of gloomy manner bent down and took the cigarette from Craven's fingers. 'Filthy habit. Didn't anyone ever tell you that smoking was bad for you, Mr Craven?' The man took the cigarette and held the lighted end over the back of Craven's hand which was being held down onto the chair, before stubbing it out. Craven gave out a short, sharp screech of pain but kept it muted because of where he was.

'Right, get up, Craven, we're going for a little walk. Come on.' The visitors were keen to press the exigencies of their boss upon this irritant. They had their instructions to carry out, however unpleasant they may be.

***

Samantha was waiting in the reception area of the Ibis Hotel to see her friend. Helen had seemed abstracted on the phone earlier when they had spoken to each other to arrange the day's activities. That worried Samantha as she knew that Helen had always been a mitherer. There was a lot on her plate at the moment: David, the kidnapping incident, the bogus police officer and her appointment with the solicitors. Her reverie was broken as Helen emerged from the lift and Samantha leaped up to greet her. They hugged at the reception desk, Samantha took Helen's arm, and they strode out of the hotel's foyer together and into the morning sunshine. 'See, I've even organised some lovely weather for you,' Samantha said blithely. 'Come on, over the road, I've found a lovely little café where we can grab a couple of cappuccinos and a croissant if you like and we can plan our day. What do you say?'

Helen smiled at her friend and cherished the way that she had decided to brighten up her day and indeed, her stay, in Leeds. They walked into *Venici's* and sat at a table by the window. It was framed by curtains that had probably been very popular in the sixties and Helen gazed at the handful of Italian images adorning the walls as someone approached their table. 'Good morning, ladies. Welcome to Venici's.' Menus were passed to them both, but Helen said immediately, 'No, that's okay, thanks. We know what we want. Two cappuccinos and two almond croissants, please.'

'At your service, ladies. I'll be back in five minutes.' This was the sort of clientele Paulo Polizzi liked in his establishment.

Helen wanted to repay her friend's act of beneficence, 'And this one's on me, Sam. I must have bored you something rotten the other night going over all of my problems and you haven't told me anything about what you've been up to in recent times.'

A young girl arrived at the table with their order. After they had stirred their coffees, Samantha prompted, 'Before I tell you about my life, tell me how you got on yesterday at the solicitor's.'

Helen looked wistfully out of the window and sipped at her cappuccino before replying. 'They didn't seem that impressed. It went all right and I know they'll settle the invoice without any problems, but I got the strong impression that they may not be knocking on my door again any time soon. The senior partner who I hadn't spoken to previously was particularly grumpy.'

'Why was that do you think, Helen?'

'Not sure,' she sighed. 'Perhaps I've taken my eye off the ball, Sam. The research that I carried out was fine, perhaps it wasn't the outcome that they'd desired. He was very imperious in his manner.'

'How do you mean, Helen?'

'Domineering and haughty, you know the type. Inappropriate for that meeting. I could see that the other partners were embarrassed, squirming in their seats. One of them said, 'Geoffrey, not now, not here.'

'What the hell did all that mean? You're a brilliant criminal psychologist, for God's sake.'

'Thanks, Sam, I needed that. Mmm, this coffee's good, how did you find this place?'

Samantha looked around the inside of the café and glanced at each of the posters in turn. 'The first time, actually. It's the nearest one to both the hotel and the railway station, so just potluck, really. Glad you like it. So, what's the plan? How long are you up in Yorkshire for?'

'Good question. I think I'll be heading south again in a few days, for several reasons: I don't know what's happening with this David situation; I want to visit my sister, Trudy, in Holbeck; and I want to spend today with you at the art exhibition. Tell me again about that, please.'

Before she could reply, Polizzi returned to their table, rubbed his hands down the front of his blue and white striped apron, and said, 'Ladies, is everything all right? Can I get you anything else?'

Helen smiled even though she didn't feel like doing so, 'No, to the second question, and the coffees are fine, thanks.'

Polizzi looked from one to the other, nodded, and then returned behind his counter.

'Now, where were we? Ah yes, you were asking about the exhibition. Okay, I studied Baroque painters at university and particularly, Caravaggio. Interesting guy, after he killed someone in a brawl, he escaped from Rome and because he was sentenced to death, fled to Naples and later, to Malta!' Samantha finished her cappuccino and then continued, 'But I digress. I was introduced to Artemisia Gentileschi, well, not her, she died in the seventeenth century! And I fell in love. She's now considered one of the most accomplished artists of her time and there's an exhibition of her work in my adopted hometown. How amazing is that, eh?'

'Sounds good to me.' Helen stood up.

'Hey, steady on, tiger. What are you going to do about David and Trudy?'

After she had sat down again, Helen, gazing out of the window and without turning to look at her friend as she replied, said, 'I will go and see Trudy tomorrow. I spoke to her on the phone last night and we're so looking forward to having a catch-up.' There was hesitation as it seemed Helen was lost in thought, weighing up her options. Samantha put a hand on top of Helen's. 'Penny for them?'

'Eh? Oh, I'm sorry, Sam, miles away. Yeah, this David situation. It's not like he's the love of my life or anything, but I guess that I'm a little disappointed. He hasn't been in touch and my pride's taken a hit I suppose …'

'Tosser. He doesn't deserve you, Helen. You know what they say, 'You have to kiss a lot of frogs to find a prince'! And he said that he was going off to see this Amanda girl?'

'No, he just told me that it was to do with her and that he would call me when he could. It's the not knowing. I haven't heard anything.'

'I wouldn't waste any more time on the bloke, but then what do I know about men? Look at my track record. What's so marvellous about this David, then? And please keep your answer clean!'

Helen sighed and then spoke in a mawkish way, 'Let's face it. I've known David on and off only for a few years. We literally bumped into each other again only recently and rushed into some kind of relationship. I certainly wasn't looking for one and he was half in and half out of one of his own. I don't know, Sam, I've just started to realise that my life is just drifting along, going nowhere.'

'You know what John Lennon once famously said, 'Life is what happens to you while you're busy making other plans'. Come on, we've finished our drinks, let's go to the exhibition and I can introduce my friend Gentileschi to you!'

'But I want to hear all about what you've been up to in recent times.'

'I'll start telling you all about that on the way to the museum and I can carry on once we're there. There's another café inside the exhibition!'

Chapter Eighteen

DS Thomas Rice looked at the two recalcitrant men in front of him, shook his head and said, 'Well, it seems as if West Yorkshire Police has never been so busy. Your friend, Paul Craven, is a minor crime wave in his own right. Hospitalising hotel staff, stalking women on train journeys, acting as a serving police officer, fleeing the scene of a crime and then going AWOL. What have you got to say for yourselves?'

Tommy and Dick looked at one another, turned towards DS Rice and said in unison, 'No comment.'

'Look, you've already been in police custody for one hour. You can't just keep saying 'No comment' all the time like a couple of parrots. You've been watching too many police dramas on television. You can't carry on like this; it won't get you anywhere. What they don't tell you on TV is that if you're caught wasting police time, you could be jailed for up to six months and possibly, fined. Instead of taking you to court, we might issue you with a fixed penalty notice under the Criminal Justice and Police Act 2001. Anything to say?'

They remained intractable and sat with their arms folded opposite Rice, so he continued, 'It may seem very funny to you to give your names as just Tommy and Dick. You've already been interviewed separately but I thought it might make sense to get you in here together to hear what's going to happen unless you decide to co-operate.' DS Rice glanced from one to the other and getting no response, began again, 'Okay, listen up. We've already got you down for stealing the Ford Fiesta from the Tesco car park. It's all captured on CCTV, so there's no point in denying it.'

'Big deal.'

'Oh, so it can speak. It's Dick, is it? You the brains of the duo then?'

Tommy sat up straight in his chair and glowered at the officer, 'It's only stealing a car, mate.'

DS Rice laughed, 'You've just corroborated my theory, whilst Dick is clearly not the sharpest pencil in the box, he outwits you in spades. A person guilty of aggravated burglary shall on conviction on indictment, be liable to imprisonment for life.'

'You've got to be joking!'

'Ah, so I have your attention now. No, this is serious stuff. It falls under the Aggravated Vehicle Taking Act, 1992.' DS Rice was reading from his notes, 'It amends the Theft Act, 1968, by creating the specific offence of aggravated vehicle-taking, which combines the taking of a vehicle without the owner's consent with driving it dangerously which, as I say, we have on CCTV.'

'All right, what do you want to know?' Dick mumbled.

'Shut up, you wanker.'

DS Rice interjected, 'Gentlemen, please. No need to fall out now. You'll be going down for this together so you may as well keep a united front. I don't know what Craven was going to pay you but I'm sure it can't be worth going to prison for such a long time. Am I right?'

'Tommy, he's correct. We'd better tell him everything.'

'Okay. What do you want?'

DS Rice carried on, 'What I don't understand is what Craven's up to exactly. What did he tell you two?'

'Not a lot. We just did what we were told. He was not someone to be messed with.'

Dick nodded in agreement and said, 'Yeah, for instance, he was obviously very interested in this girl, in particular. We didn't know why. He was very secretive in that way. He didn't trust us. Why would he?'

The interview was being recorded but DS Rice continued to take notes. 'And he didn't say why?'

'No, he's the type of person who doesn't want to be questioned. He made that very clear.'

'I'll give you an update on your mystery man now,' Rice was interested to gauge the reaction of the two men in custody. 'When you drove away from the service station, a few minutes later, a private hire car rolls up, Craven gets in and it drives north.'

Tommy was first to respond, 'It seems as if he had a plan, but it was kept firmly in his head, locked up and not to be shared, not with us at least.'

'Nah, it's not like we was friends or anything, we was just lackeys to him. Not a nice man at all.'

DS Rice continued, 'Did Craven ever mention any plans he may have had for going abroad at all?'

They both looked at each other and frowned simultaneously. Dick commented, 'He did ask us if we had our passports with us, but when we told him that we didn't, he just said, well it didn't matter anyway. Nothing made any sense to us! Tommy shook his head to concur with him and then asked, 'Has he fled the country then?'

Rice ignored the question but did say, 'Okay, surprisingly, you've been quite helpful. We'll retain you here for now. Our inquiries are ongoing. If I need to question you further, I'll know where you are.'

He picked up the receiver of the phone on his desk and quietly passed on some requests and comments to his colleague at the other end of the line.

***

The taxi had picked me up from home and within half an hour, I had arrived at the Novotel in Stevenage near the A1. As instructed in the text message I'd received, I went to reception and announced, 'The key to Room 11, please. Mr Smith has sent me.' The young woman at the counter swiftly looked me up and down and then pressed a button below the countertop. 'One minute, please.' In half that amount of time, the door behind her opened and a middle-aged man emerged. 'Please come through to my office,' he waved his hand towards the open door. Once we were seated, he began, 'So, Mr Jones, can you provide me with some form of identification, please?'

I took out my wallet that had been returned to me by the police which included my driving licence and credit cards. The formalities over, Stuart Pearson, according to the plastic name badge in company livery on the guy's jacket pocket, proclaimed, 'It's a pleasure to meet you, Mr Jones. You will be pleased to know, I'm sure, that your friend who is staying in Room 11 has been looked after admirably. Food and drink have been provided to her, all expenses paid.'

'Tell me more, Mr Pearson. I'd like to know what the arrangements were, exactly.'

'Mr Pearson?'

I pointed at the badge on his jacket and he looked down, 'Oh, I see. Ha, this isn't my jacket. I felt a bit chilly, so I put it on. It was in this office. It belongs to one of my colleagues. Anyway, you've nothing to worry about. I was handed five-hundred pounds in cash to cover your friend's lodgings and any consumables. I am supposed to hand over any balance.'

I glanced at him sardonically. This was farcical. Now I felt my hackles rising. This character may be genuine for all I knew but I couldn't be sure. I fought off my negative feelings and stood up. 'Right then, I want to see Amanda now. Let's go.'

'Please remain in the office, Mr Jones. I will need to see if everything's ready for you first. Can I get you some coffee, or tea, perhaps?'

'No!' I shouted. 'I don't want any of your frigging coffee. Just lead me to Room 11. I want to see my friend. You've admitted that you've been paid and I'm here, as arranged, to collect her. No more prevarication, mister whatever-your-name-is.'

'Please calm down, sir. You don't understand. If you sit down again, I'll explain.'

I sat down heavily and folded my arms. He didn't look too stupid, so hopefully, he would tell from my expression how I was feeling.

'Your friend,' he glanced down at some notes in front of him, 'Miss Amanda Somers, was brought here in an agitated state, unfortunately. She had to be sedated, I'm sorry to say. When I was told you were on your way here, I summoned a nurse to attend Ms Somers and she's still with her. As soon as she has finished, I have requested that we be informed. Okay?'

'Okay? No, It's not bloody okay. And you're quite correct, I don't understand!' I had raised my voice again, instantly regretted it and felt that my blood pressure must be rocketing skywards. 'Take me to her now, please. I can't believe that I just said please to you.' I stood up again. 'Come on, we're going now.' As I moved towards the office door, the hotel manager shot out a hand and grabbed my arm to restrain me.

'I'm sorry, you have to wait, sir.'

'Who the hell do you think you are? Let go of my arm!' I didn't appreciate his bellicose attitude and we struggled together in the doorway. He was stronger than me and threw me down onto my chair again. 'Wait there while I tell you the facts of life. I received a payment to bring this lady to the hotel and to keep her subdued, and unharmed, pending further instruction.' He stood with his back to the door barring any further attempt of escape. 'It seems, plans for the young lady have changed for some reason. My contact was due to have collected her and then I get a message to say that you will be here instead.'

'Miss Somers had better be all right.'

'You're not in any position to make any demands, sir.'

'And you can cut out the "sir" crap too.' There was an uneasy stand-off between us and I was quite appreciative when my mobile phone trilled. I answered, now pleasantly, 'David Jones'.

'Mr Jones, good afternoon. It's Stanley Paterson from Gambon & Clarke. We got cut off the other day. I'm looking forward to seeing you. Are you still all right for Monday? Just going through my diary.'

I paused and felt uncomfortable in this confined space with this hotel person. 'Yes, afternoon, Mr Paterson.

Monday should be fine. I'm sorting out a few things at the moment but I won't bore you with any of that.'

'Please bring your storylines for the Christmas-themed book with you. And I'll have some news from the States to share with you.' At that moment, the phone on the desk rang and Pearson leaned across and answered it. I quickly told Paterson that I was needed elsewhere and thanked him for his call. I vowed to bring the requested notes with me to London. What I hadn't shared with him was that at present they were non-existent! Pearson replaced the receiver and said laconically, 'We're off.' He turned and exited the room and I took it that he intended that I should follow him. We made our way past reception and down the first corridor. The door of Room 11 was ajar, and we entered. Amanda was sitting in the chair by the bed and as soon as she saw who had entered, looked at me with domestic felicity, 'Oh, David!' The nurse standing next to Amanda pressed a hand down on Amanda's shoulder and said lightly, 'Now, Ms Somers, please remain seated for another fifteen minutes.' The nurse glanced at me, smiled, and said, 'You must be Mr Jones. Afternoon.'

'Never mind all that,' I moved towards Amanda and my arm was restrained once again. 'You do that once again, Pearson!' I shouted, 'and I'll take a swing at you.'

'Pearson?' the nurse also moved towards me. 'It's all right, Sandy, he's harmless, or will be in a minute!' Pearson pointed at his badge for Sandy to see and raised his eyes heavenwards.

'Right, listen to me, Jones. In fifteen minutes, you'll be able to take Ms Somers off our hands. As I said earlier, the original plan changed. I'm sure she'll be fine and then you can be on your way.'

I struggled with him again and he said, 'Oh, go and sit on the bed near her.'

Amanda held out her hand and I sat down. 'Hi, you okay?'

'Oh, David, I've got so much to tell you.' Tears filled her eyes and I handed her my handkerchief.

'Yeah, same here. When we get out of here, we'll get as far away as possible. But I'm worried about you. You've been through one hell of an ordeal. And what on earth have they been doing to you?' I jerked my thumb towards the nurse.

'Oh, she's been all right. Sandy's been giving me some medication and looking after me for the past few days.' They smiled at each other, and I reacted, 'Medication? What have they been doing to you, Amanda?'

'Shut up, Jones, or we'll have to give you some medication too!'

'First of all, it was Mr Jones, then sir, and now simply, Jones. I sense a change in your affections for me, Pearson, or what should I be calling you now that we know that's not your real name?'

'Pearson's all you need. I have carried out my duties, as have the hotel staff, as has nurse Sandy. Thank God, we'll all be out of here in a few minutes and we can get on with our lives. I know I've got better things to do even if you haven't.'

The nurse took Amanda's hand and felt the pulse on her wrist. 'That's okay.' Turning to her cohort, 'We can go now.' Pearson nodded. 'Jones, you and your lady friend can go when you want.' He stood away from the doorway and I grabbed Amanda's hand. We withdrew as quickly as we could and made our way back to reception.

On our arrival there, the red-headed receptionist handed Amanda a Novotel carrier-bag. 'There you are, all the possessions that you had when you arrived here the other day; handbag, purse, and mobile phone. There's also a voucher in there which will enable you to have a complimentary one-night's stay at any Novotel in the UK.'

I snatched the bag and took out the voucher, ripping it into pieces which I flung into the air. 'Are you fucking serious? Do you think my girlfriend would want to relive the horrific memories she's encountered at this establishment?'

Amanda went and sat down in one of the chairs in reception. She quietly started to sob into her handkerchief as I continued to talk to the red head. 'What is this place? Are you real?' I pointed towards Amanda, 'She'll probably have psychological problems for years because of all this. Are you lot proud of yourselves?'

'I'm Carol, and I've been here at the Novotel in Stevenage for the last two years. I just do what I'm told, sir. I'm very sorry if your friend has been harmed in any way. My manager got the team together and told us about a special undercover police operation that involved the arrest of a female suspect who was being brought here to be taken out of circulation for a few days was how it was described to us.'

'Stuart Pearson, you mean?'

'Him? No, he came on the scene at the same time. We've never seen him before. It was all part of this police operation, we were told. Mark said that once the captive, this Stuart Pearson, and the nurse had left us, everything could get back to normal.'

'Mark?'

'Yes, Mark Reed, the manager. Most of the responsibility for keeping the hotel on an even keel has been on my shoulders.' Carol gave a snort of derision as she started to pick up the litter that I'd created on her reception desk.

'So, where is this Mark, then? I'd like to have a chat with him.'

'He's gone off with the police, back to the station.' She glanced over towards where Amanda was sitting and continued, 'Please go and look after your friend. She's done incredibly well. Delivered here already comatose, locked in her room, and then tended by, or guarded by, a so-called nurse. I don't think I would've coped as well as she has. And I'm sorry about the voucher business, it's automatic, I wasn't thinking.'

I sighed, shook my head, and went and sat down next to Amanda. I touched Amanda's hand and said quietly to her: 'Before we go to the police about all of this …'

'We're not going to the police, David.'

'What?'

'I've had enough. I'm worn out. I feel dreadful if you want to know. I just want to go home …'

'Okay,' I smiled at her although she didn't witness it. 'Before we make a move, can you tell me something. Who was it that brought you to the hotel?'

'It was that horrible man; the one who calls himself Pearson. I had received a request to come to the Novotel by someone purporting to be from the police and they told me that you had gone walkabout again and they had followed you to the Novotel, in Stevenage.

'What's that got to do with anything?'

'Well, it was clearly a ruse to get me here. I was ushered into the back office on the premise that you would be there waiting for me. This Pearson character grabbed me from behind and Nurse Nasty jabbed something in my behind and everything went black.'

'And you ended up in Room 11?'

'Apparently.'

'Good God, how long were you in there?'

'No idea. Hours, days?'

'No wonder you're not willing to go to the police, Amanda.'

'Exactly; in my fragile state I don't know whom I can trust, apart from you.' Amanda smiled at me and I squeezed her hand again. 'I've got a couple of answerphone messages on my mobile from Stollards, where I work, but that'll wait till later. Can we go now, please?'

***

Susan Parkes had taken a fairly leisurely drive up to the north Norfolk coast. She'd arrived at Sheringham for her meeting with Keith Craven, the retired Superintendent, and father of Paul. Parkes had decided to make a day of it and had left her flat early that morning in the knowledge that the interview with the former police officer wasn't scheduled until two o'clock, after his lunch. She remembered having had a couple of holidays up here as a child with her parents and her brother Charlie and as she looked out to sea through her car's windscreen, some of the memories started to flow back. Susan had parked her Nissan Juke in the small public car park close to the beach, the same one that her father had used all those years ago.

The car park in Morris Street was very convenient, ideally placed for her to spend some time by the sea and just a short walk later on up to Superintendent Craven's cottage in South Street.

DC Parkes wandered along the front to find a café. She was desperate for a strong cup of tea and a pastry and needed a comfort break after her journey. *Fairweathers* was a typical seaside café with an 'A' board outside promoting its teas, coffees, cakes and scones. It wasn't too busy and Susan was able to select one of the tables near the window overlooking the beach and sea. As she waited for her order, she picked up a leaflet promoting the town and its many attributes, including its history as a fishing village and its beach front.

It went on to explain its Viking origin, its many carnivals and festivals and the Heritage North Norfolk Railway. Parkes put the leaflet down as the café owner placed the tray down on her table. She was pleased to see the traditional China crockery, silver teapot and milk jug. The home-made scones looked delicious. She pushed the hair away from her face as she addressed the owner, 'Thank you. Tell me, on the reverse of this leaflet it says, *Mare Ditat Pinusque Decorat.* ' Parkes frowned, querying the legend.

'It's Latin for *The Sea Enriches, and the Pine Adorns*. Jean Poplar smiled as she placed the cup, saucer and plate in the traditional configuration, 'Yes, it was granted to the Council in 1953. You can see the phrase appearing all over the place. So, you here on holiday?'

'No, sadly, just here for the day. Got a meeting to go to. But I love Sheringham, well, the whole of the north Norfolk coast. I used to come here as a child with my family and again in the early years of my marriage,' Parkes turned and looked wistfully out to sea.

'Well, enjoy your tea, dear. Let me know if I can get you anything else.'

It was a lovely view. The sun was shining out of an azure blue sky from behind fluffy white Cumulus clouds. No one was in the sea. It was too cold for that today, but it was beautiful. She was happy to stay there for the next two hours. Jean Poplar was happy too, her new customer had had more tea, a cappuccino and a cheese and tomato sandwich. Parkes had been able to make calls to her colleagues in Kempston for updates on their investigations.

Craven's cronies had been rounded up and were currently helping the police with their inquiries. However, whilst they were pretty sure that Craven had been heading to a local airport, presumably in an attempt to evade capture, he hadn't yet been apprehended. A local taxi firm had confirmed they'd dropped him off at the airport's concourse, but officers hadn't located him yet.

She paid the bill and left *Fairweathers* to make her way up the road away from the shoreline. The sun was in her eyes as she walked south down the High Street and she was grateful for the police-issue polarized sunglasses. A mild breeze blew her blonde tresses as she glanced down at the street map in her hand. DC Parkes was soon at The Boulevard on her right and South Street was the first turning on the left. There was a mixture of house styles in the road, three storeys, two and bungalows.

Former Superintendent Craven had provided his address on the phone and a rough description of his cottage to Parkes. She spotted it about a hundred yards away and, of course, he had described its look accurately. Susan

Parkes had done some homework of her own as well, on the man she was about to meet. Superintendent Craven had had a stellar career in his thirty years in the force. He had chosen to take early retirement for several reasons. He wanted to spend more time on the yacht moored down in Poole Harbour but he was needed to help nurse his wife of twenty-five years, Mary, as she was bravely battling stage four ovarian cancer which had consequently spread beyond the abdomen to other parts of the body. It hadn't been pleasant, especially for his late wife. Craven had received much kudos for the time, care and effort he had extended to Mary in her final five years and for his fundraising for the main ovarian cancer charity. But the period had left him bitter and twisted. No, he hadn't been able to sail his yacht but more importantly, he had lost his soulmate. He rejected the approaches from former colleagues and their offers of help because he wasn't interested in their attempts of appeasement. Nothing would assuage his feelings. He wasn't in the police force to make friends and that had become evident quite quickly.

But he now had a plan. He liked the cottage where he lived and following Mary's passing, he'd had most of the rooms redecorated and the garden landscaped. Craven Snr had already decided to travel down to Poole for a few days the following week.

The doorbell rang and he put his *Daily Telegraph* to one side on the dining room table. In the hallway, he viewed the porch CCTV screen. His two o'clock appointment had arrived, ten minutes early. Well, at least she wasn't late.

Keith Craven checked his appearance in the hallway mirror: Shirt and striped tie, as usual; his thick head of hair a bit wayward, as usual; fresh flowers in the vase on the hallway table, as usual. This month, Mrs. Jenkins had included Anemones, Tulips, Iris, Forget-Me-Nots and Hyacinths. It looked stunning; Mary would have loved this arrangement ... His reverie was broken by the ringing of his doorbell again.

He opened his front door and the young woman on his doorstep gave him a winsome smile.

'Afternoon, sir.'

'Detective Constable Parkes, I assume?'

'Absolutely.'

The formalities over, Craven stepped to one side and said, 'Please come through, first door on the left.' As Parkes walked past, he became aware of the perfume that she had applied, too heavily in his opinion. He sat in an armchair and he indicated the sofa opposite, a coffee table between them and he opened the conversation, 'So, DC Parkes, you said on the telephone that you wanted to speak to me about my son, Paul.'

'Yes, sir. We'd like to hear as much information about him as you can, please. Where he might be at the moment, when you last saw him, that sort of thing.'

Craven frowned and then shouted, 'Is this some sort of fucking joke?' His words were inflammatory and filled with pejoratives. Getting no reaction at all, after thirty seconds he continued, 'I haven't seen hide nor hair of the little shit for about seven or eight years. Yes, he deigned to pop in to see us Christmas 2004. I know the date because I keep all my diaries. He'd been abroad somewhere, France or Italy, I think. He told us that he was shortly going away somewhere else, didn't say where, of course. We were only his parents.'

Susan Parkes felt very uncomfortable. 'I'm very sorry, I didn't realise.'

'When you said on the phone that you wanted to meet up to discuss Paul, I thought that you might have had some information for me, but you wanted to find out more about him, from me!'

'Yes, I should have made things clear. Excuse me, you keep saying we?' Parkes looked down the room, through the windows into the back garden. Craven was more tranquil once again now, 'I lost my wife, Mary, six months ago, cancer.' He took a cigarette from the pack in front of him and lit it, the irony not being lost on him. 'I couldn't get in touch with our son about Mary's illness, I didn't know where the hell he was and of course, he'd chosen not to stay in touch.' He took a deep drag on the cigarette, then said, 'It was the writer, Harper Lee who stated, "You can choose your friends, but not your family". What say you, DC Parkes?'

She paused, shrugged, then replied, 'From my own experience, I'm probably a poor judge of character. One marriage and one divorce; several relationships with members of the opposite sex; a few girlfriends but none of them close. So, I'd say I'm blessed with having a good family. I guess I'm the exception that proves the rule.'

'Anyway, it looks like we're not going to be able to help each other.'

'You were pivotal in getting your son a role with the police force, sir?'

'Yes, don't remind me. And forget the "sir" business. I'm not there now.'

'I suppose one does anything for members of one's own family …'

Craven moved uncomfortably in his chair, 'I did then, but I wouldn't now! What's he been up to then? Why do you want him?'

'He's been up to no good, I'm afraid. He'd been put on gardening leave by Bedfordshire Police, then was reported to have headed north. He hospitalised a hotel worker in Leeds, then travelled up to Leeds-Bradford airport where local police lost all trace of him.'

The former Superintendent shook his head. 'I thought I was doing the right thing, you know. I suppose Paul had never wanted to be a police officer. I helped him out after his RAF debacle – I presume you know about that – in the big scheme of things, one does what one can.' He leaned forward to obtain another Marlboro from the pack on the table. 'At the end of the day, he'll be made to pay for all his misconduct.'

'Well, I agree, it doesn't seem that we're in a position to help each other out.'

'No, he went off my radar years ago, all the addresses and phone numbers I had for him weren't any good. I tried to trace him through the force. I left messages, former colleagues told Paul I needed to talk but for some reason, he chose to ignore me. I'm afraid I'll never be able to forgive him, because of the Mary situation. He's not interested, I don't know why.'

Parkes pushed some hair away from her face, picked up her briefcase, and started to stand up.

'Before you go,' Craven said, 'I want to apologise to you for my caustic outburst earlier. Your opening remark took me by surprise, that's all.'

'That's all right, sir. There I go again, sir! I just can't help it. I think that you deserve due deference. I was brought up to be polite, can't say it's helped me with my police career though!'

'I have something to tell you, DC Parkes.'

Susan raised her eyebrows querying the remark.

'After you decided to come and see me here today, I was interested to try and find out a little about you. I spoke to an old friend of mine, Chief Constable Colin Stanhope.'

'The most senior officer?'

'Omnipotent! No, he was very complimentary. Apart from being reminded about Mary and my asinine son, I've quite enjoyed your visit to my humble home, DC Parkes.'

She looked around the room and said, 'It's a lovely home and I'm sorry about your loss. It's in a nice part of the world too. *Mare Ditat Pinusque Decorat.*'

'Oh, the town's sobriquet, the sea enriches and the pine adorns.' Craven stood and extended an arm to shake her hand. 'I wish you well in your quest in trying to find my son. If you succeed, "You're a better man than I am, Gunga Din" if you'll pardon the expression!'

Susan Parkes left the cottage with Craven still in his doorway where he stayed until she turned a corner in the road and was gone.

Chapter Nineteen

We were now back at my house in Langford or what was left of it. Amanda and I hadn't talked much during the taxi ride back from Stevenage. We just sat in the back seat, holding hands. I'd made a pot of tea and I brought it through to the living room. Amanda was, understandably, shaken up by the tribulations of the past few days and had declined an offer of food at this stage.

'David, there's so much I want to talk to you about,' she gave me a limpid gaze. Quietly, she said, 'Before I tell you my news, can you please explain to me what the hell's going on?'

'First of all, are you sure that you've recovered after your ordeal? You said in the car that you didn't want to go to the hospital or anything …'

'No! I'm fine. Just tell me about these gangsters and how you're mixed up with them. I've tried to resolve everything in my mind and I'm struggling to make sense of it, so help me out.'

'This arsehole Paul Craven, a serving police officer, don't forget, has gone rogue, it seems. He'd identified me for some reason as someone who could provide him with some easy money. I don't know how he found out about my modest bank balances, insurance policy pay-out, ISAs, etc.'

'Well, he is a policeman.'

'Yes, of course. Anyway, it seems that he'd got himself into financial difficulties.'

'Who isn't?'

'I mean serious financial difficulties with some serious bad guys. It was driving him to take more and more risks, kidnapping you and blackmailing me. Time was running out for him. He'd pressured me to get quite a lot of money together in short order.'

'What do you mean, exactly?'

'Craven was operating to a strict deadline and he was passing on to me the pressure that he was under. I did everything I could to get what he wanted. I had to. He told me about your internment, Amanda. I pulled out all the stops to get the ransom money together.'

'And how much am I worth then?'

'It's not a question of that. I drained my accounts, sold my Shell shares, did everything I could to meet this bastard's demands.'

'Go on then, how much?' Amanda sniffed and took out a handkerchief from her handbag. She waited for an answer and sipped from her mug of tea.

I sighed, '£105,000.'

'Oh, that's good to know,' she said irritably.

'It's all I could get in such a short space of time.' I got up from my chair and moved around the coffee table and sat down next to her on the sofa. I squeezed her hand, 'I would have got millions if I'd got it. I hope you know that.'

'So, what happened then? I was bundled up and taken to this hotel on the A1, kept comfortable, fed and watered, awaiting the ransom demand money to be paid, presumably?'

We both turned and were looking at each other now. 'That's just it. The money was never handed over to Craven. He was being pursued by two parties and time was running out for him. I arrived back here and I received this in the post.' I handed Amanda the handwritten note from Craven. As she read it, I topped up our tea mugs. 'It was a question of who got to him first, I think. In the end, he wasn't prepared to hang around any longer for my money. He wasn't worried about the police, I don't think. He was fearful for his life.'

'Where do you think he's gone then?'

'No idea. He was on his way to the airport so he could be anywhere by now I suppose.'

Amanda handed the note back to me and started to sob into her handkerchief. I put my arm around her and tried to placate her. 'You've been through so much; you haven't deserved any of that. Listen, I've got a couple of things I want to say.'

'No, wait, let me go first. I've got something I have to tell you.' Amanda put the hankie away and took a sip of tea. 'That's disgusting. Haven't you got anything stronger? No, it's all right, forget I said that.' She looked more earnestly at me now, 'David, the last six months that we've been together have been really good, haven't they?' I nodded in accord and she continued, 'I'm sorry that I was a little petulant with you a while ago, you know when Steph and I saw you here.'

'Hey, don't worry about it. I'm just glad you're okay.' I shifted in my seat, 'I need to talk to you, Amanda.'

'No, let me carry on, please.' She smiled warmly at me. 'I was very stressed that week. We'd had that problem at the police station but then Steph was there for me over a medical matter.'

'Medical matter?'

'Nothing to worry about. I'm going to have a baby, David.'

'You mean?'

'Yes! I'm going to have a baby David!'

I didn't exactly look ecstatic on receiving this news and I realised that this was not the reaction Amanda had hoped for. I said, 'Sorry, it's such a surprise, that's all. How do you feel, everything okay?'

'Oh, don't worry, I'm fine. Keep your hair on. We can talk about this later. Now, you had a couple of things you wanted to discuss with me.'

I was still a bit shell-shocked and it took me a few minutes to gather my thoughts. 'Yes, I've had a call from the MD of Gambon & Clarke, in London. He wants to see me about my story-writing. I'm off to see him on Monday.'

'Can I come too? I've got the next week off work.'

'Oh, it wouldn't be of any interest to you. I shouldn't be there long.' I smiled reassuringly but Amanda didn't seem too pleased to have her request rebuffed so swiftly. 'David, I've got something else to tell you.' She reached out for my hand again, 'I realise now how much I've enjoyed, no, loved being with you these past six months. I didn't realise, I didn't appreciate, that there was a void in my life. My life trundled along just like most people; I suppose. Work's okay, I go out with my girlfriends, shopping, lunches, coffees, etc. But I realise now that I want a relationship with someone of the opposite sex, you I mean!' She leaned forward and kissed me. I didn't say anything and Amanda continued, 'For an intelligent guy, surely you can see where this conversation is leading? I love you, David Jones! And it's got nothing to do with my becoming pregnant, either. But it does add a frisson of excitement to the situation and something to the recipe, don't you think!'

'Amanda, we've got to talk.'

'Oh, my God …'

'I said that I had something else to tell you.'

Amanda composed herself, then said, 'I think that I will have that glass of wine, after all. What have you got? I'm sure one small glass won't hurt me.'

I stood up, relieved to have an excuse to escape, 'I've got a Pinot in the fridge, already opened. That okay?'

Amanda was gazing out of the window, 'Perfect.' I returned within minutes and handed a glass to her. 'Good health, Amanda,' I said as we chinked our glasses together.

'Don't keep me in suspense any longer, David. It can't be that bad. It's not as if you've been unfaithful to me or anything, is it?'

A sense of fight-or-flight started to kick in and my speech speeded up as I nervously tried to explain my life in recent days. 'Look, you remember when I told you about my time at university down in Brighton?' Amanda frowned, nodded and I ploughed on, 'Well, this girl I met down there, Helen, bumped into me in town recently and we went for a coffee.'

'Well, that's all right. No harm there then. How was she?'

'Fine. The point is, she works at a solicitor's. You know all my problems recently with the police?'

'How could I forget? It was only the other day.'

'Helen was able to recommend a lawyer she knows who was able to advise me at the police station.'

'That's good, isn't it?'

'Yes, and I was very grateful.'

'How grateful, exactly?'

I paused and had another good gulp of the Grigio. 'Just need some Dutch courage!' I broke the hiatus with, 'We just picked up things where we'd left off. We went for a meal and then she told me about a trip up north that she would be taking and invited me to go too.'

'What? This can only have been a matter of days since we parted in your house.'

'That's the whole point. I thought that our split had been so acrimonious and final.' I spoke garrulously and nervously.

'So, you had a good meal, a couple of bottles of Beaujolais and Bob's your uncle?'

'It wasn't like that. With the police trouble and our breaking up, it seemed like the troubles of the world were on my shoulders. I guess I was vulnerable. One thing led to another, I suppose.'

'Oh, poor you. Are you saying that this was all my fault then?'

Silence descended on the room and enveloped us like a shroud.

'I've never done things just to keep people happy, you know. The Helen situation was a mistake. I see that now. The juxtaposition of my error, my confession, the happy news about your baby and you're letting me know how you feel about me, well …'

'Our baby! It's our baby. How do you feel about that, David?'

'Do you know what Sigmund Freud said about the love between husbands and wives?'

'No, but I know what I think about people who quote Freud. And by the way, we're not married, yet!'

'Let me tell you how I feel, Amanda. I was so worried about you when you'd been taken by those ruffians. On my way down to rescue you, I was frantic with anguish and concern about your welfare. I couldn't wait to see you, as I realised what you meant to me.' I took her hand and said, 'Of course you can come to London if you want to. My appointment shouldn't take too long as I said, so we can make a day of it, get a bite to eat, take in a show or something. What do you say?'

'Oh, whoopee-do! I can go out for a day to London with you and have some fun.' Amanda finished her glass of wine and picked up her handbag. 'I've got to get home, sort myself out. My life is going to go through some monumental changes in the next few months. Perhaps we can get together over the weekend, I'm sure we've got things we can discuss!'

We were standing up and I put my arms around her and kissed her on the lips. 'I'll let you know where I stand right now. I love you too, Amanda. I'm here for you if you want me!'

***

The small group made their way from the airport lounge area, away from the walls of plate glass windows overlooking the runways with their jets arriving and departing. They made their way back towards the entranceway and the arm of Paul Craven was grabbed forcibly by one of the mobsters. He hadn't spoken yet but chose to now. 'Okay, Craven, not long now. We mentioned earlier that we'd be going for a little walk. That time has now arrived. Go towards that doorway on the left.' The man with a face like a smacked arse pointed with his folded newspaper towards a grey door some thirty yards in the distance. 'Keep quiet, you've been very well-behaved up till now.' Craven suddenly tried to manoeuvre himself out of their clutches and one of the two men who had been leading the small procession turned around and kneed him in the groin. Craven fell to the ground clutching his injured manhood and his pride. He was unceremoniously hauled back to his feet and Boris Karloff exploded at him, 'Listen, jackass, we're going outside now near the airport vehicles and emergency service cars. I'm going to ask you a couple of questions and once you've answered them satisfactorily, you'll be able to go. How does that sound?'

Craven groaned but nodded in agreement. 'Matteo, Luca, bring him, quietly, outside.'

They went outside between vehicles and the industrial back-up generators. Craven was thrown violently to the ground and his captors started mumbling to each other in Italian and he looked up at Boris, the one he presumed to be the ringleader and shouted, 'Well, what do you want to know?'

The leader crouched down to speak and Craven spotted some movement over the leader's shoulder beyond the row of airport utility vehicles parked in this underground parking lot. This area was used to house pushback tugs, catering vans, de-icing vehicles, snow ploughs, apron buses, belt loaders, water and fire trucks. 'Sadly, your time is up, my friend.' As he put a hand inside his jacket, Craven stuttered, 'You said that you had some questions you wanted to ask.'

'I lied.' The leader smirked, withdrew his hand from inside his jacket and the last thing Craven saw was the flash of a small blade as it was plunged forcefully towards his chest. At this moment, all hell broke loose as six armed police officers wearing police caps, full bulletproof body armour, carrying Heckler & Koch MP5 submachine guns started yelling, 'Armed police! Drop your weapons! Put your hands behind your head!' Two of the hoodlums decided to ignore this warning and pulled out their handguns. It was the last thing they did. Four of the police officers immediately opened fire fearing potential harm and probable death and carried out an action that they had been trained for. The two that had made a bad decision crashed to the floor and the other half of the gang obeyed the instructions given and stood obediently with their hands on their heads. Those two were pounced upon, hands dragged behind their backs and handcuffed. The inspector leading this armed team shouted out, 'I am arresting you on suspicion of kidnapping and causing death. You do not have to say anything, but it may harm your defence if you do not mention when questioned something you later rely on in court. Anything you do say may be given in evidence.'

The noise of the gunshots and the shouting had attracted attention from airport security guards, workers and passengers. A sergeant in full riot gear was deputed to clear spectators away.

Following a call to the emergency services, police cars from West Yorkshire Police and three ambulances from Leeds General Infirmary sped into this underground facility and screeched to a halt. The two suspects had been driven away for interview at Leeds Central Police Station at Park Street and the remaining detritus of the recent mayhem could then be dealt with. The two gunshot victims and Craven were seemingly beyond saving and Scenes of Crime Officers were now attending. Once they were finished with their duties, it would just be a question of removing the bodies from the scene and taking them to the hospital's mortuary. Photographs of the scene had been taken and senior officers were talking to members of the armed response unit. They were keen to establish that the correct procedures had been followed as, quite rightly, there would be an inquiry into the circumstances of the three deaths.

***

The Artemisia Gentileschi exhibit at the museum had been stunning, well, for Samantha Brand at least. She was leafing through the souvenir catalogue in the café whilst Helen, had been queueing to order some coffees.

'There you are,' Helen sat down opposite and smiled weakly at the posters on the walls of the cafeteria. 'Not exactly your milieu, is it?' Samantha said sympathetically.

'No, it's not that. I really enjoyed seeing the paintings. Thank you. I mean, it's true, I wouldn't have come in here to see them unless you'd suggested it. It's your field, Sam and I can see why you love it. I get it. I do. My mind's been on other things.'

'What's happened? Have you spoken to David on the phone?'

Helen looked down at her coffee and pushed it away before replying, 'No and that's the point. He said he'd call me when he knew more. I haven't heard from him.'

'Perhaps, he doesn't know anything.'

'Whose side are you on? You were saying that you thought he was a waste of space! The point is, he hasn't been in touch at all. What I'm upset about is that I've left him three voicemail messages.'

'That speaks volumes, doesn't it? You worry me. You're obviously keener on him than I thought,' Samantha responded.

'Yeah, we were getting on so well, Sam. I was wary at first. I'll give you two examples: On the way up here, he wrote me a very romantic poem; secondly, over dinner, he grabbed my hand, looked into my eyes, and said, 'Helen, the face that launched a thousand ships', so you'll see why I'd been given a certain impression or been misled.'

'Oh, Helen, I've got so much love and respect for you and I want to let you know that you're the least naive person that I know, but did he say those things before or after …?'

'I see where you're going with this,' Helen stood up, 'but you'll have to excuse me now. I'm going back to the hotel. David might be there waiting for me, or there might be a message or something.'

Samantha watched the retreating figure of her friend as she left the museum's café area and shook her head. She'd call her later but knew that Helen wouldn't want to listen to her misgivings about this so-called relationship.

***

It was nine o'clock on Monday morning in the small conference room at Bedfordshire Police Headquarters. All available detective ranks from Detective Constable upwards had been summoned to attend the meeting called by Chief Inspector Duncan Bryce. Once assembled, Bryce had been advised that his audience was awaiting his arrival and he swept into the room with his formidable conceit. Accompanying him were two men dressed in dark business suits who sat behind Bryce, to his right. The atmosphere in the room was palpable. A silence had descended and Bryce ran one hand through his blonde hair before he addressed his colleagues.

'Good morning, ladies and gentlemen. Thank you for attending this impromptu meeting, as I know that you are all very busy, or should be!' This was not an attempt at humour and the assembled gathering knew this. These congregations were few and far between, held maybe two or three times a year, so everyone knew that it must be important. Some of his colleagues looked furtively at one another but it was mainly a rapt audience. DCI Bryce pressed a button on the laptop in front of him and an image appeared on the screen behind him. A large head and shoulders photograph of Detective Sergeant Paul Craven, Bedfordshire Constabulary, was displayed. A cumulative intake of breath could be heard as Bryce continued, 'I have some very bad news to impart to you this morning. Yesterday evening, I received a telephone call from the Assistant Chief Constable of West Yorkshire police in which he informed me of the death of our colleague, DS Paul Craven.' Bryce paused and looked around the rows of the seated, fifty or so, police officers before him. He continued, 'I am sorry to have to share this terrible news with you all about the loss of a very brave and dedicated, law enforcement professional.'

There were some mumblings and grumblings amongst the audience and a hand was raised from someone in the third row.

'Yes? Can I help you with something?' Bryce appeared irritated at this unwelcome intrusion so early on in his talk. 'Please state your name, rank, then your query.'

Looking from one side to the other along the rows of his fellow officers in an attempt to attract some support, this self-appointed spokesperson stood up and replied, 'Yes, sir, thank you. Er, Duncan Pratt, Detective Constable and we, I, had assumed that DS Craven had, first of all, been reprimanded, put on gardening leave and had then emerged up north and had caused some mayhem, run amok, sir,'

DCI Bryce bristled and smoothed his finely trimmed moustache. He had often been compared to some of the old Hollywood film stars like Ronald Colman and William Powell. 'I can understand why some of you may be feeling that way and I was coming on to that, DC Pratt, so thank you. You can sit down now.' Bryce glanced behind him at his two associates before continuing, 'Unbeknownst to you all, Paul Craven was working undercover for this country and indeed the rest of Europe. Paul was very much operating in a Catch-22 situation really. He often had a dilemma or difficult circumstance from which there was no escape because of mutually conflicting or dependent conditions. I need to tell you more. We pretty much gave DS Craven a free rein but ostensibly he was working under the auspices of Operation Stiletto. I think at this point in proceedings, it would be a good opportunity for me to introduce my two guests.' He put his right arm out to indicate the two middle-aged men behind him. They rose from their seats and stepped forward. As they were introduced, each man nodded towards the gathering before them. 'Mr Hagen Janssen, is our representative from Europol and M. Louis Badeaux, is representing Interpol.' DCI Bryce held his hand up to quell the muttering in the officers before him. 'As you can surmise, Operation Stiletto was a major undertaking and consequently, if it was to succeed, had to be kept very hush-hush.'

Louis Badeaux smiled and in excellent English and with only a mild but pleasant French accent interjected with, 'To go undercover is to avoid detection by the entity one is observing and especially, to disguise one's own identity or use an assumed identity for the purposes of gaining the trust of an individual or organisation to learn or confirm confidential information or to gain the trust of targeted individuals to gather information or evidence.'

Hagen Janssen, this time with the familiar Dutch twang to his speech carried on, 'As I am sure you all will know, traditionally, it is a technique employed by law enforcement agencies or private investigators and a person who works in such a role is commonly referred to as an undercover agent. In this respect, your colleague, Paul Craven, was one of the best.'

'Thank you, gentlemen,' DCI Bryce smoothed back his hair once again and continued to address his colleagues, 'Full disclosure of DS Craven's activities and the reasons for them will be made aware to everyone in due course. He was chosen for this role because of his resilience. He was tough and recovered quickly from any difficulties he came across. Operation Stiletto was a complex, yet delicate, police investigation. When we looked at potential candidates to carry out the role successfully, Paul Craven stood out from the crowd. He was smart enough to be able to use clever but false arguments, especially intending to deceive. It was pure sophistry.'

In the front row, DC Susan Parkes raised her hand requesting to speak.

'Please go ahead.' Bryce smiled at his attractive female colleague.

'Thank you, sir. Detective Constable Susan Parkes. I worked closely with DS Craven on several investigations and therefore, I was more surprised than anyone when Paul appeared to turn rogue. So, all of the bad activities that he's been involved with these past few months were all part of his cover so that he could carry out these clandestine tasks for Operation Stiletto?'

'That's correct, DC Parkes. And perhaps you would see me in my office once this meeting has ended? I'll have a lot more for you then.' He then returned his focus to the rest of the delegates in the room. 'DS Paul Craven was very brave, but he wasn't just an action-man. Part of the brief was to supply regular feedback on activities and I have to say that the detail gave his reports some credibility. Unequivocally, his information was at the cornerstone of our attempts in bringing the bad guys down. There are several Italian Mafia crime families and I am not prepared to say which one we are after at this stage as this is still an on-going investigation. Sadly, we lost our friend and colleague the other day. It was a high price to pay but we took out four of these bastards at the same time; two shot dead, two held in custody at Leeds police station, now helping us with our inquiries. For operational reasons, UK police forces could not be alerted to the activities that we were involved with in tandem with our colleagues from abroad as we couldn't afford that Operation Stiletto be compromised.

'Because of the noise and mayhem that had been created at Leeds-Bradford airport, a local press statement had been given out and a short bulletin had been broadcast on BBC *Look North* that evening. We placed an embargo on the item being circulated nationally or internationally until members of Paul Craven's family had been contacted with this sad news.

'Okay, thank you for your time, that's all for now. As and when I have more information, I'll make sure you have it. Back to work now!'

Bryce turned to speak with Janssen and Badeaux during the collective scraping of chair-legs on the conference room floor as the majority of delegates collected their folders, pens and mobile-phones before making their way back to their offices.

Susan Parkes made her way to DCI Bryce's office and didn't have to wait too long before he joined her. Bryce sat down behind his desk and smoothed down his moustache, something he did habitually, but unconsciously. He removed his reading glasses and looked at Parkes for a few moments before starting, 'Thank you for coming to see me, DC Parkes. Just a couple of things to ask in connection with our friend, DS Craven. I'll be assisting with the inquiry into Paul's activities, his evidence gathering, reports and ultimately, his sad passing.' Bryce unscrewed the top of his fountain pen and wrote something on the sheet of paper before him. He looked up at Parkes again, 'So, how well did you know him, exactly?'

'I'm not sure I know what you mean, sir.'

'It's a very simple question, DC Parkes. I'm sure that you will appreciate that I need to build as full a picture as I possibly can. As a professional, I'm sure that you would approach the task in the same way.'

Susan Parkes crossed her legs and looked her superior officer squarely in the eye. 'Of course, I want to assist you in any way that I can. Paul, I mean, DS Craven and I, had a very conducive and productive working relationship, as I am sure you will have seen when you checked my annual appraisals. Apart from that, I liked him and I think that helped engender the good working relationship that we had.'

'I'm glad to hear that, DC Parkes. By the way, there's no need to be defensive. And yes, I've seen your work record. Impressive.' Bryce wrote another sentence, which he ended with a final flourish and full stop. 'I have to ask these questions, as there are so many strands to try and tie up. They all feed into one another and become concomitant. One of your colleagues has told me that you had a close working relationship with Paul Craven. What do you think they meant by that?'

Susan Parkes felt indignant at this insinuation and she breathed in heavily which only seemed to accentuate her already curvaceous figure. 'I don't know what you mean, DCI Bryce, and I don't think that allegations of some sort of potentially improper conduct should be made against a former, brave, your words, police officer, who is no longer around to defend himself. And I don't suppose for one minute that you'll share the name of the scum-bag spreading these malicious rumours?'

Bryce screwed the lid back on to his pen and put it back into his jacket. 'There's absolutely no suggestion of any impropriety here, DC Parkes. So, it sounds like he kept himself to himself, then?'

'Very much so. He was an enigma. Paul kept surprising everyone. And, yes, I liked him. If that's a crime, guilty as charged.' Parkes folded her arms across her chest.

'Thank you. That's all for now. You can re-join your colleagues and I appreciate your candour.'

'One final thing, sir. You mentioned in the meeting that we've been unable to make any sort of public announcement about the death of a police officer and the circumstances, because his or her next of kin hadn't yet been contacted. I know for a fact that Paul Craven's only living relative is the father, who I went to see recently in Sheringham, retired Superintendent Craven. I'm sure that you'll agree that news like this can't be communicated by telephone. I respectfully request that I make arrangements to return to his home,' Parkes looked pensive, 'to convey this devastating news. An explanation of the undercover work that he was involved with over the last few years will go some way to assuage some of the feelings Superintendent Craven has been holding about his son.'

DCI Bryce stroked his moustache, and smiled, 'An excellent suggestion, DC Parkes. Let me know when the arrangements have been made and let's get together once you're back.'

Chapter Twenty

I had travelled down to the Holborn underground tube station in central London from Cockfosters, as I had done on my first journey to Gambon & Clarke Ltd. My mood was certainly different on this occasion though. Firstly, I had the pleasure of having Amanda's company for this journey and secondly, I was going to meet up with this book publisher's managing director, Stanley Paterson, who had requested today's meeting.

Amanda had said that she would go shopping in Oxford Street whilst I was tied up, but later we could meet up for afternoon tea at my favourite haunt in town, *Richoux*, in Piccadilly. On my rare visits to London, I always tried to patronise this elegant restaurant and coffee house and I have continually extolled the virtues of this haven to my friends. 'David', they would say, 'I hope the management pay you for all of your public relations and solicitations!' One always worries when something you praise doesn't live up to expectations, but that hadn't been the case here. I was looking forward to taking Amanda there and we had arranged to speak on the phone once I had emerged from 21b Red Lion Street.

I approached the black door at street level and pressed the buzzer for Gambon & Clarke Ltd. I stated, 'David Jones, to see Mr Paterson.' After a click, the door was unlocked. I pushed it open and retraced my way upstairs to the first floor where I entered the reception. The first impression on me, of course, was in seeing a new girl behind the reception desk. Gone was Julie, with her bubbly blonde locks of hair. Her replacement, on the telephone, beckoned me to enter. The redhead pointed to the sofa where I had sat on my previous visit. I went over and sat down and looked over at her and she mouthed, 'Sorry!' Glancing down at the magazines on the coffee table before me, I noted that a new selection of reading material was on offer: *The Lady, Architectural Digest* and *Macworld.* I picked up this third journal and started flicking through its pages. Within a matter of seconds, I discovered that these pages were not offering me advice on the latest styles and prices of gaberdines, raincoats, or waterproofs, but if I wanted a plethora of information about Apple watches, iPhones, or the latest iMac Pro, then this was the magazine for me! I put it back on the table so that someone else could enjoy it and simultaneously to my left, the 1960s telephone receiver was replaced on its holder.

Redhead stood up and smiled broadly at me, 'Mr Jones, I'm so sorry. I'm Clare, pleased to meet you.' I went over to her desk and we shook hands. 'I'll let Mr Paterson know that you're here.' She turned and disappeared through the doorway behind her. As I stood, I gazed once again at the artwork of book covers of the recent releases. Jeremy Browne had told me they published about one new title each month. I wasn't sure if that was good, or not. I had guessed that the average all depended on the size of the book publisher. My reverence for these books and their authors was interrupted by the office door opening and a smartly dressed middle-aged man popped his head around, 'Mr Jones, do come through.'

As I entered the room, the one that had previously been occupied by Browne, I noticed that Clare was seated to the side of the managing director, at Jeremy Browne's old desk.

'Please sit down, Mr Jones. My larger office upstairs is currently being used by my editors who are going through the latest batch of manuscripts that I've accepted for publication. We have these meetings monthly and it's serendipity, I guess, that this office has now become available for our little chat today.' Paterson took out a blue folder from his drawer. 'Before we commence battle,' here, he chuckled to himself at the little in-joke he had made, 'only kidding, have you been offered a drink of anything?' He looked at his colleague, 'Er, tea, coffee?'

Once again, I had walked past *Antonio's* outside and consequently was now desperate for a decent cup of coffee. 'No, but if you're offering …'

'Coffee?' Paterson asked and turned to his colleague, 'Would you like one too?' As we had both nodded, he picked up his phone, 'Hello, Paula, could you rustle up three cups of coffee, please?'

He ended the call and opened up the file on his desk. 'Now, Mr Jones …'

'David, remember?' I smiled first at Paterson, and then at his colleague.

'Of course, David it is. This is Clare, whom you've already met and she's kindly helping out occasionally on the front desk out there. As you know, we recently lost our regular receptionist, Julie,' here he looked towards Clare and shook his head, 'we've begun our search for a replacement, but as you will appreciate, it's not been easy and it's a rather sensitive subject.'

'I can understand that,' I confirmed.

'The drinks will be here shortly, but before we get into the nitty-gritty, let me introduce Clare, properly. Been with Gambon & Clarke Ltd these past five years and we couldn't survive without her!' Paterson smiled at Clare and she reciprocated in turn. 'Why don't you tell, David, what you do here so magnificently?'

Clare was quite abashed as she said, 'I'm one of the manuscript readers and an editor.'

'The best reader and editor, we've got.'

Paula knocked on the door and entered the office to interrupt the embarrassing commendation of the MD's favourite member of staff. She carried a tray holding three coffees, a milk jug and sachets of sugar. Paula was thanked and the mugs of coffee distributed.

'Now, Mr Jones, David, how well did you know Jeremy Browne exactly?'

I shifted uncomfortably in my seat, 'Not very well at all. What makes you ask, Mr Paterson?'

'Well, a few things. Let me re-cap if I may. He'd identified you as someone who should write a Christmas-themed book for G&C and on completion, he agreed to publish your manuscript for *The London Boys*, which, of course, he had dismissed originally.' I nodded in agreement and he carried on, 'To help with your research and to develop some sort of plan, he'd sent you about a dozen Christmas films on DVD to assist you! That sounds like he knew you quite well. It was a case of you-scratch-my-back-and-I'll-scratch-yours, wasn't it?'

I took a sip of coffee and placed the mug down heavily, on the table. 'He was no friend of mine, believe me. Jeremy Browne had caused me nothing but angst if you want to know the truth. He and his partner-in-crime came round to my house and when the local police arrived, it was like a scene from *Gunfight at the OK Corral*. Firearms were discharged, bloodshed ensued and my property was damaged. So, no, I didn't know him that well!' I was becoming over-excited and decided to shut up.

'And yet he ended up presenting a book-publishing contract to you, which, of course, was not a part of his remit. As I said to you over the phone recently, having gone through the desk and files that Jeremy Browne had left behind when he did a bunk.' Here, he tapped his pen on the desk before him, 'I've subsequently read a couple of manuscripts, one of which showed no promise at all, but your one, *The London Boys,* I was very impressed with and I could see how it may be an attractive proposition for us. It's not the typical book for us. You've probably seen the usual genres we consider for publishing: Action and Adventure, Classics, Detective and Mystery, Historical Fiction and Literary Fiction. I then gave it to Clare to peruse and I am glad to report that she concurs with me.' He looked over at his colleague who smiled in return. Paterson then took out a sheet of paper from his blue folder. 'This isn't how I meant today's meeting to proceed, David. Thank you for clarifying your position as to your relationship with Browne who, as I'm sure you are aware, is currently being held on remand, pending his appearance in court.

Now, for the good news, which is why I wanted to have a chat with you in my office.' The managing director held up two sheets of A4 paper. 'I've received an email from Treasure Chest Films Inc., based in Burbank, California. It follows up on a telephone conversation I'd had with their Vice-President, Michael J. Hoffmayer III.' Paterson glanced at his colleague, Clare and laughed out loud. 'Can you believe that? My name is Stanley Forester Paterson and I'm the third generation with that name, but I would never style myself Stanley F. Paterson III. What is wrong with these Americans?'

I hoped that he would get to the point soon, but I asked, 'Forester?'

'Yes, it means Forest guardian, goes back years.' He passed the sheets of paper over to me, 'Have a read for yourself, see what you think.'

I read through the message as quickly as I could, then returned the papers to Paterson.

He continued, 'So, as you can see, they're pretty keen to press ahead with a joint publishing project for a book, then they'll work up the story back in Hollywood to turn the script into a movie. Louis B. Hoffmayer confirmed that they would have to do a treatment on it!'

'A treatment?'

'I've really had to pick up Browne's baton on this one and run with it. He spent ages on the phone to the States about this project and so have I, recently. I'll tell you what I've discovered,' Paterson removed a typed sheet from the folder, 'A treatment is a document that presents the story idea of a film before writing the entire script. Treatments are often written in the present tense, in narrative-like prose and highlight the most important information about the proposed film, including title, story summary and character descriptions.

Treatments are a way for a writer to test out an idea before investing their creative energy fully into a new screenplay. They also allow writers to summarise their story idea so they can present the story to studio executives or producers who might want to finance the film.'

'Wow. They seem very serious about this.'

'Very, and I need to get back to them tomorrow with our intentions. Again, I said on the phone that I'd read *The London Boys* and was willing to consider publishing it, David. But it's definitely quid pro quo, you know? We need a Christmas story out of you.'

'If I can jump in here?' Clare fixed me with a dazzling smile, 'You haven't emailed any of your ideas about a Christmas book, David. May I presume you've got some notes with you? Just the basic plotlines, characters, that sort of thing.'

My mobile phone buzzed and I took it out of my jacket and ended its noise without looking at the caller ID. It had been a welcome interruption in the discussion, but I apologised anyway, 'I'm so sorry, I thought that I'd turned this thing off.' I looked from Clare then to Paterson and back again. I had nothing with me. Indeed, I had been preoccupied with other things in recent times and in any case, Browne had given me a deadline for the final manuscript of next April. But now, I expressed my doubts concerning the veracity of anything he had told me. 'Perhaps you could clarify something for me.'

'Of course,' Paterson had closed the blue folder, 'How can we help?'

'It sounds like our American friends are prepared to back the project with some much-needed funding, which leads on to my query. I'm clearly going to need to invest some time and effort into writing this manuscript. In fact, I've decided to concentrate solely on it, ditching any other work commitments. You see where I'm going with this?'

'Give Browne some credit where it's due, I suppose. He must have done something while he was here!' Paterson guffawed, 'His dealings with his contacts in the States seem to have paid off and rightly or wrongly, he's convinced them that Gambon & Clarke Ltd has someone here, you, to write a Christmas-themed book which can then be turned into a movie for them to produce. And they're willing to co-publish the book and then finance the film production. It's what they call a win-win situation.'

Clare added, 'You know what they say, 'Don't look a gift horse in the mouth'.'

'Ha! Let me tell you what my grandmother used to say in a situation like this. "If something seems too good to be true, it probably is. Grab the jaws of the horse, force them apart as wide as they'll go and stick your head in to have a damn good look",' Paterson said contemptuously.

'I'm confused. Are we going ahead with it then?'

'That's largely down to you David, isn't it? Don't worry about the money side of things; the contract between Treasure Chest Films Inc., and ourselves, is currently with our lawyers, Gravesons. Initial feedback has been quite positive and a final decision will be with me by the end of the week. I think that we must go ahead on the basis that it's going to be all right. I'll talk with you privately about some remuneration, David. I understand totally and let's face it, you're the linchpin in the potential success of this endeavour. So, tell us, what progress have you made to date? How did you get on with the Christmas DVDs? Were they useful?'

Fortunately, my mobile buzzed again and this time, I took it from my jacket and turned it off.

'I've never been so popular! Seriously, I've switched it off, so no more interruptions. I've named it *Tinsel in Tinseltown* and I've made some preliminary plans, a roadmap, some characters with the obligatory love interest included and a much-needed joyful ending.'

'Tinseltown? Joyful ending?' Clare had raised her eyebrows.

I smiled at them both, 'Yes. Tinseltown is also known as Hollywood, the section of Los Angeles that is the site of many US film studios and companies, like Treasure Chest. I'll set the scene for you both: The story starts in a snow-covered New York City and later on, the male protagonist has to move across the country to California where he meets his love interest for the first time.'

'It all sounds a bit corny to me.'

'That's the whole point, Clare. Look, I've done my research. I've got square eyes watching all those films. 99.9% of them have plot lines of a girl not liking a boy, or a boy not liking a girl, but inevitably, ending up in love, getting married, having babies. There are deceased parents, ruined businesses and charities being saved, along the way. It's a winning formula. What's not to like? It's a bit hackneyed, I agree, but why try to change things?'

Stanley Paterson opened up the folder again. 'Have you got all of that down on paper for us, David? I'm sure that Hoffmayer would like to see it.'

'No. I've been a bit tied up these past few days, my hastily arranged trip up to Leeds and back; the anniversary of my wife's death; and discussing the refurbishment of the internal décor of my house with the police. So, as you can see, I've got a few good excuses. Oh, and a magazine publisher wants to see me about editing a couple of their titles.'

'I can see that this could place you in an invidious position.'

'Don't worry, I'm sure that the financial arrangement between ourselves will be mutually acceptable and consequently, I've already made my mind up to decline any offer that they make to me.' I sighed relief, as I had come to this meeting totally unprepared and had made the Christmas story up pretty much on the spot. I would check out the *Tinsel in Tinseltown* title when I returned home!

***

Holbeck is a mixed industrial and residential area with small, terraced houses, local shops and pubs, a theatre at The Holbeck and a traditional working men's club. The regenerated enclave, Holbeck Urban Village, has offices and studios in former Victorian warehouses and factories. It's also home to Granary Wharf, a development of modern apartments, cool bars and eateries overlooking the Leeds & Liverpool Canal. And it was to this bucolic setting that Helen had arrived just a few miles from Leeds city centre to see her sister Trudy and niece.

Helen hugged her baby sister, 'It's so beautiful here. You're so lucky!' They walked down the hallway and into the large, open-plan living space. Large windows afforded them a spectacular view of the canal with its cafés and restaurants overlooking the water.

A little girl ran into the room to see who the new visitor was. Helen rubbed the little girl's curly red hair and said, 'And who on earth can this be, not Sophie, surely? Why, my niece can only be a toddler, about two years old?'

Sophie giggled, and shouted, 'I'm four, Auntie Helen! Four!'

'I'm sorry, Sophie, silly me.' Helen turned to her sister and quietly said, 'Seriously, Trudy, where does the time go?'

'I'll go and get the coffees. I saw the taxi pull up and I put the kettle on. Is that all right for you?'

Helen nodded and when Trudy left the room, she turned to Sophie and said, 'Wow, you'll be at school in September then! What a big girl.' She continued making small talk about Sophie's blue and white dress and the colouring book she had in her hand until the coffees had arrived. 'Right, Sophie, Mummy and Aunt Helen want to have a little chat now. You go to your room and do some colouring for us, there's a good girl.'

When they were alone Helen smiled, 'Oh, Trudy, I love this. When you told me a couple of years ago that you'd moved into a Victorian warehouse, I had no idea it would be something like this!'

'Never mind all that, young lady. I'm glad you like it but tell me your news, please. You said on the phone that you'd travelled up here with a boyfriend. I notice that he's not with you. Where is he then?'

'It's complicated, Trudy. And he's not exactly a boyfriend. I met him originally down in Brighton at university years ago, caught up again recently and seemed to hit it off. I wasn't seeing anyone and he told me that a relationship that he'd been having was probably over.'

'Probably? What does that mean?'

Helen turned her gaze from her sister and looked out of the window at a beautifully painted narrowboat chugging peacefully down the canal outside. 'I'm sorry, I was distracted for a moment, it's so nice here. I'm very jealous, Trudy.'

'Don't try and change the subject.' Trudy didn't want to be deflected on the matter.

'Well, as I say, we were staying in the Ibis up the road from here in Leeds and this David gets a call on his mobile about his friend, Amanda.'

'So, not from her but about her.'

'Yes. Anyway, he didn't stop to tell me what it was all about. He packed his bag and high-tailed it out of town! He promised to let me know when he knew more, but he hasn't bothered. He's quickly disabused me of any fanciful notions I might have had about a long-term relationship.'

'Have you tried calling him?'

'Of course, I have. I've left six voicemails for him to call me back, I'm embarrassed to say.'

'Oh, Helen, you certainly know how to pick them, don't you!'

'I'm not happy.'

'Who are you then?'

'Don't try to be funny!'

'Just trying to lighten the mood.' Trudy decided to change the subject, 'How's the job going, then?'

'Ironically, that's what bought me up to Leeds this week. I'd put together a report for a firm of solicitors in town and had to make a presentation to its partners.' Helen's eyes and mind meandered off towards the canal again. 'You know, I quite fancy having a narrowboat, living that sort of life. Know nothing about the lifestyle of course, or how to steer the boat, if you even need to! And there's the locks and lifts to negotiate too …' Helen sipped from her mug of coffee. 'My life's a mess, isn't it? Tell me your news, Trudy. How's life with your area bank manager?'

She paused before replying, 'I didn't want to say anything on the phone.' She then looked behind her towards the doorway to make sure that they weren't being overheard; carried on, 'George isn't here anymore. Well, not at the moment, anyway.'

'Trudy! Why, what's happened?'

'It's the same old story, I suppose. George has been doing quite well at HSBC since his move from Standard Chartered Bank in the city. The last five years have been great with him being more local, spending more time at home, even turned down a move to Hong Kong. We'd found this place,' Trudy opened her arms taking in her surroundings, 'and of course, Sophie arrived, bless her. George is the area manager, a local director really, covering the whole of Yorkshire. You know what the banking culture is like though. I've told previously, lots of training courses to go on, technical conferences to attend, days away in hotels and nights.' Trudy took out her handkerchief, dabbed her eyes and blew her nose gently.

'Oh, Trudy,' Helen empathetically pursed her lips together before continuing, 'I'm so sorry. We're a right pair, aren't we?'

'I'm okay, it's not the end of the road by any means. It only happened last week. He took some of his work clothes with him to a small flat in Leeds. We talk every day on the phone, mainly about Sophie and I'm hopeful that things can be patched up between us and that he'll return.'

'So, presumably George has gone to be with this other woman.'

'Well, this Christine was certainly the catalyst, the bitch! But George isn't happy, I can tell.'

'Good! What is wrong with men?'

'Don't worry. He'll come to his senses. He's an intelligent man.'

'And you'll just welcome him back?'

'Not before I give him another piece of my mind, if I've got any left!'

'I'm so angry, Trudy. You seem to be taking this so calmly.'

'I look at the bigger picture, I suppose. It's not just about me, is it? Anyway, that's why I didn't want to say anything on the phone about this, knowing that you were visiting me today. You know me, onwards and upwards!'

'It's his loss anyway. If, sorry, when George returns, I don't know how I'll be with him after this.'

'I appreciate your support but please don't concern yourself, Helen. I'll get Sophie in to show us what she's been up to in a few minutes. What's the plan then, do you have one?'

'More of the same really, but I do have one exciting thing to tell you! Through some of the work that I've done previously assisting scriptwriters on their dramas on legal issues, I got the call recently to help with the technical detail for the next series of *Line of Duty*. There's a character in it called Philippa Dix who's a criminal psychologist. So, I'm script editor and dialogue coach.'

'Wow, the BBC police drama. I love it!'

'Yes, and when I've made my contribution, the production company have told me that I'll get to go out on location and see it all being filmed! The episodes are recorded in Belfast. They'll pay for the flights to Northern Ireland and put me up in a hotel for a couple of days.'

Trudy smiled, 'Good for you. It's nice work if you can get it! Listen, it's almost lunchtime why don't I grab Sophie and we all pop out for a bite to eat?'

'Just to let you know, I'll need to get back to the Ibis to get my case and head back down south. There's a train leaving at 4.10pm.'

'That's okay then. There's a lovely little café on this side of the canal just along from us. We've taken, *I've taken*, Sophie there a few times. Very friendly, some great food.'

'Sounds lovely, and what a view! While you get Sophie ready, I'll just try and give David a quick call.'

Trudy left the room to collect her daughter while Helen made the call. On her return and seeing Helen putting her mobile back into handbag, 'No luck?'

She looked out of the large living room windows to the canal and the fields beyond, and shook her head, 'Straight to voicemail again. I didn't leave a message this time. It'll come up on his phone as a missed call. Come on, all the girls together, let's get some lunch. I'm famished!'

***

I met up with Amanda outside *Richoux* in Piccadilly and we walked inside this fabulous eatery together. The staff welcomed me as if I was one of their best customers, or a long-lost friend, which I wasn't, of course. Although I always loved coming here, I did not get the opportunity to frequent this slice of a by-gone age as often as I would have liked. We were shown to some seating by the windows to sit down while our table was being prepared and to look over the menus. Amanda then started to look around the ornate chandeliers, the chintz fabrics and the ornate tables.

I leaned forward and pushed my fingers gently under her chin to close her mouth. 'It's a common reaction, Amanda, don't worry! Awe-inspiring, isn't it? This is such a gracious location. On my visits here, I always try to behave with a bit of savoir-faire.'

This magical mood was broken; my mobile phone trilled – at least with a classical music theme now – and I looked at the caller ID: an unfamiliar London number and I answered it to cover my embarrassment and to end the noise in this intimate, hallowed place, 'Hello?'

'Yes, afternoon, is that David Jones, by any chance?'

'Speaking.' I couldn't hide the irritation in my voice.

'Yes, hello, my name's Jill, from Big Cat Publishing, I'm just calling to …'

I jumped in to curtail the conversation. It wasn't in my nature to be rude but this wasn't the time or the place, 'I'm sorry, Jill, I really can't discuss anything at the moment. I'm in a meeting right now. I'll contact you tomorrow. Sorry.' And I ended the call, placing the phone back into my jacket.

'You were a bit short, David. Why didn't you want to speak to her?'

I gazed about our environment, 'This place is like a church to me. It's the scourge of our society in my view; the ubiquitous mobile phone ringing, trilling, screeching, wherever you go. It's the height of rudeness speaking to people on a mobile in a public place with an audience and I'm as guilty as the next person before you say anything. I must admit, I thought I'd switched the damn thing off.'

A liveried waiter approached us and said, 'Mr Jones, madame, if you would like to follow me, please, your table is now awaiting you.'

This magnificent, narrow room with about twenty small, round tables, ten on each side, welcomed us. Our table was situated halfway down the room on the left. A small bar at the farther end was attended by a very well-dressed barman. As soon as we were sitting down, Amanda and I held one another's hand and looked into each other's eyes. A mutual moment of passion and tenderness passed between us. We started speaking simultaneously and stopped abruptly to let the other go first.

'Sorry, Amanda. You first.'

She smiled in a winsome way that she tended to do, 'David, I've got something that I want to tell you.'

'So, you've decided what you want from the menu then?' I said capriciously.

'Not yet, no. I'm being serious, David. For once in your life …'

The moment was broken by the hated noise emanating from my jacket pocket again. 'Shit,' I said, fairly quietly and extricated my mobile and looked at the phone's display. I turned the phone off to eliminate further interruptions.

'It's off now, Amanda.'

She frowned, 'Who was that then?'

I paused, picked up the menu and put it down again. 'Sorry, that was a call from Helen. No message left this time, at least.'

'How many times has this Helen called you and left messages then?'

'I don't know, half a dozen I suppose.' I looked around the restaurant, which was busy as usual, and I glanced at the couple to our left who were feigning interest in their menus as they took in their surroundings, which included us. I continued, held Amanda's hand again, 'There's no excuse really. I've been a bit tied up and just didn't want to enter into any lengthy dialogue, I suppose. I'll have to return one of her messages, I know that. It's understandable, isn't it? I left Leeds in short order to get away and rescue you. I told her that I'd let her know where I'd gone, and why which I've ignominiously failed to do and she knew that it was to do with you, Amanda. I feel a real shit if you want to know.'

I turned abruptly to my left at our immediate neighbours who had animatedly started prodding fingers at their respective menus. 'I've got a lot to tell you, let's order our food and then I'll start.'

'There's so much choice, David. Light snacks, Welsh Rarebit, burgers, main courses, cakes and teas. I don't know where to start!'

'Well, we've got to. The waiter's coming over. I know what I'm having.'

The waiter glided over to their table, 'Afternoon, absolutely no need to rush things. If you're ready to order, fine. If not, I can come back, no problem.' His discourse although in almost perfect English had that romantic lilting French accent that ladies found so appealing.

I looked at Amanda, 'You first.'

'I'm not sure, you order first and then I'll choose.'

'Okay. By the way, would you like a good red wine to go with your main choice?'

'Sounds great! You choose. You're the expert in the wine department.'

I looked up at the waiter and gave him an affiliative smile as I made my pronouncement.

'I'm going to pace myself today, I'll start with a Croque monsieur. I had it here the last time that I was here and it was excellent. Looking at the wine list, I notice that you have a Sonoma-Cutrer Russian River Valley Pinot Noir 2018 and a 2016 Brion Oakville Cabernet Sauvignon, impressive. Oh, I'll go with the Cabernet, please.'

Amanda smiled and said, 'I'll have the same as you. Croque, please.'

Once the waiter had disappeared, Amanda smiled wanly at me, 'I know you've got something you want to say, David, but you look very sad. Something's bothering you.'

'Ha, not you as well. Someone said to me the other day that I looked lugubrious. No one's said that to me before, well, not since the time of Donna's passing, anyway.'

'Come on, spill the beans then, before our lunches arrive.'

'I like to think of myself as being quite a positive person, you know. I'll give you a precis of my meeting at Gambon & Clarke. As you know, I had sent them my manuscript for something I'd written called *The London Boys* I'd been given a contract by this guy, Jeremy Browne, which subsequently turned out to be worthless and he doesn't work there anymore! But he'd asked me to consider penning a Christmas-themed book as well which I've now been told by the managing director, Mr Paterson, that that is genuine. He wants me to go ahead with that as he's been contacted by a film studio in Hollywood as they, in turn, want to write a treatment to turn it into a movie!' I paused for breath as the Cabernet had arrived and I took a sip of the proffered glass to sample it and it was as lovely as I'd hoped. I nodded to the waiter and he poured out two glasses of this heavenly nectar. We chinked glasses and I carried on relating my story. 'Anyway, this Stanley Paterson is very keen for me to get something together about Christmas for these Americans as they seem very keen to get something tout suite. Mmm, this wine is gorgeous, isn't it?'

'Don't change the subject, carry on, please.'

'I don't know what these guys from Hollywood are offering but Paterson has said that if I come up with a synopsis of the storyline, characters, romantic ending, etc. he'll agree to publish *London Boys* as well as part of the deal.'

'Hang on, hang on, this is all a lot for me to take in. You're talking at me like a machine gun. Let's go back, you said something about a treatment. What's that?'

'A treatment is a document that presents the story idea of a film before writing the entire script. Treatments highlight the most important information about a film, including title, story summary and character descriptions, that sort of thing.' I took another healthy gulp of the Cabernet. I felt that I deserved it!

'And have you done that yet?'

'I was in their offices about an hour and a half ago and I felt like I was being placed on the spot a bit when being asked that very same question. Yes, I'd received some Christmas films on DVD to go through to give me an idea of the genre and they were dreadful by the way, so I thought of something on the spot, on the spur of the moment, as it were. Talk about thinking on my feet! I busked it a bit and I came up with the title, *'Tinsel in Tinseltown'*, no plot exactly, no characters yet, but I pledged to go away and get something together.'

'And you said they wanted a romantic ending?'

'Yes. It sounds like you're not familiar with the Christmas movie fare either! The stories from all of the movies on the DVDs all ended up with a young woman-young man falling in love and ending up together. I'll let you see them. I don't want them anymore!'

'You're a talented guy. I'm sure you'll be able to come up with a cracking storyline. You're well-versed in the language of amore, David,' Amanda said acerbically.

The food arrived and an unspoken agreement to carry on any discussions later, enveloped us as we ate. After an hour and a half in *Richoux,* we had consumed the main meal, a selection of cakes from the trolley and coffees.

'They're fairly relaxed here but I think that we should vacate this table and move to their sociable seating area to continue our discussion.'

Once we were relocated, Amanda said, 'That was lovely, David. Thank you. It was everything that you said it would be. Going back to your meeting then, it sounds like you're going to be busy! Are you going to be able to write this book and potentially edit two magazines?'

'*Mea culpa*! I've never been so popular.'

'Tell me about it …'

'Don't be like that,' I laughed, 'no, I've made a commitment to Stanley Paterson to concentrate my mind and my time on this Tinseltown book and I've checked out my original idea for a title and it's available! He's made a very good financial offer which I've accepted. That means I'm going to have to give Stephen Ketts, the MD of Big Cat Publishing, a call.'

'Oh, dear. He won't be happy. He was quite keen to see you about his magazines, wasn't he?'

'Que sera, sera.'

'What will be, will be, eh? Is that what's bothering you? The reason you're so sombre?'

'No, I've got a couple of things on my mind. I'm going to have to get in touch with Helen. And I received a letter this morning …'

'You didn't say anything about that on the journey down to London this morning.'

'You'll think it's silly,' I replied ruefully. 'I got a rejection letter from the Athenæum club, in Pall Mall. The membership application form called for applicants who were considered to be an aesthete may apply.' I spread my arms out wide. 'Well, that's me isn't it!'

'I don't understand. What is this club then?'

'I went there once in my role as an associate editor of a scientific journal. It's an anachronism, all leather seats, a great library, a small bar area, liveried staff milling about. I love it! It was founded a couple of hundred years ago and the original members of this new kind of non-partisan club, with its close connections to the learned societies, were selected based on their achievements rather than their background or political affiliation.'

'But would you use it very much?'

'You may have hit the nail on the head there, Amanda. Perhaps their membership committee wasn't convinced of my bona fides. I don't know, I just wanted to be able to tell people, I'm sorry, I'm not available today. I'll be at my club! Originally, the club was created to serve as a meeting place for artists, writers and scientists, along with cabinet ministers, bishops and judges.'

'Oh, David, what are you like!'

'No, I see myself moving in such elevated circles. It stated on their promotional literature that today, influential men and women, drawn from a wide range of professional fields, are still attracted to a club that nurtures civilised conversation and companionship and access to a great library and high-quality cultural and social events. So, you understand, hopefully, why I was so attracted to being a member?'

'Yes, using one of your words it's your type of milieu, isn't it?'

I sighed and gazed out of the window at the people walking down Piccadilly outside. 'Yes, the same aristocratic milieu as Sidonius,' I saw the expression on Amanda's face and I carried on, '… he was a poet, diplomat and bishop, the single most important surviving author from fifth-century Gaul.'

'Oh, thank you, Mr Jones. Do you know, the headmaster at my grammar school was called Mr Jones too? You remind me of him a bit, I wonder why …'

'Anyway, I'm not worried about this letter,' I took it out from my jacket pocket and screwed it up, 'You know what Groucho Marx said, "I refuse to join any club that would have me as a member!" so, whilst I'm clearly disappointed today, I know that I'll get over it. Hey, I've got a surprise for you. Let me settle up here and we can nip across the road and visit Burlington Arcade, another one of my favourite haunts! Fancy that?'

Chapter Twenty-One

DCI Duncan Bryce quickly put the mirror away in the right-hand drawer of his desk when he heard the rat-a-tat-tat on his door.

'Come in,' he shouted.

'Ah, DC Parkes, it's good to see you. Please take a seat. I won't arrange any drinks as I know that you're keen to make your way to Norfolk again soon. When you get to see Superintendent Craven to gently break the news to him of Paul's death, I just wanted to let you know something which may help him at this sad time.'

'I've got something to ask you too, if I may, sir.' DC Parkes responded.

'Fine. But let me go first. Because of Paul Craven's courageous and heroic activities, I have put his name forward to be considered worthy of being awarded the Queen's Police Medal.'

'Oh, sir, that's terrific.' Susan Parkes crossed her legs and used both of her hands to push the hair back away from her face. 'Even given posthumously, it will underline the lengths he was going to, undercover, to help fight crime. His former colleagues and his family, well, his father, at least, can then know how brave he was in working, as I say, sometimes undercover, and anonymously.'

'You're right. Only a very few, at the head of our organisation, were aware of his covert activity. I have been charged with the responsibility of putting a detailed proposal together. It will be clear, concise and to the point. I know what they'll be looking for, a QPM is awarded to policemen and women in the UK for gallantry or distinguished service. I've seen these citations before, so I'm confident that it'll be fine.

Indeed, the Metropolitan Police Commissioner, Dame Cressida Dick, herself a recipient of a QPM, is aware of Paul's efforts and his ultimate sacrifice. I'm pretty sure that it will be sanctioned, so I don't see any harm in telling Superintendent Craven that his son has been put forward to be considered to receive such an award. Now, how can I help you, Susan?'

DC Parkes was caught unawares by her superior officer addressing her by her Christian name and the fact that he kept looking at her legs. It made her feel uncomfortable but for the time being, she decided to ignore it, pulling the hem of her skirt down over her knees. She commented, 'A number of the officers have been talking about the case and were speculating as to why both Interpol are involved in addition to Europol, sir.'

'Good question, but an easy one to answer. When Operation Stiletto began, the UK worked with our European partners investigating the underhand and despicable activities of criminals, some Mafia, based mainly in Italy, France and Spain. We soon realised that this was organised crime on a massive scale, likened to a pandemic, if you like. This was a worldwide problem and went way beyond the capabilities of just Europol which of course is the European Union's law enforcement agency. We needed additional help and decided to wheel in Interpol so that we could all work together on this one. Interpol enables police in one-hundred and ninety-four member countries to work together to fight international crime. So, Mr Hagen Janssen and M. Louis Badeaux were with us the other day representing those organisations and were on hand to handle any questions in the briefing you attended.'

'So, DS Craven was an important part of the investigation?'

'Absolutely. Indeed, he was so integral to the overall scheme, that it was Monsieur Badeaux from Interpol who suggested we name the investigation Operation Stiletto. It's a nod towards the Mafia's favourite weapon and also our joint intention to come down hard on these bastards.'

Bryce screwed up his right hand, mimicking his holding a knife, and bringing it down in a stabbing motion. Bryce leaned back in his chair and smoothed his neatly clipped moustache with the thumb and finger of his right hand and smiled at his blonde colleague.

DC Parkes continued to feel uncomfortable, now coming under the direct scrutiny of DCI Bryce. She glanced at her watch and started to rise from her seat as she said, 'Well, thank you for that, sir, now if …'

He raised his hand to halt her attempt at fleeing, 'Just one or two things you might want to be made aware of, Susan.' She sat down again as her superior officer droned on. 'It had been decided to give Paul a certain level of protection towards the end. Unfortunately, he wasn't able to use it as much as he could have done. A new identity and name had been created for DS Craven.'

'Like a Witness Protection Scheme?'

Bryce smiled again, 'That's right. As a force, we realise that in some very serious cases, the risk is so great that an individual may need to relocate to another part of the UK and even change their identity. As in Craven's case, it's the means of providing protection measures for people involved in the criminal justice process who find themselves at risk of serious personal harm.'

'But in DS Craven's case, he couldn't or wouldn't avail himself of this protection?'

'I assume that he realised the ramifications of such protection can be immense. He'd been given a new name, a new identity and he'd even been given a new home, a new location, which of course, sadly, he never got to use.'

'That's so sad,' DC Parkes took out a tissue and blew her nose gently. 'Well, if that's all, sir, I think that I had …'

'Hey, hold your horses, Susan, wait there a sec.' DCI Bryce stood up and turned to go to a small cabinet behind his leather chair. The chinking of two small glasses against a bottle kicked in Parkes' basic instincts and she took out her mobile phone and pressed the audio recording button. She then placed the phone on her lap and pulled the seat in closer to the table, the phone and equally importantly, her legs now out of Bryce's line of vision.

He placed the glasses and a bottle of sherry on his desk and Parkes said, 'What are you doing, sir, what's going on?'

'Sherry! Croft Original, I always keep a bottle on the go. Thought you might like to join me in a little pre-prandial?'

'No, thank you. I can't stand sherry.'

'I've been very worried about you, Susan. I know that you're divorced and now you've lost your friend, Paul Craven, too.' He poured himself a glass, sipped it, and said, 'Bottoms up, eh?'

'Can I ask you something, sir? Are you married?'

'Well, yes I am, but Mrs. Bryce doesn't enjoy the best of health. She's not a well woman, hasn't been for a few years now.' He poured himself another glass of the pale gold, rich, smooth liquid.

'I'm sorry to hear that.'

Bryce held up the glass and contemplated his world through its ambient light, 'Yes, she had a baby five years ago. Hasn't been happy since, been to see a number of doctors and hospitals, oh, it's a mental health problem; you know the score. It changed her, very annoying.'

'For her, or for you? And you said that she had had a baby, not we.'

'Everything changed. She looks after young Timothy, does it as best she can apparently.'

'According to whom?'

'Her, of course.' Bryce poured out a third glass of sherry for himself and waggled the bottle enquiring whether Parkes would like to join him.

'Once again, I don't appreciate sherry, not like you anyway.'

'Your loss, all the more for me! I'm going to say something to you, Susan, that I want you to keep between us, confidentially please.' Parkes raised an eyebrow, and he carried on, 'There's very little physical interaction between Mrs. Bryce and myself if you know what I'm saying. So, you'll understand why I would like this information to be kept just between the two of us.' Bryce narcissistically did his moustache-smoothing activity once again. A classic case of self-centredness.

'I am not a gossip, sir, so no worries on that front. What I can tell you, I'm a very professional police officer who takes her responsibilities extremely seriously. So, I won't apologise to you for not wanting to share your bottle of sherry with you. Now, if you'll excuse me …'

'No, I won't. Please sit down again, Susan. I have one more question to ask you.'

DC Parkes folded her arms and looked her boss squarely in the eyes. She held on to her mobile phone which continued to record everything.

Bryce placed the sherry glass down heavily on the tray in front of them. 'Whoops, silly me, nearly broke the thing. Of course, I'm sorry that you didn't want to join me in having a glass of sherry but that's all I've got here. I've got other choices at home, but I digress,' Bryce smirked sarcastically. 'What I was going to ask is about your trip across to Norfolk. What car will you be taking?'

Parkes frowned wondering where this was going exactly, 'I have a Nissan Juke.'

'It's just that my car's a bit more comfortable. It's the new Audi A5.'

'Oh, I couldn't possibly borrow that, sir, I'll be all right.'

'No. I thought I'd drive over to the coast with you. We could spend a couple of days in north Norfolk together.'

'I don't think so. I don't know anywhere up there to stay.' Parkes anxiously gazed through the glass office partition walls and could see some of her colleagues starting to appear to be curious, presumably because of the length of time she'd been in Bryce's office.

Bryce continued, 'Ha, leave that to me. I can book something.'

'I'm getting mixed messages here, sir. Are you saying that you want to visit Superintendent Craven with me to break the news of his son's death to him?'

Bryce ran a hand through his chestnut-coloured hair, 'Let me stop you there and it's Duncan, by the way. I've got no interest whatsoever in meeting up with Mr Craven, but I'd certainly like to use this trip as an opportunity of our getting to know one another better.'

DC Parkes didn't respond and Bryce carried on not having received any resistance to such a proposal. He wanted to press home this potential advantage, 'I think you'll agree that it wouldn't do your promotion prospects any harm either!'

'I see what you mean. And if I refused?'

Bryce laughed sardonically, 'But why would you, Susan? I've looked at your HR record and seen that you've stated that you have ambitions to progress in the force and I could be of use to you in that respect, if you know what I mean.'

'I hope that I haven't given you a wrong impression in any way. I'm not that sort of woman.'

'No, not at all. Don't worry, you haven't led me on and please don't worry, our little trip will be kept confidential between the two of us.'

'And you say that it could even be good for my career?'

'Absolutely.'

'And if I don't agree?'

'Oh, Susan, please don't be difficult. I tell you what, I'll make the decision even easier for you, shall I?' Bryce continued in an avuncular way which made Parkes squirm even more, 'If we don't go to Norfolk together, not only will it be detrimental for your future progression through the ranks; you may not even remain here as a detective.'

Susan Parkes smiled at Bryce and held up her trump card for him to see. She had never before appreciated the allure for people who played high-stakes card games, but she did now.

'What's that you've got?' Bryce was unsettled by Parkes' confidence and his voice was raised. Two heads popped up in the open-plan office adjoining Bryce's to see what was causing the commotion.

'I'm glad that you've explained everything so clearly for me, DCI Bryce,' Parkes held her phone three feet away from him and said, 'The last twelve minutes and fourteen seconds of our conversation have been recorded. And, as I'll be handing this over as the evidence of your unprofessional and quite frankly, sordid, behaviour to the Assistant Chief Constable to take action against you, I suspect that you won't be available to join me on my trip to Sheringham.'

He made a grab for the mobile and in a splenetic rant shouted, 'Give me that thing, you bitch!' Parkes stepped back and Bryce lunged at her, failing to get the phone, he pushed Parkes to the floor. Two detectives arrived in the doorway incited to investigate and saw their colleague on the floor, her skirt pushed up high to her waist, exposing her legs.

DCI Bryce incensed now that his bombastic actions had been witnessed, called to his male colleagues, 'Ha, look lads. She's not that sexy. She's not even wearing stockings and suspenders!'

The two officers, taking in the scene before them, simultaneously came to the same conclusion and stepped forward, each firmly taking hold of Bryce's arms.

'What the hell do you think you're doing?' Bryce screamed, 'Let go of me. I'm the senior police officer here.'

'Well, you should know better, shouldn't you!' one of them said. As they manhandled Bryce out of his office, a female detective arrived and helped Susan Parkes to her feet once again. 'Phew, that was a lucky escape, Liz. Thanks for your help, I'll be all right now. Hopefully, that misogynist pig will get what's due to him.'

***

Home again, I felt that it was time for me to get serious about a few things. I had a few calls to make and then I would need to get down to writing up some more ideas for *Tinsel in Tinseltown*. Amanda and I had had a wonderful time together in London. I was over my disappointment concerning my missing out on membership of the Athenæum Club, I'm an empiricist, after all. I sipped the coffee that I'd made in my cafetiere and picked up my mobile. The two most urgent calls that I needed to make this morning were stored in the phone and as I didn't want to call either of them, I took a fifty-pence coin out of my pocket and flipped it in the air. Ha! Heads. Why did I do that? My least favourite option had won and I couldn't prevaricate any longer.

'Hi Helen, it's David.' Silence. After about five seconds, I carried on, 'Sorry, I know you've been trying to get hold of me. I've been a bit tied up recently.'

'Like I was, you mean?' A pause ensued again.

'Helen, I don't blame you for being angry. I feel that I ought to tell you something …'

'Well, I'll go first, if I may. I think I deserve that at least, David. Even though you didn't bother to return any of my messages; I think that I got yours anyway! Your silence actually speaks volumes. I've one question for you though, what the fuck were you playing at? I totally let my guard down with you. I trusted you. I believed what you told me. You wrote me a poem. You took me to bed. I am ashamed of myself if you want to know. I started to believe that we could have some sort of future together …'

'Helen, let me …'

'Don't interrupt me,' Helen said truculently. 'What a fool I've been. I'm a professional, with a good degree and that's why I'm so sorry that I've demeaned myself. I've never felt so embarrassed. It may not have meant much to you, David, but it took a lot for me to do what we did so early on in our relationship.'

There was a lull in the conversation and I tentatively ventured, 'You did mean a lot to me, Helen. It's just that other things seem to have now got in the way for us.'

'You said that I *did* mean a lot to you. Past tense, sounds a bit final.'

'Look, I've got to tell you about the Amanda situation. That message I had to investigate. It's unbelievable. All linked to that character on the train, Craven. He'd kidnapped Amanda and was holding her to ransom.'

'Not another one!'

'And he wanted as much money out of me as possible. I had to sell my shares, clear out the balance of my ISAs, bank accounts, everything. He told me that he was in some sort of major trouble. He wanted all of the money by a certain time on a particular day and Amanda was his bargaining chip.'

'Well, you must have raised the funds as I presume you ended up with your bounty.'

'No, that's the weird thing. I contacted him about the funds being available and he said that it didn't matter anymore and even though I'd got the money together, it wasn't enough anyway! He wrote me a letter, a kind of farewell note, I suppose. Very friendly. He said that I could keep my money! Bizarre.'

'So, Prince Charming rides off into the distance to rescue his damsel in distress! What happened to the bad guy then?'

'I think he must have got away; he was going to an airport. He had told me where Amanda was being held, and that's where I went.'

'Oh, how romantic. I bet that she was so pleased to see you, David and very grateful, no doubt.'

'There's no need to be like that.'

'It's all right. I'll let you off the hook now. I've had enough time to process all the information. It's not all your fault, I may have misread some of the signs and don't flatter yourself, it wasn't a big love job. It could have been, but it wasn't. As they say, onwards and upwards!'

'What will you do now, Helen?'

'Oh, I'll probably end up an alcoholic, homeless, all alone, but don't you worry.'

'Helen, please don't.'

'Can I ask you just one thing? What made you decide to end up with Amanda?'

'I suppose it was when she confirmed that we will be having a child together. I guess I'm at the age now where I need to take stock of my life and be a more responsible adult. This probably won't help you, or you'll think it crass of me to say it, but I'm reading the Grahame Greene book, *The Comedians* at the moment and only this morning, I found this, "Like some wines our love could neither mature nor travel".'

'I didn't stand a chance, did I? What's it all about then?'

'Three men meet on a ship bound for Haiti, a world in the grip of the corrupt Papa Doc and the Tontons Macoute, his sinister secret police. Brown the hotelier, Smith the innocent American and Jones the confidence man. These are the comedians of Greene's title. Hiding behind their actors' masks, they hesitate on the edge of life. They are men afraid of love, afraid of pain, afraid of fear itself.'

'I won't keep you much longer, David. Indeed, I've got to pack my bags again. I'm off to Luton Airport this afternoon.'

'You didn't mention anything about going away when I saw you a few days ago.'

'I think you'll agree a lot has happened since then.'

'Yes, but I still care about you, Helen. Are you going to go anywhere nice, to get some sunshine?'

'Belfast,' she replied laconically.

'Belfast?'

'Yes, that's right, Belfast. I'll read you something from the back of the airline ticket, Northern Ireland's capital city is perhaps best known for the sectarian strife that took place here during the era of the Troubles and as the birthplace of the Titanic.'

'It sounds lovely …'

'Look, it's work, okay? Not that it's any of your business anymore. Sorry, I just sounded rather bitter and I'm not.'

'You know what they say, "Hell hath no fury like a woman scorned".'

'David. Stop it. We've both got better things to do today, well I know I have. I'm glad you still care about me and I wish you well too. I'd like to think that if we bump into each other somewhere in the future, it won't be too embarrassing and that we can catch up on news, like good friends.'

'You're amazing, Helen.'

'Thank you and I thought that you were too. Oh, well. I was told recently that you have to kiss a lot of frogs to find a prince. I guess I've got to pucker up again! But it won't be for a while. I've got to go away and lick my wounds first.'

Chapter Twenty-Two

Assistant Chief Constable Barry Thresher paced the room holding a dozen of his detectives. He turned to the screen behind him showing the faces of the two male suspects. The lack of progress in finding any meaningful, substantive, information in the last two days had made him a little testy, to say the least. Transferred to West Yorkshire Police five years ago, he had made a big impression on the practices of the force in Leeds and its officers.

'Right, I think I've decided on these two characters, but first of all, can someone update me on all of the aspects of this investigative process?'

A female officer seated in the front row stood up and said, 'Yes, sir, I can confirm that all of the steps, from evidence gathering to information analysis, to theory development and validation, have all been carried out. Unfortunately, partly because they're Italian, they're refusing to co-operate. We've got interpreters here, but they resolutely refuse to answer our questions. And of course, the documentation held on them was false.'

She sat down again and was thanked by Thresher before he continued, 'I'm going to hand them over to the specialists to get them off our hands. As you know, high-profile terrorist suspects are often taken to Paddington Green Police Station for interrogation. I've been in touch. They're ready to receive them. They can use more rigorous methods to extract information, shall we say. This is all related to something called Operation Stiletto and waiting to receive them in London are representatives from Europol, a Mr Janssen and from Interpol, a Mr Badeaux.'

Thresher put the aide-memoire back into his pocket. 'So, let's not waste any more time, ladies and gentlemen. We can get back to our current caseload.' The Assistant Chief Constable swept out of the room ending this short conference.

***

I had done my homework on Big Cat Publishing, before my call to Stephen Ketts, another item on my checklist of things to undertake this morning. A relatively small company, Big Cat had been trading for seven years and currently had a staff of twelve employees. It was based in Hendon, north London, on a small industrial estate. Their website portrayed a photograph of their offices, probably built in the 1970s. It displayed front covers of the six magazines they published and a group shot of Ketts and his seemingly delighted staff. Ironically, it would have been an ideal organisation for me to work with, but now I was going to have to deliver the news that I was not now going to attend an interview, or indeed edit two of its journals.

I was put through to him at the first attempt. 'Morning, Mr Ketts. It's David Jones. How are you?'

'Very well, thanks. I'm glad you called. I wanted to ask you to do a couple of things before our meeting here, on Friday.'

'Ah, that's why I'm calling, actually,' I paused. 'You see, I won't be able to be with you on Friday, as arranged, I'm afraid. I'm very sorry.'

'Are you still away in Leeds? Or have you had a better offer, Mr Jones!'

I felt very embarrassed and I didn't know why exactly, as I responded, 'No, it's not that. I'm back home now, but everything in my life has gone a bit topsy-turvy at the moment.'

'Well, okay, we can re-schedule. How does the following week look for you?' Stephen Ketts was trying to hide the irritation in his voice.

'No, I'm sorry, that won't be possible either. Something else has cropped up and I'm afraid that all of my spare time is going to have to be utilised on that.'

'But Alan Wade told me that you were a very accomplished individual with huge potential.'

'Yes, but did Alan also tell you about my book-writing ambitions?' It was a rhetorical question and I carried on, 'After a few years of my trying to get someone interested in my work, a book publisher in London has asked me to write a manuscript for a new book.'

'And can't you work on this book idea and work for me? Isn't that the perfect juxtaposition?'

'Unfortunately, I've been given quite a strict deadline to come up with this for them. I won't go into it all now, it's pretty complicated, other people are involved, movie producers, Hollywood.'

'I can see why my humble abode and potentially involving yourself in the worlds of Spanish property and mechanical engineering, could never compete with your new world order.'

This conversation was never going to end happily, so, I decided to bring it to a close. 'It's not just that. My partner and I are going to have a baby and therefore, my priorities have changed since our initial discussion.'

'Right, I must get on, Mr Jones. I wish you well with both of your new projects'.

The call was ended and I looked at my mobile. That call had gone as well as I could have hoped. I replayed the dialogue in my mind. It had been the first time that I had used the words partner and I.'

My reflection on the importance of the recent discourse was interrupted by Vivaldi and his four seasons, at least my mobile's ringtone was now subtle and not squealing anymore. I answered it.

'Hi, speak of the devil!'

'I've heard better idioms, David. What do you mean?' Amanda purred.

'You know, I was just thinking about you and then you call me!'

'Bless you, I think about you too! Thank you again for our lovely day in London together. So many happy memories. I'm calling you from work. I'm having a coffee break.'

'Let's get together this evening. We've got lots to talk about. I can update you on my call to the magazine people and I've scribbled out a few notes for the Christmas book. Of course, we can also talk about our baby!'

'Crikey! I've never heard you speak so animatedly about little Chloe or little Charles …'

'… or little Tamsin, or little Liam!'

'Hey, where did they come from?'

'What about yours? See, we've got a lot to talk about. I've had another idea. If you're free to come here tonight, I'll do my signature dish for us.'

'I've landed on my feet with you, haven't I! Your signature dish?'

'I'm quite unpretentious really. I'll get my publicist to send you my latest biography, together with a copy of my entry in *Who's Who* for you to become more au fait.'

'Oh, David, I never know when you're being serious.'

'Yes, you do. I'll have a red Burgundy open for us, even if you can only have one glass now, in your condition! It's a classic match for coq au vin.'

'You'll think I'm a Philistine; I don't think I've ever had that.'

'Mmm, my favourite, I'll try and describe it for you. Coq au vin is a classic French stew of chicken braised in red wine with mushrooms and crispy pancetta. It's rich and brimming with flavour.'

'I can't wait. It sounds delicious. I think I love you!'

'Well, it's going to take me a few hours to prepare, but it'll be worth it, I promise. And guess what, as with most stews, it's even better the next day and it freezes well, too. Shall we say eight o'clock?'

'I'd better get back to work now, David, but I'll see you later. Thank you.'

***

Interview Room 4 at Bedfordshire Police HQ in Kempston was slightly larger and more comfortable than Rooms 1, 2 and 3 and had state-of-the-art audio-visual recording systems for interviews and interrogations. The weather outside had changed again. Wind swirled around and the branches of the trees in the grounds were taking a hammering. The heavy rain beat against the large windows and seemed to compliment Bryce's gloomy disposition.

The preliminaries had been completed and sitting opposite Detective Chief Inspector Duncan Bryce across the other side of the smart, graphite grey table, sat Deputy Chief Constable Douglas McBride, Chief Superintendent Sean Piper and Detective Inspectors Frank Lee and Philip Ennis.

The implacable McBride started the interview in his Scottish brogue, 'Well, this is a fine mess, DCI Bryce. You've made an infraction of so many of the rules, I guess we'll have to make a start.' His irritation was evident as he went on, 'As you know, this interview is being recorded both visually and audibly and because of the seriousness of the situation, I am assisted by my colleagues in front of you. We've all got far more important things to do and I want to say, on record, that I am personally horrified, disgusted and extremely disappointed by your actions, Bryce. After the early successes in your police career, I had great hopes for you, hence my disappointment.'

Chief Superintendent Sean Piper stepped in to try and calm the waters of this febrile atmosphere, 'I will ask you to respond when I finish speaking, DCI Bryce. You've been on a number of training courses and been given copious amounts of literature on sexual harassment and workplace assault. Any decent person with the morals to enable them to have the correct standards of behaviour shouldn't even need to go on courses and read books about good behaviour.'

'It all depends on what you deem as sexual harassment,' DCI Bryce snapped.

'It's what's according to your police training. I'll reiterate the basics to help you.' CS Piper referred to the blue pamphlet in his hand which summarised the issue for employees and read it out loud.

'Is that clear enough, DCI Bryce?'

'Yes, but what one person calls feeling uncomfortable, another can take as a compliment.'

CS Piper responded acrimoniously, once again referring to his booklet, 'I'm going to skim through this but pull out the salient facts. The Equality Act categorises sexual harassment under unlawful discrimination. It describes it as unwanted conduct of a sexual nature which has the purpose or effect of violating someone's dignity or creating an intimidating, hostile, degrading, humiliating, or offensive environment for them. I hope that makes things clear for you.'

'Not really. I've seen her having banter in the office with some of her colleagues and her close relationship with DS Paul Craven was an open secret.'

DCC McBride shouted, 'That has been denied, Bryce and unless you have evidence to the contrary, I suggest you drop that one. And if DC Parkes chose to have an amicable relationship with others, that would suggest to me that she simply didn't want the same with you! For whatever reason.'

'That's just it. I think she was flirting with me. All I was doing was responding to that.' Bryce folded his arms and sat back in his chair.

'Is that your defence then?' McBride gently took the booklet from his colleague and glanced down the list. So, are you saying there was no inappropriate touching; sexual comments and jokes; comments on her body and clothing; questions about her sex life; intruding on personal space?'

Bryce paused, then smiled, 'Well, you know what it's like in a police station among friends. I suppose some of that might have happened, not the touching, but the jokes, yeah, office banter, of course, we've all done that.'

'No, we haven't,' said CS Sean Piper. 'Now, before we go onto the transcript of DC Parkes' mobile phone recording, I think that we ought to go over the assault charge, witnessed by DI's Lee and Ennis.' He glanced at his colleagues.

'Assault! That's a joke.'

'In attempting to wrest the phone from DC Parkes, there was an altercation between you and you pushed her to the ground. We witnessed this, DCI Bryce, which was why we chose to remove you from the room. You made a scornful remark about her clothing if you remember.'

'Ha, it all comes back to me now. Don't forget, I was a little under the weather that day.'

'We'll be coming to that in a minute.' DCC Douglas McBride took out a piece of paper from the file in front of him.' He read out the definition of a workplace assault. 'This includes verbal abuse, DCI Bryce, but in your case, you went the whole hog, didn't you! Now, as you say, you weren't exactly at your best that day, so I'm going to be very helpful. I'm now going to play us all the 12 minutes, 14 seconds of DC Parkes' mobile phone recording, a copy of the transcript of which is in front of us all on the green A4 paper.' He nodded at DI Ennis who pressed play on the device by his side. When it finished, McBride said, 'That is a recording of the conversation that took place between DC Parkes and yourself, DCI Bryce, in your office, is it not?'

Bryce laughed, 'I can't deny it, can I?'

'I suggest that you take this matter a little more seriously. Your police career is effectively over, DCI Bryce. Putting that to one side for one minute, we are probably looking at a potential criminal prosecution here as well. What on earth were you thinking of, drinking something alcoholic in your office whilst on duty! Then offering a colleague the opportunity of joining you! Then trying to take her to Norfolk in your posh car and suggesting that you both stay together in a seaside hotel! The list goes on, DCI Bryce.'

'Is that all you've got?' Bryce laughed again. 'Please tell me that we're not all here, wasting our time, listening to this crappy recording, on which you're going to try and end my career with some sort of trumped-up criminal charge against me!'

'It sounds like you've been hoisted by your own petard, Bryce! You've admitted that it's your voice on the tape recording and you haven't denied anything either.'

'I was unaware that our conversation was being recorded, ergo, my permission was not requested and consequently, the tape, as evidence, is inadmissible.'

'Oh dear,' CS Piper interrupted him, 'you do need to keep up to date, DCI Bryce. Mind you, as your career is about to end, it's probably too late now. Let me put things straight for you. Recordings obtained without someone's consent can be used as evidence in legal proceedings. They are admissible. Indeed, it is even possible to make covert recordings of meetings and conversations. Initially, this evidence is all going to proceed to a disciplinary hearing. In accordance with your employment contract – which I suggest you scrutinise fully – but I will remind you now, that you should be given the chance to: set out your case, answer any allegations, ask questions, show evidence, call relevant witnesses with good notice, respond to any information given by witnesses and choose if a companion can speak for you at the hearing.'

Bryce looked shell-shocked and said nothing.

'I let CS Piper state the facts of life for you as he's been involved in a few of these interviews in recent times. Thank you, Sean, for spelling out the axiom.' Deputy Chief Constable McBride observed Bryce before him whose body language had altered dramatically, 'Have you got anything else to say? The wind seems to have come out of your sails.'

Bryce gave an indifferent shrug, ignored the question and turned to look at the window which continued to be beaten incessantly by the storm outside.

McBride wanted to get the interview back on track and he slapped his hand down on to the table-top immediately making everyone in the room focus acutely on the matter at hand. He shouted, 'Be quite clear, no one in one of my interrogations can be allowed to drift into obfuscation.'

DCI Bryce sat up, 'That's why I don't play cards, I suppose.' He closed his eyes and buried his head in his hands. 'Oh, God, what happens now, what's the next step?'

Sean Piper took up the story again, 'After the hearing, we could decide that no further action is necessary; discipline you in some way, for example, give you a formal warning; ask you to improve your performance within a certain period of time; suspend you without pay; or demote you or dismiss you. In your case, DCI Bryce, I think that you should prepare yourself for that last option, based on the seriousness of your misdemeanours.'

Bryce put his arms on the table and placed his head down on top of them and started sobbing. After a minute, he started to calm down and he raised his head again and looked DCC McBride squarely in the eyes. 'I know I've done wrong, but what is clearly not on that tape recording are the conversations between her and me leading up to the meeting in my office.'

'And what do you mean by that, DCI Bryce? What are you alleging took place on those occasions?'

Bryce looked from one officer to the other and shook his head. 'I realise how bad this looks for me, on the face of it. She'd been leading me on, basically. I don't have to tell you what it's like. The coquettish little look here, an innuendo there.'

'No, Bryce, I obviously don't have your charisma,' McBride said in his very pleasant lilting Edinburgh accent, 'I can honestly say that that never happens to me or I don't notice it. And I certainly would never act upon it, man!'

CS Piper followed his superior, 'A very serious allegation has been brought against you, DCI Bryce and the reason for today's meeting is to get your initial reaction and statement of the facts, according to you. The other party, DC Susan Parkes, is not here to defend herself or respond to your statement. She will, of course, be afforded that opportunity in due course. Can you back up, in any way, your assertation that DC Parkes had been egging you on in recent times? Any witnesses?'

'No, of course, I can't.' Bryce took out a handkerchief from his trouser pocket and blew his nose loudly. 'These tarts are very clever. They cover their tracks. They're like wild cats, staking out their prey. They use stealth to carry out a kill.'

'Are you all right, DCI Bryce?'

'No, not really, but why do you ask, sir?'

'You seem very twitchy, playing with your moustache and looking towards the doorway. The door isn't locked, but let me tell you, you wouldn't get very far, DCI Bryce.'

'No, it's just that this is a very stressful situation.'

'Without prejudicing any future inquest, you seem to have brought this all upon yourself. Do you see that?'

DI Frank Lee added, 'When DI Ennis and I arrived at the scene, having heard the commotion emanating from your office, one was met with a very unedifying spectacle. DC Parkes was on the floor, her clothes in disarray, and you were there grappling with her, shouting obscenities. With evidence like that, no one is going to be accused of jumping to any conclusions!'

Bryce glanced once more at the door behind him. The four other officers in the room were sitting down on the other side of the table. If he was going to make a move, now would be the time. He placed his hands on the arms of his chair to give him extra purchase as he propelled himself from his chair to a standing position. Bryce turned and grabbed the doorknob, the door unlocked, as promised and he flew out through the doorway into the outer office. DI Ennis looked at his colleagues and said, 'Don't worry, sir, you're quite right, he won't get far.' He spoke into his police walkie-talkie, 'This is an alert warning, DCI Duncan Bryce of Bedfordshire Police, here at Kempston, has chosen to take leave of an internal investigation meeting. I will post a copy of his image on the PNC. He is to be apprehended and is thought not to be armed at the present time. He was last seen on the third floor of the Head Office building. Please let me, or DI Frank Lee, know the moment Bryce is caught, and secure.'

Chapter Twenty-Three

Susan Parkes had had an uneventful drive across country back to Sheringham to see Superintendent Keith Craven. She had arranged the meeting on the phone the day before, saying that she had something to hand over to him and had some more information that she felt should be said face-to-face rather than over the phone. His interest piqued and Craven Snr had immediately acceded to the request. Parkes felt shaken not stirred, like her favourite film hero, James Bond, by her recent run-in with her colleague DCI Bryce. His abhorrent behaviour had surprised even her and she was glad that he was now in a secure place, being interviewed under caution for his outrageous activity towards her. Parkes felt that she had done nothing to warrant such unwanted attention. On this second visit to see Superintendent Craven, she hadn't needed to park in one of Sheringham's car parks as he had said she could park her Juke on his ample driveway in South Street.

Once the formalities were over and coffees and biscuits were on the coffee table between them, Susan Parkes opened up the conversation, 'It's very good of you to see me, sir. As mentioned on the phone, I've got a couple of things to hand over to you and a few things to tell you.'

'I've told you before, whilst you're in my home you've got to remember that I'm a retired superintendent, and if you feel the need to address me, please call me by my Christian name, Keith.'

'Thank you,' DC Parkes shifted uncomfortably in her seat as she tried to settle herself. 'This isn't easy for me and it's not something that one is ever prepared for, despite the excellent training that officers go through at the London Policing College.'

'Susan, what on earth is the matter?'

'I said to you on the phone that I wanted to come over to Sheringham again to see you as I had several things to discuss, and to give you.' Susan put her hand on the bag next to her on the sofa. Swallowing hard she fixed her violet eyes on the man opposite. 'I'm so sorry, Keith, but I have some very bad news to impart to you. I felt duty-bound to come and see you today and to tell you in person, as it were.'

Craven Snr remained silent as many possible scenarios for discussion raced through his mind with one candidate in particular. The uncomprehending expression on Craven's face compelled Parkes to continue, 'Bedfordshire Constabulary has received the devastating news from the force in West Yorkshire that following an undercover operation a major incident occurred the other day – at Leeds-Bradford airport – which culminated in the arrests and fatalities of several people.' She paused and turned her gaze away, and stared at the ceiling as she continued, One of the victims, sir, was your son, Paul.'

Craven stood up and as he made his way across the room, said, 'Excuse me.' He exited the living room and Parkes was left alone for a few minutes. She gazed around her comfortable environment and started to admire the three framed oil paintings of, presumably, the north Norfolk coastline. As he re-entered, his demeanour had, unsurprisingly, altered dramatically. His brows were knitted and his face was now looking very stern.

'I'm sorry, Susan,' and after he'd lit another cigarette, said, 'Who heads up the force now in Leeds?'

DC Parkes frowned as she attempted to recall the information correctly, 'Well, we heard from Assistant Chief Constable Barry Thresher, sir.'

'Noblesse oblige.'

'I'm sorry?'

'Privilege entails responsibility.' Craven nodded, 'I know of him, don't know him as such, but heard some good things. Right, I'm ready to learn some more.'

Parkes smiled wanly, 'Paul had been working for some time on the undercover Operation Stiletto, a joint initiative involving MI5, Interpol, and Europol.'

Craven nodded as the information filtered in. 'Well, that explains why he wouldn't, or couldn't, share much of his life with his family.'

'It must have been difficult for Paul, and yourself, obviously.'

Craven took a final drag on his Marlboro and as he stubbed it out in the cut-glass ashtray in front of him, said, 'You know what's difficult, Susan?' Parkes shook her head, and he continued, 'The task you've carried out today. It hasn't been easy for you, and I appreciate it.'

'I've been told that Paul has been very brave these past two years, juggling a so-called normal police role alongside a secretive one.'

'Do carry on, Susan.'

DC Parkes nodded and leaned down to pick up a Bedfordshire Police carrier bag. She extricated a framed picture and a bunch of keys. Handing them over she said, 'This is a copy of Paul's certificate handed to him on the day of his passing out parade. It was just thrown into the back of one of his desk drawers. It wasn't displayed on a wall at his home!'

Craven looked down into his coffee cup, 'You know, he never even wanted to be a policeman.' Looking up at DC Parkes, he added, 'You were very close to Paul, weren't you?'

'I'd like to think so. I don't have to tell you that when you're in amongst twenty, thirty, or even one-hundred officers you work very closely sometimes. Fairly quickly, you can make your mind up as to who the good guys are and the bad ones. I divorced recently. He wasn't one of those who sidled in to make a move on me. And I appreciated that.'

Superintendent Craven took out a cigarette from the packet of Marlboro on the table and lit one. 'For whatever reason, Paul had decided to alienate himself from me and his mother, Mary, in recent times. Wait there a minute, I've got something I'd like you to have.' He got up and moved over to an antique Georgian bureau and removed something from one of its drawers.

He handed Parkes a small blue box. 'It's the last thing that Paul gave to Mary. It's a silver St Christopher medallion on a silver chain. I'd like you to have it, DC Parkes.'

'Susan, please.'

'It'll help protect you on your travels and be a reminder of Paul too, hopefully.'

'Thank you, Superintendent, sorry, Keith.'

'You said on the phone that you wanted to tell me something face-to-face?'

'Three things, actually.' Parkes made herself more comfortable on the seat opposite Craven before continuing, 'I just didn't want you to have negative feelings about Paul for the rest of your life.'

'Well, that's my problem, isn't it?'

'I'm hoping that by the end of my visit here today, you'll have gained a better understanding and appreciation, if you like, of Paul's lifestyle that will to a large extent ameliorate for his actions in your eyes.'

'I was pretty damn good at my job if I say so myself throughout the thirty years of my career. So, I would like to think that I'm not so close-minded that having analysed all the evidence, I may come up with the wrong conclusions. And, if it's to do with Paul, I'm interested. Fire away, Susan.'

She smiled as Craven had used her forename. 'The three things that I'm going to share with you are all related to one another and consequently, are not chronological. So, unless you have strong objections, arrangements have, appropriately, been made to hold Paul's funeral at the Civic and County Church of St Paul in St Paul's Square, Bedford. It's apposite and will be held at the end of next week, on Friday. Bedfordshire Constabulary has an area dedicated to their fallen comrades and I am here to tell you that he will be honoured in full as a consequence of his activities during his short, but illustrious, career.'

'Illustrious?'

'Which brings me to my second point. For his brave and gallant efforts, I have been authorised to tell you that Paul has been put forward to receive a Queen's Police Medal and the indications are that the submission is almost certain to be sanctioned, at the highest level.'

Superintendent Craven spluttered and grabbed his packet of Marlboro to light another cigarette. 'A QPM? I don't understand. He never said to me anything about his work which could lead to …'

'He couldn't.' Susan was gazing at the St Christopher in the box which would always bring back fond memories of Paul Craven, 'You see, a lot of his work was undercover, clandestine. He had to remain secretive to protect the operations he was on, people's lives and ultimately, his own.'

'Well, he failed there then, didn't he!' Craven took a deep draw on his cigarette before Parkes continued, 'I don't want you to think about him like that. I'll give you some more background information. He had been working down in Monaco, as you know, for a while before you got him a job with the police.'

Craven nodded in concurrence.

She added, 'But he kept his contacts and eventually, he was seconded to work on this Operation Stiletto. He was working undercover to penetrate a mafia network with connections all over Europe, Russia and the Americas. He was so brave.'

'Unbelievable. These bastards make money by participating in virtually any activity that's illegal. I do know a bit about them; over the years, mobsters have dealt in alcohol during Prohibition, illegal drugs, prostitution, extortion and illegal gambling,' Keith Craven was starting to get rather agitated, 'What upsets me is that Paul was involved in all of this and I didn't know a damn thing about it.'

'Please don't get distressed about this.'

Craven dragged on his cigarette and shook his head, 'You told me previously that he'd become some sort of a rogue in the force, indeed, had been placed on gardening leave. But this volte-face seems extraordinary to me. He was a hero, after all …'

'Yes, no one was aware of what he was up to. That's the nature of the beast I suppose.'

'From my time as a detective and working ostensibly on these types of cases, we had specialist branches that briefed us on what it was like for those who went undercover. It was all about how to avoid detection by the entity one is observing and especially, to disguise one's own identity or use an assumed identity for the purposes of gaining the trust of an individual to learn confidential information or evidence.'

'That's what I've been looking into concerning what Paul was involved in. It seems to me that there are two principal problems that can affect those working in undercover roles. The first is the maintenance of identity and the second is the reintegration back into normal duty. Living a double life in a new environment presents many problems. Undercover work is one of the most stressful jobs one can undertake.' Parkes paused and looked at her St Christopher medal again, 'I was informed that everything had been set up to protect Paul towards the end of his assignment. You know, a new identity, home, lifestyle.'

'What, like the witness protection scheme that's run by the National Crime Agency?'

'Absolutely. It was all set up for him, but he didn't quite make it.'

'In my experience, for many people entering the scheme, the threat to their lives is so great that they must say goodbye to friends and family, sometimes forever.

'Going back to Paul's funeral in Bedford next week, I haven't got a problem with the location and I agree, it sounds like his final resting place is appropriate. And I would like to be there, so should appreciate it that all of the details be sent on to me, please.'

Craven sighed, 'All of his sins were paid for by his ultimate sacrifice then.'

Susan Parkes started to feel that after an hour in Superintendent Craven's bungalow, she had conveyed all that she had intended and that perhaps she was now, unintentionally, starting to outstay her welcome. As a consequence, she said, 'Keith, thank you for your time today. Hopefully, you'll have understood why I wanted to come back here to tell you everything in person and of course, to hand over Paul's certificate. You're his only living relative. I didn't want it ending up in a skip at head office. The bunch of keys relate to Paul's house, the address is on the tag. We haven't found a Will yet, so we don't know what his final intentions to do with his estate are. We'll stay in touch on that basis if that's all right.'

Craven stood up, extended his hand to shake Parkes' and said, 'Susan, it's been a real pleasure to see you again. I know that it can't have been easy for you and that's why I have appreciated your efforts today. And, Susan, I'm glad that the St Christopher medallion has gone to such a very good home.'

***

It was a very pleasant Wednesday morning in the Bedford area, with a bright azure blue sky that had a smattering of wispy cirrus clouds. On his walk from the car park to the Kempston offices of Bedfordshire Police, several different bird types were cheeping and chirruping away to their heart's content, the names of which were unknown to

Detective Inspector Ian Thompson and that embarrassed him.

It was going to be a very busy morning for several reasons. Workloads were always shifting, with cases being handed over when colleagues were away either on holiday, on sick leave, or court duty. Today was a case in point. His immediate boss, DCI Duncan Bryce, had gone AWOL recently but had been recovered to base very quickly. Gross misconduct for this leave of absence and Assault occasioning Actual Bodily Harm (ABH) against a fellow officer had been added to his list of misdemeanours. Some of these were deemed so serious that he had been placed in custody for twenty-four hours pending further inquiries.

Thompson abstractedly stroked his goatee beard as he opened his desk diary and fired up his computer. Penny, one of the canteen staff, brought in a tray with a teapot, milk jug, cup, saucer and a plate of assorted biscuits. She placed it gently on the desk in front of him. This was his daily ritual. No coffee for him, unlike the rest of the team.

He checked his emails whilst the tea brewed in the pot. One message, in particular, stood out. The Chief Constable had confirmed that all arrangements for DS Paul Craven's funeral had been made with the Bishop of Bedford for this Friday at the Civic and County Church of St Paul How appropriate, he mused. He poured himself a cup of tea and added a little milk. Thompson was about to pick up his phone to make a call when it rang.

'DI Thompson.'

'Hello, sir, it's DS Jim Miller.'

'Hi, Dusty. Hopefully, you've got some good news for me.'

'Well, I've got some news. I followed up on a few things with the Met yesterday but most importantly, Superintendent Alistair Walsh has advised that the Jeremy Browne and the Tom Foster cases are going to be heard at Highbury Corner Magistrates' Court on December 14th. They will be in touch again about which officers from Bedfordshire Police will be expected to attend the court.'

'Thanks for that. That's one thing to cross off my list. Tell me, what's the latest with DC Pratt?'

'He's still at Bedford Hospital South Wing. Let me get my notes,' Miller found the correct page. 'Yes, here it is: Dr. Carmichael is the A&E consultant who first treated Duncan when he was first admitted. He's received some terrible facial injuries from Bryce's handgun when he was attempting to flee. At least, he didn't decide to discharge the weapon but unfortunately, used it as a club instead. As you know, Bryce was taken down by three other officers, minutes later.'

'What an ignominious end to his career, Miller. I'll try and make a visit to see DC Pratt tomorrow. Thank you for that.' Thompson ended the call and returned to the emails on the screen before him. Another had been received in the last few minutes from the Chief Constable about DS Craven's funeral. The secretive nature of Craven's work was clouded in mystery and apparently would remain so. The email message had been sent to the six officers who, it had been decided, could attend the funeral, including DI Thompson. This exclusive group, apart from DI Thompson, would be the Chief Constable, Chief Superintendent Sean Piper, Craven's father, retired Superintendent Keith Craven, Detective Inspector Frank Lee and Detective Constable Susan Parkes.

'In an attempt to avoid any obfuscation, it went on to detail that this was such an important matter that strict protocols would be followed in accordance with both Home Office and MI5 guidelines. In Thompson's view, this email message failed miserably in its attempt to clarify matters. It carried on, to explain that DS Craven's undercover activities, whilst in the employ of the British police force, had meant that he was about to be immersed in a protection programme affording him a new identity. As was now clear, Paul Craven did not live long enough to partake in its alleged protection.

Thompson looked around his office and his gaze focussed on a recent police recruitment poster, one that had been circulated to schools, colleges and universities. He read the words which had a strong emphasis on care for the community and service to everyone involved.

As he sipped his tea, the poster's sentiments had made him reflect upon what little he knew of Craven's career and indeed, his own. His reverie was broken as his phone rang again.

'Hello, DI Thompson.'

'Morning, sir, it's the custody sergeant, I'm sorry to trouble you.'

'What's the problem, John? How can I help?'

'I'm afraid it's DCI Bryce. He's kicking off down here, literally,' he replied mordantly.

'Oh, for God's sake, what's his problem then?'

'He wants to be let out. He's screaming and shouting.'

'Well, you manage the custody suite and are responsible for the care and welfare of detained people, so you're in charge.'

'That's what's so stupid. He's a police officer, for the time being at least! Bryce knows the rules. We can hold detainees for up to twenty-four hours before we have to charge them with a crime or release them. He knows that.'

'You've done all you can, John. Just tell him to shut up.'

'I've done all of that, sir, but it's not as simple as that. These days, I have to monitor the health and safety risks. I just thought that you ought to know.'

Thompson stroked his goatee and after a brief contemplation said, 'How long has Bryce been locked up?'

'Twenty hours, so he's got another four to wait before we have to let him go or charge him with something.'

'We're currently writing up a charge sheet. As you can imagine, it's taking a while. We've got to decide whether Bryce can go home until the court hearing, on bail or be kept in police custody until he's taken to court for a hearing. Of course, the first court hearing after he's charged will be at a magistrates' court.'

'I don't think he's going to last another four hours, DI Thompson.'

'All right, John, I'm sure you're doing all you can,' Thompson laughed, 'I'll tidy up here and then I'll be down to join you. I want to see if his reactions and emotions are real, or fake.'

***

I always liked to do things properly and whilst my signature dish had always turned out well in the past, I could not afford to be complacent or to leave anything to chance. My philosophy was to allow sufficient time to get everything ready, not to rush anything. It was a bit like decorating, it was all about the preparation. And in the case of coq au vin, there was quite a bit to do. Being self-taught, using cookery books, watching TV chefs and being fairly diffident about my own ability, I had received high kudos for my culinary attempts.

I had a bottle of Beaujolais on the go and I savoured a mouthful as I sat down for a breather. The smoked back bacon rashers and the shallots had been fried and were now on the side draining. I sipped at the nectar and contemplated my day up to this point. I was pleased with myself without being too self-absorbed. I had made good progress on ideas for the Christmas-themed story. The DVDs that I had viewed over the past week had enabled me to extract some important details as to the style of writing and storyline that the Hollywood filmmakers seemed to desire.

I took another sip of the red wine; I would soon have to deal with the chicken component of the recipe. I looked at the clock: Three o'clock. On course, no need to panic.

The phone in my house started to ring. Oh, what joy! 'Hello?'

'Hi, David, it's only me. I miss you. Can't wait 'till this evening. Had a good day?'

'Yes, lots to tell you. I'm in the middle of cooking you a sumptuous meal, Amanda.'

'Oh, sounds wonderful. I'll let you get on. Love you.'

The call ended and I replaced the phone to its home on the cabinet top and returned to the kitchen to get on. I still had quite a bit to do. Hopefully, I wouldn't have any more interruptions.

The aroma was marvellous and when I got the chicken out of the fridge and placed it on the worktop, the kitchen all went dark. I looked at the cooker, the overhead strip lights, the fridge. Everything was in darkness. Stupidly, I walked over to the light switch flicking it on and off to see if that would have the desired effect on the fluorescent tubes. Of course, it did nothing. Oh great, a power cut!

The meal! My signature dish! I ran back to the lounge to my bureau to get the latest British Gas electricity statement and my mobile phone, to call them. I got connected to a gentleman with a foreign accent who confirmed that there had been an outage in my local area and that he was terribly sorry.

'Sorry? More importantly, when do you think the power will be back on?' I asked.

'No idea. We have sent a team of engineers out to the location to investigate the problem.'

'Fantastic,' I said sarcastically. 'Perhaps you can tell me what to do with my uncooked meal and please be polite.'

'I am very sorry about your meal.'

'Yes, you said you were sorry. What about the cost of all my food?' My stress levels were going up.

'If this problem is our fault, you will be able to claim some compensation, Mr Jones.'

'If?' I spluttered, 'Well, it certainly isn't my fault!' I cut the call off. I couldn't even get a cup of coffee now. I sipped at my wine and smiled wryly. I decided to call Amanda. 'Hi, an update about this evening. I'm a bit upset, to say the least. I haven't got any power here, Amanda.'

'Well, don't worry, David. I'll cook something at my place if you like?'

I drained my glass of Beaujolais and put the glass down on the coffee table and paused. Because I hadn't responded immediately, Amanda said, 'You all right? Come on, it's not the end of the world. You can always do your signature dish for me another day!'

I sighed, 'It's not like I can even do a re-heat of last night's meal, either. You would have liked that too. It was only lasagne, but there's plenty left for us but I don't have any electricity, no oven, no bloody lighting! Agh.'

'Nip over now. I've come home early from work to tart myself up for you, David!'

'I can't drive though. I've been drinking wine all afternoon. I feel fine, but I suspect I'd be over the limit. I tell you what, I'll get a taxi because I've got loads to tell you and hey, if you're really nice to me, I might even stay the night!'

'Cheeky sod!' Amanda chuckled, 'You'll be very welcome. See you soon.'

When the call with Amanda ended, I phoned the cab company I'd used previously and asked them to pick me up in an hour. I wanted to change my clothes and put an overnight bag together. I also had some more ideas to write down for *Tinsel in Tinseltown*. I didn't know why exactly but this little story had revitalised my joy of writing. It was my raison d'être, after all. The disinterest in my book about Samuel Franklin Cody and then *The London Boys*, albeit I'd now been given the incentive to produce this Christmas story whereby *London Boys* would also be published, had certainly inspired me. Wasn't blackmail illegal? Anyway, I wouldn't be driving, so I poured out the remainder of the bottle into my glass. Shame to waste it. I grabbed my writing pad and started pouring out my ideas onto the paper. I'd already got the plot, the characters; I now wanted to flesh out the storylines. I'd do some more when I got back home tomorrow.

Chapter Twenty-Four

Detective Inspector Ian Thompson walked down the four flights of steps to the custody suite, the area within the police station designed and adapted to process and detain those who have been arrested. This modern building had much better design qualities and facilities than the old Victorian cells, some of which are still standing and in use today in various parts of the UK.

Thompson was shown to Cell C3 where DCI Bryce was being held but he would have located him without any difficulty because of the noise being emanated.

'Shut up, DCI Bryce!' Thompson shouted, 'What the hell do you think you're playing at? Keep the noise down, you're upsetting the other inmates.'

Bryce discontinued his rant and calmed down briefly. He stood facing Thompson on the other side of the bars, hands holding onto them, separating their faces by only a foot.

'Let me out, DI Thompson.'

'You know I can't do that, DCI Bryce. You've been very silly. You must realise that.'

'Please! I can't stay in here. I've got a wife and son. They need me. You've got to let me go.'

'Can't do it, sorry. We're going as quickly as we can. You've committed so many crimes it's taking us quite a time to type up the charge sheet against you, for it to be ready for the court in which you're going to appear. Understand?'

'No, *you* don't understand, Thompson.'

'It's difficult not to pre-judge your pending court appearance, DCI Bryce, but I suspect that not only is your police career at an end but that you will be spending a considerable amount of time at Her Majesty's pleasure to pay for your crimes. Until that time, I suggest you afford me the respect that I've earned over the years and deserve. Consequently, address me as DI Thompson or sir.'

'I will not be put away. Do you know how long I would survive in prison as a convicted police officer?' Bryce said in a vituperative outburst, 'I've had enough, sir! This job gets busier and busier and no one gives a shit. I've covered up my drinking, but I don't know why I bothered, frankly.'

DI Thompson retorted, 'Listen, you've got to calm yourself down. Go and sit down. I'll return within the hour.'

'Fuck you, the police force and that Parkes bitch.'

Bryce, still holding the bars in his hands leaned his head back as far as he could and hurled his head forward into the iron bars. He slid to the cell's floor and Thompson immediately saw the damage. He turned to his right and shouted, 'Sergeant Coombs, a doctor down here; get an ambulance! Quickly!'

***

I had got the taxi driver to deposit me at Amanda's smart, Victorian terraced house, via Marks & Spencer's where I had purchased a handsome bunch of flowers. Sade's song *Smooth Operator* was playing in my head as I knocked on her front door brandishing the bouquet which included roses, gerberas, orchids and carnations. It certainly looked lovely and so it should have done for twenty-five pounds!

The door opened and I thrust the bunch towards Amanda as I said, 'Quelle surprise!'

She let out a whoop, carefully received the bouquet, and exclaimed, 'David! Wonderful ... and the flowers! Right, you sit down there and I'll take these into the kitchen. I've got just the vase for them.' As she was disappearing through the doorway, she turned, 'When I come back in, I'm going to give you a big, wet one!'

That caused my eyebrows to rise. I wasn't sure how to take that!

Amanda returned with the flowers, arranged beautifully in an Art Deco ceramic vase. She placed it on top of the grey-painted wooden sideboard and sat down next to me on the settee. 'I knew granny's vase would come in useful one day. It just needed the right occasion. Thank you!' Amanda decorously kissed me on the cheek.

'So, no signature dish tonight then. What's the latest on the power front?'

'On the lack-of-power front, you mean. Just before I left Langford, British Gas sent me an update by text apologising for the current outage. I don't know if that was meant as an oxymoron or their simply being ironic. Normal service would be reinstated as soon as is possible. Honestly, I give up. All that food wasted and a special evening ruined.'

Amanda placed her hand on my thigh and sighed, 'Don't you worry, I promise that you won't be disappointed how this evening turns out.' She swivelled around and kissed me fully on the lips unequivocally leaving me in no doubt about her feelings for me.

'However, I have a confession to make. When I rashly jumped in to save the day when your marvellous plans crashed to earth, I thought that I had enough food in the house to at least put something together tonight.'

'Well, we could go out somewhere, I suppose.'

Amanda gave me one of her winsome smiles, 'No, it's all right, all taken care of. Hope pizza's okay, David.'

'Love it, great idea, it's been ages.'

'Okay, we've got a Hawaiian arriving here at around seven o'clock.'

'Will he be bringing the pizza with him?'

Amanda playfully hit my side, 'Beast!'

'Before then, I've got a few things I want to discuss with you, Amanda.' I held her hand and looked into her eyes.

'Oh dear, that sounds serious.'

'Yes, it is. Have you got your diary handy?'

Amanda leaned down and retrieved her A5 desk diary from the shelf beneath her coffee table, as I continued, 'Fine, please turn to December. We'll have to keep the middle of December free from our trip to Barbados, I'm afraid, Amanda.'

'Barbados?'

'Or Bali, or Bermuda, or Brighton, that's nice too!'

Amanda took a deep breath, 'So, what's happening in December to interrupt our ideal holiday?'

'I'll come back to that, it's not just a holiday. But I received a call because I'll be receiving court appearance details for the Jeremy Browne and Tom Foster case. It's going to be heard at Highbury Corner Magistrates' Court on 14th December. So, I've ruled that week out in my diary.'

'Oh, that would be lovely, David. After the hearing, to go somewhere warm and our first holiday together! I'll book that time off with work when I go back tomorrow.'

'Holiday? Our honeymoon, darling.' I paused, 'Actually, perhaps we ought to get married sooner rather than later in view of your present condition!'

It was now Amanda's turn to pause before replying, 'Am I to take it that you just asked me to marry you, David?'

'If I was to ask you, what would you say?'

'Well, are you asking?'

'Yes.'

'Then, it's yes!' Amanda threw her arms around me and we kissed.

'I want to say something. You've really helped these past six months and made me so happy. We've had a couple of blips over that period, I admitted a little hiccough recently when I went away with …'

'Helen.'

'Yes, we had a brief fling but it didn't mean anything. I hope you know that!'

'What! It didn't mean anything. Charming!'

'Amanda, what's the problem, what do you mean?'

'Well, if you're unfaithful with someone, please don't tell me it didn't mean anything to you. It's disrespectful to me and the other person.'

I felt very chastised and the change in mood had made me look very pensive as Amanda then said, 'Hey, come on, I'm pleased that I've made you feel happy and I've got a couple of things I want to say to you too. The flowers were a lovely surprise. Now, I've got one for you.' She once again dipped down beneath the coffee tabletop and retrieved a paperback. 'Don't get excited, it's only second-hand. I picked it up in a charity shop recently. It's very funny.' Amanda handed me the well-read copy of a book entitled, *Greek Night*. 'I do hope that you'll enjoy it too.'

I turned the book over and over, and quickly read the synopsis on the back cover.

'Sounds good. Not my usual type of choice but I like its basic premise. Thanks. Good timing, actually, I've just finished the Graham Greene one.' I placed the book down on the seat next to me, and continued, 'As I was saying, I've never felt happier. Putting the power-cut debacle to one side, I'm in love and going to have a child and I've got a contract to write a Christmas-themed story, for which I've got a good idea.

I'm going to treat this period as a new epoch in my life.' I laughed to myself, 'You know how adroit I am?' This question elicited no response from Amanda, so I carried on, 'I've been sitting here trying to come up with a poem for you and about you. It's so embarrassing, I won't bore you with it.'

'No, please tell me, no one's ever written a poem for me before.'

I hesitated, 'It's a work-in-progress, all right? And don't forget that I've got a bottle of wine inside me! Here goes.

> *I walked out onto the veranda*
> *And who was there? Amanda!*
> *Under her arm, a cuddly Panda*
> *Has she read the memoranda?*
> *Where to go next, Casablanca?*
> *Better ask my friend, Miranda*

Anyway, as I say, it's a work-in-progress. Hackneyed, mawkish, or what?'

Amanda threw her arms around me again, 'I love it and I love you!'

When I was able to prise myself away, I said, 'Well, if you like that, then you're going to love this! We can choose where we want to go for our romantic, warm, honeymoon and arrange our wedding day, but I've got another surprise for you!'

'You're awesome.'

'Concerning this court case business down in London in December, I've been able to borrow an apartment from my best friend, Gary. He's got a pied-à-terre down in Holloway which is minutes away from Highbury Corner Magistrates' Court. It's so convenient. As this case may go on for some days, it'll be brilliant to be able to use his flat as a base. And, as I hope you'll be Mrs Jones by then, I hope you'll be there too! I'm hoping you'll become inured in being my constant travelling companion from now on.'

Silence ensued. Amanda started to flick through the pages of her diary during the hiatus in conversation. After two minutes, I asked, 'You all right, Amanda?'

She looked up, 'I was just contemplating the next year of my life. Scary. When I made my new year's resolutions on the first of January, they certainly didn't include falling in love, getting pregnant, getting married, foreign holidays, staying in London. My little brain's struggling to process all these changes!'

'I hope they're all pleasant considerations. I've already marked our big dates in my Oscar Wilde pocket diary.'

'Oscar Wilde?'

'Yes, I buy one online every October so that I can start populating it with all the important dates in the coming year,' I started going through the pages, 'Oh, here's a good one, 6th June.'

'You mean, D-Day?'

'Correct, but more importantly, my birthday!'

'Yes, I know that. Remember?' Amanda retorted, sarcastically.

I went back to the frontispiece of the diary which, under a photograph of the great man himself, had the following quotation which I read out to Amanda, 'I never travel without my diary. One should always have something sensational to read on the train.'

'I'll put these dates in my diary and I'll talk to my boss at Stollards tomorrow to book the time off. They'll be fine. But you've got to promise me something, David.'

I frowned, 'What's that then?'

'No more surprises!' Amanda laughed, 'A girl can only take so much!'

Paradoxically, I had always felt that one's surprises and shocks in a person's life tended to be balanced out by the boring and mundane.

***

Bedford Hospital has had a number of improvements, additions and facelifts since it first opened in 1803. A light drizzle had commenced the moment Detective Inspector Ian Thompson had started on his drive from Headquarters to the hospital to see a brace of Duncans. That must have been a first and he smiled wryly to himself.

He intended to visit South Wing first to check on the condition of the recipient of the despicable assault by DCI Bryce, DC Duncan Pratt. He would then check on DCI

Bryce, if he had the inclination, or even be bothered. Asshole. Thompson was met in reception by the A&E consultant whom Thompson had met the other day, Dr Chris Carmichael. They shook hands and Carmichael led the way down the corridor to Shuttleworth Ward where DC Pratt was settled.

DI Thompson listened to Dr Carmichael as the doctor picked up the clipboard at the end of the bed and reviewed the latest data. 'Well, Inspector, the patient is doing remarkably well. Please don't be shocked by the apparent mummification of his face.' He looked up at the officer, and smiled reassuringly, 'It was a nasty injury, he's received about thirty stitches. Don't worry, he'll be almost as good as new in a few months' time. He'll have to have some reconstructive, plastic surgery, obviously. It's all right, he's sedated at the moment and can't hear us.'

'I didn't know that you could get cosmetic surgery on the NHS?'

Dr. Carmichael was a charming man and a popular member of the team and he grinned once again, 'No, no, no, you can't. Definitely not. Plastic surgery is different from cosmetic surgery which is surgery carried out solely to change a healthy person's appearance to achieve what they feel is a more desirable look.' He pointed at some of his other patients lying in the other beds on Shuttleworth Ward, 'The main aim of plastic surgery is to restore the function of tissues and skin to as close to normal as possible. These unfortunates are here through no fault of their own and improving the appearance of body parts is an important, but secondary, aim.'

Thompson nodded, 'And important for their mental health too, presumably?'

'All patients at Bedford Hospital that require mental health input or assessment are referred to the Psychiatric Liaison Service, operating twenty-four hours a day, seven days a week for people aged sixteen years and over. So, we really do look after people here, inspector.'

'Yes, I can see that, Dr Carmichael. Thank you for that.' DI Thompson nodded towards the sleeping figure in the adjacent bed, 'When Rip Van Winkle stirs, would you mind telling him that his colleague, Detective Inspector Thompson, came to check up on his progress?'

'Of course. Now, I'll walk you back to reception as I understand that you're here to see someone else at Bedford Hospital?'

'Thank you once again, Dr Carmichael, I appreciate your time today as I know that you're a very busy man.'

In reception, Thompson awaited his turn and then approached the middle-aged female whose name badge identified her as Margaret Taylor, Receptionist, Bedfordshire Hospitals NHS Foundation Trust.

'Morning, Margaret, I'm Detective Inspector Ian Thompson from Bedfordshire Constabulary,' he said, flipping open his warrant card to confirm his credentials. He blithely continued, 'Bedford Hospital seems to be patching up half of the local police force at the present time!'

'And who are you here to see?' she replied, reciprocating the pleasant ambiance of their conversation.

'DCI Duncan Bryce. He was brought here last night by ambulance.'

Margaret quickly turned to look at her computer screen and Thompson saw her eyes scanning down the list of current incumbents. He sensed a change in attitude as she perceptibly seemed to go pale in front of him. After a brief interval, she said, 'I'm sorry, DI Thompson, would you mind taking a seat over there,' pointing to a row of soft blue, fabric seats, ranged against the wall opposite the reception desk. 'I'll get someone to see you as soon as possible, sir.'

Thompson went and sat down obediently. He watched the receptionist pick up her phone and spoke for about thirty seconds, occasionally looking up and glancing at Thompson before continuing with the conversation. When the call ended, she got up and left the reception area, walking past DI Thompson as she carried on with her duties.

Ten minutes went by and DI Thompson was starting to get irked when two doctors in their white coats approached him. A distinguished-looking, grey-haired Indian doctor in his late fifties, sat down next to him. 'Morning, I am Mr Dinesh Ahuja, a consultant neurosurgeon.' He paused. His colleague remained standing, looking at the police officer, with a very austere look on the younger doctor's face.

Mr Ahuja stood up and put his left arm out to his side. 'Detective Inspector, if you would kindly follow me and Dr Nesh to my office, please. It's not far. I have something to tell you.' He set off and led the small party some fifteen yards to an unmarked office door. He flashed a credit card-sized piece of plastic at a sensor in the wall adjacent to the door handle which unlocked the passage to the neurosurgeon's inner sanctum.

The two doctors made their way behind the large wooden desk situated in the centre of the office and indicated the seat opposite them on the other side was intended for Thompson.

'I am very sorry, Detective Inspector, we cannot let you see your colleague at the moment. He has suffered a severe TBI, I'm afraid.' Mr Ahuja looked at the image of an MRI scan of someone's brain, presumably Bryce's, on the computer screen before him.

'You're already blinding me with science, doctor. TBI?' queried Thompson.

The younger doctor, who sported an amazing shock of red hair, leaped to the rescue, 'That's a traumatic brain injury. It occurs when an outside force disrupts the brain's normal function. Falls, car crashes, assaults, and a blow or strike to the head are the most common causes of a TBI. I understand that this injury occurred in your prison cells, DI Thompson.'

'That's right. It was self-inflicted!'

Mr Ahuja turned the screen towards Thompson in order that he could see the image. 'As you know, this nasty trauma occurred to him at the very front of his brain. As a whole, the frontal lobe is responsible for higher cognitive functions such as memory, emotions, impulse control, problem solving, social interaction and motor function.' He paused in the middle of his prognosis to make sure that Thompson was taking everything in, 'Damage to the neurons or tissue of the frontal lobe can lead to personality changes, difficulty concentrating or planning and impulsivity. Treating frontal lobe injuries isn't easy because everyone responds differently. The key is for both the patient and their family to have patience. Full recovery can take weeks, months, years or may never occur, so you need to be patient. It also may not be easy. Has DCI Bryce got any family? If so, have they been contacted because no one has turned up, detective inspector?'

'I'll contact headquarters to find out, Mr Ahuja, but I understand that he and his wife may have been having problems in their marriage.'

The doctors looked at one another and Dr Nesh said, 'This is a very serious situation. It's impossible in a case like this to make any concrete promises. I feel that we need to warn you, DI Thompson, that despite our best efforts, it may be impossible for DCI Bryce to make any sort of recovery in terms of getting back to his previous life.'

'To be very blunt, inspector, I think that you and your colleagues should prepare for the worst.' Mr Ahuja held Thompson's gaze firmly, 'It's more than likely that he won't survive. I'm very sorry.' Ahuja put a folder away in his desk drawer, and stood up, closing the meeting.

'I thank you for your candour, sir.'

Chapter Twenty-Five

St Paul's in Bedford was formerly a medieval collegiate church, a large building of cathedral proportions with its later additions and iconic spire which dominates the town. Arrangements for the funeral of Paul Craven had been made between the Bishop of Bedford and the Chief Constable of Bedfordshire Constabulary.

It was always going to be a fairly intimate affair with only six police officers in attendance which would include his father. It had been established that he had no other living relatives, his mother having passed away a few years previously. Craven had no personal life to speak of. There was his time in the RAF and then his sojourn overseas and he had not gleaned any sort of coterie of friends, as such. Investigations of his former air force colleagues had discovered that whilst popular, he did not suffer fools gladly and this demeanour had not done him any favours as far as gathering a band of brothers.

Consequently, the small gathering of six for this service was rattling around in the vast space of the Grade 1 listed building. There was sufficient space for the half a dozen officers to all fit on one pew without feeling cramped in any way.

Canon Michael Weaver led the service, the order of which had been arranged, discussed and altered over the past few days, with concurrence by all parties concerned.

After a musical prelude, scriptures and prayers were followed by the obituary read by Chief Superintendent Sean Piper. The Chief Constable made an acknowledgement of Craven's time with the force and all of his efforts, some of which could not be stated today. He could confirm that Paul Craven was to be awarded a Queen's Police Medal which, as the assembled audience knew, was only given to those in recognition of gallantry or distinguished service.

Finally, DC Susan Parkes rose from the pew and went to the pulpit to deliver a eulogy. She composed herself, took a deep breath and, looking along the line at each of her colleagues, began, 'Paul Craven was much more than a brave and trusted police officer.' Parkes paused and looked up into the vast dome of the medieval church. 'It has been difficult to put together a comprehensive list of the key points of Paul's life. So much is not known. Sadly, he didn't have much of a family life; his career achievements, I suspect, will largely remain unknown too, for all sorts of reasons, best known to the Chief Constable only!' Parkes smiled, but suddenly felt guilty, this being a solemn occasion. 'And who knew what his hobbies and interests were? Certainly, no one in the force. I tried valiantly to find out to put together a fitting tribute to the man and I've failed miserably.' DC Parkes gazed heavenwards, 'All I will say, is that Paul, you were an enigma, private, loyal and the best friend to those in times of need.

'If you wanted, you could make every person feel like they were the most important person in the world. And, I'm thinking, here, of my audience in St Paul's. You showed courage in the face of adversity and I'm sure I don't even know the half of it. I will miss you, Paul. I'll always hold onto the amazing memories we shared together.'

Susan Parkes made her way down from the pulpit to return to her seat, where her colleagues were still looking at each other contemplating what they had just heard.

Canon Michael Weaver returned to the pulpit and looked at the small gathering before him. 'I want to close today's proceedings with a prayer,' he continued.

Everyone bowed their heads as he ended with, 'Thank you for Paul Craven's life and all the years we shared with him. We lift him to you today, in honour of the good we saw in him and the love we felt from him. We give thanks for the service he gave to the community in helping to maintain law and order and protecting members of the public and their property and preventing crime. Please give us the strength to leave him in your care, in the knowledge of eternal life through Jesus Christ.'

Canon Weaver stepped down from the pulpit and joined the officers for more private conversation and carefully chosen words of comfort, before leading them to the prepared graveside.

The dedicated spot in the far corner of the cemetery where other brave or worthy former policemen and women had fallen in the course of carrying out their duty, was not insubstantial, allowing for any future graves to be added over time. And, unsurprisingly, tremendous thought and assiduous time and effort had gone into the planning and continuous maintenance of its topography.

For such an important setting, it had been decided, at some point, to concentrate on bordering the cemetery and arbitrarily populating it with evergreens. New arborvitaes, junipers and yews had been planted approximately ten years previously. The arborvitae had been chosen particularly for its natural pyramidal or conical form, boasting dense, rich, green foliage that darkens or bronzes slightly in the winter.

The very proud sexton moved away to an inconspicuous position and bowed his head as the chosen party made their way to Paul Craven's graveside. He had chosen to remain on site, to pay his respects and to be on hand in case Canon Weaver had any last-minute concerns or queries. Patrick had always taken his role as sexton extremely seriously. He always told his mates at *The Rose* public house, how important he was being in charge of such a major, local, cemetery. 'Call me the caretaker!' was his mantra. This space, he felt, could be regarded as sacred, in that it acted as a focus for the pilgrimage of friends and family. And St. Paul's in Bedford, was the crowning achievement of his career.

The six mourners were not lined up uniformly, but each had picked their own position, DC Susan Parkes a little away from the others, towards the rear.

Michael Weaver, with hands holding his bible down at the front of his body, looked up and addressed everyone. 'To everything there is a season and a time to every purpose on earth, a time to be born and a time to die. Here in this last act, in sorrow but without fear, in love and appreciation, we commit Detective Sergeant Paul Craven to its natural end.'

Susan Parkes dabbed a tissue to her eyes and once composed again, looked at her fellow officers. All, except Paul's father, stood staring ahead resolutely, either at the hole in the ground into where the coffin had just been lowered, or down at their feet. Superintendent Keith Craven stood close to his son's grave with his eyes tightly shut, in quiet contemplation.

Of this intimate gathering, only the Chief Constable knew the true veracity of today's event. Only five others:

the bishop of Bedford, the director general of MI5, the home secretary, the president of Interpol and the executive director of Europol knew that the body that had just been interred was not real and certainly not that of Paul Craven, who was now elsewhere living under an assumed identity, with a new name, to all intents and purposes living in hiding.

The Chief Constable had previously advised his colleagues, including Keith Craven, that Paul Craven would be appropriately honoured by the UK's Police Roll of Honour. Once officially sanctioned, a ceremony to present the Queen's Police Medal to Paul's father would be arranged. He had further stated that those who so wished, could repair to a local hostelry to raise a glass to toast the passing of their former colleague.

He called his deputy - DCC Douglas McBride - as the only person that he could confidently have one hundred per cent trust and faith in. And sadly, even McBride wouldn't and couldn't, be told everything: 'Douglas, have you got a minute, it's Edmund.'

'Of course, sir. What do you need?'

'Things are being brought to a close on all lines of enquiry concerning the Paul Craven case. We seem to have had officers running this way and that, and as you know, I was concerned that there was a potential leak of information and, if there was, I wanted to know who was responsible. I suggest that we reconvene, in my office, tomorrow morning at 10.00am to go over the case notes.'

***

Detective Inspector Ian Thompson returned to work the next day, having taken the afternoon off after the funeral of DS Paul Craven. He'd had limited dealings with him over the last two years: one murder investigation (unsuccessful); one rape case (successful, conviction); and one each of the following, cyber-online crime, fraud-economic crime, international-organised crime. They had worked well professionally but had not exactly gelled together socially. Consequently, the news of Craven's passing hadn't been devastating news. Tragic news, obviously, but not exactly a personal loss to him.

Thompson sat down at his desk with cup of strong tea that was his staple start to the day and switched on his computer. Within the first minute, the phone buzzed, and he picked up the receiver. Deputy Chief Constable McBride spoke unhurriedly, disguising the obvious importance of the reasons for his call.

'Ah, Thompson, you're there,' McBride spoke in his mellifluous way, conjuring up an image of a cartoon cat enticing a mouse out of its shelter. 'I need to see you in my office, ASAP.'

'Of course, sir, I can be with you any time this morning. When would you like to see me?'

'Now. I've got a number of things I want to discuss,' he replied with an amount of haughtiness.

'I'll be right with you, sir.' Thompson took a sip of his tea and stared at the telephone on the desk. He speculated on what the number of things of DCC McBride's possible agenda might be, his voice, whilst pleasingly smooth and musical to the ear, belied the man's famous reputation and steely determination to get results.

Five minutes later, he had presented himself to the office on the top floor and was sitting down in one of the two chairs opposite the Deputy Chief Constable.

'Thanks for coming in to see me this morning, DI Thompson. I know that you're a busy man and I wouldn't have called this meeting unless I had felt it was important enough to do so.'

'I realise that sir. How can I help?' Thompson nervously stroked his beard.

'Three things. The first two are updates on two of our colleagues and the third relates to a situation with a colleague that I would like you to investigate and report back on, please.'

DCC Douglas McBride turned to his computer screen. 'We've received an email communication from a Dr Chris Carmichael whom I think you've met recently?' McBride put on some very stylish round vintage reading glasses as he read out, 'DC Duncan Pratt is responding well to his facial trauma, also known as maxillofacial trauma, it says here.' He looked away and wrote something on a pad next to him before continuing, 'This involves the soft tissue, lacerations and bruises, or fractures of the facial bones. Our friend suffered all of those, of course, bless him.'

'He didn't deserve any of that. Does the doctor say how long they expect Duncan to be with them, sir?'

'Hard to say, really,' McBride didn't look away from the screen as he spoke to DI Thompson, 'Facial bruising and swelling may be cleared up in only two to three weeks. Nerve damage affecting physical sensation may take weeks or months to heal. In some cases, it may only partially heal or there may even be no recovery at all. But DC Pratt's fortunate that he had early evaluation and treatment, because that will have helped to prevent further complications.'

Thompson shifted in his seat, 'Would you like me to go and see him again in hospital, sir?'

'Not right away, no. We'll talk again in a few days once we've had another update from Dr Carmichael.' DCC McBride put the glasses in their case and slipped it into the inside pocket of his jacket. He looked at the officer before him and went on in his dulcet tones, 'Now, I want you to prepare yourself, DI Thompson, as I have some shocking news to share with you.'

Thompson tugged at his goatee once again and frowned as a number of conspiracy theories raced through his mind. He was desperate for another drink and was conscious that one was not in the offing in this particular office.

McBride took out a piece of paper from his jacket, unfolded it and smoothed it out on the desktop before him. 'My shift started early this morning, DI Thompson, which is just as well, as it happens,' McBride's smile had altered to a look of gloom as he read through his document once again.

'Bad news, sir?'

'I was in situ when we received some devastating news here, at seven o'clock in the morning. I immediately made my way to Bedford Hospital to see a Mr Dinesh Ahuja, consultant neurosurgeon.' He turned and looked towards DI Thompson who had already guessed what was coming next. 'Mr Ahuja had apparently warned you to expect the worst and I'm sorry to say, DCI Bryce never recovered from his severe brain trauma. Mr Ahuja didn't just want to fire off an email or tell me over the telephone, so we met up in his office. He explained in great detail what had happened to DCI Bryce and also set out the salient facts here.' DCC McBride waved the letter in the air then placed it down again, summarising, 'In Duncan Bryce's case, the skull was fractured badly. As the injured vessel bleeds, blood collects in the space between the skull and the dura, the outermost of the three membranes that cover the brain. This collection of blood is called a hematoma. The hematoma can expand within the skull and press on the brain, causing death, which is what happened in Duncan Bryce's case.'

'I'm sure that Mr Ahuja and his team did all that they could,' Thompson opined. 'I was very impressed with what I saw the other day. With your permission, I would like to pay him a visit to offer our thanks for his efforts; the same day I go to the hospital to see Duncan Pratt.'

McBride nodded and looked into the middle-distance as he commented, 'Bedfordshire Constabulary hasn't had a few days like this for a long time. First, we lose, DS Craven and now DSI Bryce. That's calamitous for a force of our size. It's a formidable blow, one of the worst since a former Chief Constable was shot in the 1930s.'

'Really? I didn't know that.'

McBride flipped open his police desk diary where all of the past Chief Constable's were listed on one of its early pages, 'Yes, here it is, I was right: Lt-Colonel Frank Augustus Douglas Stevens, CBE. Accidently shot in 1939.'

'I'm very sorry to hear about Duncan Pratt, but hopefully, over time, he'll get better and return here. I have to say though, sir, I'm not at all sorry concerning the news about Bryce. What a tosser! I know that's not a very Christian thing to say, but then again, I suppose you could call me an atheist.' Thompson folded his arms and sat back in his chair.

'DI Thompson, you know that DCI Bryce was aware that there was going to be a potential employment tribunal, subsequently a criminal case against him and he was going to have to atone for his misdemeanours. Additionally, his marriage was probably at an end, or so he thought. Prison was not an option for him, in his view, so he took the only way out, I suppose.'

A moment of silence followed as they both processed these developments, each in their own way.

To break the impasse and to help them both move on, Thompson said, 'You had three things to tell me, sir?'

Irked partly by his officer's attitude towards his fellow colleague's demise and the fact that he'd felt McBride needed prodding into action, he replied with his best patrician face, 'I am well aware of that, Thompson. I'm also now contemplating whether you're the right person to carry out this next task in hand, or not.'

Suitably chastised, Thompson apologised immediately, 'I'm sorry, it's been a very stressful time. Please let me know what you want, I'll do whatever it takes.'

'We'll see.' The Deputy Chief Constable took an A4 sized piece of paper from the top of his growing pile of paperwork that sat in a wire filing tray on his desktop. 'This week has been the worst of my thirty-two years in the force and this,' holding the sheet aloft, 'is the icing on the cake, for me! It's a letter of resignation from a very trusted, and assiduous, police-officer, Detective Constable Susan Parkes. Presumably, because of recent events, the loss of her close colleague, Paul Craven, then the unwarranted attentions and subsequent attack by Bryce. It's all got a bit too much for her. And I can't blame her.'

'And you want me to help?'

Yes, if you're able. DC Parkes has provided us with one months' notice in accordance with the terms of her employment contract.' McBride retrieved a glossy blue Police Federation card showing the salary scales of the various ranks of police officers, from his top drawer. 'Here, take this. DC Parkes has been given a discretionary leave of absence of ten days, by the human resources department because of her ordeal and to provide her with some time to consider her action.' DCC McBride shook his head, 'I sincerely hope she re-considers and this is where you come in DI Thompson. Give her a few days, then contact her to arrange a meeting between you. I've checked her performance records and discussed my wishes with HR. DC Parkes is overdue a promotion for her diligent efforts over the years, in my view. At thirty-five and after fifteen years with the force, if she can be persuaded to stay on, she will return as a Detective Sergeant.'

'That's very generous, sir. Her salary will rise by about fifty per cent.'

'It's not just about the money, Thompson, it recognises her efforts. I'm perplexed that this has slipped through a crack and been missed. I have ordered an urgent review of all police officers' records so that we try to obviate this situation happening again. That's all, DI Thompson.'

McBride turned to look at his computer screen and Thompson took this hint that their meeting was over. He stood up, saying, 'I'll report back in due course.' There was no reply, so he left the office, softly closing the door behind him.

***

The BBC *News at Six* programme contained an item which may have been of mild interest to its four million viewers, but it was of huge fascination to the UK's home secretary, and the director general of MI5, both of whom had been primed to watch by the president of Interpol.

The attractive female newsreader had started the piece by saying, "And now, before we go over to the weather, with Stephanie, there was some excitement on the streets of Lyon, in France, today."

The bulletin carried on over footage provided by the French TF1 channel showing a struggling prisoner being manhandled from a prison transport van.

"The National Gendarmerie, armed with automatic weapons and dressed in full riot gear, can be seen escorting one of Europe's most wanted mafia mob bosses, Aretino Esposito, into court, for a hearing this morning. Apparently, arrested in Yorkshire earlier this month, Esposito, suspected of murder, extortion and drug importation on a grand scale, was in court to confirm only his name, age and address. A full trial is expected to take place at the end of the year. Espirito had been brought to Lyon originally for questioning as it's the home of Interpol's headquarters. And now, over to Stephanie. When is this drab weather going to go away, Steph?"

***

Susan Parkes had spent yesterday in her flat doing some of the jobs she'd been putting off. It was time, she felt, for spending some time on herself for a change. Whilst she'd enjoyed most of her police career, the last six months, or so, had been different and she hadn't regretted quitting, in the least. They'd allowed her a period of time to calm down and to reflect on her decision, but Susan was pretty certain she'd made the correct choice. She was even enjoying her one glass of Prosecco she felt she deserved after tidying up her bedroom. Her mobile phone rang and glancing at the ID, the caller was unfamiliar to her: 'Hello?'

'Hi, DC Parkes, it's DI Thompson. I've just parked up outside your flat. I've come round to have a chat if that's all right?' Parkes didn't reply so he continued, 'DCC McBride has asked me to come round to see how you are.'

'Well, that's all very nice, I'm sure, but it's not convenient at the moment. Look, I need a few days off to think things over, DI Thompson. You probably know that I've resigned my role with the police force.'

'Yes, that's why I'm here. We'd like you to re-consider, DC Parkes.'

'It's too soon, I'm afraid,' she replied truculently, 'you really should've called to make an appointment to see me, you know?'

'Please don't get upset.'

'I'm about to go out if you want to know. I'm going to see my doctor. I've got to be there at half-past.'

It was a white lie but the first thing that had popped into Parkes' mind.

Thompson would not be put off and pressed on regardless, 'It'll only take a few minutes and I promise you; it'll be worth your while.'

'No, DI Thompson, you've got to listen. I've had enough stress this week to last me a lifetime. Please leave me alone!' Parkes ended the call and flung her mobile down onto the sofa opposite. She drained her wineglass, sighed and put her head back. Five minutes later, her musing was interrupted by an urgent knocking on her front door, she banged the glass down on the coffee table and strode to the door, yanking it open. 'What!?'

'Well, not exactly the welcome I was hoping for.'

Susan Parkes grabbed the side jambs of the doorframe to help support her and screamed, 'Paul!'

'Er, can I come in, Susan, I think I've got some explaining to do!'